Prais

"[A] red-hot read sure

"Naylor gets off to a comically wicked start. . . . Amusing."
—*Publishers Weekly*

"Readers will stay on Naylor's scent as she devises surprising ways to break up and repair brightly drawn characters. . . . Yip, yip hooray!"

—*People*

"Liv is a likable Everygirl, with whom many twentysomething female readers will identify."

—*Booklist*

"Liv and her new world are cute, hip, and quirky. . . . [A] charming novel."

—*Contra Costa Times*

Catching Alice
"Delicious . . . A refreshing, sexy, and funny novel."
—*Publishing News* (England)

"Naylor has fun in this send-up—surely only in Los Angeles would old-fashioned wooing with chocolates, flowers, and love notes be interpreted as stalking—and her readers will, too."

—*Booklist*

Love: A User's Guide
"A perky tale of a glossy magazine fashion assistant's adventures in wonderland."

—*The Guardian*

"Lighthearted and assured . . . [Naylor] has created a comic heroine with a difference. . . . With the sharply intelligent wit of a modern Elizabeth Bennett and the imagination of Ally McBeal, Amy is the best excuse yet for surrender . . . to the [British] invasion."

—*Publishers Weekly*

By Clare Naylor

Published by Ballantine Books

LOVE: A USER'S GUIDE
CATCHING ALICE
DOG HANDLING
THE GODDESS RULES

Dog Handling

by Clare Naylor

BALLANTINE BOOKS • NEW YORK

This book contains an excerpt from the forthcoming hardcover edition of *The Goddess Rules* by Clare Naylor. This excerpt has been set for this edition only and may not reflect the final content of the forthcoming edition.

A Ballantine Book
Published by The Random House Publishing Group
Copyright © 2002 by Clare Naylor
Excerpt from *The Goddess Rules* copyright © 2004 by Clare Naylor

www.ballantinebooks.com

ISBN 0-345-46539-3

Manufactured in the United States of America

First Trade Paperback Edition: May 2002
First Mass Market Edition: June 2004

OPM 10 9 8 7 6 5 4 3 2 1

Chapter One

Francesca Honeycomb, International Beauty, Philanthropist, and Academic, 1972–2060

Francesca Honeycomb [oh, come on, if you think that in my fantasy life I'd be noble enough to keep the name my parents gave me you've got me all wrong] *lived a life without compromise. There were times she was so wasted on fabulous substances that the morning after a night of unparalleled hedonism she'd hitch a ride home on the milkfloat only to discover she'd lost her house in a game of blackjack with a Russian card shark. Fortunately, Francesca was the kind of girl that the card shark would fall madly in love with and serenade with "Down the River Mother Volga" at four in the morning. He would give her back her house and a bitten fountain pen that had belonged to Karl Marx and leave her to concentrate on her study of neoclassical armoires. But study alone couldn't hold Francesca's attention for long—she was diverted along the path of academic brilliance by the appearance of a lethal rock star and a glittering aristocrat, neither of whom she had an iota of respect for but both of whom knew how to twinkle her toes in every sense. In fact, it was not until her forties and an exhausting decade of being pursued by the most eligible and delicious men in the world that the girl who boasted the unique accolade of appearing as a guest star on* Eastenders *and as a panelist on* Newsnight *finally met the man she was to settle down with—marketing guru turned yogi Tim Evans—a man in the Terence Stamp mold [Francesca figured Terence himself may be a little past it as she approached her forties and he his seventies]. She is survived by two children with piercing blue eyes, a daughter who has just been awarded the Turner Prize and a son who lives in Falmouth with his boyfriend and their eight cats. A distraught friend said last night, "Frannie was the greatest. She spent every last penny in the bank account of life." Mourners are asked to send as many flowers as the hearse will hold but none of those awful supermarket carnations.*

It was another day in the accounts department and Liv Elliot was thinking ahead. Thinking ahead to the day she died, to be precise. Newspapers across the land would be splattered with coverage of her life well lived. Her obituary would read like the blurb on a fantastic novel and everyone would agree that she hadn't wasted a moment.

"Like hell," moaned Liv, and quickly flipped the computer screen from her fantasy obituary to the work she was meant to be doing. But instead of a spreadsheet detailing company profits she was confronted by the XXX-rated pictures of Naked Brad she'd been glancing at earlier. She didn't always spend her mornings ogling electronic images of movie stars in the buff, but she was getting married in a few weeks and the strain was wreaking havoc with her brain and hormones. In short, she wanted to have mad sex with every man who walked past her desk or banged into her trolley in the supermarket. It was all getting a bit ugly.

"Liv, we need the monthly accounts before lunchtime. We've got a meeting with the board at Selfridges and I want ammunition!" Fay shouted as she bristled past Liv's desk. And what Fay wanted Fay got. Fay was Liv's superwoman, superenergetic, super-bloody-human boss who lived on Nutri-Grain snacks alone while she reared a fourteen-year-old child whose first play in Greek had just opened the Royal Court. Luckily, she'd flown past back into her office before Brad's lack of skivvies had time to register on her double-first-from-Cambridge brain.

"Sure!" Liv yelled out, and maniacally began drumming figures into her keyboard. She hated numbers. Which wasn't very useful for an accountant. If Liv had to tell a total stranger what she was all about, it wouldn't be algebra or equations or anything even remotely resembling the senior financial executive she was. She'd have a way with a musical instrument that would take her to Albert Hall for a solo performance in a taffeta dress or, even closer to her heart, she'd be the milliner out on the studio floor nestling organza into a trilby. Somehow, though, she'd become an accountant. Albeit a good one. In fact, her life could be described, to the casual onlooker, as a bit of a success story.

Liv pretty much has it all: a flat—small but great location-location-location in the heart of London's fashionable Notting Hill—a job that, even if a bit dull, is definitely better than a kick in the teeth with a cheap stiletto. And to top it all off she's got a man. To whom she's engaged to be married. So Liv's hardly a candidate for a charity sale. With half of what she's got most people would be counting their blessings and planning their next winter sun holiday. But not Liv. Not that she's ungrateful or anything, just that she's starting to panic a bit. Wondering whether she's doing the right thing, et cetera. Worrying that this is it, the end of the road, and she'll never know what it is to sleep with someone who has a record in the Top Ten or discover whether bald men really make the best lovers. This really is where the train of romance and lust stops and Liv gets off.

The trouble is, this bit is a source of embarrassment and she's never admitted it to anyone, but she's never had a one-night stand, which kind of tweaks the nipples of bra-burning feminists really. What did they get saggy boobs for if not so that girls like Liv could know the joys of regretting that last glass of wine and wondering why they hadn't noticed he was wearing a wedding ring last night?

When Liv started working at Goldsmiths, the most dusty and prestigious milliner in London, she planned to learn how to magnificently trim a boater at night classes; then one evening she would stay late, ostensibly to work on the annual financial report. The next morning everyone would come into work unsuspectingly clutching cappuccinos and crois-sants as usual and discover the most magnificent hat that any-one had ever seen outside of an Audrey Hepburn movie. The Hat would be resting insouciantly on a dummy, and croissants and Nutri-Grain bars would remain uneaten as everyone merely marvelled, wondering who, but who, had given birth to The Hat. For Liv's Hat would be the Platonic Ideal of hats. A prototype of wonderfulness that would have Philip Treacy, creator of the most beautiful headwear in his-tory, meeting seedy figures in overcoats in subterranean bars negotiating just how much it would cost him to have The Marvel's legs broken. Or maybe her arms. No, on second thought, both. . . .

"It'll run late, too. Could you book us both a cab home for nine?" Fay did a few quad stretches as she whirred past Liv's desk again. She was off for her lunchtime run around Hyde Park. All of it. When she heard the doors of the lift close safely, Liv flipped back to Naked Brad and thought of her upcoming wedding. Her lust obsession had coincided, to the day, with her engagement. Since then she hadn't been able to stop looking at other men. And not in a "lucky me I'm marrying the only man in the world for me" type way. No, she was wondering what it would be like to . . . if she were being honest with herself . . . shag them senseless. Not very blushing bride, is it? Much more lusty, perspiring, panting in some locked stationery cupboard / seedy motel room / quickie in the back of his Audi woman-you-wouldn't-want-to-marry-in-your-darkest-nightmares type thing. But that said, she and Tim had been together for five years and she'd never once been unfaithful. It was just that simply wanting to on her wedding day would be an act of treachery and not the act of a newly married woman. A newly married woman who would never again until her dying day as long as ye both shall live know what it was like to so much as kiss someone else. So, you see, apart from that small, niggling doubt, she was blissfully happy to be getting married.

"It's not that I'm sex-mad or anything, just that I'm curious." Liv spilled Sweet'N Low all over her skirt as she and Alex settled down for a lunchtime catch-up in Patisserie Valerie.

"Had one, you've had them all," said Alex Burton, Liv's closest friend and a ferociously smart woman trapped in the body of a supermodel. "I promise that the second you so much as kiss another man it'll be like déjà vu. One tongue's the same as another and the more penises you see the more repellent and frankly ridiculous they start to look."

"But at least you can use the plural—in my life it's just a penis. Only the one. I just want to know what it's like out there."

This was a conversation that Alex and Liv had been having every day since May, when Tim had taken Liv to Blakes Hotel and proposed. In bed on a gorgeous Sunday morning, with a beautiful tombstone of a ring. The only problem was that to Liv it might as well have been a tombstone. A huge gaping grave, a creaking coffin with her inside it all bridaled up. Bridle. That's what horses wear, isn't it? Man's faithful servants. "I mean having to take his name. I'm not ready to

be someone's chattel. I'm not ready to be Liv Evans. Shit,
I'm not Welsh."

"You don't have to take his name. Keep your own. But
you're twenty-seven; isn't it about time?" Alex sipped the
froth of her cappuccino and glared in a schoolmarmish fashion at Liv.

"Time?" Liv's eyes rolled wildly in panic. A huge gong
signalling Doomsday. Time to give up all your dreams and
ambitions, girls. Time to admit that you're just another one
of the little ants that scamper round the earth eating, getting
married, procreating, and then snuffing it. No matter what
you think, you're just the same as the woman who serves
you in Woolworth's. You're no different from the superconfident housewives stocking up with salmon *en croute* in Put-
ney Sainsbury's on Friday evening. You have the same
dreams and desires as the next clone. Time? How dare Alex
(who was about to collide headlong with thirty) threaten her
with Time? Since when had her best friend decided that it
was time to put the clock forward to GMT, Get Married
Time?

Liv fiddled with her spoon and tried to resist the urge to
run to Thomas Cooke across the road and book the sixty-
four-pound one-way ticket to Málaga. Weren't those holiday
reps for all their sunburned drunkenness at least flying in the
face of convention by not exactly longing to run down the
aisle at the drop of a hint from their mother? Liv simply
wasn't ready. She hadn't lived the life she fantasised about.
She'd never had a studio flat of her own with knickers hanging from the antique chandelier that she'd bought with her
own money. For heaven's sake, she'd never even kissed a man
whose name she didn't know. "Will you marry me?" is the
sumptuous curtain call of a romantic encounter that has
taken in shifting sand dunes and desert storms; sex and sun-
sets on beaches in the South Pacific; ecstatic kisses atop some
mountain that only you two and a few Aztecs have ever

climbed. This hallowed question is meant to be the full stop at the end of a life less ordinary. Not the beginning of a life pretty much the same as before save for a few more sticks of furniture and the addition of an infant in the box room.

"Let's go and look at some frocks," said Alex as she bolted down her Florentine. "I've seen the most amazing McQueen gown in this shop round the corner." In case you were wondering how Alex manages to bolt down Florentines and still be slim enough to utter the words *Alexander McQueen* you have to understand a thing or two about Alex. Mostly, that she's not like me or you. For one, she's the kind of girl you see in South Kensington patisseries and Gucci and wonder how. How come she doesn't have inky cuffs and a bullying boss? How come she can buy trouser suits in three colours and one for evening? How come life is so unfair and I have to shop in French Connection? The short answer is that if you knew how, you might be prepared to settle for French Connection.

She makes a very decent living having very rich boyfriends and immaculate hair. Her Gucci is always paid for by someone called Richard who has the same surname as a large American bank. Dinner is usually courtesy of a shipping tycoon, and the penthouse in Holland Park was a goodbye present from a seventies rock star who wanted his past to remain a secret when he got married to a French heiress with a Catholic mother. See, it's easy when you know how.

Alex discovered how by accident really. Her natural habitat as a book reviewer led her to late-night conversations with many a literary lion who would thrill at her knowledge of allegory but much prefer the journey around her Amazonian body. Alex would fall in love and give them five-star reviews and then they'd suddenly remember that they had a lioness and cubs in some den in Primrose Hill. Adieu, literary lion. Soured and fed up with men who evidently preferred her bra size to her IQ, Alex tumbled along with the old maxim if you can't beat 'em beat 'em up and sometimes whip 'em, too, as long as you never have to see your own credit card statements. Which she'd been doing lucratively for the past three years to some of the most powerful and rich men in the world. Though she claimed not to do much sex anymore.

"You just don't have to. It cheapens the product." And she would never kiss before the third date unless he was under forty and passably sexy. What's more, all her spending money came in useful for her brothers. Alex's parents had died a few years ago, leaving her solely responsible for her two younger brothers, Luke and James. She'd kept them in trainers, driving lessons, private schools, and university since that day. They didn't come cheap and they didn't get any cheaper. Luke had just been accepted to Yale University in the States and James was about to start his second year at Exeter. All bank-breaking stuff, so she gratefully accepted all the help she could get from her suitors.

Liv and Alex met via one of the literary lions five years ago. Liv was his accountant and teaching him to collect as many receipts as possible from lunch dates so they could all be written off as business expenses. Alex was his current mistress, whose shoes and salads were being written off as a business expense. The girls met in his hallway one day when his wife was in the Mull of Kintyre. They were instantly bonded in hilarity over his misconception that shiny trousers made him look taller than his five-foot-two in Cuban heels.

"It's the happiest day of your life. You can't wear black." Alex, for all her career choice, was much more an old-fashioned romantic than Liv in many ways. Just a frustrated, hard-bitten, cynical one. She hovered outside the wedding shop changing room as Liv emerged looking like a trussed-up governess who had just escaped a grim Victorian novel— austere, harassed, and deep in mourning.

"It's slimming. And I can't wear cream or I'll look like a bedspread." Liv scraped back her hair into a governess's bun.

"Definitely virginal, but you look more like a candidate for female circumcision than a wench longing for a rampant deflowering." Alex walked over to the rails and plucked out a few shimmery, ethereal nightmares for Liv.

"Ees such a shame your friend is not getting married. She would make ravenous bride, eh?" Delilah, the irritatingly pretty French assistant who was begging to have her face slapped, stepped forward and tittered.

"Sorry?" bristled Liv.

"She would wear these dresses well, *non?*" Delilah assessed Alex's perfect proportions, which were only enhanced by combat pants, and longed for her to try on the Dolce number she couldn't bear to sell to any old person. "Per'aps you keep it simple, eh?" Delilah's face pinched with horror as Alex handed Liv the diaphanous numbers. Thankfully Liv was spared the guillotine stare when a gleaming beauty strode in through the door and Delilah hurled herself to the other side of the room.

"Ciao." Beauty kissed Delilah on the cheeks and tossed her handbag onto a nearby sofa. "Is it ready?"

"Ees 'ere." Delilah hurried into a back room and emerged with a wedding dress so perfect that Liv thought perhaps she'd forget weddings altogether in the face of such unfair competition and plan her funeral instead.

"Alex, I just can't do this. Look at me. I'm not a bride. Unless Frankenstein's up for it."

Alex stared long and hard at Liv as she stood before the mirror in a delicate dress that showed off everything she had and hid what was better left unsaid. "Yes, you can. You look gorgeous." And Liv really did. "But this isn't about dresses, is it?" Alex shoved her hands seriously into the pockets of her combats and assessed the damage. "It's Tim. Do you really not love him?"

"Love him? Yes," Liv granted. "In love? Not exactly. You can't be, can you, after all this time? Which is why I really shouldn't be doing it, should I?"

"Let me explain something to you, Livvy. It's Darwinian, you see." Alex gave her the look that the lions hankered after. Authoritative and sexy. "Love as we think of it is a chemical imbalance. Humans were designed to have babies. A couple meet and have mad sex for three years. No rhyme or reason; often they hate one another. Then if no babies are made they stop fancying each other. It means they're not compatible mates. If, however, you actually get on with that person but still have no babies you're consumed with doubt during the sex drought. It's a common problem in the post-permissive era of the pill."

"Which means what exactly?" Liv pulled the thread off a delicately embroidered rose until the whole flower vanished.

"Nobody has sex after the first three years. And at least you *like* Tim, which, trust me, is a huge blessing." Alex took the thread from Liv's hand and hid it in her pocket before Delilah could accuse them of shoplifting an embroidered rose.

"But sex? Passion?" Liv looked forlorn. "I want to have lunch with a man I hardly know and not wear any knickers."

"It's overrated and chilly. You'll have a fantastic life with a man you love. Tim is that man. Someone you can trust not to shag the chief bridesmaid. He'll still love you after childbirth. It may not be passion, but god, it's the most romantic thing ever. You've no idea how much I envy you that."

Liv looked back in the mirror. Give or take the odd flower on her bodice, maybe she could be the fancy dress version of a bride at least. The bodice looked passable with her pale skin. A bit of lipstick, and all would be well on the big day. And Tim? Well, he was completely great, really; she'd never thought otherwise or she wouldn't have been with him for all this time. She just had to learn to appreciate him a bit more. Remember how much she loved his fluffy boyish looks and how cute he was when he fell asleep on the sofa during *Friends*. And try to imagine how devastated she'd be if he was hit by a bus tomorrow. Anyway, who wanted a man who bought you dagger-heel shoes and asked you to wear them in the bedroom? How awful would it be to have a husband whom women at cocktail parties flirted with as they elbowed you out of the way to try to wrest his mobile number from him? And just what was it with these aftershave-commercial-type men who kissed your neck passionately in front of the mirror as you cleaned your teeth? At least Liv knew Tim loved her for herself. He wouldn't be stupid enough to stand for her tantrums. To buy her jewels "just because." He knew his own mind and they laughed together. Curled up deliciously in bed. Knew their respective chopping and stirring roles in the carbonara recipe by heart. That, as a poet must have said, was love. She'd make a beautiful bride, she thought as she eased the zip down on her corset, with maybe a whisper of a diet before the big day.

"You see, darling, I've sampled the soup. Licked the cones. I have lived life. And now I will give myself: my extended, travelled, fulfilled self, to my husband." Beauty was twirling around the shop like a remake for the twenty-first century of a Doris Day movie.

"C'est parfait. Parfait." Delilah was practically panting with the ecstasy of it all. "Roger ees lucky man, *non?*"

"It's been a thrilling affair and it will be a thrilling marriage." Beauty was the kind of girl who took her luck and flawless looks for granted. Presented with one smidgen of her charms on a silver platter by the tooth fairy, Liv would have evaporated in a puff of I-am-not-worthies. Beauty just frowned at an imaginary dark root on her head. "I love love

love him. I swear the second he puts that ring on my finger I'll just growl with pleasure."

"And you just know that Roger will be precisely three-foot-six of mangy, bearded, impotent, but oh, so wealthy arms dealer," Alex whispered into Liv's ear as she looked at Beauty with her golden ponytail and Bulgari engagement ring. Liv giggled; Alex was right. So what if Beauty had sampled the soup and licked the cones? She wasn't likely to be truly in love with the old dog she was marrying. Just bluff. Passionate marriages with wonderful, kind men who were also handsome were just a myth devised by advertising agencies to sell more chocolate.

Liv pushed all thoughts of breathtaking one-night stands and having Eric Clapton write songs about how wonderful she was looking tonight to one side and concentrated on how she was going to make Tim the happiest husband in the world. And there was always Tantric Sex Counselling and stuff if they ever got really desperate. For heaven's sake, she hadn't even resorted to buying exotic undies yet. Much less had one of those conversations that magazines always advised: talk through your fantasies and if you're comfortable with them feel free to chuck an old scarf over the lampshade and act them out. The only hitch was that Liv's fantasies usually involved other men: Naked Brad, the in-house photographer at work, various newsreaders.

"Oh, my god. Look away; look away." Alex closed the curtain on Liv and began to whistle loudly.

"What? Why?" asked a muffled Liv, thinking that maybe the arms dealer was just too hideous a sight to behold. Perhaps he'd been maimed by one of his own weapons. Perhaps they'd had to stitch his face on inside out after a mishap with a Kalashnikov. "You know I'm much better at stomaching the gory scenes in *ER* than you. I can take it." Liv groped her way round the curtain and stuck her head out. "Fuck me." She whistled slowly. Before them stood a clearly smitten Beauty but not a beast in sight, only the most divine leather-clad Frenchman that money could never buy. His hair was cropped, black, and ruffled and his criminally blue eyes creased with joy as he watched Beauty emerge in her very small smalls.

"Darling, you're not allowed to see me in the dress. Now go away or I won't marry you at all." Beauty shooed him away like a gnat; he tossed his head back and laughed.

"Me, please. Me, please. Next in line if she doesn't want you." Alex panted quietly. "There is a God, isn't there?"

"Yeah, and he's wearing a seventies biker outfit and smells of petrol." Liv's bodice was too tight now. She hacked the zip down a few notches and continued staring. "Why is life so unfair?" she moaned. Alex suddenly swivelled round and pulled the curtain over her.

"Okay, hang on a minute. Let's just say that even if that fiancée of his was hit by a bus, or even just an old green BMW in the street outside, *you* are getting married. He'd be mine. You can't have your cake and eat it."

Liv didn't care. She just wanted another look. She ripped the curtain from Alex and stuck her head out. The girls panted and gawped until the trinity of beautiful people in the corner turned and stared at them in horror. Did such unfortunate people really exist? they wondered as Alex wiped her sweating palms down her thighs, her tongue lolling bovinely next to Liv, whose boobs spilled out of her bodice onto the Fulham Road. The beautiful ones quickly looked away, terrified that such dreadfulness was contagious and having no intention of being afflicted.

"*Cherie,* my bike 'e is throbbing in the street outside. I wait there for you. Comme toujours." Roger pulled on his helmet and creaked through the door.

"But you just know he's impotent, don't you?" Liv ventured hopefully. "I mean all that throbbing between his thighs. It can't be good for it. Can it?"

Chapter Two

Where Was I When
Everyone Was Sampling the Soup
and Licking the Cones?

Liv rang her parents six times before she finally gave up and decided to cut her losses and walk the two miles from the train station to their house. It would give her time to think and work out just what she was going to say to them. To ask them whether they really thought she was doing the right thing in getting married. Shouldn't it be undying passion or not at all? Liv had convinced herself that her mother would know what was best for her. But her faith in her mother's ability to help her out suffered a minor setback ten minutes later when she was accosted by last year's rotting Christmas tree and three empty boxes of Waitrose's own brand wine in the driveway of their house. Ordinarily Liv would have cleared them discreetly away into the wheelie bin, but she was dying for the loo.

Seeing the curtains still drawn despite the bright autumn sunlight outside, she pelted round the back of the house in the hope that someone had left a door open for the cats to get in. Liv's mother and stepfather had no concept of security—Lenny, her stepfather, had worked with reforming criminals for many years and had it on good authority from several burglars that the more signs of life in a house the less likely you were to be broken into. Hence all the neighbours with bolted garages and crooklocked cars were forever having their homes stripped of video cameras and computers. Meanwhile Lenny and Elizabeth, with their open doors and garage spewing lawn mowers and trampolines and unlocked cars with tantalising stereos, had never been relieved of so much as a garden hose. They just knocked on wood occasionally and wondered who'd want their LP collection anyway, much to their smart neighbours' crooklocked dismay.

But today the door was firmly locked.

"Lemme in, quick." Liv hammered on the French windows and crossed her legs. Still no sign of life. The cats were scattered on assorted surfaces, Oedipus on the kitchen windowsill, Tom on the mouldering patio table, and Blair, the youngest, on the mat. Blair had been named in the heady preelection frenzy of April 1997 when Labour seemed like a good idea and before Tony had become Tory. Lenny had subsequently wanted to change her name to Karl, but Elizabeth deemed it cruel to confuse her, so he'd only call her Karl under his breath while breaking open a can of Sheba.

"I'm dying for a pee. Quick," Liv pleaded, and looked around the garden for an opportune hedge or bike shed. Then she crossed her legs again; the neighbours were notoriously nosy and it'd be all over the local paper the next week. Lenny and Elizabeth were already a rather unusual addition to the quiet Berkshire street. On a good day they were deemed a breath of fresh air—the Tom and Barbara Goode in a neighbourhood of Margot and Jerrys. But when the good life wasn't going their way the Margot and Jerrys would huff and puff at the lowering tone of the neighbourhood. After January storms, fence panels lay scattered across the garden for months harbouring entire universes of wood lice; the front wall that Lenny had started in 1983 had never quite seen the light of day, and those who actually ventured into the house left with tales of dislodged bathroom tiles and splotches of paint samples all the way through the house, "And on top of perfectly nice wallpaper, too." But Elizabeth and Lenny would barely have noticed. They had eyes only for one another and their minds were filled like recycling bins with the economic implications of organic farming and adult literacy issues. To them a splotch of paint sample was as good as decorating the house in Primrose Glory.

"Oh, it's divine. Isn't it Lenny? I could look at it all day," Elizabeth would marvel for a while at the patch of yellow on top of twenty-year-old lilac and then read a book, glancing up every so often to envisage Primrose Glory wherever she looked.

"Good god, we thought Oedipus was having another stroke. Come in, Livvy." Lenny opened the French doors in his Betty Ford Clinic T-shirt. A rangy, bearded man who could have passed for the messiah on any day other than a hungover Saturday, he scratched away his hangover and kissed Liv as she hurtled past him to the downstairs bathroom. After much sighing and a minor civil war with the flush on the loo, she emerged smiling and relaxed.

"I'll put on the kettle. Your mum's in bed. Go say hello." Lenny went to boil the kettle but remembered he'd had to use the cable as a makeshift door handle last week, so he boiled a saucepan of water instead.

"Black, loads of sugar please." Liv left her stepfather humming to himself and wandered upstairs to say good morning to her mother. Lenny and Elizabeth had been married for twenty years now, but still, sometimes Liv had a pang of just wanting her mother to herself, of which Lenny was acutely aware. He was an achingly sensitive man who had endured all manner of tantrums and resentment from his stepdaughter until she was in her early twenties and she suddenly stopped struggling and saw his messianic qualities and twinkly blue eyes instead of an imposter who wanted to take her mother away from her and hurt her as her father had done. Liv's father had left when she was only five; she'd only ever had a cursory holidays-on-Scottish-islands-type relationship with him. Liv had looked after her mother and protected her for so long that it was finally a relief when she relinquished that mantle to Lenny and began to have a life of her own. Liv thought that part of the reason she'd become an accountant was just as an extension of her protective, coping role in life. It was ordered and financially secure, neither of which had been features in her childhood.

Her mother was at the top of the ramshackle house, behind a door with an old part from a kettle for a handle.

"Mum." Liv tramped in and sat on the end of the bed. Her mother's sleepy blond head rose confused from beneath the sheets.

"Darling. I thought you were coming tomorrow. Now what's this big thing you want to talk to me about?" She kissed Liv on the forehead and settled back into the pillows. "If you're thinking about inviting Aunt Flora, you know I hate, but hate, her." Liv had come down to her mother's for precisely this reason. Elizabeth was wonderfully childlike and had absolutely no idea of how to behave in the real world. She had no regard for convention for convention's sake, and if she thought the wedding was a bad idea then she'd say so with no anxiety that it might provoke frowns of disapproval from elderly relations. To Elizabeth a wedding wasn't a big deal, just a lot of fun. She wanted to be surrounded by lovely people, Liv's friends, and Tim, who she thought was the most handsome man since Gregory Peck, and if it had been up to her would just have sent everyone off into the garden to eat barbecued sausages from paper plates as they sat on tree stumps chatting. Liv would wear some old ballet tutu they had lying around in the loft, and the nuptials could have been taken care of by a friend of hers who was a tarot reader. It was all the same to Elizabeth; the children loved each other and wanted to make a commitment—no matter if it was in St. Paul's Cathedral or her dilapidated pagoda. Liv, however, felt entirely differently.

"She's Dad's sister. We have to have her," said Liv as Lenny came in with a tray of coffee and some Bombay mix.

"Thought you might be hungry after the journey," he said as he laid the tray on the floor, the only available space in the dark and chaotic bedroom.

"Thanks, Lenny," said Livvy as she shovelled down a hand-ful of Bombay mix gratefully. "Besides, she's my godmother, isn't she?"

"Dog mother more like. She never even called when you had whooping cough when you were four, Livvy. But it's your day, petal. If you want her there, then I promise not to pull her chair away when she sits down." Elizabeth giggled and hugged her mug of coffee. Liv sighed.

The wedding would also be stressful because Liv's parents hardly ever saw each other. The last time had been the fu-neral of a mutual friend and had resulted in the hurling of in-sults and ham sandwiches at the wake. Even if Liv managed to keep tempers sweet, she still had to cope alone with the decisions on peach or cream napkins and lox or melon and prosciutto for the starter. Her mother had no concept of the etiquette of these matters, and her father, being snob extra-ordinaire, would forever moan if Liv got it wrong. Perhaps coming home hadn't been such a great idea after all. Instead of her mother's insouciance rubbing off on Liv, she'd just sunk further into the mires of misery as she realised that the weight of the world was resting squarely on her shoulders.

"Can we give you a hand making the invitations or any-thing, love?" asked Lenny as he settled down on the bed. Liv thought of the look of horror on her father's face as he opened an invitation to his only daughter's wedding that had been crayoned with a lettraset and had Prit-stuck glitter wedding bells on. Perhaps not.

"I think maybe I'll just go to a printer's actually, Lenny. Probably cheaper in the long run."

"In which case, we'll make the cake, won't we?" Elizabeth turned to her husband proudly, obviously having forgotten the fact that her fairy cakes had been rejected from Liv's school fete three years running. In the end, she had to send tinned peaches to the nonperishable stall instead.

"Mum. Lenny." Liv took a huge breath in. "Do you think that perhaps I'm too young to get married?" There. She'd said it. Her lungs visibly deflated.

Her mother and stepfather took in the question for a long moment, then in unison said, "Oh, of course not, darling."

Then her mother added, "I was your age when I had you." Something Liv was only too aware of.

"Exactly," Liv volunteered cautiously.

"Well, you're beautiful, darling. And so far as I know not pregnant yet?"

"No. Not pregnant. But, well, you and Dad . . ." God, it was like getting through to someone snorkelling in the Solomon Islands on a mobile phone. "I just wonder if I shouldn't ought to live a bit more first. Maybe, you know . . . just a bit." Liv had thrown caution to the wind, she'd lain her life and destiny in her mother's lap more firmly than the time she had whooping cough.

"Well, darling, if you think so. Perhaps then you're right. What did you have in mind?" her mother asked as she collected spilled bits of dried spicy pea off the duvet cover.

Well, sleep around a bit, find out if I really do like oysters or if it's only because Tim says they're so wonderful, discover whether I could design a hat that somebody wanted to wear. Live a life worthy of an obituary in the *Telegraph*. Be involved in a political sex scandal that would justify my appearance on *Desert Island Discs.* Join the French Resistance if it's still around. Be a latter-day Joan of Arc. That kind of thing.

"Dunno really," Liv mumbled.

"Livvy, you know that whatever you decide to do, Lenny and I will support you. If you want to ask your dog mother to the wedding, or your father for that matter, then I promise to be civil. But if you want to call the whole thing off, then I'll be here with chamomile tea and a large steak."

"A steak?" Liv was puzzled.

"Well, to put over the black eye that Tim's going to give you." Her mother could barely control her laughter.

"And a packet of frozen peas for the bruised shin that his mother will give you." Lenny joined in the hilarity.

"What about your father? Well, he'll just disinherit you . . . that is, if the mean bugger's left you anything in the first place."

"All right. Very funny." Liv sulked into her now-cool coffee. "I happen to think it's quite a serious matter, guys."

"Oh, darling, I know. But you're young. Divorce is easy these days. Just don't fret about it. Tim's a dreamboat; he'll be a wonderful husband. But if you want to dally a bit more, then do. We love you no matter what."

Liv pouted a bit. She wanted a braying, bossy mother in a body warmer and knitted socks to tell her to marry Tim or the family would disown her, put her up for adoption. Or she wanted a militant feminist mother who would leave stickers on light switches and bathroom cabinets imploring her daughter not to enter into the exchange of property and shameful exploitation of womanhood that is marriage. Did she get either? No. What Liv got was a big, loving liberal kiss on the cheek that was the same one she'd been given when her mother and Lenny told her they'd still love her if she went to Aberystwyth instead of Bristol. If she dropped out of her A levels and became a hairwasher in A Cut Above in the High Street. If she decided to give up six years of piano lessons because her teacher smelled of parma violets. Just as long as she was happy and not hurting anyone else Lenny and Elizabeth were fine. In fact, if she weren't so practical and capable Liv would probably be in therapy right now declaring Tough Love on her parents for turning her into a well-adjusted adult at the age of seven. Crying because if she hadn't spent her life being so grown-up she might not be in this mess. She'd have been thrown out of the Groucho Club for getting diabolical on cocaine, had at least one trip to an STD clinic, and have taken up a promising career in something underpaid and pointless like fashion journalism. There, it was all their fault. Liv scowled over the Bombay mix and longed for the wasted youth she'd never had.

Chapter Three

Be Careful What You Wish for Because You Just Might Get It

Liv's bag kept leaping out and thwacking people as she ran full tilt down Westbourne Grove to meet Alex and Tim in the pub. She was feeling much brighter since her weekend of indecision at her parents'. She and her mum had got out the old biscuit box full of pictures and she had looked back over five years of Liv 'n' Tim until her anxieties had evaporated. Of course he was the man for her. There he was smiling out at her from under his snorkelling mask in the Bahamas; raising a pint of Guinness in a pub in Dublin when they were still students, grinning his crooked-toothed smile as he celebrated Liv passing her accountancy exams. He was, quite simply, part of her. Part of her past, present, and now her future. It had all sunk into place. She put her wedding jitters behind her as she realised how ridiculous she had been to think that vanishing into the sunset with a Frenchman on a motorbike might make her happy. So what if she never had an obituary in the *Telegraph* describing the nights she'd spent with Noel Coward sipping gin and tonic in Jamaica? Noel Coward was dead. And wanderlust was all very well, but you usually ended up with malaria if you set foot outside the EU, so exotic climes could go take a hike, too. No, Liv had found her milieu. She would be content to be remembered by all who knew her as a wonderful wife and mother, for her very accomplished dinner parties, and for her ability to juggle accountancy with gnocchi making. What more could the modern woman ask for?

The Bonaparte was heaving with the usual Friday night crowd. In the corner a table of Britpop's finest downed pints and bangers and mash while the Notting Hill Glossies and home-for-the-weekend supermodels tried to hide their sheen beneath woolly bobble hats and parkas. On a prime table beneath the television set Tim, Alex, and Liv flicked beer mats and shouted to be heard above the din.

"So I think I'm going to go to Sydney for a month or two," Alex said as she stirred up her seabreeze with her finger.

"A month or two? How come?" Liv asked. "Are you going to be back for the wedding?"

"Yeah, of course I will, sweetheart. It's just this Australian guy Charlie that I'm seeing. He's going back on business and his mother has this beach house she hasn't used for twenty years that I can stay in, so I thought I'd go and finish my thesis in the sunshine."

"Don't like it too much and stay forever, will you?" Liv said. She was used to Alex jetting off at a moment's notice, but Australia wasn't exactly a hop, skip, and a jump away.

"So who's the new bloke? Is he marriage material?" Tim asked.

"Marriage?" Alex laughed. "Timbo, I haven't been out with a man who was marriage material since my father took me to Thorpe Park aged seven. But he is sex in a sports car and owns seven newspapers and three glossies. Oh, and a news network."

"What's he called? I might have heard of him," Liv asked.

"Charlie Timpson"—Alex pouted contemplatively—"and

his ears are a bit on the flappy side, but he's sweet as a dough-nut and not too dumb."

"And quite rich, too?" asked Tim with blissful male naivete.

Alex gave him her Is the Dalai Lama Buddhist? look and carried on, "There's some horse race thingy in Melbourne, so we'll probably go and see that. Should be fun."

"So when are you going?" Liv asked.

"In a couple of weeks. I'm really looking forward to it."

"That'd be great—you could meet his family." Tim smiled brightly.

"Yeah, right," said Alex unconvincingly. "That's not ex-actly what I have in mind. But I could wear some great sun-dresses and I could go and check out some of the galleries in Melbourne," Alex prompted Liv, who nodded and squeezed Tim's knee affectionately.

"Sure. Maybe we could even come out for the honey-moon, couldn't we, darling?"

Tim smiled blankly up from his pint and nodded. "Sure. Why not?"

Liv had forgotten Tim's blankness when they got back to her house later. Also the fact that he had gone as stone deaf as her grandfather at the mention of the Paul Smith suit she'd picked out for him for the wedding.

"It would be fun, wouldn't it, going to Sydney on honey-moon? Don't you think?" she called out as she clambered under the duvet. "And if Alex was there with this new boyfriend—"

"Um, Liv." Tim walked out of the bathroom and through the bedroom door still wearing his suit.

"What? You're not even undressed yet? Aren't you tired?" Liv propped herself up on one elbow as she rummaged in her bedside drawer for some vitamin C tablets she'd bought last winter. She had to keep spots at bay if she were going to be scrutinised by a church full of her father's picky family.

"Liv, I've been thinking," Tim said calmly.

Liv called off the hunt and looked up. Tim was perched on the edge of her bed looking like he wasn't going to be clambering in next to her anytime soon. "Have you now?" she asked, wondering why he was looking so sober after five pints.

"I think we should call the wedding off."

Liv squinted at him, then gave him a sidelong glance. For signs of a joke or panic or silliness. None of the above were evident in either his tone or his expression. "Sorry?" She frowned.

"The wedding. I just don't think it's right. I know that I should have said something before now, but . . . well, I thought maybe I could work it all out in my mind. But I can't. It's not that I don't love you. I do. You're my best friend and the most important person in my life. But I think we're more like brother and sister now. I don't think that I'm in love with you anymore. I'm sorry."

Liv continued to frown. Was she meant to say something? She swallowed and stared at Tim, who was looking at her steadily, awaiting her response. "Right. Well. So you're not in love with me then?" she whispered. Her body began to shake as though she were very, very cold.

"No." Tim was suddenly a stranger. Not fluffy, snorkelling, beer-guzzling, bad joke–telling Tim. She didn't know this serious man in a suit who claimed not to love her. Or want to marry her. "I think I should go," he said, and stood up gravely.

"Excuse me?" Liv finally said, her voice cracking. "You sit there and tell me you don't want to marry me and then think you're free to go?" She shook her head as though someone had just slapped her hard across the cheek. "Somehow I don't think so."

"I don't know what else there is to say," Tim said, his composure slipping so that for a second he looked like *her* Tim again. Not the imposter who had just shattered her world.

"We can start with why," Liv uttered as Tim sat back down on the bed and ran his hand through his hair.

That had taken the better part of a night. The uncontrollable sobbing and sleeping pills had taken about a week. Alex had cancelled all her bikini waxes and trips to the library and appointed herself clearing-up-the-tissues monitor and running-out-to-the-shops-to-buy-more-whisky girl. Alex had also been the one to call Fay and tell her that Liv would be taking a bit of unofficial compassionate leave and was the one who slipped all the vital platitudes to Liv as she huddled under the duvet.

"You know that this is what you wanted deep down. It's just that Tim's a bloke and he was ruthless enough to do it, whereas you're a woman and you're too kind. Anyway, he did play golf and somewhere that has to make him an incredibly dull fuck really, doesn't it?"

"But I love him. How could I not have known what I had until it had gone?" Liv wailed plaintively.

"Remember Roger, the beautiful biker frog in the wedding dress shop?"

"Yes."

"Well, there are loads of Rogers out there. And let me tell you another thing: Men always think the grass is greener; they always think that once they're free life will just be one big bloody pitcher and piano full of women with big breasts and small underwear who want to shag them senseless. Then what happens is that they discover that not only is the grass not greener; it's *mud* on the other side of the fence. Then in three months' time when you've moved on they come back with their tail between their legs and stalk you and beg you to have them back and marry them."

"Oh god, is that true? Please let it be true, Alex." Liv sat up in bed. This was the only glimmer of sunlight on her horizon right now, and it had to be true.

"Always. But the thing is, Livvy love, that women cope and men mope. When he does drag his soggy golf bore of a tail back here you'll have moved on. You'll have Roger in your bed and butterflies in your knickers and you'll say, 'Tim who?' when he rings your doorbell in the middle of the night and begs to be let back into your life."

"But he's the only man I could ever, ever love. What am I going to do now? I'm never going to meet anyone again."

Alex forgave Liv these needlessly pessimistic thoughts as this was her first real heartbreak. Absolutely everything that Alex had said about grovelling men steeped in regret was true. It was simply that Liv had to live through the inter-vening three months of hell before the stalking began and she was forced to remove the batteries from her doorbell and serve a restraining order on him. "Damn that bloody ruth-less bastard," muttered Alex as she dropped Rescue Remedy onto Liv's tongue and handed her another tissue.

And, sadly, it didn't make Liv's pain any easier to bear when she remembered that she, too, had wanted to head for the hills and sand dunes and sunset and whatever other horizon her imagination had on special offer on that particular day of the week. She knew that it was all for the best somewhere very deep down inside her, but right now it was buried be-neath all her dreams of Tim-style babies and a life signing her cheques as Mrs. Timothy Evans. She couldn't get past regret. Regret that she hadn't appreciated him more when he'd been around. Regret that she hadn't noticed something was wrong when sex had gone from tepid to somewhere-as-exciting-as-plucking-your-eyebrows a couple of months ago. As Tim had sat on the bed, everything he said had been true and was really just an echo of Liv's own thoughts: they had lots of other things to do in life; they should live a little more first, perhaps travel; the passion had just ebbed away; they were better friends than lovers. All that stuff she totally agreed with. Just why was it him who got to say it? "Ruthless bastard," she sobbed again.

Chapter Four

You May Have Been Dumped on Your Ass by Your Rat Bastard Boyfriend, but Life Goes on, Baby

Alex was also right in another respect: women coped and men moped. Within a fortnight Liv was back behind her desk at work with a packet of Handy Andies in her fist and barely a tidemark on her finger where her engagement ring had been. She had decided to throw herself into work and become an index-linked businesswoman. For the fourth day in a row she'd been the the first person in the office.

The office came to life in instalments—a few designers who either had dreamed of a hat so fantastic last night that they just had to get to work on it straightaway or hadn't made a decent headpiece for months and who were fuelled by hatter's-block anxiety, were the first. Then an intern whom all the nongay designers and men in the postroom fancied. It was always that way with work-experience people. Limbs, hair, pouty lips, beautiful husky tones. It didn't matter if they were male or female. They'd grace the photocopy cupboard with their sublime presence for two weeks, then evaporate. When it came to new recruits, fully paid up members of the staff, there were always a great deal of spots, chipped teeth, and personal hygiene problems. What happened to all the beauteous youths? Liv wondered miserably. It was a metaphor for life. It all just crumbles and gets ugly. (Her body may have been sitting upright behind her desk, but her heart still felt as though it were being trampled under a herd of migrating buffalo.)

She tapped into her voice mail hoping that there would be something from Tim: a trembling message of regret. "Sorry, I went to the doctor today and was diagnosed as having temporarily lost my mind, but I've got some antibiotics and the wedding's back on. I've realised that carbonara sauce just isn't the same without you." Instead she got:

"Message One.

" 'Liv, babe, it's Alex. Just to remind you that you're gorgeous.'

"Message Two.

" 'Liv, darling, it's Mum. Hope you're feeling better, pumpkin. As I was taking the compost out this morning I suddenly thought: Catherine Zeta-Jones. Now she may have been heartbroken years ago by that Blue Peter person, but look at her now, lovely black hair and Hollywood at her feet. And there *he* is spinning the wheel of fortune on afternoon telly. Do you imagine that if she were Mrs. John Leslie she'd be on the cover of my *OK* magazine this month? I don't think so. So there you go, love. It all comes out in the wash.'

"Message Three.

" 'Hi, Liv, it's Alex. Just arrived in Sydney this morning. I can't tell you how blue and beautiful it is. Charlie's mum's house is amazing. You'd love it. The guys here are incredible, too, in case you were contemplating a bit of cone licking or whatever it was you were talking about the other week. I miss you, sweetheart, and I hope you're well. I'll call you at home this evening to check in. Love you lots. Bye.' "

For a split-milli-barely-counts-at-all second Liv thought of the men in Sydney. In fact, she thought of one in particular. But god, that was ten years ago. Ben Parker had been her one and only holiday romance. The love of her life. The man who when she was eighteen she was going to marry and have kids and dogs with. Her family had gone with a group of other families with teenagers to Aix and stayed in the most enormous low-ceilinged farmhouse with a mosquito-infested lake in the woods nearby. The adults would stay up till midnight imbibing the local brews and playing boules while the teenagers either sulked in their rooms or, in Liv's case, experimented with hash and heavy petting in the ramshackle outbuildings of the farm. Ben Parker's parents had been staying in a mill up the road, and on their last night, as the rain poured down outside and clung to the jasmine, Liv and Ben sheltered in a barn and they probably had sex. Though she'd never quite been sure if this was the night she lost her virginity or not, because either the fine Moroccan was dope or Ben wasn't having quite an effect upon her. She still had the occasional dream about his very wonderful lips and surfer's legs teasing her into a frenzy of adolescent passion.

Liv's heart did a whistle-stop tour of a life ahead—it came in flashes. Liv going out to visit Alex and the pair of them drinking margaritas on a beach. The sunlight on her face making her strong again. Ben Parker kissing her in the surf. The two of them holding hands in front of the Sydney Opera House. But of course there was Tim, too. Tim watching the whole thing and being made sick with jealousy. Tim thinking how beautiful and have-backable she looked. Tim scuffing the knees of his Paul Smith wedding suit as he crawled around on his knees in abject misery while she touched Ben's taut tummy and then accidentally trod on Tim. I'm losing it, she snapped at the whistle-stop tour and jumped off the bus.

"Liv, are you okay?" Fay was standing behind her looking at the tepid lemon tea Liv had spilled all over her desk.

"I'm sorry; it was an accident." Liv hastily mopped up the

tea with her shirtsleeve and reached for her lavender oil to apply to her temples for calm.

"Liv, I'd like a word if you don't mind," Fay said, examining Liv's disarray: spreadsheets and how-to-win-Tim-back strategies pasted damply to her desk with Liptons. Even though she knew her work was up to scratch, Liv felt slightly nervous as she followed Fay into her office. Perhaps her pink eyes were proving an embarrassment during meetings. Or Fay had decided to put a curfew on trips to the loo, which still, despite the bottle of Rescue Remedy and hip flask of Saint-John's-wort that Liv was averaging a day, amounted to around three an hour. Which was quite a lot of wasted work time, given that each trip involved a snotty sob on the loo seat, the bashing of her head against the wall, a liberal splash of cold water on the face, and a pause to wonder if Tim would have stayed had she not had a balding patch on her right eyebrow.

"Take a seat," said Fay as she closed the door softly behind her. Unaccustomed to such time wasting as sitting down and closing doors on Fay's part, Liv felt mildly claustrophobic and nervous. She perched perilously on the edge of a low filing cabinet in an attempt to defuse the situation. "The sofa's all yours." Fay wafted her hand in the direction of the butter-soft suede objet d'art and swivelled her own chair to face Liv. "How are you feeling, Liv?"

"Getting better every day. Really. I've almost forgotten about the whole thing. And I'm sorry about the mess out there—I just got a bit light-headed. I came in early and haven't had breakfast yet."

"It's probably not wise to skip breakfast, Liv," said Fay. "But I think that's just a symptom of skipping other things, isn't it?" she added meaningfully.

Liv sprinted through a list of things she could be accused of skipping . . . lunch: never. She was terminally hungry and, try as she might, had never been fashionably anorexic—even the breakup had just forced her headlong into the cookies. Missed periods: only once and that was because she'd misunderstood the instructions on her packet of pills and consequently endured a month of "I'm too young to have a baby" hysteria. Though now she wished she had got preggars, because Tim would have had to stay and love her. Work: Liv used to skip work occasionally when there was a decent Wimbledon game on television or for emergency Christmas shopping, but it wasn't something she made a habit of. Therefore, what on earth could Fay be talking about?

"I don't think I follow, Fay." Liv thought that judging by the look of compassion on Fay's face she wouldn't *want* to follow, either. Perhaps Fay was going to ask her to skip coming into the office for the rest of her life. Skip being paid and skip down to the Jobcentre to sign on. She hoped not; now she was a spinster she was going to have to put some money away for her pension and the one-bedroom bungalow she was going to live in with her cats when she got old. A tin of Whiskers was going to be the price of a small car by the time she was sixty, the way inflation was going.

Fay picked up a tidy pile of papers and stroked them flat on her immaculate lap.

"I found these in my in-tray." Fay shuffled the pile of papers in Liv's direction.

Liv squinted at them, wondering if she'd managed to fill the spreadsheets with Tim's name in the throes of devastation. Rows of Tim and columns of fuckwit.

"I left them there this morning. I double-checked and they looked okay to me," said Liv, instantly rising to her own defence.

"The spreadsheets are fine. As immaculate as ever." Fay remained unsmiling. "It's not the spreadsheets I'm interested in, Liv. You also left these on my desk." Fay handed Liv a pile of poorly spelled documents: her fantasy obituary, a grainy Internet printout of Naked Brad, her desert island discs, her short story about Francesca the French resistance fighter, her day in the life as milliner to the stars. Liv wished for death by water. Death by lemon tea. Death by rushing headlong into the lift shaft. She wanted very much not to be in the room right now. She couldn't imagine how her dream life had got caught up with the spreadsheets.

"I'm sorry. I'll work late every day for the next year. I'll sweep the workroom floors in my lunchtime. Only please don't fire me. I need this job. It's a distraction. God knows if I were at home right now I'd probably have drowned in my tears."

"You need this job like a hole in the head, Liv." Fay's stony-faced boss look was beginning to grate on Liv's nerves. What the hell did she know about heartache with her randy husband and perfect kids?

"No. You can't fire me. Please." Liv saw only mornings at home when she'd be reduced to calling daytime television phone-ins with psychiatrists and cotton-wool-haired agony aunts.

"Liv, I have no intention of firing you. Listen, love, I think this is all a bit deeper than you think. And in a way a lot more exciting." Liv was beginning to doubt Fay's sanity now. On the scale of fun-stuff-to-do, how exciting was getting dumped? And she was cringing as she realised that Fay would now know what a sad loser she was and that Spandau Ballet's "Gold" was one of her all-time favourite songs and that she fantasised about wearing A-line skirts in a wartime bunker. Christ, she hadn't even confessed that to Tim and he was, as she now knew, the only man she would ever love in her entire life. "So I'm going to help you." Oh god, Liv just didn't want to be Fay's latest mission. She wasn't a Bosnian war child. She wasn't keeling over with chronic alcoholism. And she didn't *think* she needed recycling. Why couldn't Fay keep her North London worthiness for another cause?

Liv contemplated slinking away, but her boss was not to be thwarted in her crusade.

"You're in pain right now. Your ego's been bruised, and you feel betrayed. You don't think you'll ever get over it," continued Fay. A tremble assaulted Liv's lower lip; this was almost as accurate as a telly shrink. "But the truth is that your relationship with Tim probably suffered because you were harbouring unfulfilled dreams of a life outside your relationship with him. You wanted out of the wedding as much as he did. Only now you're making yourself into the victim, which is fine for a moment or two, but then you have to tell yourself that this happened for a reason and the reason is that you have shit to get out of your system, young lady."

"I do?" Liv asked. She felt a flash of strength. "I do!" she repeated. Then she realised that actually, she would never utter those words while gazing lovingly into Tim's eyes and went a bit floppy again.

"You do." Fay didn't notice the collapse of spirit. "Which is why I'm sending you on a sabbatical."

"You're firing me?" Liv squeaked.

"I've watched you practically crawl into work every day for the last week; you're wretched and pathetic" (Liv would have told Fay to go easy had she not caught sight of her stringy-haired, baggy-eyed reflection in Fay's computer screen) "and I know that if I don't persuade you to go somewhere, anywhere, then I won't be passing on the benefit of my feminine wisdom. You need to get off your bum, stop dreaming, and start living. Now blame it on the fact that I went to university in an era of ludicrous idealism and hope, or blame it on the fact that I still wonder what would have happened to me if I'd married Gus the cowboy I fell in love with in Arizona in '73. But please. For me, Liv, go. Go anywhere. Just for a while. You're a free woman."

"You want me to go away?" Liv was having trouble comprehending. Did *sabbatical* mean "bugger off" in Greek?

"How about France?" Fay was resting against the book-shelf now with her hand on Liv's shoulder.

"The French resistance thing was just because they all had great forties hairstyles and pretty noses." Liv felt a dash to the ladies' for the sob-bash-splash routine coming on but resisted.

"Anywhere, then. Do it for me. Go somewhere amazing; then come back and tell me all about it over a glass of wine, eh?" Fay pleaded.

"That's okay for you to say," Liv sniffed. "Your life's all sorted and you're amazing."

"But I never rode bareback with Gus." Fay smiled softly. Liv remembered what Alex had said about getting back in the saddle, and thought about Australia—it was the last place she wanted to be right now, but it was as far as she would ever, ever get from Tiny Tim (as he'd come to be known on account of his small-minded-not-able-to-love-Liv ways).

"Australia. I might be able to go there, you know. If you like." Liv wiped her snotty hand on her skirt and stopped crying for a moment.

"Australia." Fay looked as though she'd just had a mouth-ful of especially delicious chocolate cake. "Perfect."

Chapter Five

New Horizons

Liv climbed out of the taxi in front of her new address. The first thing she learned about Sydney was never to trust a taxi driver to know the way. They'd already visited 34 Seinfeld, Sussex, and Dillon Streets, taking in Sydney's harbour, North Shore, and red-light district. All of which were perfectly picturesque but proved not to be her new address. Finally they alighted on the leafy little street near the ocean in Bronte—an area that for all she knew could have been the Acton of Sydney. Liv tipped him the grand sum of seventeen dollars, which seemed extreme even for a dumb tourist, but she wanted to be sure that he wasn't going to come back and slit her throat at nightfall. After all, a foreign city is a foreign city, and until she knew the precise location of the nearest places to buy newspapers, tampons, and beer she wasn't taking any chances. As the taxi rattled away down the road she hoisted the suitcase onto the pavement and paused to look at her new home for a moment.

The address had sounded fairly ordinary when she'd copied it down from her mum's address book: Bronte Beach, New South Wales. But this was as far from Wales as it was possible to stray. For one thing, when she'd left, the other Wales was enduring the coldest October since records began and children were going to school in boats due to floods, et cetera. The usual stuff of British winters. Here on the flip side of the world it was the beginning of summer. Liv rolled up the sleeves on her fleece. The air smelled warm and sweet and the evening sky was a pale velvety blue. The cottage, though partly obscured by the most verdant jasmine tree imaginable, was painted pale buttery yellow. There was a lace ironwork balcony upstairs and the windows had been shuttered against the sun earlier in the day. Cicadas murmured in the air as Liv hauled her luggage behind her.

Liv had been right and Alex had been loving Sydney more than she was letting on. So when Liv had called after her little chat to Fay and asked if the offer of getting her bum out there still stood, Alex was delighted. Alex was going to be away in Melbourne with Charlie for a few days and wouldn't be there when Liv arrived, but she'd left the key to the cottage with the girl who squatted in the beach hut next door.

Apparently, Charlie had let the girl stay even though she didn't pay any rent because she was all brokenhearted and emotionally disturbed, having been dumped by a friend of his. Alex said it was a bit like having a cat. Occasionally she'd stroll in and use the bathroom, and she stored her milk in the fridge and stuff, but she was pretty quiet and did the odd bit of housework, so Alex was delighted to have her. Alex said that her name was Laura and though she was an emotional train wreck at the moment she was actually quite sweet really. Liv thought that a train wreck of a girl was exactly what she needed to take her mind off her own woes. She only hoped that Laura wasn't quite as glamorous as most of Alex's friends—just in case Tim should do the tail between the legs trick after three months and come and ring her doorbell in the night . . . only to decide that he preferred her neighbour instead.

But there was no sign of life at the window of the hut. Liv wondered what Laura Train Wreck might be up to on a Saturday night in the sunniest city in the world. Sitting at home being disappointed in love and playing wrist-slitting music, perhaps. Liv took a deep breath and pressed the doorbell.

"Yeah?" a woman's voice breezed out of the hut, which was actually more of a barn painted cornflower blue. A light was filtering through a window and it looked pretty cosy.

"It's Liv Elliot. Alex's friend," Liv stammered back.

"Righty ho," the voice drifted down.

Liv waited for someone to come flying out at any moment. She assumed that the voice must be on her way to give a hand with the luggage, so she waited quietly, checking her hand for drug-induced shakes from the melatonin she'd scoffed on the plane. She could only hold her hand out for three seconds before it began to wobble dangerously. She wondered how she was going to cope when the time came for her to experiment with Ecstasy, as she'd invariably have to do in her new life as a girl who lived life and kissed cowboys. Or jackeroos or whatever the Australian equivalent was. Her liver would probably pack in. She anticipated life ahead with a yellow tinge to her skin, which, oddly, wasn't nearly as terrifying to her as the idea that she might actually do something she'd regret on drugs. Flash her tits, fall into a trifle, be a terrible dancer. Still, wasn't that the whole point? It would be tough being a legend without doing anything legendary.

Liv sat on her suitcase and assumed that Laura Train Wreck must be in the shower or something—or perhaps she was prising herself from a hammock and drifting heartbrokenly through the hut. But ten minutes later, by which time even Elizabeth I could have made her way through the hallways of Hampton Court in a difficult dress with a neck ruff, Liv decided to bang on the door again.

"Yup?" the voice answered.

"It's me, Liv. I just wondered if you could let me have the key to Alex's cottage!" Liv called out.

"Oh, right. You want me to let you in?"

"If that's all right."

"Coming," the voice signed off. And didn't materialise for another five minutes. Then, just as Liv was wondering how much of a brain cell deficit one person could exist on, the mosquito net flew open and a small red-haired girl with china-white skin and paint-splattered overalls stood before her.

"I'm Laura. Follow me. It's all a bit hectic at the moment." She led Liv to the cottage and through the front door. "Your room's over there. Do you think you can sort yourself out? I'm really late for an appointment with my shrink," she blurted out at breakneck speed before vanishing back to the hut and slamming a door. It was like an encounter with the white rabbit in Wonderland.

Liv sat on the floor on top of her suitcase and caught her breath. Which was when it all began to sink in. Here she was, on the other side of the world, boyfriendless, in fact altogether friendless, her mother, though a bit flaky and useless at the best of times, was now an impossible twenty-four hours away, and her new neighbour, and the only person she knew in the whole goddamn city, was unfriendly and had abandoned her for psychotherapy. Liv closed her eyes for a second and contemplated tears. But she was a bit bored of that whole crying scenario. Depression had taken over where tears left off. Alex told her that it was the next stage of grief, which was a good thing because now there was only Anger and Closure to look forward to. So in the face of encroaching black gloom and a month in an institution Liv did the British thing and went to make herself a cup of tea.

The beach house was possibly the most beautiful place Liv had ever seen. And while Charlie stayed at his flat in Bondi so he could keep his infidelity options open, he'd let Alex move in here and stay as long as she wanted to. It had belonged to Charlie's mother, Jemima, in the midseventies when she was going through a sticky patch with her husband. He was spending too long at the office and flitting around in helicopters and she was sick of playing the corporate wife. So, much like Marie Antoinette, she reasoned, she moved into the beach house with just a few bikinis and kaftans and rediscovered herself via Germaine Greer and Erica Jong and with a little practical help from the nineteen-year-old lifeguard on Bronte Beach. The house was bohemian in the way that only billionaires can afford. Each room was an extension of the beach and the sea—driftwood, plaster walls encrusted with seashells, a sandpit for a garden surrounded by reeds and rushes. There was a small log fireplace, and mementos of Jemima's Awakening littered the house: a white sheepskin rug before the hearth—undoubtedly well used—Frederick's of Hollywood lingerie in the beachwood drawers, some Leonard Cohen LPs and a Barry White 45 of "Hang On in There, Baby," and the telltale pair of yellow swimming trunks size XXLarge.

Liv had instant respect for Jemima, who until now she had only glimpsed in cream suits and clutch bags with a bouffant at some gala ball in the pages of *Hello!* Yet here was the woman twenty-five years ago, reckless, disgraceful, and, if the black-and-white photo of her next to the water bed in Alex's room was anything to go by, plain rather than beautiful but cool and sexy as hell. Quietly Liv determined that she would try to live her time in Sydney with Jemima as her patron saint.

Just as Liv located the kettle there was a rap on the mosquito net and a blond girl dressed all in pink down to her handbag stood in the doorway.

"Hi. I'm Jo-Jo, Laura's girlfriend. You must be Alex's friend." She put out a pink-nailed hand and reached for Liv's trembling one. "I saw the light on and thought Laura might be in here."

"I'm Liv. I think Laura sort of went that way." Liv pointed, drinking in the pink and longing for some human company. "Cup of tea?" Liv offered as a bribe.

"No thanks. We should go—you know shrinks; they get all agitated if you're late and start saying it's Freudian." Jo-Jo turned and yelled with unexpected volume for someone so pink, "Laura, you ready?"

"Here." Laura reappeared, kissed Jo-Jo on the lips, and they left. Liv was alone once again but felt slightly more encouraged. Did pebbles on the beach necessarily have to be male pebbles? she wondered. Shame she didn't even slightly fancy Alex, for then life would be sorted: Alex was pretty and cleaned her teeth more frequently than most men. They got on brilliantly and Liv's parents adored Alex. Except, sadly, Liv wasn't rich enough for Alex and they both liked sex with men too much. Double shame. Liv downed her tea and plodded off to fall asleep on the nearest bed, dreaming of the day when Tim couldn't help himself from calling her and hanging up just to hear her voice on the machine.

When Liv woke up, her throat hurt and her eyes seemed to be clamped shut. There was someone moving in the shadows of her room. She opened her mouth to ask who it was, but nothing came out. Eventually she raised a limb and then heaved open one eyelid.

"Eepppp," she slurred, wanting to make her presence felt.

"Oh, well done. I was wondering whether to give you a bit of a shove or not. If you'd slept any longer your sleep pattern would've been buggered up for days." The quiet Australian voice seemed to be moving around in the cool darkness of the room. "Suzanne, my therapist, suggested that helping others was a good way of deflecting my own pain and anguish, so I've unpacked your stuff and put a white wash in. Do you fancy a boiled egg and toast?"

"Breakfast?" Liv squeaked, marvelling at her ability to adjust her bodyclock so cleverly through what must be at least seven international time zones.

"Actually, it's teatime. We can have some toast soldiers, too, if you like."

"Sounds lovely." Liv shifted her body to ascertain which limb was which beneath the somnolence. Also, she was a bit peeved, because if Laura was going to help Liv, then who was Liv going to help to forget her worries?

"Sorry about last night, but I still get nervous about the counselling sessions. Even though Suzanne's lovely and I've got Jo-Jo to come with me now," Laura said, pulling back the curtains and drenching the room in bright blue. Sea. Cloudless sky and a glare that sent Liv back under her bedclothes.

"Bloody hell. What was that?" asked Liv. "Some kind of alien invasion?"

"A cracking Sydney afternoon," said the voice, which, in the light, indeed belonged to the same Laura as last night, though it was hard to see anything much given the green stripes of paint across her temples.

"So the counselling?" Liv tried diplomatically to find out whether Laura Train Wreck was clinically insane or merely brokenheartedly insane like herself. She noticed that Laura was folding Liv's oldest knickers into a careful pile in a chest of drawers.

"Yeah. Therapy's getting me through. Only three nights a week now, though, and once on the weekend. And there's a great telephone hot line that's stopped me doing something stupid quite a few times," Laura announced proudly.

"Actually, I've just split up with my boyfriend and I'm feeling a bit wobbly myself," Liv confided. "Which is why I'm here really. Trying to forget about him and find myself or something mad like that. I thought I'd try to work it

through myself rather than going to see a therapist, though."
In the blackest moments of the last couple of months it really
had occurred to Liv to seek professional advice, but shrinks
were surprisingly expensive and when it came to a toss-up
between therapy and a pale blue cashmere cardigan it somehow hadn't been such a hard decision to make. Which had
led her to feel, with a surge of triumph, that she just might
be on the mend.

"Oh, counselling's great, but it's no substitute for self-
help," Laura recited in fluent recovering victim speak, a language Liv realised she was going to become very familiar
with. Soon she'd know her Issues from her codependencies,
and she'd be able to verbalise her guilt in no time. See, she'd
already learned something and she'd only been in Sydney a
day. Or night. Or whatever. God, five minutes with Laura
and she'd be all cured. "I'll tell you all about it over tea." And
with that she was gone, leaving Liv basking in the startling
afternoon sunshine.

Liv's room was a beautiful cream-walled haven filled mostly
with the enormous white bed that she was lying in. Next to
the bed was a table of candles: jasmine-scented, raspberry-
coloured garden candles in terra-cotta pots, and beside that a
bookcase filled with film star biographies, a chest of drawers
in perfectly distressed blue nestled in the corner, and an antique Indian rug embroidered with giant peonies lay over the
uneven white floorboards. All a far cry from her fraying car-
pets and Picasso posters at home in London.

She shoved back the covers and made her way towards
the window, feeling a bit like the old people going towards
the spaceship in the movie *Cocoon*. The window was at
least the length of Liv's entire flat in London and opened out
onto a little terrace littered with pots of geraniums and lilies.
Liv held her breath as she took in the view. A cityscape
straight off a postcard: Centrepoint Tower rose high above

the mirrored buildings and office blocks; then if she turned her head farther to the right she could see the water bounce diamonds of light back at her. After a few minutes of drinking in the brilliance of the view she pulled an old sundress out of the wardrobe and over her head and made her way into the other room.

"So how do you know Charlie?" Liv asked as she cracked open the top of her perfectly runny soft-boiled egg.

"I was going out with a friend of his. Then we had the most traumatic breakup. I don't really like to talk about it, but it was the worst thing that ever happened to me. Complete bloody carnage. Well, I guess you'd understand. Anyways, Charlie offered me the flat. He's been fantastic. Even introduced me to Jo-Jo."

"So do you and Jo-Jo go out together?" Liv asked.

"Yeah, it was pretty much love at first sight. If it weren't for the fact that you should never rely on another person to make you happy and that it has to come from within, I'd say that Jo-Jo makes me really happy," Laura related. Liv totted up the money she was going to save on self-help books just by living next door to Laura.

"Have you always lived in Sydney?" Liv asked, bursting to ask about the horrible witch who had dumped her but trying not to sound too much like an ambulance chaser. Certainly the way Laura was talking and based on the few horrific details Alex had shared with her it sounded like the roughest breakup since Romeo and Juliet. In fact, before Liv had even met Laura she had sometimes drifted off to sleep chanting, "At least I'm not Laura Train Wreck."

"It's all right, isn't it, this place?" said Laura, giving Liv her first taste of the Australian knack of playing things down. Elle Macpherson? Yeah, she's an okay-looking chick. The ninety-degree cloudless weather? Not bad going today. A spider the size of a Shetland pony? He's a big bloke. Liv would get used to it in time.

"Yeah. At least it's not Golborne Road in the pissing rain," mumbled Liv. Which was exactly where she had spent last Saturday night. Walking backwards and forwards in her only item of designer clothing. Which happened to be a Chloe corset designed more for seducing rock stars than prowling up and down wet streets hoping to bump into your ex-boyfriend on his way out to buy a pint of milk and convince him that you were completely over him and now had a full and active social life full of seducible rock stars whom you were on your way to meet at Woody's. Thank god for Alex and Sydney, was all Liv could think as she looked back on perhaps the worst way she'd ever spent four hours. In fact, looking back made her realise how far she'd come. And not just the gazillion or so miles. She was only thinking of Tim every hour or so now and not every ten minutes. Maybe things were looking up.

"I'm dying to explore," Liv said, suddenly curious about the city that, until five minutes ago, had existed in her mind as a faded postcard of an odd-shaped opera house and a whole load of men with sunburn and stringy long blond hair. Judging by her view, she was going to have a hard time keeping the promise she'd made to Alex not to explore the best bits before she and Charlie came home next week.

"Well, I'd love to give you the tour, but I'm in the middle of painting Venice, I'm afraid. Maybe tomorrow?"

"Venice?" Liv asked.

"Sure, come and have a look." She put down her spoon and led Liv into the hut. Propped against a wall was the Grand Canal, Harry's Bar in the distance, and the unmistakable brickwork of Venice. A floor-to-ceiling city, stretching across the entire room. The bed had been shoved into a tight corner and the floor was strewn with open paint pots and a chaos of brushes. "I'm a set decorator," Laura said, grabbing a paintbrush and touching up a gondolier.

"This is amazing. What's the play?" asked Liv.

"Death in Venice. . . . It opens at the opera house tomorrow night, so I have to push on." Laura was unable to resist getting back to work. Within moments all talk had ground to a halt and she hummed away to herself as she mixed some more brick colour. Liv tiptoed back to the cottage.

As Liv finished off her tea, leaning over the balcony, she was beginning to remember all those stirrings she'd had: Roger, Ben Parker, any old random bloke on the tube. Yes, the sap was definitely rising. I mean was she just going to abandon all those dreams she'd had of wearing no underwear to lunch and having sex in the afternoon just because Tim didn't want her? Absolutely not. No, the time had come to boot the accountant from her soul and get kicked out of nightclubs for raucous behaviour. Bugger Tim. Liv's life was about to take off so dramatically that she'd turn into one of those women who never seemed to have a pair of clean knickers so she had to turn yesterday's inside out. Well, she didn't literally hope for this because it might be a bit foul, but theoretically she dreamed that she'd be so busy being socially indispensable that knickers would be the last thing on her mind.

The only problem was she didn't really know how to kick-start this knickerless social whirl. Given that she knew nobody in the city save a linguistically impaired cabby and Laura Train Wreck. There was always the option that she could just leave it up to fate. Perhaps she should be Zen and take to the streets and see if she bumped into Ben Parker or a similar candidate for fun and love to end all love. Someone to have sex with on sheepskin rugs while eating pomegranates. Not that there was anyone similar to Ben Parker. She slid into a reverie and wondered what he was doing now. Maybe he really was in Sydney. Certainly his parents had

lived here. And let's face it, who in their right mind would
want to leave? And if he did live here and was, let's just say,
girlfriendless, then he, too, might be wandering the streets in
a similarly Zen-like manner. Though in her experience men
with spare time on their hands tended to make plans involving beer, not destiny. So what did one do in a strange city
without a car, map, or friend? She would get dressed first.
Something fun and sexy. She pulled on her shorts and some
great flip-flops decorated Carmen Miranda–style with fake
cherries that Tim happened to think hideously tacky and set
out in search of Sydney and herself. Well, she had to start
somewhere.

Actually, the only place she could think of to go was to the
local shop for a pint of milk. Until Alex arrived, that might
actually be the sum total of her social life. But it was definitely a start. Liv walked out onto the street and stopped to
pick a flower of jasmine from the tree in a jaunty fashion.
Had she been in New York or Paris she'd have simply
walked in the same direction as the best-dressed person and
followed the neon lights. But there were only lots of frangipani trees, a man walking a dog, and some temperamental
streetlights. She just went the opposite way to the man with
the dog, knowing that wherever he was she didn't want to
be and also that if she followed him either he'd accuse her of
being a stalker or she'd step in his dog's poo with her flip-
flops on. So she walked up the hill past a street of beach
houses all similar to her own, some done to fabulously rich
banker standards, others more dilapidated and run-down, but
all variations on a theme and most painted all ochres and um-
bres and sandstone colours, with the odd pink or cobalt blue
thrown in. There were a few cars parked on the streets and
the occasional cockroach scuttled underfoot, but otherwise
there was no sign of life.

The uphill became a downhill and the road wound until
Liv found a buzzing intersection and a fluorescent-lit super-

market glaring out at her. She wandered in and found the fridge, thinking she may liven up her night in by buying a pint of Ben & Jerry's, too. She had hoped that she might inadvertently wind up on some beachfront bar sipping a piña colada that matched her flip-flops, chatting to an eclectic bunch of locals—maybe a shark catcher with leathered skin. Most definitely there'd be a lifeguard and a bikini-clad waitress who'd tell her the best place to get your tarot cards read and the hippest beach to spread your towel on. But Rainforest Crunch was the next best thing.

"Just gorgeous. Where did you find them?" Liv looked up and saw a six-foot man smiling down on her. Wearing a polka-dot dress and a black wig. He was pointing, with a nail that put even Alex's French manicures to shame, at Liv's foot.

"My flip-flops?" She smiled. "Little shop in London."

"Well, they're very special," he commented, and eased his corseted waist and pneumatic bosom up to reach the top shelf for a bottle of wine.

"Going to a party?" Liv asked.

"Just a club night in Oh so low," he replied.

"Oh so low? What's that?"

"It's what we call Soho, honey. Real dive, but I've been at the office all day so needed a little deeee-stress." He smiled. "I intend to get totally arseholed tonight. So you're new in town?" he asked.

"How can you tell?" Liv picked up the ice cream and grabbed a packet of Oreos, too, as they headed for the checkout together.

"Your skin's blue. Clearly not a native." He examined her shopping closely. "Night in alone, eh?" he asked sympathetically.

"Yeah." Liv confided, "Had quite a few of those lately. I was pissed on from a great height by the man I was supposed to marry."

"Never? But you're gorgeous, darling. What was he thinking?" He pouted as Liv loaded her shopping into a plastic
bag. This was exactly the kind of response she loved. Yeah,
dumbass Tim.

"That he could do better. Clearly. You know, I haven't so
much as kissed another man for five years." Liv was beginning to know how people felt on *Springer*. Once you got into
the habit of confessing the stuff of your soul to total strangers
it was hard to stop.

"You are kidding me?" He stopped dead in his tracks and
his eyes lit up. "Well, fate could not have been kinder to you
tonight, sweetness. We are going to a party." He took Liv by
the arm and led her out of the shop. "I'm Dave, by the way.
Venture capitalist by day. Miss Pussy Whiplash *par nuit.*" He
held out his Schiapperelli pink–nailed hand; Liv wasn't sure
if she was meant to shake it or kiss it.

It wasn't until several hours later that Liv realised that the
sticky mess at her feet signalled the sad demise of her Rainforest Crunch. And as it was by now one in the morning and
she'd been on the Orgasms for the last few hours, neither did
she care. She was perched on a bar stool in a sweaty room
surrounded by drag queens and the cutest taut-chested, high-
bottomed men she had ever seen. And bar a few females who
looked like they could be the bouncers, she was the only
woman in the place. Not that this improved her chances of
anything other than being able to shamelessly ogle the talent.
Some men were dressed as devils, others glittered as angels,
and one was Monica Lewinsky with attendant cigar and large
hair. The floor show was about to begin and the lights
dimmed in preparation for Dave's entree.

For Dave just happened to be the most spectacular live act
this side of the opera house, and, having introduced Liv to
all his friends and plied her with innumerable Orgasms (the
alcoholic variety, he had reassured her when he offered her

one and she looked dubiously at his frock), was now about
to entertain her. Along with about five hundred gay men.

"Ladies and gentlemen, Miss Pussy Whiplash. Please give
her a warm hand." The compere pouted as the strains of
Cher's "Life after Love" began. Dave exploded into the
room and began to belt out his number. With sucked-in
cheekbones he mimed his way through the song, and Liv
couldn't help thinking that if Cher were there she might be
very flattered. Dave had the best set of legs this side of a
Sports Illustrated calendar and all the men, and even the
bouncer-women, were enthralled. As the audience whistled,
Dave leaned across the bar and flicked one fake-eyelashed
eye at the man standing next to Liv. Liv had already deduced
this was Dave's boyfriend, James.

"Lucky you," laughed Liv, and waved her hands in the air
in what passed for a dance to the untrained eye. The last time
Liv had moved to music with such abandon had been to
"The Land of Make-Believe" by Bucks Fizz when she was
eleven.

"Ooh, baby, he was great. So, James, how long have you
guys been together?" Liv asked as the lights went up again
and Dave, alias Cher, clicked his heels backstage to disrobe,
or whatever one does after a bout of Cher-ness.

"Call me Greta, darling. I'm only James when the sun's
above the yardarm." James smiled. He had arched eyebrows
and a cigarette in a holder. "About eight years, which doesn't
seem to have been even slightly impaired by the fact that we
work for rival city firms."

"Two investment bankers in one night." Liv pondered.
"So it is possible to work in finance and be interesting. Must
just be me who isn't."

"Oh, for sure." James—sorry, Greta—smiled. Actually,
James pronounced it "Greeter" with a heavy Aussie accent
and it was a reference to his Greta Garbo apparel, which was

disturbingly convincing. Except for the fact that Greta was beginning to sport a two-in-the-morning shadow—but Liv figured that just added to his moody Swedish allure.

Two hours and even more Orgasms later, Liv was trying very hard to focus on Greta, but her eye had begun wandering in a spastic fashion to Dave and a member of the New Zealand Ballet Company, who were rhumbaing the early hours away on the bar.

"All over the world women are being slowly murdered by their lingerie," Greta whispered. "Too tight. Too constricting. Which is fine for a night like tonight. But for day wear? A woman needs comfort and support."

"You can say that again," said Liv, now downing her seventh Orgasm. "And not just from her bra."

But Greta wasn't in the mood to discuss emotional dalliances. Greta had business in mind. "Which is why Greta's Grundies are going to be headline news internationally. A bra that looks binding but fits like it's not there at all. Know what I'm saying?" He winked at Liv and she nodded seriously. She made a point of never laughing when paralytic. It was the only rule she could remember, but it stood her in good stead. It meant that she didn't offend anyone and therefore never got her nose broken. Unless, of course, she tumbled headlong into a bar stool or table.

"So if I pay, you promise me you'll do it?" Greta asked. What felt like minutes but must have been hours later, given that Liv now had no feeling in her left leg and the Rainforest Crunch was now just a cluster of nuts. Liv found herself staring into the heavy-lashed eyes of He-Greta and trying to remember what terrible thing she'd agreed to do.

"Sure. You've got my number. Just call me," she said, trying to cast her mind—well, what was left of it—back to a moment earlier in the evening when Greta had offered her money for something. Not old rope. Not her body, she didn't think. Though that was pretty old rope–ish itself. God, she had to remember. Think, Liv. Think. What was the meaning of life and what on earth have you promised you'll do for this Greta Garbo with facial hair?

Chapter Six

Liv Makes a Clean Breast of Things

Liv had taken the precaution of closing the shutters so that a random Peeping Tom on his yacht on the ocean couldn't get a butchers at her through his telescope or on his radar or whatever. Then, recollecting a *Blue Peter* recipe, she mixed up some flour-and-water paste, took out a copy of yesterday's *Sydney Morning Herald,* and began to mould the papier-mâché to her chest. What she had drunkenly agreed to do was be at work at their market stall on Saturday mornings and be the sample size for Greta's Grundies lingerie. The boys had made some very pretty but, understandably, rather distorted underwear because it had been modelled on Dave, who had only foam boobs and more round the front than round the back in the knickers department. They'd spotted Liv's very average girl shape at once and, dressed in business suits and city attire at lunch the day after the big night, had persuaded her to offer her body up for their services.

Though working in a market stall and flashing her tits wouldn't have been her career of choice, it was a lot more fun than spreadsheets. She gasped as she slapped the papier-mâché on her skin, but the cold was quite soothing in the outrageous midday heat and so as not to crack the mould she lay down on the sofa. Every ten minutes she knocked on the newspaper, but it wasn't drying. Eventually she picked herself up and shuffled over to the bathroom and took the hair dryer to her chest. But just as it was setting, just as the newspaper and glue hardened over her bust, Laura walked in the door, trailing a ceiling-scrapingly tall woman. Not wanting to seem rude, Liv reached out to shake her hand.

"I'm Liv Elliot. Nice to meet you," Liv said as though having Laura Train Wreck and her friends wander through the house as though it were an art gallery was the most normal thing in the world. Well, it was certainly a regular occurrence. And as she held out her hand the papier-mâché chest fell to the floor, leaving Liv decorated only by a few columns of weather forecast and the cricketing news.

"I'm Suzanne. I'm a psychotherapist," the woman replied, and nodded sagely at Liv. A grimace formed on Laura's brow.

"Just helping a friend out," Liv twittered, plunging to the floor and reapplying the cast before it set. "Now if you'll excuse me, I just have to go and finish myself off." Liv closed the bathroom door behind her and splashed some water onto her mould to soften it.

When Liv turned the tap off she heard hushed and urgent tones filtering in from the living room.

"She's English," Laura whispered.

"I think that girl probably has some issues," Suzanne muttered. "Serious case of exhibitionism. It's a power thing, I think. In keeping with the lingerie fixation. The lingerie is about placing a veneer of unattainability between herself and the world outside."

"But did I tell you that I think she could be abusing substances, too? It stinks of glue in there. And that talk about finishing herself off. You don't really think she'll commit suicide, do you?" Laura asked grimly.

Needless to say, Liv couldn't imagine who Laura and the woman were discussing. She presumed that it must be an actress from Laura's theatre company. Though she couldn't think why they'd be surprised at an actress being a pathological exhibitionist. Just as long as they didn't bring her anywhere near the house; otherwise Liv's position as acting landlady would be severely compromised.

When Liv finally emerged from the bathroom wielding the perfect impression of her average breasts which James could use to make his bras, Laura and her shrink had gone, leaving Liv free to test-drive the leopard print G-string in comfort and privacy for the rest of the afternoon. Though it wasn't a comfortable experience at all. She realised at once that if these knickers were for women, the first thing to be done was to remove the sagging pouch of fabric from the front and add it to the back, where a woman was grateful for all the coverage and support she could get.

"So you've met Laura then?" Alex asked as she swept across the airport car park with a slick wheelie suitcase in tow, looking sickeningly tanned and relaxed after her trip away with Charlie.

"She's really sweet—all that therapy stuff's a bit much, though. What happened to her?" Liv asked.

"Dunno. Charlie hasn't said. But I guess we'll worm it out of her eventually. Have you hung out with her much?" Alex walked to the front of the taxi queue and jumped into a waiting car ahead of a dozen businessmen. This was a perk afforded only to those confident few who had never had to suffer the indignity of camel-toe when they tried on their jeans.

"Nah, she pops up occasionally like a piece of toast, but I haven't really seen anyone all week," explained Liv.

"Well, I'm here now." Alex gave Liv a huge hug. "Aren't

you glad to see me? Bet you've been bored out of your brain," Alex said as the taxi sped away.

"Actually, I've sort of got a job. And I know I said I'd go sightseeing with you tomorrow, but I've got to work," Liv said, feeling guilty at getting Alex over here on emergency standby and then dumping her.

"Not tomorrow you haven't," said Alex, pulling a couple of badges out of her bag and waving them under Liv's nose. "I've got tickets for the gee-gees."

"Horseracing?" Liv took the bright orange badges and examined them. Judging by the gold trim and little safety pin on the back, they were the business. Royal enclosure. Undoubtedly sitting on the Queen's lap. Champagne, et cetera. Though she expected no less from Alex, Liv was actually quite looking forward to her first day of work.

"Well, I suppose I'd quite like to meet Charlie. But I reckon you'd have much more fun if you came to the stall with me," Liv said, slipping the tickets back into Alex's bag. "You're going to love the boys."

"What stall?" Alex pulled on her sunglasses and took in the blue sky as the driver went haring down the road.

"I've become a muse." Liv tried to make her new job as a professional chest model sound glamorous. "This designer, James, wants me to be at the stall tomorrow to be the approachable face of high-fashion lingerie."

"Who's James?" Alex asked as they tore along the Pacific Highway.

"James is a designer. He's part of a they. James and Dave. A gay they. I just should be there. It starts at six in the morning."

"No way. We need our beauty sleep. It'll be so much fun at the races. Charlie can give us some money to put on the horses with cute names and we'll drink champagne until we fall over. That beats standing in the rain on some grotty market stall, doesn't it?"

"Correction: Charlie will give *you* the money. I haven't done anything to earn Charlie's money and I'm going to the stall to make some dollars to feed myself. Plus this is Sydney, not Leeds. It won't rain," Liv reminded her.

"So where is he now?" Liv asked.

"Oh, he's gone down to Royal Sydney for a round of golf. So have you heard from Tim?"

"Not a word."

"Bastard probably thinks he's being kind. Well, only a couple of months to go till he's on his hands and knees grovelling in the gravel on our front path. I promise."

But Liv was gone. Until now she'd not really had anything to remind her of Tim. Except of course for the collage of photos she'd pinned of him next to her bed and the Tiffany bean necklace he'd bought for her birthday, which she wore every day, and the fact that she could smell him on the T-shirt she wore at night that she deliberately hadn't washed yet, though it was beginning to rot just a bit under the arms. Liv wanted to ask Alex if she'd heard any news of him from her network of globe-trotting friends, whether he'd been spied in any Notting Hill watering holes with unidentified blondes. Been seen in tears at the wheel of his car as he waited at traffic lights listening to "Can't live if living is without you. . . ." But she couldn't bring herself to ask. She had specifically instructed Alex not to tell her if she did have news of Tiny Tim, so unless she brought up the subject herself she'd never know.

She bit her lip and wondered if he was wondering what she was up to. Wondered whether he was jealous of the men she was meeting in Sydney (well, he didn't know, did he, that he needn't be jealous of James and Dave et al.?), whether he was having piercing pangs of regret at four in the morning, hating being single and devising ways he could win her back. Flowers, chocolates, stalking the aisles in Van Cleef and

Arpels looking for just the gem to secure her heart. Yeah, right, she thought miserably. And when exactly was the last time a leopard changed his spots? The guy used to split dinner with her and bought her soap for Christmas. She was lucky to get a beer, let alone De Beers.

Later the girls ordered a takeaway from Arthur's, absolutely the best pizza in the Southern Hemisphere, and while Liv looked at glossy perfume ads featuring stunning couples for whom life could not involve more togetherness if they were sewn to each other, Alex leafed through *Cleo* magazine's list of eligible bachelors, putting rings around the most promising for Liv before she realised that it was a 1992 issue so most were either married or sagging horribly by now.

"I don't fancy anyone else. It just wouldn't work," Liv dismissed the bachelors that Alex was waving under her nose.

"I know, but it's hypothetical. If you had to have dinner with someone else. Suppose Tim came back to you and you discovered that you didn't want him back. . . ." Alex ignored Liv's oh-come-on-get-real look and persisted, "Then who would it be?"

"There is no one else." Liv was defiant. Not only was it bad enough that she was in pieces inside, but she was suddenly being deemed single and therefore suitable fodder for all and sundry to fix up with life's leftovers. All those blokes who had a "nice personality" or were "perfectly good-looking" were going to be offered up on a plate for Liv to sample. Sadly, the platter was not made up of Tiny Tims or even Wayward Williams or Sexy Simons. Dreg city from here on in, Liv imagined. So best embrace spinsterhood here and now.

"Okay, then the last person who you fancied before you met Tim. Though you'll notice that I'm very sweetly overlooking the fact that you've had about sixty thousand crushes over the last five years *while* you were deeply in love with him, which must tell you something."

"That was because I didn't know what I had until it'd gone." Liv took a sip of her VB and churned with regret and guilt. Surely Tim chucking her was just bad karma for the time she'd imagined what it would be like to have Jude Law lick the inside of her thigh.

"So before you met Tim," Alex demanded.

Liv cast her mind back over the years of bliss and happiness. Unconsciously leaving out the afternoons she'd been bored senseless while Tim played golf, the evenings she'd wanted to go on from dinner to some party and he'd preferred to go home to bed (not *that* sort of bed, either), the fact that he hadn't bought her a bunch of flowers for about three years and picked his nose in front of her in a way that suggested he'd begun to take her love and adoration very much for granted. That kind of stuff she edited as she skimmed over the love story to end all love stories.

"Okay, but I was a baby. It wasn't really love like Tim and I had," Liv insisted.

"Don't care. Tell me all about it," demanded Alex as she lay back and listened.

"He was called Ben Parker. It was sweet. I mean we were really young so it was all kind of puppy love, but . . . ," Liv protested.

"From the moment you met him. Just tell me."

"It was at the farmer's market in Aix-en-Provence. I was on holiday with Mum and this troop of Mum's friends. A few of the families staying at our cottage had piled into a convoy of Volvos and hired Renaults and driven into town. When we got there, all the Sloaney parents wandered off to buy local art at a little gallery and Mum and Lenny got pissed and played boules with these tobacco-stained seventy-year-olds in the square. So all us kids went off to some American bar that had MTV and we were ordering Diet Cokes and trying to score Es from Pascal the waiter. I was feeling pretty ropy after a night on the cognac, so I went for a wander around the market to practise my Franglais. I looked around a few of the stalls and asked the woman who owned one of them if I could have a *pomme de terre*. But what I really wanted was an apple. Anyway, she stuffed a mucky potato into a bag and just grunted at me. I wandered off not realising and was perfectly happy thinking that I was Emmanuel Beart in *Manon des Sources*. I remember feeling really sorry for the cockerels in pens and wondered whether Lenny and Mum would agree to take a beige baby goat back home with them if I spiked their *vin rouge* with Ecstasy.

"Then I saw this guy buying this huge Brie. He had a perfect French accent and was so tall and beautiful that I almost took a bite of the potato. Anyway, after haggling and swearing he walked away from the stall with his cheese under his arm. I followed him for a bit around the stalls. He had this body that no English boy could ever compete with. Really strong tanned arms and these beautiful long, almost hairless legs. Anyway, I decided that he had to be called Serge and he must be home from the Sorbonne for the summer with his *famille*. I just knew that he lived in a cigarette butt–filled garret near the Seine. I imagined living there with him. Sometimes in the dream he'd get irritated because my French vocab was wrong, but it was a sexy irritation; he'd just toss back his hair and then give me a patronising French snog.

"Anyway, by the time I'd followed him to the square it was so hot that my sundress was sticking to me and my feet were killing. I'd managed not to make him notice me when my mum yelled out, 'Liv, darling. We're over here. Come and meet Florence.' She was so loud that I dropped my *pomme de terre* in shock. God, it was so embarrassing. She might as well have yelled, 'Put out more flags! The British are coming!' Everyone stopped and stared. So I was rooted to the spot and when I looked down there he was, Serge, kneeling in front of me, and he picked up my brown paper bag. He lifted it up, looked inside, said, 'What did you want to go and buy one potato for? Couldn't you afford a pound?' And I swear to god he sounded like Brad from *Neighbours*. He was about as French as Skippy the Bush Kangaroo. I thought how can he make French love to me in a contemptuous way if he isn't French? So it turns out he was born in Woolloomoolloo. And he was holding out my *pomme de terre* in its bag with this hand that was so tanned and so breathtakingly gorgeous that I nearly fainted.

"Anyway, we went off to have an Orangina and it turned out that he was in the final year of his degree course studying Russian and I forgave him for not being French because he said *merde* like a native and smoked Gauloise Blonds. His name was Ben Parker and his lovely hands weren't even the best thing about him. He was staying at this place just next to our place, so we agreed to meet up. And when he came round he had this bag of red apples that made me keel over with love.

"And the rest is pretty much just teen angst. A few walks along Provençal riverbanks, a couple of nights in Saint-Tropez with the others, where we could only afford a glass of house wine between three of us, the fooling around in a barn, and in an abandoned tree house we found on the grounds of this château and then in the back of the hired Renault parked in the drive outside the cottage. And then the summer was over and I thought about him for the whole of my first year of university. Until I met Tim." Liv pulled her beer bottle from the table and took a swig. Slightly flushed at the memories she thought she'd forgotten.

"Wow." Alex rubbed her eyes and looked at Liv. "You were really into him."

"In an eighteen-year-old sort of way, yeah, I suppose that I was." Liv stretched her legs out in front of her.

"So you never heard from him again?"

"Nah," said Liv.

"But he's from Woolloomoolloo?"

"No, actually, he was from Sydney. He was only born in Woolloomoollo because his mother's car broke down and her water burst there."

"Liv!" Alex cast off her jet lag and leaned forward. "Ben Parker lives in Sydney and you didn't tell me?"

"Well, as you'd never heard of him until three minutes ago there didn't really seem to be much point. Anyway, I don't know that he lives here. I mean he could have emigrated to Utah or anything."

"Once a Sydney-sider always a Sydney-sider, so they say," Alex said enigmatically. "And all the years you were going out with Tim did you ever think about him?"

"Sometimes. I mean occasionally I would have a dream about him and I'd get the photos out the next day and have a look. Just for old times' sake. He was the first guy I ever slept with."

"God, that is so romantic I want to cry." Alex sank her teeth into a slice of pizza and looked wistful. "We absolutely have to find him."

"Oh, for heaven's sake, the thought hadn't occurred to me." Liv flicked her hand nonchalantly in a way that meant of course she'd thought about it; she was just too shy / nervous / didn't know how to go about tracking him down, and anyway, if she did and he was married with three kids, then her only pipe dream, the only man she had dared hope she might be able to love as much as she'd loved Tim, would be shattered and she'd have to kill herself.

"Listen, Livvy, you are a beautiful girl. I've watched you so sad these past few months that at times I didn't think I could bear it anymore. Now here we are and the sun is shining and you've made nice friends and you're starting to smile again. I want to see you have fun. You came here for adventure, not to dwell on some hokey tosser who just may or may not get his act together. One day."

"Hmmmm." Liv shrugged meekly. But she had to admit that feeling the sun on her face and laughing with the boys had made her feel just an inch or so better.

"You know what? You deserve to have your rocket fired, for Christ's sake. You've been a dutiful daughter, a high-earning accountant, never been fat, addicted to drugs, or promiscuous in your life. You're halfway round the world now and I think you should give it a go." Alex was now sitting on the back of the sofa looking fired up and excited. It was like watching footage of Eva Peron.

"Actually, I'll give fat a miss, Alex." Liv smiled, secretly wondering whether Ben still had those legs that she'd fantasised about through many an applied maths lecture or whether . . . ? Well, she supposed he did still have his legs. At least, she hoped so.

Chapter Seven

The Stripper Wax

When she woke up in the cottage on the beach the next morning it was all Liv could do to stop herself from galloping into the ocean in her nightie as Alex lay flat out on the water bed. It looked so cool and inviting as the sun rose and a huge tractor trailed across the sand preparing the beach for the hordes who'd descend on it later with their factor 25 and bottles of Volvic. Liv managed to restrain herself for the poor tractor driver's sake and put on a swimsuit first. She pulled an ancient Missoni one from the back of the laundry cupboard in the bathroom and squeezed into the string bottom and crocheted top. In fact, she might have to borrow this for the boys to copy as a Greta's Grundies prototype; there was no reason on earth why they couldn't launch a swimwear collection, too. They'd be on the market stall now without her, she thought guiltily, then remembered that according to Fay and Alex she was meant to be one of life's doers rather than an observer, so banished the regret and ran across the sand hiding her bottom with her hands.

The water was fantastically cold and, apart from a cluster of surfers farther out, there was nobody else to be seen. The

air was milky and warm and Liv just lay on her back and let
the waves bob her up and down, her hair plastered wet to
her shoulders and her toes peeping up out of the water. Last
night she'd gone to sleep thinking that she would never be
able to lean over and run her fingers through Tim's blond
hair again. But this morning she knew there was absolutely
nowhere else in the world she should be right now. She even
took time to remember how full Ben Parker's lips were.

"You might think that looking at the sky is a bit soft, Alex,
but I tell you it was awesome." Liv shovelled her hips into a
cerise shift dress that Alex had demanded she wear.

"It sounds great. Now we have to work out how we're
going to get Ben Parker's phone number," Alex said as she
cast off her bathrobe and stepped into her linen dress.

"Like I said, he's probably married." Liv didn't want to get
her hopes up just yet. "And I'm not really over Tim. The last
thing I need is some rebound fling." She poured herself a
glass of mango juice from the fridge and felt the warm sun
trapped under her skin and realised that even though she'd
only been on the beach an hour she'd managed to burn
slightly. But right now she didn't care. Worrying about an
ageing neck and wrinkles was not her bag today, she decided,
and reached into the fridge for a bite of cold pizza.

"It's ten o'clock, by the way. What time were we meant to
be at the racecourse?"

"Oh, not for ages. Which is perfect, because I've got a bit
of a treat lined up for you," Alex said as she picked up her
handbag. "Come on; let's go."

"No way. Nope. Nope. Not on your life," Liv hissed under
her breath as Alex took her seat in the waiting room of the
beauty salon.

"It's the most wonderful thing you'll ever do to your body.
Once you've had one you'll be hooked; I swear," Alex said

as she shoved Liv towards a woman in a white coat who was wielding a little display card with pretty pictures on it. Until Liv looked closer.

"Choose one of these for me, darlink." The woman handed Liv the laminated card. On it were six different pictures, which were not pretty . . . six bikini lines in various states of undress, the Mohicana, alias the Stripper Wax, and a multitude of others that Liv was just too prudish to spend more than a second studying, but one was undoubtedly called the Japanese Porn Star and would have made for a very chilly time inside anyone's knickers. Blimey.

"Erm, that one please." Liv lay back on the couch and kissed good-bye to her curls as she pointed to the one that looked most au naturel.

"Okay, darlink. Here we go." And there followed a good twenty minutes of snipping and yanking and yogic-type positions and gynaecological scrutiny that left Liv pink-faced and full of hatred for her bloody friend who was probably sitting in reception flicking her way through *In Style* magazine without a care in the world save whether she should go to a new aerobics class designed to give her the buns, but not the bank account, of Jennifer Lopez or just carry on with her Sports Fucking and hope it left her with an equally toned bum. Sports Fucking was actually Alex's preferred choice of exercise at the moment and, like all the best crazes, originated in LA. All you had to do was be especially energetic during sex, incorporate a few press-ups as part of the usual bump and grind, and try to keep it up for at least twenty minutes for maximum aerobic impact.

"Don't you think it's really erotic, though?" Alex asked as the girls climbed the steps of the main pavilion of Randwick Racecourse.

"What? Sore pink skin that makes me look like a bald eagle? No, I don't think that's particularly erotic and neither do I find it amusing going to the loo and not recognise myself anymore," Liv snapped as she tried to walk normally. To put it bluntly, she'd been scalped. "In fact, I'm bloody glad I haven't got a boyfriend, because I'd be really embarrassed."

"Trust me. By Monday you'll be thanking me. It's all smooth and sexy. Men will be transfixed by it." Alex steered Liv towards the members enclosure flashing the stewards with badges and smiles on the way.

"Which ones exactly?" Liv wondered, failing to spot the queue of admirers forming behind her.

"We've been waiting for you," Charlie said rather soppily when Alex sauntered into the upstairs lounge. "I put a few bets on for you." He handed over some tickets to Alex, who kissed his cheek tenderly. Charlie actually wasn't anywhere near as Rumplestiltskin-like as Liv had imagined he would be. And he reached out and shook her hand perfectly politely and without staring either scornfully or lustily at her. This made a huge change from all Alex's other men, who generally spent any conversation they deigned to have with her looking over her shoulder at the new arrivals or cornered her on her way to the loo and put their hands on her boobs.

"So, Liv, can I get you a drink?" Charlie asked.

"Champagne would be lovely." Liv nodded, thinking that even though she was wearing cerise and looked like a boiled sweet, she might stand a chance of getting to know and maybe even like Charlie. And as she looked around she thought she might even get to know and like one of his friends. She knew Alex condemned them one and all as shits with money, but they were definitely better-dressed than most of the men Liv came across and if, just if, she were ever in the market for a nameless, blameless fling to make Tim jealous then at least she'd be able to identify him by the designer name in his underpants. She downed the chilly champagne until her ears popped like those of a deep-sea diver.

"He seems nice. And his ears aren't that big," Liv whispered to Alex, who had flipped into professional mode, smiling winningly and forgetting she had a brain.

"Sweet, isn't he?" said Alex with a little pout. "Come and meet some people."

And with that she swept Liv into a survey of the room. Liv was used to the scene and wasn't sure if she recognised most of the people from magazines or the odd time she'd been with Alex to the Met Bar. Mostly, though, they had those generic Smart People looks. All the girls had buttery chunk highlights and approximately no hips and the men worked out and then splashed on Creed aftershave. The conversation was generally just . . . la la staying at the Hempel; la la holiday in Harbour Island; ho hum, she's put on a lot of weight. Not particularly inspiring, but then Liv decided not to judge so hastily. If you lured a whole load of accountants into one room it might not be an appealing sight, but individually they might all be as fun-loving and adventure-seeking as Liv hoped to become.

Certainly by the end of the afternoon she felt like she was the most fun that could balance (but only just) on two legs. But then by the end of the afternoon Liv was atrociously drunk. Still, if she did say so herself, she was in sparkling form and keeping everyone amused. In fact, she was feeling so insouciant that she decided that she was going to practise flirting. Perhaps it was the bikini wax kicking in or merely the effects of so much champagne that she couldn't even pronounce Tim's name, let alone have time to lament his passing, but she was feeling a bit saucy. And she'd never really had much cause to flirt before, having been with the same man for so long. She'd occasionally tittered helplessly and run her fingers through her hair when confronted with a ticket-wielding traffic warden, but she was absolutely hopeless when it came to holding the gaze, slowly stroking the stem of her champagne glass, making double entendres out of in-

nocent remarks, and laughing wantonly. Flirting was as alien
an art to her as jujitsu, but she'd picked her target and wasn't
going to let her lack of skill stand in the way of her
Labradoresque enthusiasm.

"So I've won enough money to buy what?" Liv leaned
over and intimately burped in the face of a man called
Robert. "A share in a racehorse?" Liv had decided that
Robert was not necessarily the most attractive man in the
room, but he had sympathetic freckles and seemed like a
good start for her to study her new art. She was also less
intimidated by Robert than the Cartier-watched Mr.
Smoothie Chops types, as he looked more like a groom than
a racehorse owner in his moleskins and denim shirt with
scuffed brown boots. She knew the Smoothies had all been
out with at least one model in their lives, and though she told
herself she had a good brain and a passably pretty nose, she
didn't want to have to deal with rejection at this early stage
of her Awakening to Womanhood.

"You wish. I can let you have a bit of his mane if you like.
That's about all a hundred dollars'll get you." Robert laughed
and hit not only his thigh but also her arm and the table. He
was proving an appreciative audience for her inebriated lech-
ery, so it was just as well that she didn't really fancy him; otherwise she'd have a lot to regret the next morning.

"Oh well. Did I tell you I was a lingerie model?" asked
Liv, not looking very much like Elle Macpherson.

"That's great. Your mate Alex mentioned it, actually. Nice
girl." Robert leaned over and smiled.

"You should come and buy some of Greta's Grundies from
my stall. For your girlfriend," said Liv, proud of the clever
and subtle way she was drumming up business and managing
to find out if he was available at the same time. Clearly the
secret of successful seduction was to remain one step ahead.

If he was hung up on someone else she would expend her not inconsiderable skills elsewhere.

"I would if I had a girlfriend." He smiled and his freckles smudged into a splodge. Sexy if you like the schoolboy thing, she thought. In fact, Robert was very lovely. He hadn't once leered at Liv, yet he was still chatting away to her and let the fact that she was clearly a pathological liar for passing herself off as a lingerie model pass unchallenged, which was the pinnacle of sweetness. Or stupidity.

"I live in the country. Don't get much time for women out there."

"The country? You're not a jackeroo, are you?" Liv asked, wondering if fate had led Robert into her path, jackeroo being the next-best thing to Cowboy and the Gus of Fay's dreams.

"Not exactly. I ride a lot, though. Got a few horses out there today. One of them won, actually," he said.

"Congratulations. All that training and getting up early must have paid off then. But no girlfriend. That's a bit sad," said Liv, who was actually just reflecting her own concerns about being a sad single.

"Maybe." He smiled enigmatically. "I've sort of got my eye on somebody, actually."

Liv was a bit taken aback at her early success in flirting. He means me, she marvelled to herself. She couldn't be so bad at all the lip licking and erotic eyebrow raising as she'd imagined. In fact, she was suddenly sober enough to feel a bit mean for leading him on. Until a second later, when Liv realised that she could not have been further away from being his object of desire if she had major cosmetic surgery, a limb extension, and head transplant with Claudia Schiffer.

Walking towards them was a girl who, although more casually dressed than any other woman in the room in leather pants and a slim-fitting white shirt, still managed to look a million times more captivating than anyone had a right to be.

She had the boyish blond crop of a twenties flapper and the kind of figure that not only would make a bishop kick in a stained-glass window but also might cause the pope to develop Munchausen syndrome and start bashing himself over the head. She smiled at full wattage and leaned down and kissed Robert on the cheek, her hair skimming his cheek and undoubtedly smelling of orange blossom. Not two kisses as an acquaintance might, but warmly and only once.

"Robbie, don't have a light, do you?" she asked, smiling fleetingly at Liv, just long enough to acknowledge her presence but not so long that she'd have to engage her in conversation. Obviously impeccably bred.

"Where's that bastard bloke of yours, Amelia?" asked Robert, glancing the end of her cigarette with his lighter as she inhaled.

"He'll be along later. Got things to see to." The gorgeous Amelia winked at Robert, nodded again at Liv, and went back to join a group of men who were slapping one another's backs, celebrating their wins. And smoking. Each and every one of them with a cigarette or cigar of his own. And not a light among them? Liv found that very hard to believe. Obviously Amelia had made the special trip over here to make sure Robert was behaving himself. Though it seemed she had her own boyfriend. So what purpose did lovely, freckly Rob serve in Amelia's life? Liv wondered.

"Well, Robert," she teased, after they'd both caught their breath, "I think I know exactly who you've got your eye on."

But instead of keeping up the jovial spirit of their conversation, Robert turned quickly to Liv and blushed. "It's not what you think. Really." And he drew heavily on his cigarette and looked the other way across the room where Alex was practically catatonic with boredom. Liv dashed Robert off her list of men to flirt with but decided that she'd keep him as a friend and then could use him for target practise whenever she wanted to try out a new flirting technique. And she hadn't had a male friend in years. Well, not a straight one, anyway.

Later, as Liv and Alex lay in a crumpled heap on a sofa and the party continued around them, with various dissidents vanishing to the loos in pairs to get high, Liv observed Robert by the bar as he talked intently to Amelia. She was nodding seriously at him and occasionally blowing smoke from her lips, to one side. A paragon of consideration. Liv thought how sad for Robert. Robert the stable hand who was clearly in love with Lady Chatterley but didn't stand a chance. Even if they were having a rampant affair, Liv didn't imagine that Robert would last long.

"Who's the blonde?" Liv asked Alex, pointing towards Amelia.

"Amelia Fraser. She's a friend of Charlie's. Her father owns a lot of property in the Western Districts. Best catch in Sydney if the boys are to be believed. And I guess that's her perfect boyfriend," Alex added as a tall, broad man walked up to Amelia and kissed her wallop on the mouth. Even with his back to Liv and Alex they could see he cut a formidable and very fuckable figure. With one arm draped casually over Amelia's slender shoulder and the other patting Robert on the back, he seemed relaxed and confident in his white T-shirt. His damp hair was straight from some Calvin Klein universe of nice-smelling men on beaches.

"Well, he looks pretty all right to me." Alex smiled, admiringly.

"Hmm, not my sort. I prefer them a bit less *obvious*," Liv said, and downed another glass of water, feeling sorrier than ever for poor Robert.

"Well, I'm going to find out. Coming?" Alex smoothed the creases in her skirt and stood up.

"Nah, I think I'll sit this one out. Take a moment." Liv

grinned. She and Alex had a mutual obsession with cheesy-speak and loved taking moments and having alone time.

"Sure thing," Alex drawled and did her panther prowl over to the bar to investigate.

But Liv didn't have even a moment of alone time to worry about poor Robert or even feel inadequate for coexisting in the same room as Amelia, because no sooner had Alex clasped the mystery boyfriend's hand warmly than there was a low whisper in Liv's left ear. "Can I get you a drink?" it asked.

Liv turned to see a small, slightly pudgy man with a raised eyebrow smiling at her. "God, no thanks," she said, then in case he thought she was being superoffensive about his clear lack of handsomeness, chimed, "I mean I've drunk so much this afternoon that it's a wonder I'm still standing. Which is probably why I'm sitting, in fact. So . . . no thanks all the same."

"Do you mind if I sit here?" he asked, sitting there anyway.

"Not at all."

"You're English," he observed as he put his gin and tonic down on the table.

"Ha. You're right." She smiled, half wanting Alex to come and rescue her but also half feeling so unthreatened by him that she didn't mind engaging in a bit of small talk with someone normal-looking.

"I'm Will." He held out his hand.

"Liv."

And it was another two hours before either of them drew breath again. Liv discovered that Will was a foreign correspondent for one of the Australian news networks and so spent a lot of time abroad and roaming war zones, and though he didn't look as though he was exactly born in khakis and could flee dangerous scenes in a sexy manner, she was beginning to detect a certain something in his eye.

"We've got a connection, Liv. I mean is that a really weird thing to say or do you know what I mean?" he asked as she paused before launching into her dreams of leaving accountancy behind for a more scintillating career and telling him why she thought *Apocalypse Now* and all those boy movies were basically just a wank in the bath. Things she'd never have dared say to Tim for fear of being thought a philistine.

"Yeah. We do get on, don't we?" Liv said, noticing that his eyes were exactly the same colour as her favourite sofa at home—a kind of velvety green. Well, he wasn't a stunner at all, but yeah, she knew what he meant; they did get on.

"It's just so easy talking to you. I love a girl with a mind." He smiled. "Look I've got to go to Bosnia tomorrow, but I'm back next week. Do you think we could maybe hook up and have dinner or something?" he asked, his hand resting on her knee.

"I'd love to," Liv found herself saying. And, even more weirdly, meaning. Will could not have been further from her ideal man if he'd tried. While Tim was tall and blond and rangy, Will was not. Most emphatically not. But there was something about him. He was smart and funny and made her laugh like nobody had made her laugh in ages. And when she looked him dead in the eye she found herself not minding that his hand was on her knee. Though with anyone else she'd have been sending telepathic messages across the room to Alex to come and save her or telling them that now was not the best time for a man to put his hand on her knee because she didn't really want a relationship, as she was bruised and battered from her last one. But not with Will. Hmmm, she thought. That's odd.

"Okay, one more drink for the road and I'd better be off. I'm supposed to be at this party . . ." Will looked at his watch and shrugged. "Oh, about an hour ago."

As he walked towards the bar Liv picked up her handbag

and surreptitiously did a few repairs to her booze-impaired complexion and unfashionably random hair. And then as she turned and watched him put his arm around some girl at the bar in a matey-friendly way she suddenly felt weird. Kind of like it should be her he was putting his arm around and wondering whose party he was going to. But that was ridiculous. She liked him, but no way did she fancy him. At all. He wasn't her type. He had stocky little thighs and sofa-coloured eyes, but . . .

Well, clearly she did fancy him somewhere. Either that or she'd been besieged by some strange Darwinian need to wrest him from the grasp of the other girl and have him for herself. In fact, she spent the next five minutes wishing to God he'd come back and talk to her again. That he'd ask her where she lived or even just press his phone number into her hand. And when he did finally come over and begin to tell her about a story he'd covered on diamond smuggling in Africa she saw not sofa-coloured but dazzling green eyes and not stocky thighs but legs she'd like to feel protected by and feet she'd like to see peeking from beneath a sheet at the bottom of her bed. So this was it. This was what happened when you finally got close enough to a man to feel the charge of chemistry. It was something that she'd mythologized over the years but never quite comprehended. And when she'd finished telling him about her first pony she took a sip of her drink (mineral water, not some drink-him-kissable cocktail in case she were looking for an excuse) and found herself looking into his eyes with all the intensity of someone hanging onto a cliff face by her fingernails. She knew what that look meant. Though she may not have used it on anyone in a very long time. She knew that any second now she was about to kiss the first man other than Tim in five years and if she were going to slap his face it had to be . . . oh, about five seconds ago.

★ ★ ★

"Wow," said Liv as she sat back and smiled a very small smile to Will. She looked at him and leaned in to kiss him again. It was nice. Really, really nice. But odd. She put her hand to his face and felt his cheek. It was a well-upholstered cheek and soft. With none of the chisely hardness and cut bones of Tim. Will's earlobes were soft and his hair kind of spikey. Liv felt like a blind person as she discovered this new man, cupped her hand around the back of his neck, explored his mouth. And she inhaled deeply and smelled the very different smell of his skin. The kiss was much the same as any other kiss, she supposed, but the taste of him was different. Was quite simply delicious. Liv wondered if other men smelled this good. Was this what she had been missing out on? she wondered as Will began to kiss her neck. Something she'd never been able to get Tim to do beyond Date Three. And something she was discovering she loved.

"I have to go." Will gently pulled his face away from hers and raised his eyebrow at her. "Just promise me you won't fall in love with anyone else before we have our first date."

"Hmm," said Liv with all that was left of her vocabulary.

"I'll get your number from Charlie." He ruffled her hair and walked off, leaving Liv watching and wondering how a man an inch shorter than she, with very unattractive tennis shoes on, could make her feel this way.

"Oh my god, oh my god, oh my god," Alex shuttled across the room chanting in a footbally " 'ere we go, 'ere we go" way.

"Yeah," said Liv, sort of looking into space and seeing stars. "What was that all about?"

"You just snogged Will." Alex was bouncing up and down on the sofa. "What was it like?"

"Nice. Really nice, Al. I mean . . . lovely. He kissed my neck, which was insanely nice. And now he's gone. That's my first kiss with anyone other than Tim for—"

"Five years, yeah, I know, but . . . well, you've broken the spell, Livvy. You've done it. I am so proud of you." Alex hugged a still grinning and slightly bemused Liv. "Do you like him?" Alex asked.

"I don't know. I mean he was funny and sweet and tasted lovely but soooo not my type."

"You liked him. Wow." Alex kissed Liv on the cheek and danced around on the sofa a bit more. "Which is a bit of a shame, actually, because, well, here you are about to have a new boyfriend already and I've just been over at the bar talking to Ben Parker."

"Whhhaaaaaaa?" Liv swivelled her head round, but the fug of smoke was now so dense that she couldn't see a thing. "Where?"

"He's living in Paddington apparently. Working as an archaeologist in the city."

"But how? I mean, Alex, oh my god."

"My god, you didn't tell me how gorgeous he is. I mean that boy is so handsome it's *wrong*. And such a rocking body."

"He's still good-looking?" Liv asked.

"I would pay money to watch him chew gum." Alex grinned.

"In which case I would probably pay money to watch the gum that he had chewed."

"Great, because we're all going to dinner, so hurry up."

Liv scooped herself together and filled in the cracks with her concealer in the back of the taxi while Alex and Charlie discussed their next skiing holiday in Sun Valley. She was glad of the break as she was able to scoop her thoughts together. Not only had she just been snogged deliciously by an unlikely man, but she was about to go and have dinner at the same table as Ben Parker. She hoped he hadn't seen her snogging Will and planned her opening gambits, which ranged from witty to saucy to prosaic. She knew she'd be chicken and have to settle for prosaic, but it was going to be accompanied by enough eyelash batting to start a wind farm and power the national grid, so it didn't really matter.

"And you're sure he's not balding? Not receding?" Liv quizzed Alex as Charlie paid the cabdriver.

"Not even slightly. I told you he's perfect," Alex reassured her.

"Maybe just a bit paunchy, though?" asked Liv. Then realised that she did seem to be doing paunch these days, so what did it matter? She grinned to herself and thought of Will and the neck kisses.

"Not even slightly paunchy. Washboard all the way. I told you—it's *wrong.*"

So all was well. Liv was well and truly back in the saddle. Bye-bye, Tim, she thought as she walked through the restaurant door. Let the good times roll.

The table was at the far end of the room and Liv strained to see Ben Parker without looking. That Could I Be More Casual If I Tried thing. She was, of course, seated in Purdah at the wrong end of the table, being neither rich nor Julia Roberts. It was the same crowd as the races but looking a bit more glassy-eyed and blotchy. There were at least twenty people munching bread rolls at the intimate little gathering, and all of them were waving so many knives and flashy watches and suntanned arms about that it was all Liv could manage to read the menu three inches in front of her face, let alone spy the last man she loved but one through the sea of swaying drunkenness.

"So we want to hear all the details about last night." Charlie slapped a short man on the back. "How was it, mate?"

As the man revealed to the table how he'd scored with a supermodel (funny how a fat wallet can compensate for a height discrepancy, Liv mused; maybe he stood on it), Liv

and Alex deliberated over Greek salad or something that
would make them miserable tomorrow for a starter.

"Deep-fried Camembert." Liv decided on miserable tomorrow so as not to look like a vain anorexic tonight. "So
where is he?" she whispered behind her menu to Alex.

"Over there." Alex pointed with her seventy-seventh glass
of white wine in the direction of a strange two-headed monster in the corner.

"But that's Amelia," Liv said, taking in the back of Amelia's
blond hair, then noticed that there was indeed someone attached to her face. "And . . . that's Ben Parker," Liv hissed as
she suddenly realised that the two-headed monster wasn't
that at all. It was Amelia and Ben. Ben Parker was the guy
from the bar earlier. Calvin Klein beach-scented Ben who
had put his arm around Amelia—Ben whom Liv could now
see quite clearly, the mouth, the long legs, the smooth back,
the green eyes that . . . she hadn't seen, hadn't gazed into, for
nine years. Ben Parker. And oh, Ben Parker who was, Liv realised with a lurch of her heart, unless she was completely
mistaken, Perfect Amelia's boyfriend.

"Didn't I tell you he was going out with Amelia Fraser? I
must have missed that bit out, Livvy. I'm sorry, babe; it totally slipped my mind. Too much of this stuff." Alex sloshed
wine from her glass onto her bread roll and giggled. Liv
didn't. "And he's quite bright, too, Robert was telling me.
Got a Ph.D.," Alex said, not noticing that Liv had ground to
a halt. She was neither chewing nor talking nor moving. But
she was thinking and watching Ben as he and Amelia got
cosy. As he muttered something delicious in her pink little
ear and she smiled and whispered something back. Liv was
thinking that Ben Parker was indeed very bright. And, true
to Liv's dreams, hadn't lost anything. Merely gained. A lot.
Including a girlfriend. Neither had he lost his effect on Liv's
glands. She nearly laughed out loud, vomited, and ran away
at the same time.

"I promised Laura that I'd help her alphabetise her self-help library tonight," Liv murmured to Alex as she feebly stood and picked up her bag. She cast one more glance over her shoulder at Ben Parker. She was nauseous with wishing she were back in that farm building lying on the straw with him now. Just one last time. So she could die happy. His hair was short and chestnut brown, his face and arms tanned, with a few freckles; he was no less and much, much more than she had remembered. Even in her dreams, the ones where he'd do all the things to her that Tim had long since stopped doing, Ben had never looked this good. "Bye." And Liv staggered, only slightly, but there was a definite weakness in her knees, out of the restaurant and into the balmy darkness.

Chapter Eight

You Have New Male Waiting

Paddington Market on a Saturday was definitely *somewhere* to be in Sydney. If not exactly *the* place, it was certainly a port of call for every self-respecting Sydney-sider who wasn't on the beach, on a yacht, or lunching *a deux* on the waterfront. As the sun rose, the stall holders would assemble outside the church on Oxford Street and lay out their wares. Not a manky cauliflower to be found anywhere. There was the inevitable mixture of muesli-type people in Birkenstocks and high fashion—candles and joss sticks next to beautifully hand-beaded bodices, corn fritters baked by chicks in dreadlocks, and a bearded Aborigine selling herbal lotions and potions. Antique stall holders locked horns with the man selling Gregorian chants and Techno whose tinny tape deck scared away potential toby-jug buyers. In a baking hot sun-soaked corner at the back of the market, dangerously close to the noodle-and-dumpling stall, Liv wiped the sleep from her eyes. Coming to, she began to fumble with a few pairs of knickers as James assembled an expert sun canopy from a piece of tarpaulin and turned the rough planks of wood into a leopard print backdrop for Greta's Grundies.

★ ★ ★

"They look fabulous." Liv lifted up her sunglasses and peered at the improved garments. And they had improved dramatically. With Liv's chest as the model 36C and Alex's as the 34B they had spent all week pinning each other into newspaper patterns and worked out the sizes in between and beyond and had the spectrum pretty much covered. They'd even designed and made up beautiful gold labels, which they'd spent the last two nights sewing carefully into the seams.

"Just as long as business is a bit better than last Saturday," sighed James. "Apart from the couple of bras we sold to Nicole Kidman, we barely covered the stall hire."

"Ah, but I wasn't here last week." Liv winked. Thankfully James and Dave had overlooked her peccadillo on the grounds that it made her One of Them, as both had, at one time or another, slept through an entire day's trading on the stock market, numerous lunches with friends, and on one occasion James had failed to wake up for his own birthday. "You see, I'm your secret weapon. I can bond with women . . . perfect ploy, eh?" she said, smoothing a turquoise bodice out onto the display.

In fact, Liv had spent the entire last week feeling good. Despite the fact that Ben Parker was quite clearly beyond reach until he realised that life with Amelia was shallow and superficial and he wanted a real future with a woman who might not have pinprick thighs but was funny and lovely and kind to animals and could balance the household accounts with the precision of a tightrope walker. Or an accountant. At which point he'd have to divorce Amelia and marry Liv. And it was okay, Liv was prepared for the fact that this may take a few years, marriage, and several children before he realised this, but in the meantime she had decided she was going to have lots and lots of sex. It was the new balm for her wounded heart, and then when Ben did come round she'd have that glint of terminal satisfaction.

★ ★ ★

"So you're having dinner with Willy tonight?" James asked
Liv, who had not wiped the smile off her face all morning.
Even when she'd smashed her shin on the door of the Greta's
Grundies van.

"Yeah. I can't wait. What I'd really like to do is skip dinner and just have him kiss my neck for a couple of hours. I
just know that he'll be an amazing lover. I mean you can tell,
can't you?"

"Pretty much. But you can't sleep with him tonight, you
know that, don't you?" Dave had just arrived back from a
wander around the market clutching a banana smoothie and
wearing his Dorothy look—plaits, gingham dress, and red
shoes in case he wanted to go home. It was Mardi Gras in a
couple of weeks and all the drag queens in Sydney had
launched into a frenzy of competitiveness, which meant that
Dave now had to shave his legs at least three times a day if
he had a hope of being invited to the best parties.

"Not sleep with him? What are you talking about? Of
course I'm going to sleep with him." Liv looked shocked.
"Why else would I be going out to dinner with a man?"

"Because you like him and want to get to know him better."

"Uh-uh. I only go out to dinner with men that I want to
sleep with; otherwise you spend all your time worrying that
they're going to kiss you and try to get into your knickers
and it spoils a perfectly nice dinner." Liv was adamant.

"I hate to say this, Liv, but how would *you* know? You
might as well have been locked up in a dark cupboard for the
last five years for all the experience you've had." Dave
slurped on his smoothie and checked his cheeks for stubble.

"I want sex. I haven't been getting any. Can't it be that
simple?"

"Sorry." Dave shrugged. "Are you going to explain to her
or shall I, James?" James pointed at Dave, but Liv wasn't pre-

pared to let them talk her out of this. She'd been religious about body lotion all week. She'd be buggered if her new soft skin was going to waste.

"This is about displacement. I kissed Will and felt great because it meant that I could actually fancy someone who wasn't Tim. I feel liberated. But imagine how great I'm going to feel if I actually have sex with someone else. I'll be on cloud nine and forget all about the pain and Tim and stuff. I'll be happy again."

"Classic rebound, darling, which is all as may be, but you just cannot fuck a man on the first date."

"Why not?"

"Men are like dogs: you have to train them. If they get what they want straightaway, they lose interest. You can't give away the goods just like that." James snapped his fingers to demonstrate how quickly Will would head for the hills.

"Boys, boys. 'Give away the goods.' This is the twenty-first century. Now usually I would defer to your better judgement, but I want sex, not everlasting love. So thanks all the same," Liv insisted as she went off for a wander around the market to ponder the problem of whether painted toe-nails or nude ones were sexier. Dave and James looked at each other.

"She won't be saying that when he doesn't call." James shook his head ominously.

"Heartache waiting to happen," Dave agreed.

Half an hour, two smoothies, and one vegetable pasty later, Liv arrived back and tweaked one of Dave's pigtails, having decided that nude was always sexier.

"I think we're breaking through. We're a success." James started hugging her furiously, kissing her madly.

"You've changed your mind and I am allowed to have sex after all. Is that it?" She chucked her cup in the rubbish bin and smiled. "Well, it's nice to have your blessing. Thanks, boys."

"Gorgeous, we just had our best-ever customer." He pointed to the almost empty stall—rows of missing lace undies, a gap where a sequinned bodice had been, and a transparent turquoise bra had vanished.

"Who?" Liv asked, suddenly worried that her own rather unique breast size might just be freaky and not fit anyone else.

"Amelia Fraser. Sydney socialite and general goddess." He smiled. "She almost bought us out."

"Amelia skinny blonde leather pants Amelia?" Liv asked.

"More like very little denim skirt, T-shirt v.small and so tight I could tell she didn't actually need a bra." He looked into the sky as he recalled the unbelievableness of Amelia, "You know, even though her tits are big enough to make you weep, they'd still stand the pencil test. Amazing!"

"What pencil test?" Liv asked, suddenly diverted and jealous and wishing she had an HB handy to measure her own amazingness with.

But James hadn't heard. "So do you mean to say you actually know her?" He turned to Liv as he registered what she'd said.

"Saw her at the races on Saturday. She's got a boyfriend, I know, but I think she's having an affair with a serf." Liv smiled, proud that though she'd been in town only a few weeks she had a handle on the gossip.

"Listen, if Greta's Grundies do the trick for her she can do the dirty with whomsoever she likes. She's always in *Vogue*, you know. Just hope she spreads the word."

James got back to work flushed with excitement, and Liv craned her neck around the other stalls, wondering if maybe she could pick up a tip or two on being a goddess by watching Amelia Fraser.

"Lush boyfriend, too, though. Can't think why she'd want

to fool around with anyone else. He's very sexy in that 'could be queer' kind of way."

"He's not queer, James. Take my word for it."

"I'm not taking the word of an ingenue on anything. Come back to me when you're all grown and maybe then I'll listen," James mused, and began to sketch a new G-string with the inspiration of it all.

Liv contemplated telling them exactly how she knew but was too caught up with the fact that Ben Parker had been here just minutes ago—she wondered if he'd left a chewed bit of gum behind or something she could take home for a keepsake, but not a relic in sight. So she pushed Ben to the back of her mind and focused on a magazine article telling her how to drive her man wild in bed. "Only revision," she told James when he asked her how she'd managed to reach the age of twenty-seven without such a necessary life skill. At least when the time came for Ben and Amelia to get divorced she'd be prepared, Liv reassured herself as she memorised one particularly complicated twist-and-squeeze routine that might well change her life forever.

Chapter Nine

You've Come a Long Way, Baby

The restaurant that Liv and Will had arranged to meet in was a classically Australian affair—tucked behind a pub—but nonetheless, the food in all these joints was worthy of a Michelin star and you didn't have to put up with stiff waiters trying to shove napkins down the front of your shirt. But as she sat waiting Liv suddenly realised that she couldn't even slightly remember what Will looked like. She knew vaguely that he was stocky and un-Tim-like but not much else. Darkish hair, ish-ish nose, but that was about it. She hadn't a clue. So it was just as well that with her dark hair and still stupidly pale skin she stood out from every other golden six-foot blond girl in the restaurant and he could identify her should he, too, have forgotten.

"Liv, you look great." Will strode across the restaurant and was far too competent to have forgotten her. "Am I late? Have you been here ages?" he asked as he kissed her very comfortably on the lips.

Good, no messing around. I like that, thought Liv.

"I only live round the corner, so I was here before I knew it." Liv smiled.

"Good. Now I figure that because we don't really know each other it's going to be awkward for about an hour and then it'll be okay," he said as he reached for the wine waiter.

"Okay." Liv shrugged. This was nice—a straight-talking, to-the-point man. Couldn't have been further from . . . oh, she wasn't going to even think about Tim, was she? No. And she didn't want to. Who wanted some shilly-shallying, polite tiptoer through tulips when Will told it like it was in that rather disarming war-correspondent way?

"Red or white?" he asked as he scanned the menu. "Or champagne. Let's start as we mean to go on."

And so they went on. And on and on. Chatting about pretty much everything, laughing properly at each other's jokes, discovering that they'd both had a penchant for break dancing as fifteen-year-olds, and Liv kept stealing glances at Will and though he was just as chubby as she'd remembered, just as not-her-type—in fact, not many people's type really in the looks department—there was definitely something about him. And when he'd taken her hand and put it palm-to-palm with his and looked into her eyes and talked about the incompatibility of life in war zones and finding the woman of your dreams, she'd almost volunteered herself: "Fear not, not-so-fair William, for I'm here. And your luck's in tonight, because I'm insta-bride—I've still got a ring at home and actually a whole bloody wedding planned, with a cake in my mum's freezer and a Bedouin tent and Carpenters tribute band because I couldn't quite bring myself to cancel it because I was in such a state of denial." Except of course she didn't say this, because the next thing she knew they'd polished off the poached pears in cardamom syrup, he was kissing her neck outside a bar on Oxford Street, they were three margaritas up, and it seemed unimportant because it was so clear that they were destined to be together. Oh, and it was rude to talk with your mouth full. So instead of discussing wedding plans they kissed a lot.

"Come back to mine?" Will asked as they walked and kissed and stopped occasionally for something a bit more heavy-duty by someone's garden wall on their way back to his house.

"Oh, I don't know," Liv mumbled, remembering what James had said about first dates. Would Will think she was easy? He pressed himself against her, making her feel as sweet and salty as a margarita inside. "Yeah, okay." Liv was persuaded, her decision owing just a bit to the blood rush to long-forgotten places.

He laughed and brushed her hair back from her face and looked at her. "You're very cute, Liv."

"Thanks." She wanted to add that he was cute, too, but as he wasn't she'd have had to qualify it with lots of stuff about great personality and quick mind and fantastic sense of humour because he so clearly wasn't an oil painting and he must know that. Still, it didn't detract from his confidence, which was so magnetic that about six minutes and forty-five seconds later Liv was lying naked on his bed as he trailed his hands over her breasts. Blimey. You've come a long way, baby, she thought to herself as she reached for Will's love handles and completely began to see the point of chubby boys.

The Walk of Shame. God, how Liv loved it. All the mornings she'd looked enviously at girls she'd passed on the street as they shuffled along in crumpled skirts and high heels and crushed-but-happy hair on their way home from some wanton encounter in Shepherd's Bush. And now it was her turn. She knew everyone would think she was a cheap little slut, but this was a novelty for Liv. She'd spent five years being Miss Sensible Knickers and she was damned well going to wring every drop out of her night of raunch with Will. She'd had a fantastic fuckfest, some real headboard-crashing, knicker-melting sex, and she was going to savour the moment. She meandered her way home along Oxford Street and tried to do fairy steps just to make it last: her eyeliner somewhere about her ears, a little cut on her lip, her nose all peeling from stubble burn but the rest of her glowing. No more expensive face creams required, either; she'd forgotten how sex made your skin gorgeous. No matter that her T-shirt was on inside out because she was cruising the Walk of Shame past the people waiting at bus stops and couples sitting in cafes picking at sun-dried-tomato muffins. Past the joggers who should learn alternative ways of firming the inner thighs. She smiled smugly. Ah, her hormones soared with the late-morning sun as she thought gratefully of Will. Never had a man been more wonderfully useful, she mused as she examined a scratch on her arm and a bruise on her knee proudly. Wounds of love. She smiled dramatically and wondered what she'd ever seen in Tim and his mundane ways. Better to be shagged senseless by a war correspondent once than a lifetime of the same old, same old know what's coming next. What a boring concept forever is when you have last night, she decided.

And so Liv's grin lasted until about Tuesday afternoon. Two and a half days of postcoital daftness, which included smiling even though her bank threatened to cut off her credit cards and laughing in the face of all her white clothes being mutilated by a rogue pink sock in the wash. And then she began to wonder why the phone hadn't rung. What exactly had happened to the man who'd turned her world upside down and pushed Tim to a dusty corner along with her Duran Duran albums and lock-up diary of 1995?

"Perhaps he's gone to Bosnia again," Liv mused to Alex as she pulled on her swimsuit with one hand and cradled the phone with the other.

"Erm . . . no . . . Charlie saw him at The Royal last night," Alex said reluctantly.

"Playing it cool?" Liv tried again, though she hadn't got Will down as the playing anything type. He was way too up-front for that.

"Probably, I'm sure," Alex reassured her.

"Okay, well, we'll talk about it later. I've got to dash to my surfing lesson—do you want to come along and watch?" Liv asked as she grabbed her towel and some factor 37,000 sun-block.

"Oooh, please. I'll just go and oil myself up." Alex hummed. "See you there in twenty."

"I can't stand up!" Liv yelled to the man who was standing up on a surfboard three feet away.

"Just kneel to begin with. Then you're away!" Justin hollered back.

Liv got onto all fours. "It's no use. I can't!" she called. "It's just so bloody embarrassing." She looked around the beach and at the small group of Japanese tourists who'd abandoned their sunbathing to watch her learn to surf on the sand. Not a wave in sight. "Can't we just go into the sea and do it?"

"Unless you can sort yer balance out here, love, you'll be batshit in the water." Justin came over to Liv and started to pick up her legs and rearrange her arms. She'd enrolled in the surf course a couple of weeks ago after she'd spoken to Fay, who had asked her what mind-altering, character-building things she'd been doing since they last spoke. What could she say? I drank too much in this great restaurant in Surry Hills last night. I discovered a fabulous cheese called King Island Vintage Cheddar, which is now enjoying a new lease of life around my midriff. Oh, and yes, I spent an entire evening flicking through Laura's back issues of *Vogue* and *Cleo* looking for pictures of Ben Parker and his girlfriend Amelia Fraser. And at the time her night of lust with War

Zone Will, now Missing in Action Man, hadn't even been a glint in her eye, so she'd had nothing to divulge on the jackeroo front. So she improvised and said she'd enrolled at Surf School. It came out of her mouth as she watched a cluster of pigeon-chested teenagers run fearlessly into the ocean with their boogie boards on *Home and Away,* which was on the telly at the time. She had no intention of really doing it, but her conscience finally got the better of her and the next morning she had signed up for a twelve-week course before she could say "dumb idiot with no sense of balance."

Justin was her instructor, who, despite his angel face, Liv was beginning to realise was as formidable as Arnold Schwarzenegger. There was no shirking, no girlish wimpiness allowed.

"We'll have you surfing Wiaimae in no time at all," he assured her, which may or may not have been a good thing depending on what Wiaimae was. This morning she'd tried to skive her class altogether, but when she came down for her midday dip and sunbathe with Alex he'd spotted her by the ice-cream kiosk and given her a ticking off.

"It's not my time you're wasting, Liv. I get to sit in the sun and watch the babes for the entire hour you're not there. But you're cheating yourself out of achievement." He looked earnestly at her from above the stripe of green zinc across his nose and told her he had a free slot at four that afternoon if she wanted to redeem herself. Liv hung her head and agreed that she would.

As she'd slunk away in disgrace Alex let out a low whistle. "Fantastic. How much do you pay him to be strict with you?" she asked, casting a glance back at his perfect young body and shoulder-length blond hair.

"Too much, clearly. If he were earning a fiver an hour he wouldn't care." Liv sulked, thinking now she wouldn't be able to watch *The Bold and the Beautiful* and wait in for Will's phone call that afternoon.

* * *

Alex had taken time out between her Indian head massage
and a trip to the library to watch Liv grow, as she put it.
Really, she just wanted to perv at Justin. She walked along
the sand looking like the perfect Australian Beach Babe—she
had on a hot pink string bikini and pair of sneakers and her
hair was getting longer and blonder by the day. Even though
sunbathing was practically illegal in Australia, given their understandable aversion to skin cancer, Alex had managed to
fake a dipped-in-something-sweet-as-honey colour. And just
to add to her cuteness—as if bonus points were needed—
Alex had brought along Charlie's new puppy. Mate was a
Jack Russell terrier who accessorised Alex's beach bag perfectly. Charlie had got him as a babe magnet but was off in
Melbourne for the day so had left him in Alex's care. He sali-
vated adorably on Alex's shoulder.

"All right, Liv? You're getting good at that." She smiled
and settled herself on a towel nearby with Mate beside her
licking her knee. Liv tried to ignore her as she toyed with a
block of something called Sex Wax, which was meant to stop
her falling off the board. She wondered what would happen
if she rubbed it on her body.

"Do you reckon lifeguards and dogs would fall in love
with me and follow me along the beach like a body spray ad-
vert?" she asked Justin.

"More like flies from miles around would flock to you.
Like a human dog-poo," he replied seriously.

Liv brushed off the insult and turned on Alex. She knew
Alex was only here so she could check out Justin's tuition
and low-slung blue board shorts. While she was a cynic
when it came to rich, older men, she did seem to come over
all romantic and misty-eyed in the presence of penniless
youngsters like Justin.

"What are you still doing here, you voyeur?" Liv barked
at Alex.

"I can look, can't I?" Alex said shamelessly. And she proceeded to look and drool and occasionally dip into her novel.

"Okay, we'll call it a day, Livvo. See you down here seven A.M. tomorrow. Thought we'd get a bit of speed work done, so put on a bathing suit that you're not going to lose in the surf." Justin dusted the sand off the back of Liv's legs as Alex's eyes practically popped out.

"I must say I completely approve of you having an affair with your surf instructor," said Alex as they made their way back to the cottage with Mate once again in Alex's bag.

"I don't want an affair with Justin," Liv whispered, turning around to make sure he couldn't hear. "Anyway, I've got a lover," Liv said, though she was far from certain. She really ought to dash home and listen to her messages.

"Yeah, but he's nowhere near keen enough. It's no good having a lover who's not around to provide da luvvin'," Alex said. "So Little Justin would be perfect. Uncomplicated lust. Keen as mustard and no chance that you'll fall in love with him—he's too young and eager."

"I don't fancy him," said Liv.

"That's because your mind isn't open to the experience yet. You're still thinking like a faithful girlfriend. You've just replaced Tiny Tim with Will the Weasel, who, it has to be said, is not known for his sense of commitment. You need to get in touch with your inner woman," advised Alex.

"There's quite enough outer woman for me to deal with first." Liv felt her bottom trail behind her like a small child. "Don't you think we should let Mate out for a bit of exercise?"

"Sure. Help yourself," Alex said as Liv lifted the panting pup from his beach-bag transport.

"Here you go, Mate. Fetch." Liv threw a nearby stick for the dog, but he just eyed her in a bored fashion and rolled around on the sand.

"You have to be firm with him," Alex told Liv. "Watch." She went and stood beside the puppy. "Sit," she said, and raised a forbidding eyebrow at the tiny hound. Mate sat and flashed her adoring eyes.

"Okay. Sit," Liv repeated, but Mate just looked at her and then began to maul her sandal. "Oy, get off!" she yelped, and tried to shake him free. He clung on for dear life with his deceptively strong jaws.

"You just don't have the knack, Liv. You're much too nice. He just takes one look into your eyes and knows you don't mean business. You have to get tough," Alex advised. "Oh, and by the way, I think that you should dump Will," she added.

"I will. I really will. Just as soon as he calls me," Liv said bravely. "It's funny, but James said this would happen. He said I shouldn't give away the goods on a first date. That I ought to treat men like dogs—train them and not give in to them. Which, judging by my success with Mate, I'm clearly crap at."

"James has a point," Alex said as they neared the cottage. "I always train my boys. Slap them across the nose with a rolled-up newspaper when they behave badly. It's the only language they understand, poor loves. And I always said you were way too easy on Tim. You should have slapped him down a lot more than you did."

"Yeah, but you're not normal, Alex. You've never been in love, so you don't know what it's like to long for a man to call you."

"I never have to long for long. Because I'm firm. They do respond to that, you know, Liv. There is such a thing as being too nice and available."

"Well, I'll be a bitch on wheels when Will calls then. Show him I'm not available. At least not that same night anyway," Liv decided as Alex opened the front door and they fell into the cool shadows of the cottage. Mate leapt up again and tugged at the hem of Liv's shorts. "Down, boy," she snarled firmly, trying to muster up a ferocious gaze. Mate stopped yapping for a moment and then looked up at her. "Good boy," she said much too soon, as he cocked his leg and peed on her ankle.

"There must be someone you're interested in apart from Will?" Alex pulled a couple of Cokes out of the fridge and Liv washed her foot and gave Mate the evil eye.

"Well, yeah, there's somebody. Ben Parker, for instance. But I don't stand a cat in hell's chance with him because not only is he otherwise occupied; he's occupied by Perfect Amelia, who I wouldn't even want to stand next to in a bus queue for fear of looking shabby. Let alone make a fool of myself by trying to seduce her boyfriend."

"Well, you never know about Will. I mean he might just be really, really busy. I'm sure he'll call by the weekend," Alex said. Which Liv supposed was a neat way of avoiding the fact that with Amelia as competition in the race for Ben, Liv was definitely going to be the horse that fell at the first fence.

Chapter Ten

If the Phone Doesn't Ring
It Can't Be Him

By Saturday, a week and still no phone call after her date with Will, Liv was rudely awakened at six o'clock.

"Oh, god. Surfing," she croaked as she turned over and knocked the alarm to the floor. Her head puttered to life like an old car on a winter morning. As she was mentally preparing to find her swimsuit and shave her underarms, she remembered, "Saturday. Thank god. Thank god." She buried her face back in her pillow and let herself drift back to sleep. As the warm early-morning sun was catching her hair and making her relish her lie-in she suddenly sat bolt upright. "Fuck. Saturday. I'm late." It was miserably true. She'd meant to get up at five o'clock this morning. Not six. She'd promised James that she'd help him drive his stock from some warehouse in the city and bring it to Paddington. Sure enough, the phone rang three seconds later and compounded her general trembliness. She shuddered and ran into the sitting room nursing the shred of hope that it could be Will. At 6:00 A.M. Yeah, right.

"Yes." She tried for husky, but it came out homicidal.

"Where are you? You were supposed to be here at six." It

was James sounding as if he'd already jogged seven miles, breakfasted on smoked salmon and scrambled eggs, and read a spectrum of improving newspapers.

"James, I'm so sorry. I'll be there. Now," she said, pulling on a T-shirt that was lying on the floor. Laura's? Probably; it was disfiguringly tight and had splodges of Venice on it, but no time to lose. She pulled her hair back into a ponytail. She'd definitely overdone the frizz-smoothing serum when she'd last washed her hair, she thought as she grasped her lank, greasy locks. And trousers. Trousers? Not a prayer. She found a pair of denim shorts that might have looked good on Naomi Campbell. But only might. Oh well. Key. Wallet. Out the door.

By midmorning on the stall Liv was flagging badly. She'd given up on life and love and it was definitely showing in her appearance. Like girls who meet a man and mysteriously lose weight and shine. Liv lost two men, gained weight, and became ugly. Her hands were purple with dye from all the crushed velvet she'd had to lug around the warehouse, and her face was a whiter shade of wallpaper paste. James had asked her if she wouldn't mind sitting in the back of the van and running through the books. He'd said it kindly, but she knew that in truth it just wasn't good for business to have someone who looked like a Goth who'd been in a smash on the M3 on the way home from a Cure gig in the late eighties as your muse.

"Liv. Are you still alive?" he asked two hours later as he opened the back door of the van and found Liv doing her sums in the comforting darkness.

"Sure. It's a bit hot, though," she said, gasping for air and blinking like a mole in the sunlight. "Only I'm off for a bit of a sandwich. Shouldn't be long, but would you mind"—he looked reluctantly at her, wondering if maybe it wouldn't be better just to close down the stall rather than have Liv peddling his wares for him—"taking over the reins while I'm gone?"

"Do I look *so* terrible?" she asked as she tried to catch a glimpse of herself in one of the van's wing mirrors.

"Best not to look, eh?" James said. "You're usually a beautiful girl, but this morning you're not far from a bushpig." He went to ruffle her hair in a display of brotherly affection but quickly pulled his hand away before it was coated in lardy gunge. "A friend of mine's got a hair salon in Double Bay. I'll fix you up with an appointment," he said sweetly, and beat a hasty retreat. "The cash tin's there. Hopefully it'll be quiet."

Liv thrust her legs into the sunlight and blinked at their terrifying pallor. Not a good look for Paddington Market, which was awash with fresh golden-baked teenage limbs. In fact, probably not a good look anytime. She plonked herself down in the deck chair behind the stall and read the balance sheet with mock fascination. If she emitted unfriendly-enough vibes she might not even have to deal with a single customer. In fact, she watched with a surly expression she'd copied from an Estée Lauder saleswoman as at least six potential customers came, fiddled with the bras, and then scurried away. Doubtless to have a few nightmares about the experience.

Then she heard another set of footsteps approach the stall. She made a few accountant noises in her windpipe and practised her own modified version of a Uri Geller spoon-bending tactic to make the invader go away. The fact that it made her puce in the face was an added bonus. But the footsteps didn't beat any sort of retreat, hasty or otherwise. Bugger.

"Is this Greta's Grundies?" a man's voice asked.

"Yeah. Feel free to touch whatever you like," Liv growled, a little surprised at the man-buying-bras revelation but without looking up.

"Great. Thanks," he replied. God, he had a sexy voice though, she thought. Different from the voices she'd heard recently. She tried to work it out while keeping her eyes fixed on VAT. "Do you mind if I ask you a question?" Chocolatey voice, she decided. Actually could be any number of other things, like warm-raspberry-jam-on-buttered-crumpets voice or treacle-poured-on-porridge voice, but she plumped for chocolatey. Interesting this, not judging the book by its cover but by what it's got to say. When she was at Goldsmiths she'd once conducted an outrageously flirtatious phone relationship with the buyer from a trendy Soho hat shop. He was called Simon and Liv had fantasised about how he was the one for her and that there was no way they couldn't fall in love the second they met. They discovered that they had both been listening to Kris Kristofferson's "Loving her was easier than anything I'll ever do again," alone in their rooms for years. They were passionate about reading in the bath and they both wanted to keep yaks and follow the Inca trail. So no way they couldn't fall in love. Except that when they met at a PR agency's Christmas party he had the nerve to have a shiny bald pate, glasses, and a monobrow. So despite thinking that the man fiddling with the lacy knickers six feet away from her sounded like he would have her dribbling lustily in no time, Liv knew that Mr. Chocolatey Voice was actually as hideous a bushpig as she herself was.

She put her black book and pen down and stood up.

"Sure, fire away," she replied as she came face-to-face with Mr. Chocolatey Voice. Alias . . . oh, Christ, well, of course it was going to be, wasn't it? Alias Ben Parker. No wonder he'd sounded different. She knew him. He was the man who'd told her ten years ago in fledgling chocolatey tones that her hair was as lovely as Belinda Carlisle's. It had been love then. What was it now? Well, actually, it was acute embarrassment.

"Haven't we met before?" Chocolatey Ben asked.

Liv grabbed a nearby bra and pretended to sniff it, hoping to cover her face. What she wanted to say was, "God, Bill. How are you? Oh, it's Ben, is it. Oh yes, now I think I remember. Spain, 1992. Oh yes, of course, France 1991. Well, you're looking great, Ben. Oh, I am, too? Well, thanks. So how aarrrrreeee you?" At least that was the cool and casual speech she'd prepared for when she bumped into him, but she had also planned to grow a couple of inches and become lovely before she said it. This morning she was very far from loveliness. And if he didn't recognise her it would be more than her currently rather fragile ego could bear. "Don't think so, mate," she snorted instead, doing her best Aussie impression.

"You're not English then?" he asked.

"Ya kiddin', aren't ya? Next you'll be accusing Skippy the Bush Kangaroo of being a corgi." She hid her pallid legs behind the stall, thinking that even if her embarrassingly bad attempt to be Clive James made her sound local, then her glow-in-the dark sausage-shaped limbs would definitely give her away as English.

"Sorry. Thought you were a girl I once knew." He smiled beguilingly.

Liv wanted to hang herself with the bra. After she'd hurt him very badly with a few metres of knicker elastic. "Yeah, well, wrong chick, sorry. Did you wanna buy something?" Liv saw James approaching from the other side of the market. He was carrying two cups of coffee and a large pizza box, obviously feeling guilty about making Liv a pariah. Only he mustn't come anywhere near here right now and give her childish game away.

"I've been advised that Greta's Grundies are just what I'm looking for." Except he wasn't looking at anyone's grundies. But she could have sworn he was looking at her chest, which was dangerously unhinged in Laura's minuscule T-shirt. He was probably considering alerting the emergency services.

"Then feel free to look," Liv said, her accent dropping slightly as she panicked about how best to avert James from his path. Ben gave her a lingering puzzled look before averting his gaze to Liv's personal favourite—a velvet-trimmed corset.

Liv stepped into "distract James" mode: She tried to wave him back with her eyes, but he merely hurried even more, knocking his pizza box into a baby snuggled in a papoose on his mother's back.

Go away, Liv mouthed when she was sure that Ben had his nose buried in underwear, but James simply hurried up and piled his box and coffees onto the cash table.

"What is it, gorgeous? Are you ill? You haven't been looking well all day."

Liv kept her mouth firmly shut and just shook her head. She gave James a thumbs-up sign and smiled broadly. Then she picked up a coffee and smiled like Marcel Marceau. Hmmm, thank you for the coffee, the smile said.

"Liv?" James shoved her down into the chair and looked at her with concern.

"Can I help?" Ben piped up from behind the stall. "I didn't think she was well before. Looked a little green and breathing heavily."

"No, she's always that colour. Must say she did seem to have the power of speech when I left, though." James felt Liv's forehead and was about to attempt to take her pulse. God, bugger off back to the other side of the stall, Ben Parker, and let me look like a cow's backside in peace, why don't you? Liv thought. *Now* what was she meant to do?

"I can take her to the emergency room if you like. I mean you've obviously got a stall to look after. I'm doing nothing this afternoon." Ben smiled winningly, the bastard.

And as he did so, James suddenly took in that he was a very edible young man, vaguely familiar-looking—and buying female smalls, too. Maybe this could be the beginning of a beautiful, if adulterous, friendship. "Oh she'll be all right. Just drinks too much. These pommy sheilas can't take their grog." He waved a dismissive hand over Liv and turned the full wattage of his smile on Ben. "Now, sir, what size can I help you to? Large, I'd imagine." He smiled, looking Ben up and down.

But Ben was too busy trying to work out how the Aussie sheila he'd just been talking to was actually English Liv. "Yeah, Large is fine, thanks," replied Ben absentmindedly, making James's Saturday. Liv picked up her figures and hastily plugged numbers into the calculator, making up imaginary sums and faking looks of concern at the total amount.

"Liv, can you hand me three ones and a twenty from the cashbox, darling?" James asked, not taking his eyes off Ben, who was now clutching a brown paper bag full of man-sized lingerie and staring at Liv, who handed over the cash and carried on doing her sums.

"Thanks so much; erm, that's great," Ben mumbled as he turned and walked away through the market, looking around just once to make sure that he hadn't imagined that whole encounter.

"Well, I think that one's truly in the bag, both metaphorically and literally." James grinned as he fingered the crisp $100 bill that Ben had handed over. "He's certainly hot enough to pitch my tent."

"What are you talking about?" Liv asked, slamming down her calculator. "How dare you put your sex life before my health!"

"Oh, darling, I knew you were faking it just to get that gorgeous beast to drag you off to be hooked up to a drip." James gave her a tart look. "But isn't he Amelia Fraser's fella? Jeez, there'll be a great big fat scandal when I tell the blokes at the Albery about him."

"He's not gay, so get over yourself. And for your information, I don't need to fake illness to make him drag me anywhere," Liv said, albeit unconvincingly. The way she looked today, the only place anyone would drag her was to the recycling plant.

"Oh yeah?" James smiled, his hands on his hips. "Dying to hear this one. And he does wear women's undies, by the way."

"We used to be lovers." She tried an insouciant flick of her hair, but it wouldn't budge. Her *coup de theatre* was short-lived, as James laughed out loud.

"Yeah, right. So why didn't he recognise you?"

"As a matter of fact he did. I just pretended not to be me so that on another occasion I can wow him with my wit and beauty. Today, as you've astutely pointed out, I'm neither witty nor beautiful." Liv slunk back into her chair and contemplated exactly where she was going to begin with this transformation that would stop Ben Parker in his tracks and make him marvel at how he could ever have forgotten Liv Elliot.

"Not witty?" James laughed. "You're hilarious, Liv. If that bloke's not a tranny, then why did he buy fourteen pairs of Large knickers?"

"That I don't know. But they're definitely not for Amelia Fraser," said Liv, thinking that perhaps as good a place as any to begin a transformation was her back end, which would have resided comfortably in each of Ben's fourteen pairs of knickers. Then she decided that she wasn't sharing a single thing more with James. And certainly not the secrets of her love life. Not that she'd had one for a whole week, but just in case, well, just in case one happened to strike her down. Like the flu.

"Oh, come on, sulky chops. Tell me what's wrong." Dave had just finished his Mardi Gras rehearsals and was looking as spectacular as ever in his Ursula Undress outfit complete with dagger. He and Liv were sunning themselves in front of the stall. "Is it because James didn't believe that you and Ben Parker had ever smooched?"

"We didn't smooch; we had sex. Heaps of it in the hay." Liv pouted as Dave sat on the deck chair next to her. "But that's not what I'm miserable about."

"What is it, sweetie?" He lit a cigarette and tuned in to listen.

"Why hasn't Will called me?" Liv bit back a tear. "Am I so awful?" She'd been holding it in since Wednesday and was trying to look on the bright side, but there was just no escaping the fact that a man she didn't even think was particularly attractive didn't fancy her. Her ego was fragile right now and the last thing she needed was to be rejected again.

"Liv, you didn't even fancy him very much. You talked yourself into it because you needed a rebound flingette. For heaven's sake, you told me that by Monday you'd decided that you'd been deluding yourself and that the sex was only about a six and that you suspected he was self-obsessed. Now, a week after he hasn't called, you think he's the most amazing man alive," Dave reminded her.

"Yeah, but even though he wasn't good enough for me it still hurts that he doesn't want me."

"It's not you he doesn't want. It's just that I did warn you, didn't I?" Dave stroked the tear away from her cheek and took her hands in his big one.

"You told me not to sleep with him, but surely that can't have been the problem."

"Liv, my love, I know it sounds Victorian, but you gave away the goods too soon. If you want a man to beg, you have to treat him like the dog he is." Dave lit a cigarette and began to ponder the problem. "There are a few rules when it comes to men, or dogs, for the purposes of this conversation, and the sooner you learn and use them the better."

* * *

An hour later Dave was half a packet of cigarettes down and Liv's legs were char-grilling dangerously in the afternoon sun, but neither really noticed, as they were very much involved in the principles of dog handling.

"Okay, now you've got the gist, I want you to repeat the dog-handling basics to me." Dave flicked his ash on the floor and watched Liv closely, hoping for great things from his new star pupil.

Liv sat up straight and took a deep breath. "The first thing to remember is that men are exactly like dogs. They pant and salivate and like to sniff your bottom and basically have loving hearts, but they have to be trained if you're ever going to get the best out of them," Liv began.

Dave nodded encouragement. "For example?"

"For example, if a dog drops a ball in your lap he wants you to throw it so that he can play. If you hold onto the ball, the dog will not go away. He'll look at you expectantly for a second, and then if you still don't throw it, he'll sit down and wait. If you continue to hold onto the ball, he'll raise the stakes and lie down and pant. If you hide the ball in your pocket, he'll come closer and sniff you and then stare at you for hours in a heartbroken way. So that when you finally toss the ball for him he's so excited he runs around and barks and can barely contain himself. By playing this game with him you've made him a happy, fulfilled dog."

"And then?" Dave quizzed.

"And then he brings the ball back to you and you're back where you started. The ball's in your hands."

"Exactemondo." Dave slapped Liv's thigh in triumph. "Hence?"

"Hence, do not give your ball away. For as long as you have the ball you are in control of the game. Be a tease. Hold onto the goods. Give a little away, but then back off. Never let them know that you want to play ball, too. Men, like dogs, prefer life this way," Liv concluded.

"And how else are men like dogs?" Dave had by now run out of matches so just chewed his nails.

"Men, like dogs, are hunter-gatherers. But like dogs they have been domesticated. They no longer have to go out and slay supper, but the instinct is still there in their genes and behaviour patterns. So in the absence of cute little deer and adorable bunnies to kill they hunt women. This is a law of nature and if you deprive them of the hunt then they will go elsewhere to satisfy that need. A man must always be kept slightly hungry, six feet away from his prey. This way he will remain in constant pursuit."

"Fantastic. You're getting there. Already all the men you want are panting at your heels. Pleading for dates. Slobbering on your sandals," Dave said excitedly. "Now all I want is for you to sustain this position of power. How will you achieve that?"

"Well." Liv cracked her knuckles in a businesslike fashion. "The thing is that dogs are pack animals. They need a leader who is firm with them. While they may gaze adoringly at the leader forever, the leader must not show signs of weakness, because they'll think he is being submissive and appoint themselves pack leaders. Then they run amok."

"Which, translated from doggy language to boy language, means what, Liv?"

"That if you want to remain in control you must never back down. Let them gaze adoringly at you and all will be well. You may sneak sidelong glances at them and feed them and be nice as can be, but you must never gaze back too adoringly at them. Never let them know you love them as they love you. If you do, the game's up. The man appoints himself leader of the pack and runs amok."

"Bravo." Dave sprang from his chair and kissed Liv right on the lips.

"And you're saying that's all I have to do to make any man want me and stay?" Liv asked, not quite able to believe it.

"Absolutely bloody right it is," Dave said. "Now the sooner we set you to work on your dog-handling exercises the better, my darling. The big question is who will be dog number one?"

Liv spent her afternoon break wandering around the stalls pondering the merits of dog handling. She loved boys generally. How would she ever manage to treat them meanly and keep them at arm's length? And wasn't that crap, that you had to spend your entire life playing stupid games and being a controlling old witch in order to make a man love you? But then she thought about what Alex had said. Certainly Alex never had trouble getting a man to return her calls. She genuinely didn't care very much and had never been known to gaze adoringly at any man. Ever. So it certainly worked for Alex.

Then Liv remembered Will. Ordinarily she would have had a bloke like Will eating Pedigree Chum mix out of her hand, but she had been so keen to rinse away the past, to kick the ghost of Tim to the kerb once and for all, that she'd been positively gagging for it. Panting desperately in his lap. And the result was that he'd vanished. Left her high and dry. Kicked *her* to the kerb like a worthless piece of rubbish. It should definitely have been the other way around, she admitted, given his propensity for self-obsession and frankly plain unattractiveness (which she had previously turned a blind eye to because she wanted sex so badly). So maybe Dave was right. Maybe she should try a bit of dog handling. Just a bit.

Liv moved over to try out one of the hand-crocheted Mexican hammocks in a nearby stall and dreamed of having a snooze. She felt a bit woozy actually—too much time studying dog handling in the blazing sun. Her earlier run-in with Ben Parker wasn't exactly settling, either. Such close proximity when she'd been so unprepared to see him had made her sick with panic. She wondered if she had managed to fool him. Had he really recognised her from that French holiday or had he caught a glimpse of her at lunch the other day or even at the races? There was no way of knowing. She hoped he'd got it totally wrong and just mistaken her for a waitress who'd served him at Hugo's last month or something. But that was a slim hope. She stuck out like a sore thumb, so he'd certainly recognise her when he saw her again. Thanks to all the sunshine and Just Right breakfast cereal, Australia seemed to grow its women tall and lithe. Liv was neither. She was convinced that she was the stoutest, palest, doughiest girl in the whole city. And being rejected by a fellow stout, doughy person, namely Will, wasn't exactly encouraging. Of course Ben would recognise her if he saw her again. In which case she was going to have to look so wow that the memory of today's weirdness would be obliterated from his mind with her explosion of gorgeousness. Not going to happen, actually, she thought as she climbed out of the hammock and tried on an ostrich feather skirt.

"Buy, buy, buy," a voice demanded behind her. Liv turned to see Alex laden with bags and almost obscured by a huge bunch of flowers. "James told me you were around and about. It'll look fantastic at the party."

"What party?" Liv asked, helping Alex to deposit a few of her purchases on the ground.

The stallholder smelled a woman on a spending spree and came over to them to encourage a sale. "It does look divine. Just the thing for a party." He grinned, paying more attention to Alex's legs than Liv's ostrich-swathed hips.

"What party? And why've you got a bagful of watermelons?" Liv asked.

"Tonight. Huge surprise. It's Charlie's birthday and that's all I'm going to say. I'm holding it at his apartment in Bondi.

So you have to come and you have to wear ostrich," said Alex, picking up her bags again and turning on her heels. "Seven-thirty at Charlie's. And only ostrich, okay?" And she vanished, leaving Liv to contend with an overexcited stall owner and the horrifying prospect of socialising when all she wanted was to phone her mum and scrape the grime from under her fingernails as she watched *Seinfeld*.

"You know, if you've not got a date for this party . . . I guess Cameron Diaz won't be too disappointed if I stand her up to come with you," the Stall Slime said to Liv as he watched Alex sway through the crowds towards Oxford Street.

"Yeah, you're right. I'm sure Cameron Diaz won't mind at all that you're not going out with her," Liv said, and prized the skirt down over her shorts. "And actually, I'm engaged to be married," she hissed, and stormed off. Sometimes Alex as a best friend was not a picnic.

As James squeezed his van the wrong way up her street he looked at Liv in bewilderment. "Why don't you want to go out tonight with that lot?" he asked Liv as he pulled up in front of her house. "They're the happening young Sydney crowd. To tell the truth, I'm pretty impressed with your social rise."

"I don't belong up there. I believe you should find your level in life and stay there." Liv scraped her bags and grocery shopping up from the crisp packet–strewn floor of the van. "I know where I belong. And it's not at Charlie Timpson's surprise birthday party. I should have taken the Stall Slime up on his offer and considered myself a lucky girl."

"I'm sorry if I called you a bushpig, honey. You know I'd never really call you that if you were," James said, salvaging a can of organic baked beans that had rolled under his seat. "I'm sure Ben Parker would fall over himself to spade you if he wasn't a poof."

"He's not gay. I told you, he's going out with Amelia."

"Yeah, right. And that's not denial? The girl he chooses has the backside of a Polynesian deck boy. Figurewise she's the next best thing to . . . well, to me, I suppose. Well, me as a boy, without my falsies," said James.

"So for a girl I'm all right?" she asked as she opened the van door and jumped out.

"All right? You're amazing. Liz Taylor before the ice cream and painkillers, I'd definitely say." He pinched her cheek, which hurt a bit, but she smiled anyway.

"Thanks, James. Sure you don't want to be my date tonight?" Liv yelled back from the pavement.

"Ta very much, but I'm going dancing with my very own Richard Burton. Ciao, bella. Oh, and by the way, Dave and I expect full reports on how the dog handling goes. No slacking, gorgeous." And he drove off and honked his horn enough times to rouse a few grunts from lawn-mowing neighbours.

"Laura, how do you fancy painting the town a lurid shade of scarlet with me tonight?" Liv yelled out towards the hut as she dumped her grocery shopping and scurried into the bathroom to pull off Laura's T-shirt before its absence was noted. She quite wanted a bit of moral support tonight in case she had to endure further public humiliation.

"Sounds good; don't think I'm doing much other than working on the colour of death. Jo-Jo's gone riding in the Blue Mountains for the weekend," said Laura, appearing at the back door and shaking her hair loose from her ponytail. When she smiled she wasn't bad-looking at all, Liv thought. If she dabbed a bit of white spirit on her eyebrows to get rid of the paint she might even be pretty.

"I'll just call Alex to check out the details," Liv said, shoving the phone down as she got Alex's answerphone. "She must be out buying balloons or something."

"Sure she won't mind?" Laura asked. "Only I feel as though I haven't seen a soul in days. It'll restore balance to my life."

"Not at all. You'll be my date," said Liv. "Mind if I have first shower?" Liv added, heaving off her shorts and heading for the bathroom before Laura could object. Even though it wasn't strictly her house, the girls felt a certain obligation to include Laura. Possibly because she was the only one of them who knew what Mr. Clean was for.

Later Liv sat on the sofa wrapping a pair of faux-cashmere socks she'd bought Charlie from the market. She wasn't accustomed to buying gifts for billionaires so had opted for almost-luxury goods, which she felt sure he'd be able to wear as he tottered around the first-class compartment on the Concorde or something.

"All set." Laura emerged from her bedroom obviously having employed a few litres of white spirit somewhere along the way. Her hair was actually wavy and auburn when not under a head scarf and two coats of Dulux and she had a face—tiny, pretty, little bit of red lipstick and blob of mascara and her green eyes went all glittery. Like the Lady of Shallot after a few glasses of red wine.

"Laura, you're lovely," Liv said, wishing that she'd dolled herself up a bit more now instead of settling for Ameliaesque minimalism, which made her feel that she should be on her way to a third-form chemistry class and not a party where she planned to fell Ben Parker with her glory and tame a few of the neighbourhood strays so she could impress Dave and James.

"Whatever," Laura drawled, replacing the rusty nails at the bottom of her rucksack with a lipstick and credit card. "Someone I know . . . used to know . . . said that being wanted I'd be more wondered at."

"What did that person mean?" Liv asked, knowing full well that it was The Heartbreaker who had said it.

"I think that I had a much bigger impact on that person when I was dressed up because I was usually covered in crap. But actually, that person was crap, so let's not go there." Laura shoved the rucksack over her shoulder and picked up her car keys. "If we're having just too good a time we can ditch the car and get a cab home, eh?"

"Sure," said Liv, still shaking her head in shock at the beautiful spitfire who was taking her to the party.

Bondi had become one of Liv's favourite Sydney places. Although it was just slightly tatty round the edges, it wasn't Sydney's most famous attraction for nothing. The beach was perfect, there was a swimming pool that sat just above the sea and was lapped and filled with water from the ocean (some called it the pee pool, but Liv chose to have more faith in human nature), and then a skip and a belly flop away from the beach were more cafes than you could shake a stick at. Or rather shake your fat behind at, as Liv had pretty much eaten her way through: macadamia nut cookies, fried breakfasts, and endless, whippy, creamy smoothies. It was very possible to spend the entire day at Bondi and be well fed, well read on the beach, and exercised by the time you caught the bus home over the hill to Bronte with the workaday crowd in the evening. Tonight all the beach crowd had gone and, apart from a lone surfer who was doing things with a board that gave Liv nightmares, the place was deserted.

Liv and Laura parked the car at the top of the hill and walked along the beach path towards Charlie's very grand house. It was dusk and Alex had decorated the garden with fairy lights and candles. Laura took off her shoes and kicked back the sharp pampas grass as they walked. Strains of music collided with the sound of crashing surf and Liv could make

out a few figures standing around in the garden as smoke
rose from a barbecue guarded by a group of men.

"Oh, there are people here. I thought we were just picking Alex up and then heading off for a night out," Laura said
as they approached the front door.

"No, the party's here. Didn't I say? It's Charlie's birthday
and Alex is having a surprise bash."

"Here?" Laura stopped dead in her tracks and turned this
weird bluey-green colour that made her look as though she'd
been embalmed. "And Charlie's mates are going to be here?"
She was looking at the front door as though it were the
mouth hole of hell and any minute now the ferryman was
going to drift up and offer them a lift.

"Well, I guess so. Actually, I hope so, because I sort of have
a bit of a soft spot for one of them. You know, this guy Ben I
was telling you about." Liv giggled, hoping that divulging her
own secrets might help Laura spill the beans on hers. But
Laura wasn't spilling anything. "Laura, are you okay?" Liv
asked as Laura took a few faltering steps backwards. But clearly
Laura had come over all train-wrecked again.

"You know what? I feel incredibly nervous that I haven't
managed that shade of red for death yet. We have a design
meeting tomorrow and god, call me a workaholic, but . . ."
And she turned round and headed up the hill. "Will you be
okay to get a taxi home? I'm sorry, Liv. I'll explain later."
And she was gone. A small figure wending her way back up
the hill to the cliff top where her car was parked.

"Laura?" Liv called up, but she raised an apologetic hand
and got into her car, leaving Liv merely dumbstruck. But before Liv could make sense of Laura's vanishing trick, the door
was opened by Amelia, who grabbed Liv by the arm and
pulled her indoors.

"Quick, Charlie'll be here in a minute. You'll give the
game away." Liv was whisked through to the kitchen by

Amelia's deceptively strong arm—obviously a few hours a day on the rowing machine came in handy.

"Where's everyone gone?" asked Liv as Amelia pushed her into the darkened bedroom. But as her eyes adjusted to the darkness she saw rows of faces of those sitting on the floor and lounging on the bed.

"Alex is going to pretend she forgot her purse and come back here. Charlie thinks they're going to see a movie—he's been whinging about it all day, but we pretended we'd forgotten it was his birthday." A voice came from beside the wardrobe. It was Rob, and Liv inched over towards him, hoping that she didn't step on Ben's toe or fall on Amelia and crush her on the way.

"Shhh. They're here," someone said, and the burr of conversation ground to a halt. Liv leaned against the dressing table and tried to make out where Ben was. She shuffled her feet so that she could see behind the man's head in front of her when the man turned around and whispered, "Do you mind shifting back a couple of inches? I'm crushing the poor bloke in front." She could feel his words on her cheek, and as he turned back around his hair brushed her lips. Liv was stunned. She stopped breathing. Then started again in case he noticed that she'd stopped breathing and took credit for it. Ben Parker three millimetres from the tip of her nose and she had begun to shake. She shuffled back again so that she wasn't thrusting her chest into his shoulder blades. Thankfully the attention of the entire room was suddenly focused on the voices next door.

"Come on, Alex. Didn't you say the reservation was for eight? What are you doing now?" Charlie's voice filtered through the crack in the door and the room stifled a snigger.

"I'll just have a quick pee. Can you get my bag for me? It's on the bed!" Alex yelled, as carefully planned, from another quarter of the house.

Everyone took a huge breath in and got ready to yell. "Surprise!" they squealed as light flooded the room, and Charlie was nearly catapulted into the afterlife with shock.

"Fuck me!" he managed to spit out before he collapsed in a nearby chair. Liv laughed out loud at his surprise and the room erupted with the sound of champagne corks popping. She'd always thought surprise parties were sick clichéd affairs and dreaded anyone surprising her with one—god, she'd undoubtedly be wearing rank jogging pants and picking her nose if it happened to her—but for someone else it was actually great fun, almost as much for the assembled surprisers as the surprisee. Charlie didn't have a finger up his nose and looked perfectly clean and crisp and so willingly accepted all the attention and the opportunity to snog Alex—and all the other women in the room—and sip champagne. The party took their glasses and toasted Charlie's birthday before filing out of the room and spilling into the rest of the house.

"Glad it wasn't me. I hate surprises," Ben Parker laughed as he brushed past Liv towards Amelia, who was being typically gorgeous and social. "Got a glass of that for me, Millie?" he asked as he wrapped his arm around her waist. Liv shook her head to try to shake off the strangeness. He clearly hadn't seen her yet or recognised her in either of her guises: the purple-lipped, Poison perfume–scented teenager or the deranged fake-Aussie chick who ran the undies stall at the market. It was one of those occasions when you don't actually know if you exist or not. When maybe you're imagining the whole thing because nobody's speaking to you, but they're all chatting away among themselves. First Laura vanished into the night like a will-o'-the-wisp and now she was hearing voices from her past.

"Livvy, where's the Big Bird outfit?" Alex bounded over and kissed Liv's cheeks, making her relieved on two counts: the first being that she did actually exist and the other that she hadn't bought that bloody skirt. Could she have borne it if she were subjected to Sesame Street and Orville jokes all night by irreverent Aussies? However, judging by the lack of interest she was inspiring among the men here, at least it would have meant she had her bottom stroked an ego-boosting number of times.

"I tried to bring Laura, but she fled just as we got to the door. You read loads of books; what do you think her problem is?" Liv asked as Alex pressed a glass of champagne into her hand.

"God knows. I keep meaning to ask Charlie what happened. Anyway, look who's here. . . ." Alex turned around and grabbed a well-muscled arm. "Ben Parker, this is my best mate, Liv Elliot."

Liv gawped openmouthed. Thanks for the warning, Alex. Oh my god, this was the moment she'd been meant to get slim for and imagined on and off for the last nine years and now here it was about to turn around and face her. And Liv's eye chose this moment to develop a twitch. Of course.

"Liv Elliot. Not . . ." Ben turned and looked puzzled for a second; then a broad smile spread across his face. "Holy shit, not *the* Liv Elliot. Bloody hell . . . you look . . . well, you look completely different. Really great, though. What on earth are you doing here?" He clasped her hand and seemed genuinely thrilled and surprised to see her. Liv had scrambled head on toast. A man who wasn't too cool for school. This was a first.

"Liv's staying with me down at Bronte. Isn't that amazing?" said Alex before slinking off to play hostess.

"Yeah. God, isn't it a small world? And what are you doing in Sydney?" He turned the full force of his sincerity on her and Liv nearly turned into a puddle of goo. God, he was practically steaming off the wallpaper with that voice and Liv hated him for it. Then, just as she was about to start preening and enjoying herself under Ben's watchful, beautiful, interested gaze, her eye began to twitch again and she suddenly noticed a familiar bulk helping itself to a margarita at the other side of the room. The bulk that'd been kissing her neck about this time last week. It was Will and any second now he was about to look over in her direction and see her. Hell, that's the last thing I need, Liv thought as she forgot all about dog-handling Will back into submission and decided to play the terrified deer and run in the other direction. She just could not face him.

"Oh, listen, Ben, I'm sorry, but we'll have to catch up some other time." Liv put on a polite smile for Ben but knew that it was embarrassingly fake. She just had to get the hell out of this room. And she flicked her little deer tail in the wind and fled for the kitchen.

"Alex, thank god you're here. You didn't tell me Weasely Will was coming," Liv stammered, and began to stuff garlic bread in her mouth to steady her nerves. If in doubt eat.

"Oh, but he's a really good mate of Charlie's. Sorry, Liv. Anyway, he's the one who should be embarrassed, not you. Don't worry."

"But what if he ignores me? God, even worse, what if he's nice and sympathetic to me? Ugh." Liv panicked as she munched her way through the better half of a baguette. " 'Sorry I didn't call you, but you're just not my type.' I'd have to kill myself."

"Oh, don't worry. Look, he's talking to Marcie. He probably won't even notice you're here," Alex said absentmindedly. Honestly, for Liv's best friend she'd been pretty bloody insensitive, Liv thought. "Now have you seen Robbie? I promised him the first bite of my pavlova." Alex was not the person to look to for sympathy, thought Liv as she slunk off to find the phone. In the absence of a single other friend at the party she might as well get James to swing by and pick her up on his way out. At least if she went out with the boys she wasn't in any danger of being fucked and chucked again.

* * *

"Liv, there you are. I've been looking for you." She felt a hand on her shoulder. She swung around ready to clobber Will or even castrate him in a dog-handling fashion, but it was Ben, his perfectly white T-shirt just skimming his broad chest as he raked his hand nervously through his hair. "It really is great to see you, you know."

Liv looked at him and doubted whether she could remain standing in his presence for long, especially if his T-shirt strained any more at his completely perfect arms. "I was about to go outside, actually; it's pretty hot in here," she said by way of an excuse. "I'm sure we can catch up another time."

"Maybe I could join you?" he asked.

"Sure. Whatever," Liv said with one eye on the Will situation. Two ex-lovers in one room was not something she'd ever experienced before, and though somewhere it made her feel a bit modern and proud, right now she didn't want a head-on collision.

"Shall I get us some drinks?" Ben asked as Liv picked up her cardigan and headed for the door.

"Yeah, that'd be great."

Ben accosted a guest with a tray and picked up two strawberry daiquiris. He was about to follow Liv outside when Amelia caught sight of him.

"Ben honey, is one of those for me?" She took a glass from his hand and clinked his. "Cheers, darling." Then she looked closely at Liv as though she were something on the bottom of her shoe she'd just trodden in.

Liv braced herself for a scene. Clearly the drinks were for Liv and Ben and clearly they were going outside to drink them on the beach, because Liv was casting off her shoes as Amelia gave her the once-over.

"Oh, you're Alex's friend, aren't you?"

"Liv and I met ten years ago on holiday in the South of

France. Can you believe she's actually living at Charlie's mum's place down at Bronte?" Ben shook his head in disbelief and smiled.

"So what do you do, Liv?" Amelia was still appraising this blast from Ben's past when she picked up another strawberry daiquiri and handed it to Liv. "I always think you can judge a person by what they do."

"I'm an accountant," Liv said, and took the drink. Thinking she may take *to* the drink as well.

"Never mind. You guys go run along and you can tell Ben all the gossip. Guess there's a lot to catch up on, eh?" Amelia had a voice as sweet and brittle as a sugared almond, and despite her intimidating dreadfulness she was utterly irresistible—even to Liv. The vision of womanhood that men would sell their souls, Ferraris, and golf clubs to possess, and that women can't take their eyes off because somehow, mistakenly, they think that if they stare hard enough and pick up just one of her mannerisms, they will somehow be as gorgeous and magnetic as her. Some hopes, Amelia's sweet smile seemed to say to Liv as she looked up into her "as seen in *Vogue*" face. Not someone anyone was going to not telephone after sex.

Amelia kissed Ben on the mouth slurpily and made her way over to a group of men in the corner who watched her lasciviously as she approached. Run along? Liv pondered the insult. How many girls would positively encourage their boyfriends to take a girl onto a moonlit beach and catch up with her over a couple of cocktails? Well, they wouldn't mind at all if the girl was a bit of a dog who stood about as much chance of attracting the said man as Liv had of giving up chocolate for Lent. Liv began to button up her cardigan. Hell, she didn't even *want* to be on the beach with Ben Parker. She couldn't even manage Tiny Tim and Weasely Will; how would she ever be able to deal with a major-league lover like Ben Parker?

She decided that the best thing to do was just ignore Ben, not even enter into his rather spectacular orbit.

"I better go and have a word with Alex," Liv said. "I'm a bit concerned that I bought the wrong-size socks for Charlie."

But Ben took hold of her arm. "Liv, are you trying to avoid me?" he asked, looking concerned.

"Don't be ridiculous." Liv tripped up the step and into the garden. "I just don't really know that I have that much gossip to fill you in on. Not that you'd be interested in anyway."

"It's not the gossip I'm interested in." He touched her arm and smiled. "And anyway, I need your professional input."

Liv was a bit baffled. "You want me to balance your books or fiddle your tax?"

"No, actually, I want to exchange all the lingerie I bought today, if that's possible." He smiled. "Amelia didn't appreciate being Large."

He had a gleam in his eye that wasn't mean, just playful, but Liv was mortified. Oh, for a beach of quicksand. He bloody well *knew*. He'd known who she was when he bought the underwear from the market stall. Why had he waited this long to humiliate her? Prize arsehole. Biggest, fattest, hairiest bum in the entire competition. (Liv was not feeling very tolerant of any man right now and call it defensive, but her nerves weren't up to all this roller-coaster stuff.)

"I'm sure she didn't." The idea of Amelia being Large was pretty hysterical, but Liv was too stressed to snigger along with him. Instead, she smarted and wondered whether she should have kept up the Aussie accent just to stop her looking such a complete moron, who'd not only lied about not having met him before but also come over all faint at the sight of him. She looked at the crowd in the garden for somebody else she knew who might provide her with an excuse to escape, but she didn't know a soul and the party seemed to be standing on its own two feet very well without her.

So instead she allowed herself to follow him down the garden and out onto the deserted darkness of the beach.

"I would have said something, but your Aussie accent was so convincing that I thought you might just have a doppelgänger," Ben said, and Liv turned and looked at him.

"Sorry, it was probably really rude of me, but well . . ."

The tide was headed out and the sand was still damp and hard. Ben sat down and threw down his jacket for her to sit on. Liv couldn't decide whether to wander moodily along the beach to give her time to make up an excuse or sit down and hope the blood flowed back to her brain. Unfortunately, her body couldn't quite interpret her indecision, so instead of performing either the sitting action or the heading-off-to-the-sunset-with-the-grace-of-Audrey-Hepburn one, she sort of did both. "Shit!" she squealed in an un-Audrey-like fashion as she catapulted bumlong onto the sand with her sunset-bound leg twisted spastically under her. "I've broken my leg." Breaking her leg was the only justification she could come up with for the decibel-crunching thud with which she'd landed. Certainly a lighter girl would not have caused quite the earthquake she did.

"Okay. Just let me see."

Liv looked up to see Ben Parker crouched beside her, his face pale with concern (or was that the moonlight?). Either way, she couldn't bear the embarrassment of the scenario that might follow if she didn't revise her condition pretty swiftly. The last thing she needed was Ben helping her across the beach.

"Actually, it's completely fine," she moaned. Which it wasn't. It completely hurt. She just could not face the idea of being trussed up like the proverbial beached whale—a couple of towropes round her ankles and one of those tarpaulin harnesses around her middle. A tractor would be hired to lug her to the nearest hospital. Meanwhile it would be dawn and the tourists would think she was stranded wildlife and snap away. Justin the surf instructor would tell her that he'd seen it coming; it was rare you came across a human being with so little sense of balance, agility, and natural grace.

"Actually, your ankle's all big and swollen." Ben was horrified as he gently straightened the offending leg out.

Liv screwed her eyes up in shame. "It's okay. I've never been known for the slenderness of my ankles. I'm sure it's fine," Liv apologised, thinking it understandable that anyone used to Amelia's pin-thin legs might fairly deem her own hideously swollen by comparison. Liv opened her eyes to assess the damage. Actually, she was disfigured beyond belief. Her ankle looked like a milk bottle, and clutched around it, softly lifting it onto his rolled-up shirt, was Ben's hand. As Liv looked down at the hand around her ankle, every second between the warmth of the summer in France and this moment seemed to evaporate. The hand she'd remembered so often undoing her bra, raising his Ricard in a toast to "us," and finally clutching her favourite diamonte crucifix, which she'd given to him as a parting gift to remember her by. The hand that was now, nine years later, taking out an ice cube from a strawberry daiquiri and rubbing it slowly against her swelling ankle.

"Any better?" he asked. God, he was so compassionate and so bloody sexy, Liv marvelled. He wasn't at all smooth and superconfident like Will, or as cocky as someone who was Perfect Amelia's chosen mate could be. He was just sweet and perhaps a bit shy. Which was a surprise to Liv, who had imagined him only as unapproachable and intimidating. While the ice cooled to water and trickled down her foot he lifted his glass to her lips, "Here, better have a swig. It'll numb the pain."

But Liv wasn't thinking pain. Only pleasure. She thought

about saying, "Sod my ankle and put your ice cube to better use." But she'd never been like that, worst luck. "That feels good," was what she managed instead, but she did string out the vowels in *gooooood* to make it sound as though she were simply coming apart at the seams with hormones.

"I once came to a party in Bristol to look for you," Ben said. As if her "goooooood" had never happened.

"You did?" Liv spat out, not being even slightly casual. God, if she'd known. The nights she'd listened to George Michael's "A Different Corner" in bed and willed Ben to get in touch. And it turns out he'd tried. God, he'd come all the way from Australia to find her, probably to suggest he transfer his final year to be near her, as all the girls in Sydney weren't a patch on his summer strumpet.

"Yeah, I was over on a summer exchange in England and I went to this club called Lakota and even got someone to go into the ladies' loos to see if you were in there." He smiled and his ice rubbing slowed down. Liv caught her breath. He'd felt the same way. If this wasn't destiny hurling them together on some beach on the other side of the world with barely a swollen ankle and melting ice cube between them, then Liv didn't know what destiny was. "Then I took three tabs of E by mistake and kind of lost the plot. Anyway, I ended up going out with some girl I met there for the next two years. King of long-distance love thing. Funny, eh?"

"Bloody hilarious!" Liv wanted to yell.

"So what do you do now?" Liv asked, trying to detonate the romance bomb that was in danger of exploding in her face any second. And which she knew would leave her in pieces as usual.

"I'm an archaeologist—mostly I deal with Aboriginal artefacts."

"Wow, interesting choice after a degree in modern languages. Do you like your job?" Liv felt like an interviewer.

"Yeah, I love it, but it's a bit of a slacker's job. Guess I'll

have to do something grown-up soon. Maybe even an office." He raised his eyebrows in mock horror and smiled.

"So you and Amelia. You'll probably get married, won't
you?" Liv forced him to admit the grisly (for her, anyway)
truth, which was that even though he was stroking her ankle
as though it were a delicate ancient artefact that he was
hugely interested in, he was still going out with God's Gift
to Men.

"I've got a few other things on my mind at the moment."
He let the ice cube slither onto the sand and began to trace
his finger around Liv's anklebone and up her calf to her knee.

Liv would have liked to rasp some throaty reply like, "Tell
me exactly what's on your mind, Mr. Parker." But once again
she didn't, because this wasn't a secretary–boss situation in a
B movie. Instead, a puttering noise rose in her throat and
found its way out through her nose. Then he leaned in even
closer to her and moved his hand toward her face. Liv recognised the vital signs now. That pause in conversation, the lips
looming towards hers. Only this time they were a hell of a
lot more beautiful than any lips that had loomed at her in a
long, long time. Perhaps, ooohh . . . nine years or so. But as
he ran a finger over her own petrified mouth, she suddenly
remembered that she'd not only had an entire onion pasty
this afternoon on the market but she'd just gobbled down
half a baguette of garlic bread. In short, she probably ponged
to high heaven. Which absolutely would not do if she were
going to kiss someone else's boyfriend.

"Ooooh." Liv gulped. "I think maybe not, hey?" But still
he hovered in front of her with an expectant look on his
face. Any second now she'd have to breathe on him and he'd
just die of garlic. Instead, she held her finger to his lips and
shook her head slowly until he retreated, almost a broken
man, she hoped happily.

"For the best, I think," she added to make him feel better.
But the poor little pup, she almost felt sorry for him.

Liv hobbled back along the sand towards the house and was grateful for the limp because it meant he didn't notice that the rest of her body was also shaking like a leaf. If only she hadn't eaten that bloody garlic bread, she thought. She could be kissing him now. But it really did have to be perfect. There was no way she could bear to have Ben Parker, who seemed to almost be quite keen on her right now, suddenly change his mind and avoid her for the rest of his life like every other man she'd ever kissed.

"Hey, Liv?" he called as he sat on the sand watching her stumble along. "I'm having a drinks thing tomorrow night. You'll come, won't you?"

"Sure, love to!" she called back. "Thanks!" Okay, score ten, she thought. Fantastic. And nothing but spearmint would pass her lips until then.

Chapter Eleven

Here, Boy

The next day Liv decided to tell Alex that she would be joining her for the evening's entertainment. She didn't usually like to tag along with Alex wherever she went, but she was happy to make an exception because she had received a very personal invitation to Ben's party and there was no way she was going to let him down. She did, however, completely forget that according to Dave, she wasn't meant to be available and offer herself at a discounted rate to the first taker. Still, what did Dave know? Hadn't Ben practically panted after her last night? Besides, he'd handpicked her. It would be rude to say no in the name of dog handling.

"So I'm going to Ben's party tonight. Shall we go together?" Liv asked as she practised her blanket stitch on a scrap of fabric. She had vowed to teach herself to sew, and then she'd be able to help the boys out with their designs. It wasn't hats for Goldsmiths, but it was a start.

"Sure, sweetie, but I thought you couldn't walk because of your ankle."

"I can't. Well, not very well, but you can just perch me on a stool and I'll be fine," Liv assured her.

"Whatever. Tell you what, I've got to dash round to Charlie's to pick up my moisturiser, so I'll get you some arnica cream to take the bruising down while I'm out."

"Fab. Oh, and we need a pint of milk!" Liv yelled back as Alex dashed out of the door. "And cereal," she added, wondering how she was going to get skinny if she couldn't walk. And in under six hours.

Two hundred sit-ups on the living room floor seemed as good a place to start as any until Laura came in and made her feel a bit embarrassed. So instead she decided to make herself a health shake with every seed and pulse and fruit she could find. It was really completely disgusting, but she just visualised Amelia's clavicle as she downed it in one. In fact, visualising Amelia could be a good way to make Liv a better all-round person. It could inspire her to learn foreign languages and make her race down to the beach for her surf lesson instead of practically crawling across the sand cursing. She grabbed a pair of scissors from the kitchen.

"How's work at the moment? Busy?" Liv asked Laura, who was on her hands and knees scrubbing the floor in what was an undoubtedly therapeutic manner.

"Fine. Got a postholocaust set to design and finish by next week, though, so I might be a bit tied up," said Laura. "How was the party last night? I'm really sorry I ran off. I just had a bit of a funny one, y'know? Bit of a panic attack."

"Oh, it was fine. Actually, it was great. I ran into this guy who I knew years ago. Real sweetie," Liv said.

"That's nice. Do you fancy him?"

"Is it that obvious?" Liv blushed a bit; she was still torn between wishing she'd kissed him back and being glad that she hadn't, as yet, had an opportunity to disappoint him. "Well, I suppose I do have a bit of a crush on him. But he's going out with some girl called Amelia, so I think it'll have to be a nice fantasy," Liv said, but really hoping to god it wouldn't have to remain in her head and that whatever strange frame of mind or class A narcotic it had taken to persuade Ben to try to kiss her last night was still kicking around his system tonight.

"I see." Laura let her sponge fall into the bucket and looked a bit pale and ill suddenly. "That's nice." Then she seemed to do some counting thing under her breath and a chant that Liv couldn't quite make out, but it was pretty miraculous, because after she'd said it she sprang to life again like a jack-in-the-box. Liv meanwhile pretended not to notice and distracted herself by taking a pair of scissors to an old *Vogue*. "Do you want some of this pasta, by the way?" Laura was now going at it with a tin of sweet corn and some tuna.

"I'd love some, only Alex is coming round soon and I'll probably have lunch with her. But thanks."

"Oh my god!" Laura suddenly yelped, and her tuna mush fell to the floor with a huge smash. Liv looked up and caught Laura staring at the picture of Amelia in a Colette Dinnigan evening dress that Liv had shoved under one of the fridge magnets in a bid to motivate her. "What on earth is *that* doing there?" Laura began to pick up her crashed bowl but still didn't take her eyes off Amelia.

"I know. She's disgustingly pretty, isn't she? I just think it might help motivate me," Liv said decisively.

"Oh, shit." Laura started her chant again but stopped. "It won't work. I can't handle it." And with that she fled from the scene as though she'd just discovered the tuna was radioactive waste. "I'm sorry." She burst into tears as her bedroom door banged shut behind her.

"I can't believe you didn't kiss him," Alex said later as Liv lay prostrated across the sofa surrounded by discarded board games and the wrappers of a 25 percent extra free six-pack of TimTams, the best of Australia in chocolate biscuit form. Laura was still acting like a train wreck in her room.

"Neither can I. And I wish you hadn't let me eat all that garlic bread or I'd probably still be lying there being all *Here to Eternity* with him," Liv said as she rubbed some more arnica cream into her still bruised but now thankfully deflated ankle.

"Yeah, until Amelia decided to come looking for her boyfriend. Despite the fact that I think you should take your fun where you find it, I also think you ought to be careful not to piss her off. She's a tough old cow." Alex turned off the television. "Shall we order in? Pizza?"

"Sure. Anyway, I don't see how Amelia can be such a hypocrite. It's not as if she isn't getting her oats elsewhere."

"Listen, Liv, I know for a fact that the Robert–Amelia thing just isn't happening. They're not having an affair," Alex said sternly. Then she softened marginally to add, "And I don't want to sound like your mother, but you do know that Ben's probably not as sweet and harmless as he seems, don't you? I know he does that shy, flaky hesitant stuff, but I mean you don't get to snag Amelia Fraser, heiress with a penchant for spitting out Hollywood actors after breakfast, if you're not a major player. And in my vast experience major players tend not to be nice. And you, my angel, are about as sweet and tough as a jam doughnut," Alex said as she rifled through Liv's drawers for a take-away menu. "Just be careful."

"What on earth is this?" Alex was trawling through the cupboard looking for the pile of take-away food bumph that nestles somewhere in every home. She pulled out a transparent plastic folder that Liv had never seen before from the bottom cupboard. "Under the telephone directories."

"Don't ask *me*. Pizza menus?" replied Liv, thinking that if Alex wanted to make her fancy Ben even more than she already did then she was going about it the right way. Dangerous. A player. When a girl just got out of a steady (terrible word) relationship with a wonderful man what was she looking for? Well, it certainly wasn't nice. And it certainly wasn't kind to babies and animals. Or even makes a great Bolognese sauce. It was danger, of course. Big red letters promising that if you go within the taped-off crime scene of this man then you're looking for serious trouble. For trouble meant lust, sex, ecstasy, and, yes, if you're not careful, a scorched heart. Which all seemed pretty tempting after five years of ishness with Tim.

"A dossier. Christ, you really have fallen for him, haven't you?" Alex sat down at the kitchen table and spread the contents of the folder across the table. "Amelia Fraser and unknown hunk at the Australian Music Industry Awards: 'Stunning heiress Amelia seemed to have put Brit-pop boyfriend Jonti Clarke behind her last night as she arrived dressed in a slinky black dress with a mystery male companion known only as Ben. She refused to be drawn on the subject, saying only, "I'm having a fabulous time tonight seeing some of Australia's finest musicians." ' " Alex flicked her way through a few more cuttings. "Could she be more bland if she tried?" Alex said.

"Thanks, Alex; you're a fab friend." Liv hobbled over to the table and heaved herself onto one of the chairs.

"Great dress, though," Alex muttered, and began to pack the Ben and Amelia Collection back into its folder. "But, Christ, all these pictures you've been cutting out of him. How long have you been doing this for, Liv?"

"Me? This wasn't me. How pathetic do you think I am? Just because I'm single doesn't make me a demented sad stalker of other people's boyfriends," said Liv. "It must have been Charlie's."

"Somehow I don't think so." Alex asked, slotting the folder back into the drawer, "But who else could they belong to?"

Liv shrugged her shoulders and looked closely at Amelia opening a possum sanctuary in Vaucluse when suddenly it hit her.

"It's not Charlie's folder. It's Laura's. And it's not Ben

Parker she's interested in. It's Amelia." Liv's eyes lit up wide as this stroke of genius dawned on her. She whispered excitedly so that Laura couldn't hear, "It's Amelia. The friend of Charlie's who broke Laura's heart was Amelia Fraser. They had an affair. It all makes complete sense now." Liv limped back to the sofa triumphantly.

"Liv, you're so full of it," Alex said dismissively as she dialled up Arthur's Pizza. "First you're determined that Amelia's having an affair with Rob, which I categorically know not to be true."

"How?" Liv quizzed her. "It still could be."

"It's not." Alex shuffled her hair in front of her eyes a bit and looked shifty before continuing with renewed vigour, "Then you decide that she's actually gay and a heartbreaker to boot. Bit of an ulterior motive here? Like Ben, for example?"

"No, I'm right. You know, I'm sure she guessed that it was Ben Parker who I had a crush on, because when I said he was going out with Amelia she looked all pale and started praying. I mean how many Amelias does Charlie know?" Liv felt a bit like Miss Marple, but with youth on her side.

"None, I suppose," Alex conceded.

"Exactly. And she freaked when she saw the photo of Amelia on the fridge, the fact that she wouldn't come into the party when she knew that Charlie's friends, i.e., Amelia, was going to be there. See, I'm right. So where, I wonder, if Amelia is a dyke, does that leave Ben?"

"Well, as he's a bloke, probably pretty chuffed that he's scored a lesbian fantasy to be enjoyed in his own bedroom. For free. Do you want pineapple on yours?" Alex asked as she doodled a loveheart on the front of the telephone directory.

Later, when Alex had scoffed her pizza and gone for a shower, Liv wondered if she should go and make sure that Laura wasn't standing on the edge of the balcony wondering what it would be like if she left this big bad world forever.

She decided that this was Laura's problem and she clearly had all the professional help and handy mantras a girl could hope for at her fingertips. Though Liv was longing to know whether Amelia did swing both ways. Actually, Liv hoped that she didn't, because that would make her a bit more interesting. Looks were quite enough without interest tossed in to ruin Liv's chances even further. Still, poor Laura. Liv would just have to be kind and let her know that she was there for her. She'd smile warmly a lot and leave nice Post-it notes around and replace all the wine that she had drunk in the last few weeks. Show she cared a bit. Right now Liv had to prepare for the night she came face-to-face with fate. "Look out, Ben," she said to herself as she softened the edges of her eyeliner and hitched her boobs up over the precipice of her trusty old bodice. Yes, the Chloe of wet streets of Notting Hill fame, though all that was now thankfully forgotten. As was her wedding to Tim. In fact, the only fantasy she was indulging anymore had this tacky happy ending that involved Liv and Ben Parker somewhere hot with a cocktail umbrella in the background. Heedless of her swollen ankle, Liv struggled into a pair of Alex's Manolos. She practised her evening in her head:

Ben Parker pushed her backwards onto a chaise longue (blissfully not the balding maroon velour usually found in pubs but a kind of soft damson velvet from Wallpaper *magazine) and deftly unlaced her corset until her bosom spilled voluminously into his large, warm hands. His kisses were salty with the taste of the oysters they'd just shared, her mouth sticky with the juices of the Persian honey cake he had just placed piece by piece between her eager lips . . . and now . . . feasting not on Turkish delight or lobster but . . . oh, the crescendo of pleasure . . . her right nipple.*

"Oh, you look fabulous in those shoes!" Alex squealed, and Liv smudged her lipstick in a bloody-looking red mess up to her nose. Alex was resplendent in jeans and a white T-shirt. Liv had on her satin trousers and hair a foot high with product. "But you do know we're only going to the Grand National, don't you?" Alex said as she scraped her hair back into a loose ponytail.

"What? For a quick drink before the party? Sure, that's fine," Liv said, thinking that it would give her time to work out the exact angle she could tilt forward so as to be stunningly sexy but not pouring her tits onto Ben's lap. "Where's Charlie tonight?" she asked.

"Oh, he's gone to some conference in Canberra. So while the cat's away I thought we'd go and play with some locals. It's crap coming all this way just to see the same old faces. I mean how many real Australian accents have you heard yet?" Alex quizzed Liv as they hopped in a cab to the Grand National.

"Well, quite a few, actually. There's Laura. Then there's Justin the surf instructor. And Ben and Amelia and Rob."

"Oh yeah, actually, Rob might just pop into the pub later." Alex smiled.

"Great. We can all go on to the party together."

But Alex wasn't really paying attention. "Which is just what I mean. Rob's about the only real Australian we know. Tonight I thought we'd leave the poncy crowd behind and meet some blood-and-guts Aussies. Dyed-in-the-wool. Okka. A bit of rough," she whispered huskily as the cabby grinned a black-toothed all-my-Christmases-have-come-at-once-type salivating grin.

"But we are going to the party later, right?" Liv asked as she thrust a tip into the cabby's hand and tried to ignore the disconcerting way he whistled his heavy breathing through the gaps in his teeth.

"What party?" Alex asked as they approached the Grand National, a pub that, despite a new lick of paint, hadn't managed to shrug off the locals.

"Ben's party. The one he invited me to last night. The one I got dressed up for. I don't usually hoik my tits up under my chin just so some bloke in a scruffy bar can have a laugh trying to rest his pint on them," Liv said anxiously.

"Oh, Liv, you never said. I've been planning this all week. Oh, shit, I'm sorry." Alex looked genuinely guilt-stricken. "We can always go along later if you like. I mean I'm sure that Rob and the boys won't mind."

"Oh, don't worry." Liv put on a brave face, knowing that later she wouldn't feel up to it and her chest would be too exhausted to perform.

"If you're sure. I tell you what. I'll invite Ben and Amelia over to dinner one night next week and sit you and him at the opposite end of the table to Amelia and feed him oysters just to make up for it," Alex promised, and looped her arm through Liv's as she and Alex swayed in through the doors of the pub like Mae West into a Western saloon. The men on the other side wished they had their pistols at the ready. Liv ran her hand through her hair in a bid to lose a few inches and followed in Alex's already-feted wake.

"Can I get you anything, love?" A man in moleskins took a step forward from the bar and offered Alex his stool.

"Holy shit, that's the first time Tom's taken his arse off that stool in thirteen years!" his mate yelled from the snug.

Liv and Alex smiled, took their glasses, and sat at a small round table under the window.

"So before the boys get here I thought we should have a bit of a chat." Alex took a sip of her wine.

"Sounds ominous," Liv said, hoping that it didn't concern men, because she was actually bloody bored of being so overanalytical right now and if she couldn't be getting hot and heavy with Ben, then she'd rather just shut the whole subject out for a while.

"Not at all. Actually, I had a business proposition for you." Alex continued, "I've been thinking about Greta's Grundies and how for James and Dave it'll always just be a hobby. Their Saturday afternoon social club. But you know, I think it could be a really successful business. The branding's bang on, the boys have so many contacts, and between you and me I reckon we could make it a really profitable company."

"Really?" Liv hadn't really thought of Greta's Grundies as a major business proposition, but well, maybe it could work. "But what would we do? Buy the boys out?"

"Exactly. We could arrange to pay them in instalments, give them shares, and then expand, expand, expand." Alex had clearly thought this through.

"I don't have any money at all," Liv thought out loud for a moment.

"Well, I can sell some stocks; you could remortgage your flat or something," Alex offered helpfully.

Wow, clearly Liv's accountancy brain had deserted her over the last couple of months. "Yeah. I think you're right. We'd have to talk to James and Dave, though. It's totally their baby."

"If you're agreed in principle then that's great. And think of the contacts we have here. I reckon Amelia will really help us, too, if we ask her. She's so well connected," Alex concluded.

"Yeah, and she'd want to call it Amelia's Adorables or something pukey." Liv wasn't too happy about this part of the deal.

Bloody Perfect Amelia. She could very well live without her. Amelia's Adorables. Adorable Amelia. Eugh. And anyway, why hadn't Liv been called Amelia? The name that tinkled like a bell when you said it, instead of Lumpy Liv, who was always just a lady's maid in Victorian England. You couldn't help but fall in love with Amelia, could you?

"Ben, meet Amelia with the tinkling name and body of the Sugar Plum Fairy." How could any man resist? Well, lucky Ben, he'd certainly come a long way since his early fumblings in that Provençal barn. Liv wondered if he ever thought back to it. Wondered if as they lay on Amelia's crisp linen sheets bathed in moonlight Amelia and Ben ever discussed their first sexual experiences and giggled fondly. Probably not. "Bloody hell, I had this English girl. Not a patch on an Aussie by the way. They're always covering up their boobs and diving under the covers. Or in this case the straw. Honestly, talk about looking for a needle in a haystack. Except not very needlelike. More of a space hopper." At which Amelia would turn and kiss his breastbone, her lithe body in no danger of being concealed. Why would you bother, she probably wondered, putting a dishcloth over the Mona Lisa?

"Liv, what on earth are you doing?" Alex asked as Liv came to her senses and realised she'd been shredding the beer mat into confetti. "I reckon you need some decent sex. That's a sign of sexual frustration."

"Thanks. Terribly helpful, Al, given my only candidate for romance is probably flirting with some other new girl in town at a party in his flat in Double Bay as we speak and will have taken my lack of appearance at his party tonight as total disinterest and will never even waste his breath speaking to me again." Liv humphed and scattered the remains of the beer mat across the floor.

"You might fancy one of Rob's mates, though," Alex said brightly, and uncannily on cue Rob and a couple of his less-than-Cartier mates walked in. Liv smiled and gave a little wave, hoping that after her embarrassing seduction efforts the last time she'd seen Robert she wouldn't actually have to look him in the eye, but Alex had other ideas. She leapt to her feet and greeted Robert with the warmth an Academy Award–winning actress usually bestows upon her little gold Oscar. She fluttered a lot and even tripped up on her way to the bar. Once there she kissed her statuette, formerly Rob, demurely. "Robbie," she said. Liv finished off the packet of Cheese Twisties in peace and watched the performance. "Come and join us."

Liv grinned as she shook hands with Tommo and Simmo, Robert's burly oil-encrusted entourage. Rob ordered the obligatory round of VBs and smiled broadly as he and his boys came and sat down at the table, their large knees and wide chests making the little corner of the pub suddenly feel very full. Liv was embarrassed for all of a second as Rob kissed her on both cheeks; then she realised he was smiling so hard at Alex that even if Liv had spent her afternoon at the races demanding he demonstrate the kama sutra with her on the coffee table and not merely engaged in a bit of feeble flirting, he would have pushed it to the back of his mind in the wake of Alex.

"So I'm surprised you're not at Benjy's party tonight." Rob emerged from the shade of Alex's eyelashes and addressed Liv.

"Why would you be surprised?" she asked, wondering just what Alex had been saying about her puppylike crush.

"Ah, just that Amelia was saying that she thought you had a bit of a soft spot for him. That you guys had something going when you were like ten years old. She thought it was really cute," Rob said, with no idea that he was felling Liv's dreams and pride like a woodcutter with a chain saw.

"Well, as for having a soft spot for him, I hardly think so," Liv snapped defensively. "Actually, the last thing I'm interested in right now is relationships."

"Oh really. That's a bit of a shame," Simmo, who until now had been gazing at the head on his VB as though it were the elixir of life, suddenly piped up.

"What are you interested in then, mate?" Tommo asked, like what else was there apart from sex?

"Actually, my work. Alex and I are going into business together and I've just got out of a five-year relationship, so I think love's the last thing on my mind," Liv said firmly.

"Yeah, Liv's really focused right now," Alex chimed in.

Thank god for some loyalty at long last, Liv thought. God knows where Alex's head had been lately, but it wasn't devoting much of its time to helping Liv. "So there." Liv sipped her drink in what she hoped was a businesswoman-type way and tried to pretend she wasn't oozing boobs everywhere.

Still, while Liv had clearly deflected the attention away from the idea that she might fancy Ben, for the time being she was secretly mortified at what Amelia had apparently said. Was that how everyone saw her, the hopeless wet English girl who used to follow Ben around? Someone to be indulged like a pathetic pet? Liv imagined that Amelia definitely thought so. Well, at least she knew now that Ben was just being charitable. Probably it was Amelia's good deed for the day to make him snog her because she'd heard that Liv couldn't even get Fat Will to call her back. Noblesse oblige or something like that. Playing Lady of the Manor seeing to the peasants' best interests. So Liv began to accept that she wouldn't ever find herself on the receiving end of Ben's lips again, apart from when he told her to get lost. And now she'd missed his party and probably wouldn't see him for decades.

Still, she craved the idea that she might run into him when she was looking gorgeous in some restaurant one night. Bump into him in six weeks' time when she was out in the surf, standing atop her surfboard looking like some goddess of the deep with miraculously Australian thighs and a golden tan. Because in six weeks she was going to be beautiful and modelesque of course. It was always in six weeks. This seemed to be the optimum time for any miraculous makeover transformation to take place. If you bought a cellulite cream you had to rub it in religiously for six weeks before your thighs were no longer mistaken for the surface of the moon by Russian space stations; if you enrolled at the gym you'd continue to wobble precariously on the treadmill until the sixth week, when you became GI Jane in Adidas leggings; and if you embarked upon a draconian detox diet you had a headache and felt weak for six weeks, then became clear-skinned and happy. There was no such thing as instant perfection. One always seemed to have to wait six weeks. In theory. But Liv knew that once the six weeks were up, if you hadn't just got bored and forgotten that you were waiting for the New You to emerge from a chrysalis, then you were generally still You. Same wonky eyebrow, same short neck, same ugly feet.

"Well, mate, it was good to see you again." Rob slapped Liv on the back and turned to Alex. "So give my regards to Charlie, won't you?" he said in a bad, stagy way. There was a lot of ham acting going on tonight, Liv noticed but was too tired to be bothered to think any more about it. They had managed to pass the evening with perhaps not the most fun you can have on a Friday night, but it was in no way too boring. Liv had quite enjoyed hearing a few dirty jokes, and Rob was surprisingly sharp and clever for a stable hand. And Alex had been in fine form, chatting about her thesis and her plans for the business and proudly telling stories about her brothers. It hadn't been too bad at all, given that it was very much not Ben's party.

"Good night, all," Liv said as she clambered into the back of a taxi and waited for Alex to glide in beside her. But instead Rob shut the cab door firmly. Alex just stood there waving. "I'm off to Charlie's. I left my toothbrush there and you know I can't get to sleep without cleaning my teeth. I'll call you in the morning." Alex smiled and watched Liv sail round the corner without her.

Liv unlocked the front door and tiptoed past the hut. She could hear the faint murmur of sobs and she noticed that there was a crack of light seeping under Laura's door, but she also noticed Jo-Jo's pink handbag on the coffee table in the cottage so presumed that whatever the current crisis, Jo-Jo would handle it. Poor Laura, thought Liv, what a witch Amelia must have been to crush her this much. Liv really did want to find out what precisely had happened, but the time never seemed right to risk another pasta-disasta or some tirade of chanting and mumbling, so she'd just kept her curiosity to herself. Liv spotted the answer machine flicking away in the corner and tapped the button, probably only her mum or Laura's shrink. The two most trusty callers they had.

"You have one new message. Message One sent at eleven thirty-nine P.M.

" 'Hey, this is a message for Liv.' " It was male, Liv could make out, but sounded a bit whispered, like the guy had wrapped a curtain round himself before speaking. " 'It's Ben. Ben Parker. Listen, I'm sorry you couldn't make it tonight. I hope everything's okay, 'cause I was kind of expecting you and I know it's late notice, but I was wondering if, as we didn't get a chance to catch up tonight, you'd like to come along tomorrow to spend the afternoon on the harbour with us. There'll be a crowd, I'm afraid, but well, I'd love to see you again. We're meeting on Rose Bay Jetty at twelve-thirty. Erm. That's it. Hope you can make it. Bye.' "

Liv thumped down onto the sofa and stared at the machine as though it were playing an elaborate joke on her and any second now would yell, "April Fool, you idiot!"

Liv looked at the clock and wondered if it was too late to call Alex. It was just gone midnight, and as Charlie wasn't there, it didn't really matter if she woke her.

"Alex," Liv said. "Still awake?"

"Sure am, petal," Alex said but sounded a bit preoccupied. It occurred to Liv for one split second that she might be indulging in a spot with Rob the groom, but she remembered that he was as poor as a church mouse so put that one into the "unlikely" basket.

"I've been invited to Ben's thingy tomorrow," Liv said.

"Ben's thingy, eh? And what would that be?" Alex laughed.

"The harbour thingy."

"Oh, the party on the *Millie*?"

"What's the *Millie*?" Liv feared she already knew.

"It's Amelia's yacht . . . named after her, naturally."

"Naturally. Listen, are you going?" Liv suddenly didn't feel like leaping up and down like a rock star on the sofa anymore as she had done when she'd first got Ben's message. "Does that mean I have to wear a bikini, by the way?" She knew it shouldn't matter, but lying seminaked in the unforgiving Sydney sunshine was only marginally more appealing than sticking hot needles under her fingernails.

"Yeah, we are. Well, I'm going. You could pretend to be an English rose and wear something floaty," Alex reassured her.

Liv looked at the abandoned pile of beading and feathers on the sofa. She'd spent the last few days trying out designs for Greta's Grundies, and maybe she could cobble something together. And perhaps, if she finished this tonight, she would be able to go to the ball after all tomorrow.

"Okay, I'll be there. What time?" Liv edged her way towards the needle and thread.

"Ohhh, I, erm, oohhhh, I don't know. . . ."

"Alex, are you having sex? Only if you are don't let me interrupt you—"

"Sorry, Livvy, no, you're not interrupting anything. I was just . . . cleaning my teeth. Now what time? Oh, I reckon about twelve-ish. See you there."

So who else could Liv call in a crisis? Suddenly she missed Tim. He used to be her late-night advice line and she felt quite capable of talking to him these days without even a glimmer of a tear, in fact, she thought, with no flicker of sadness, which was pretty amazing. Still, what would she say? "Hey, whoopee dooo, I've been invited to expose my pallid flesh on Ben Parker's girlfriend's yacht, which is named after her, tomorrow. Do you reckon I stand a chance of scoring some love?" Not exactly, she decided. Ah, Liv knew who'd she'd call, her boys.

"Dave?"

"Livvy?"

"Can we talk?" she asked.

"Okay, fire away, but you do know that you're interrupting a pretty impressive dream scene where I was about to seduce Brad Pitt right in front of Jennifer, don't you?"

"Sorry, but my need is greater than Brad's." Liv lay back on the sofa and began to sew herself the dreamkini.

"Brad just doesn't know his needs yet. So what's the problem?"

"Problem is that . . . well, did I tell you about the beach thing? About Charlie's party when I went and sat on the sand with Ben Parker and he tried to kiss me?" Liv asked.

"Okay, now you have my attention." Dave audibly sat up and listened.

"When did I last speak to you?"

"Yesterday morning when you were being a sad bint because the fat boy hadn't called."

"Oh my god . . . okay, well the thing is this: quite a lot has happened since then. . . ," Liv began.

And Liv related, to the strains of much oohing and ahh-hing and "lucky bitch"-ing on the other end of the phone, her past twenty-four hours. She relived it all in glorious Technicolor herself and when she was finished put her needle down and waited for Dave to say, "Lucky you. Go for it, baby." Which was, after all, the only reason she'd called him. To confirm that she wasn't morally bankrupt for wishing that

Ben would kiss her even though he was going out with someone and that her karma wasn't going to be kaput for all eternity because she wouldn't be the one making the phone calls and the moves. She'd be the innocent party slayed by Ben's devastating charm and entirely blameless. Hell, from what Rob had said earlier on it sounded as though Amelia might even sanction Ben's seduction of Liv.

Sadly, though, Dave said no such thing.

"Dog handling, dog handling. Didn't I tell you, darling?" he practically sang down the phone.

"No, I'm not interested in dog handling anymore, Davo. What I want is to know if it's really awful to be wanting to kiss someone else's boyfriend. I mean I know that it is, but he was once mine and possession is nine-tenths of the law and so maybe I still have a stake in him and I'm really only reclaiming my right. Right?"

"Shut the fuck up a minute, honey. For starters, where Amelia Fraser is concerned we have no qualms about morality. She wears fur and once shagged a friend of mine whose pregnant wife was actually *in labour* as she was getting her gums around his plums. So lose that concern."

"Holy moley. That's fantastic. God, thanks, Dave, now it's all going to be fine and—"

"I said hush. Has something really significant not occurred to you here?" Dave asked, now getting out of bed to locate a can of Coke—this was going to require energy.

"Like what?" asked Liv, but she was losing interest. She'd heard all the good bits, and the best was surely just filler. Now she needed her beauty sleep.

"Like the fact that you have completely proved my theory on dog handling."

"How?" Liv wondered.

"Okay, you went to the party and because you saw the fat guy at the other end of the room you were so busy trying not to be seen by him that you completely abandoned Ben Parker. Right?"

"Well, yes, but I didn't mean to. I mean I would have stayed and talked to him if I hadn't seen Will."

"But Ben didn't know this. All Ben sees is a girl who doesn't want to talk to him. A girl with a ball who doesn't want to play." Dave was very excited at the confirmation of his closely held theory. "So naturally our dog is intrigued. He wants more, so he comes back to the girl as she's about to run out of the door and leave the party and begins to sniff her."

"I was only going to leave because I was so worried about escaping Will." Liv frowned; she really should be asleep now if she wasn't going to have shopping bags under her eyes in the morning.

"And then . . . god, my darling, you were abso-bloody-lutely wonderful. Because then came the pièce de résistance. My clever dog handler gave away just a little; she strolled out onto the beach in an insouciant fashion with her cardigan cleverly buttoned up and she chatted sweetly and showed our dog what a lovely, loveable girl she was and then . . . she refused to kiss him. Perfection. I couldn't have done it better myself."

"But, Dave, I would have kissed him if I didn't pong to high heaven," Liv said, though she was beginning to see a pattern.

"But he was still on your case, wasn't he? He didn't think oh, she doesn't want to kiss me, so I'll go eat worms and die. He invited you to his party and then—how I love you, my darling clever Liv—when you didn't show tonight he dashed into the bedroom when Amelia wasn't looking and called you, desperate to know you better, to have you. And all because he thinks he can't have you." Dave collapsed back on the bed in a heap. "This is almost better than Brad's perfect little legs wrapping themselves around me in my dream. I'm so glad you called me."

Actually, Liv wasn't terribly glad she'd called Dave at all now.

"Does that mean that he doesn't fancy me and it's only because I'm dog handling that he wants me?" Liv was a bit concerned.

"No, he doesn't do this to check out chicks in the supermarket. Just that if he does fancy you and you press the right buttons and don't give him what he wants when he wants it then *YOU RULE.*"

"I do?" Liv was unconvinced and nervous. "Then how do I get to kiss him and carry on ruling?"

"So simple you'll choke. All you need to do tomorrow is rock up on the jetty wearing something divine, not look at him at all, and barely even acknowledge his presence. But when you do, you have to be heaven on a pole or he'll just think you're a bitch."

"But do I get to kiss him?" Liv was bursting to know. "Or else really what's the point?"

"The point *comme toujours* is that you make him fall in love with you. You're not just a one-night stand or some floozy in a bikini. You're the real McCoy. The love of his life. But the good news is that you do get to kiss him tomorrow. But then you have to back off. Right away. Say thanks, but no thanks, I could not possibly, as you have a girlfriend and, frankly, this isn't on my agenda right now."

"I say that?" Liv was not convinced.

"Not in so many words. But this isn't until you've shown him that you're a very competent girl in the bedroom department and can do whizzbang tricks. Or at least just give him the impression that you might. Don't actually perform for him yet."

"Fuck. Like what?"

"I don't know. Improvise. But make it good. Listen, I have

to go, otherwise I'll never be up and I've got to paint my float for Carnival tomorrow, but call me and let me know how it goes, okay?"

"Promise. And thanks, Davo." Liv put down the phone. "I think."

Chapter Twelve

And Sit

By the time the party began to assemble on the harbour, the sun had scorched the mist off the morning and climbed to dazzling heights over the city. Rose Bay was dotted with tiny craft and the neighbouring beaches were dappled with languid prone bodies. Liv had been up for her surfing hours ago. Spurred on by nerves and romance, she'd even honed her skills somewhat, and today had been a breakthrough for Justin, as Liv hadn't screamed and swum in the other direction when the wave came towards her.

Still flushed with triumph, she'd gone home and decided to wear her new swimsuit. Before she'd fallen asleep last night she'd finished a latter-years Liz Taylor number that was designed to hide all the places Betty Ford couldn't reach. Thus with the help of the purple feathers and expanses of something new and formidably tough called techno-fabric Liv had fashioned a swimsuit-and-sarong ensemble that boasted a cleavage-to-lower-body ratio of something like 7650000:1. You see, mathematical ability was good for some things. Cleavage was good for others.

An hour later, Liv wasn't sure that she'd done the right

thing in wearing her new bathing suit on the bus. She'd had one proposal of bigamy, two offers to carry her bags (she had none, merely a rolled-up towel under her arm), and an invitation to join an agency for surrogate motherhood between the Oxford Street stop and Watson's Bay. Quite how the upper echelons of Sydney society, namely Amelia and crew, would react to Liv's Liz look remained to be seen. Thankfully, the second she stepped off the bus the first person Liv spied was Alex, sitting on the jetty with her head buried in a book.

"Hey, Ally Bongo, it's me." Liv sauntered towards her, though the spring of elastic in her suit could well have catapulted her all the way.

"Ooh, baby!" Alex yelped as she caught sight of Liv. "And God created Liv."

"It's not too much?" Liv scowled shyly.

"Of course it's too much. But it's heaven." Alex winked.

"So why were you so distracted last night? What's going on?" Liv asked Alex as they clambered aboard the *Millie* with the help of the harbourmaster. None of the others had shown yet, but Amelia had staff who arranged the boat in her stead.

"I'll have to tell you later. Too many spies," Alex said, grinning wickedly. They found a shiny piece of deck with an unparalleled view of the harbour and laid their towels down.

"Then I can't tell you my news, either, in case anyone hears. God, I had such a funny chat to Dave last night though; he's still going on about all that making-men-fall-in-love-with-you-by-treating-them-like-naughty-dogs stuff. I know you think it works, but honestly, I can't do that manipulative thing. Anyway, I reckon it's just coincidence that it's worked so far. Really, it's a load of crap," Liv said, readjusting her techno-fabric.

"Actually, I totally agree with you, I think. I mean with some men it probably works, but love and romance can't be engineered; it always happens when you least expect it," Alex said, and looked towards the car park, where the guests were beginning to arrive.

"You've changed your tune."

"Just living and learning," Alex said mysteriously. "So I assume that Ben called you and asked you to this? Clearly has the hots," Alex whispered to Liv.

"How do you know he called?" Liv asked. "I didn't tell you that."

"No, you great idiot, who do you think gave Ben your phone number?" Alex said as she lay back on the towel.

"Well, I don't suppose I did think. Was it you?" Liv asked.

"Actually, it was Rob. It was quite funny, 'cause Rob called Ben from the mobile last night to see what time we had to be here this morning and they were chatting and Ben wanted to know what we'd been up to and, anyway, somehow Rob ended up telling what you'd been saying about being dedicated to your career and didn't want a boyfriend and stuff, so Amelia didn't have to worry."

"Amelia was worried?" Liv asked.

"Nah, not really I don't think. She only worries about her roots showing. Anyway, then Ben asked for your number and said he wanted to invite you along today. So we gave it to him," Alex finished.

"Great. Now I'm a charity case," Liv groaned in embarrassment.

"Oh, come on, Liv, stop being so down on yourself. You reckon that you'd never stand a chance next to Amelia, but she's not as amazing as you think, you know. She's really a bit rough, and I think she takes Ben totally for granted. You're sweet and lovely, so get over yourself. Have some faith."

"Well, he'll be completely put off anyway, as he thinks I'm a celibate workaholic thanks to Rob. Just my bloody luck."

★ ★ ★

The boat began filling up. Liv turned casually to see who was there. Amelia was just coming up the gangplank onto the gleaming deck, followed closely by Ben, who seemed to have assumed the role of porter, carrying at least two hand-bags, a picnic hamper, and a small suitcase.

"G'day, ladies." His brown arms swinging, propelling him expertly up the ladder, Rob appeared at their side. "Bit late 'cause I've been mucking out at the stables and fancied an early-morning ride. Alex, you want to borrow my shirt? Your arms are gonna fry," he said as he unbuttoned his shirt and draped it over Alex's shoulders. Liv waited for Alex to hand it back in a fit of feminist pique, but she didn't; she merely smiled sweetly at Rob.

"So, Robbie, can I come and help you with the horses one day? I haven't been on a horse since I went to Bridlington on holiday when I was seven," asked Alex enthusiastically.

"Yeah, but we have to muck out before. I'll lend you a pitchfork. Mind," he said, scratching the back of his calf with his foot, "it might muck up yer clothes a bit."

"Oh, I love getting mucked up." Alex laughed and turned back to admire the harbour view. Liv looked at Alex and then at Rob and wondered if they really could be having a fling. Alex's bit of rough? With his filthy fingernails and workman's torso Rob certainly qualified.

"So what was that all about?" Liv asked as Rob wandered over to help the deckhand haul in the anchor.

"He's sweet, isn't he?" Alex neither confirmed nor denied. "And really interesting, Livvy. I was telling him all about my thesis last night. He gave me some good ideas." Alex watched as Rob's back muscles flexed under the weight of the anchor.

"So a bit of rough with a brain. Where does that leave Charlie?" Liv asked.

"Exactly where he's always been. In my bed but eyeing up other women. Rob's just like my brother. And he is quite sexy, isn't he?"

"Who's sexy?" Liv looked up to see Ben Parker's crotch presiding over them. She turned away but not before he caught her looking. Well, if he *would* wear white shorts, have long brown legs, and stand inches from her head.

"Well, not you, that's for sure. Could you move the obscenity from my line of vision?" Alex yelled as Ben laughed and sat down next to them.

"Oh, by the way, Ally, Charlie's just arrived. He was looking for you a minute ago. Over by the bar." He pointed over to where a group was forming: sun hats, beachwear, and ubiquitous sunglasses at the other side of the boat. "I'll look after Liv if you like. How's the ankle?" He smiled as Alex wandered off giving Liv a told-you-he-fancied-you glance over her shoulder.

Liv sat up and decided that his concern and phone calls had been purely medical. And actually, she wished he would go away. He made her feel about seven and all shy and stupid, and suddenly the last thing in the world that she wanted was to kiss him; it was all much too scary.

"Fine, thanks." Liv nodded curtly and pretended to concentrate on a mosquito bite that was assuming epic proportions on her arm.

"It was fun last night. It's a real shame you couldn't make it." Ben made himself comfortable beside her on Alex's towel.

"Yeah, I'm sorry," she said. "So, erm, how's work?" She thought she should make a bit of an effort, though she could only seem to manage dumb things.

"Great, but actually I want to hear about yours. I gather you're really into this business idea with Alex. Rob said you guys are going to have some huge empire in no time."

Liv just smiled; she couldn't think of a single interesting or even dull thing to say. Her vocabulary had totally deserted her. So instead of being scintillating, she just lay down on her towel like a mute idiot and pretended to be enjoying the heat rash that was breaking out on her cheeks.

"Have you seen much of Australia yet?" Ben persisted. God, he just wouldn't give up, would he? Like a terrier with a rat . . . or god . . . even a dog with a ball. This was so weird; maybe Dave was right. Ben was behaving like a total panting dog. Even if she were to lie down and die she suspected he might just sit there in the same way that faithful Alsatians sit by their dead masters' graves for years and years. Liv couldn't quite believe it. It just seemed that as long as she smiled sweetly occasionally she didn't actually have to do anything else to keep him hanging on there, trying to win her round. I mean there were about twenty other much prettier, definitely more interesting girls on board who would be willing to dance attendance and hair-flick adoringly at him and he was sticking to her side like a limpet. But Liv wasn't fooled for a second. She contemplated telling him that he'd got the wrong girl; in case he'd forgotten, she wasn't five-foot-eight in stocking feet and when she took her hat off she was—surprise, surprise—a brunette. No leggy blonde about her. But it was a hot day and the last thing she wanted was to be made to walk the plank into shark-infested waters for having a barney with the boyfriend of the yacht's namesake. And besides, she was quite enjoying her day on the ocean waves. The *Millie* was almost as lovely as her owner. In fact, they could have been separated at birth. They were both a glossy teak colour, phenomenally expensive to run, and safest kept on the right side of. So Liv opted for civility.

"Oh, I've been pretty flat out on the stall, seeing friends, don't seem to have time to breathe," she said without raising her head for fear he'd see her disgusting rash.

"That's a shame," Ben said as he looked out onto the harbour. "I mean you not being around. You really should see some more of the country. You know, Sydney's great, but it's a playground. You need to check out some of Melbourne, Queensland, Alice Springs. See the real stuff."

"I think Amelia's about to be eaten alive. If I were you, I'd go and rescue her," Liv muttered, and cast a glance at Amelia, who was indeed being circled by seven predatory males.

"When it comes to sharks it's the ones who travel alone you have to watch out for. And they usually get their prey in the end." He laughed and tried to catch Liv's eye, but she pretended to immerse herself in a book she'd found in Alex's bag, *The Brothers Karamazov* by Dostoevsky. In Russian.

"Later," Ben said finally as he got up to leave, getting the message, she hoped. The gulls circled the mast hoping for a mouthful of filet mignon or sushi canapés or whatever delights everyone else seemed to be tucking into at the bar. Too shy to go over and ask for a bite to eat, Liv attempted to ignore the mouthwatering smell of the barbecue and tried to get some beauty sleep.

In fact, it was a hugely successful attempt at sleep. But a little more beetrooty than beauty sleep. Liv woke up two hours later to find the boat totally silent. She lifted her stiff head and rubbed her cheek. She'd fallen asleep on her watch, and, sadly, had Marks and Spencer imprinted on her jowls. If she'd been any of the other glamour-pusses on the boat it would have been Cartier, naturally, but the only thing they were ever likely to fall asleep on was the finest goose-down pillows. Certainly they wouldn't dream of waking up with the kind of sunburn Liv had managed to achieve across her shoulders and the backs of her legs.

"Hell." She sat up quickly, the proverbial scalded cat, as if another second in the sun would make any difference. She was fried and there was little else to it. But, actually, of more concern to her right now was that she seemed not to be aboard the *Millie* anymore but the *Marie Celeste*. As she stood up and wrapped her jeans around her shoulders for emergency sun protection she saw no sign of life.

"Hello?" She whispered at first, looking down the staircase into the berths below. "Anybody there?" Her voice got louder as she approached the bar. Champagne glasses sat untouched. A Fendi baguette bag glittered abandoned on the floor and a gold macramé bikini bottom. But no apparent owners. The deck was gleaming in the sun, and in the distance the Harbour Bridge stretched across the horizon. Other yachts bobbed on the flecked surface of the water, but Liv was very definitely alone on board. She thought of the possibilities: either they were sinking slowly and everyone had jumped ship in a lifeboat, mistaking her sleeping form for an inflatable Day-Glo raft, or they'd been picked up by some glamorous friends in a helicopter and taken to the bar at The International for cocktails while she slept.

"Oy, Liv, you not coming in?" someone yelled from somewhere far away and muffled. Liv ran towards the edge of the boat and looked out. There in the water, dotted like currants in an eccles cake, were the heads of the entire party. Laughing, doing duck dives, splashing one another. Liv waved down as Stephanie, Amelia's personal assistant and dearest friend, bobbed up. At Liv's feet was a pile of the finest undergarments and bathing suits money could buy. As she smiled down on the watery fun she contemplated picking up a few of the bits and bobs and examining them for stitching and lining and any other details that might help her further in her design of Greta's Grundies. She longed to know whether the interlaced Gs on a Gucci bikini were real gold or just clunked like plastic when you knocked them against your front teeth. But it might be inviting just a little too much attention if she were caught munching heartily on Amelia's bikini bottom.

Instead Liv took the opportunity to slink off and find a real bite to eat. Something other than $400 bikini bottoms or

Ben Parker's boxers. And besides, she'd feel a bit like a spare prick at a wedding if they all came back on board in the nude and she was standing there with her jeans wrapped around her shoulders. Even though she would dearly have loved a dip in the cocktail blue water, she dismissed the idea before it could even form. How, but how, she would ever manage to leap into the water in the altogether without those down below getting a full gynaecological viewpoint was too perilous to contemplate. She did have a supercool Stripper Wax to her name, but she'd be buggered if that was going on public view.

Instead she negotiated the steep, polished steps down into the berth and sighed with relief as the cool darkness soothed her scorched skin. In fact, this was much preferable to bouncing around in the refreshing waters of the harbour because she got to have a peek through the keyhole of Amelia's life. A glimpse of which Liv knew was going to be just like flicking through the pages of cuttings again, but with the added bonus of being able to check out what brand of mascara Amelia really wore when she wasn't being bribed by Chanel to say it was thanks to them that her eyelashes had been voted Most Battable in last year's *Cleo* magazine's readers' poll. In fact, as she glanced around the glistening glass shelves of the tiny but perfectly formed bathroom Liv discovered it *was* Chanel. She couldn't resist; she picked up the wand and stroked a little onto her piggy pink morning eyes to see if she became Battable. Not a hope but certainly an improvement. She ran her hand over the cool marble and checked out her sunburn in the mirror behind her. Ooh, if her piddly little eyes didn't make her a complete pig, then the broad pink rump she was looking at now did. She didn't dare touch it for fear of unimaginable pain.

She walked along the low, cream silk–lined corridor hoping to find the kitchen and a few leftover canapés. What she found instead was the main bedrooom, lit as dimly and flat-

teringly as if by candlelight. She dreamed she would be allowed to spend the rest of her days in here. Not your average superyacht-type ensemble of naff luxury and dripping
gold. Not that Liv really knew what the inside of the
Christina or the *Britannia* or any old oil tycoon's yacht would
look like, but she had seen her share of biopics of the rich
and famous and had to say the decor on those silly-money
boats was generally pretty vulgar. Miserably, Amelia didn't
seem to have a bad-taste bone in her body. The bed was
draped in acres of white and cream silks and the small mountain of cool linen pillows was made for lounging like a languid courtesan. In fact, the whole place was bloody amazing.

Liv plumped down on the antique stool at Amelia's dressing table. She reached over and picked up a jar of something
cool and moisturising-looking and slipped off the lid. She
inhaled deeply and practically passed out with pleasure at the
smell of white jasmine. Knowing she shouldn't but feeling
the backs of her legs begin to prick, she stuck in a fingertip
and rubbed the small blob of cream onto her forearm. It was
so cool and soothing, she gasped. Then she stuck in a few
more fingers and began dolloping the cream on her shoulders. As she rubbed it gently into her searing skin she heard
a noise outside the door. Probably someone come to use the
loo. She was about to put the cream back on the dressing
table and fake a fit of heatstroke when the door opened.
God, talk about being caught with your hand in the cookie
jar. She turned around hoping that it would be Alex or, at
worst, Rob. It was, unfortunately, worse than worst. It was
Ben. Naturally. And god, he looked natural. He was wrapped
in a towel and his chest and face were covered in glistening
drops of water. His hair was damp and a small pool of water
was forming at his feet.

"It was a first-aid measure," said Liv, juggling the cream
from one hand to another as she tried to look as innocent as
possible. He smiled as he rubbed his arms with the thick

white towel. "I mean, I wouldn't have cared if it was cold cream or fresh cream or Savlon; I just needed to rub something cool into this sunburn," she warbled on, and tried to rub the vast, expensive, *stolen* blobs of cream into her legs and shoulders before he could make out the extent of the theft and perform a citizen's arrest.

"Christ, you're fried there." He left his pool of water and moved closer to her.

"Shouldn't you be drinking champagne or swimming or something?" she said, and covered up her legs with the pair of jeans she was still wearing around her neck.

"Can I help with that cream?" he asked as he took the jar from her hand.

"You know what? I think it's very expensive and I probably shouldn't have taken any in the first place, so why don't we just put it back and go upstairs for something to eat?" Liv blabbered, and as if on cue, her stomach rumbled like an air-raid siren.

"Not a chance." He pushed the flopping wet hair out of his eyes and reached towards her. Liv jerked back and Amelia's perfumes and potions clattered behind her on the dressing table. "That shoulder needs attention," he said as he rested his hand on the sunburn. "Painful?" he asked.

Liv nodded and held her breath in fear. Painfully embarrassing. "Listen, Dr. Kildare, I think we should go back upstairs. You've tended to my wounded ankle and that was very kind of you, but I reckon this is taking things a bit too far. Besides which, you have a girlfriend about six feet above us."

"Yeah, well, Amelia's a problem I'm going to have to face up to eventually." He sighed and Liv thought actually looked miserable. Yeah, right, the big faker. Like any man could call Amelia a problem to be faced up to.

"Nice try," Liv muttered under her breath, and walked towards the door. But he put a hand out on her arm and she really did just stick to the spot.

"Just let me rub some cream into your back. I promise I'll
be a complete gentleman."

Oh, hell, what could she say to that? Now he was being
all Victorian and honourable and she *had* to trust him. And
besides, it would look bigheaded if she said, "No, sorry, but
I think I'm so irresistible that you're going to have to pounce
on me because you won't be able to help yourself." And last,
well, there was no denying that she wanted him to do it.

"See, it feels better already, doesn't it?" he said, lightly
stroking the gorgeous cream into the back of her neck.

"I suppose," Liv murmured like a petulant teenager.

"Okay, so trust me. Lie down and I'll give you a proper
massage. I took a course in Thailand a few years ago. Purely
professional."

Liv looked at him and he did look disappointingly professional. His towel was now pulled tightly, almost chastely,
round his waist and there wasn't a hint of suggestiveness in
his eye. Oh well, she'd well and truly peed on that bonfire,
she thought, and decided to comply. Clearly she'd taken her
be-cool-and-don't-play-ball dog-handling behaviour too far.
Whether she meant to or not.

Still, though, having Ben Parker rubbing delicious-
smelling unguents into her limbs had been her dream before
she even knew she was coming to Australia. The idea of such
a thing had left her too weak to finish her sandwiches on
several lunch hours. And she was saying no? Like hell. Last-
chance saloon for this cowgirl, she thought as she lay on the
bed and gave way to Ben's admittedly expert hands kneading
her shoulders and back. She'd discarded the jeans and shyly
discarded her top, too, when he suggested it might be a little
difficult to reach the really important places if she was wearing her smock top. She bit her lip and whipped her top off
with her back to him. This may be a professional massage,
but she wasn't going to let him see things that he might one
day be able to use in evidence against her.

"This bit looks really sore. Is it?" he asked as he stroked his fingers over Liv's burgeoning red bits.

"Ouch. Yup," she acquiesced. Even though her tongue was practically lolling out with the sheer bliss of the massage. Her head was buried deep in the folds of the cool linen pillows and the boat bobbed softly up and down. She drifted off and would have been lying if she didn't admit that she did find herself imagining slightly that this wasn't purely professional. The delusional fantasy of a lovestruck woman, she knew, and she realised that she wasn't being any more realistic than the women who chucked underwear at Tom Jones thinking that they'd be tucked up under the sheets with him later that night and making his scrambled eggs in the morning. She'd definitely blown it by being such a cold old cow. If not by just being herself.

Liv turned her head the other way so he could reach the left side of her neck. His stroke now felt slower and he'd shifted his body weight closer to her. She tried to ignore the fact, too, that every time his hands effleuraged down the sides of her body they slid a little farther, brushing the sides of her breasts. She wasn't complaining. Though maybe she should have complained about the morality of his kneading as it got a little lower down, his thumbs exploring the skin just beneath the waistband of her shorts while his girlfriend was doubtless regaling eager partygoers with charming anecdotes just feet above them.

By this stage Liv had almost stopped fantasising. Hell, she didn't really need to. He was definitely stroking her inner thighs in a fantastically unprofessional way.

"Feeling better?" he asked as she felt a soft tickle on her left shoulder.

"Mmsshh," she murmured. An indecisive sound that couldn't make up its mind whether to be honest or sexy or disapproving so just came out plain silly.

"And this?" he asked as she felt a softer, slightly more

damp sensation trailing down her back. Christ, wake up and smell the jasmine, Liv. It's his lips. It's his tongue. She craned her neck around to see if she was completely seasick and delirious only to be met by his lips. Square on hers. The second that happened she found herself flipped over deftly like a pink omelette, tomato and bacon perhaps, and her chest pressing close to his. My god, the hairs against her burning skin, the weight of him on top of her, the bloody shock as he slipped one hand down the front of her shorts and kissed her. But this was all a little bit too real to take in. As though after years of imagining this moment, of imagining that Tim was Ben Parker, here he was and it was all some hyper-reality acid trip. Liv shook her head to get him off her face; she put her hands on his shoulders and tried to look him square in the eyes, though, to be honest, her gaze kept wandering distractedly to his lips and his scary sexy chiselled nose.

"You are so incredible." He looked right down into her face and for an atom-splitting second Liv believed him. Well, with one hand down her now-unzipped shorts and his other stroking her hair back from her face it was pretty easy to believe him.

"And incredibly, I'm going to say I think we'd better go back upstairs," Liv said briskly, sitting up and reaching for her smock top. Lovely though it was, this wasn't really what she wanted, because she was just too damned afraid that the minute this went any further she would end up on some scrap heap of Ben Parker rejects. Clearly Alex was right and he was a player, albeit in the guise of a very sweet guy, but if he was a player he really would discard her the second he'd had his way. She knew that Dave had been right about that much. Quit while you're ahead, Liv, she told herself firmly. She'd been battered around quite enough lately and couldn't face it happening again.

"I'm sorry, Ben, but this will never work. It mustn't happen again," she said firmly as she scraped her hair back into a ponytail and headed up the stairs to face the others.

"Liv, that looks so painful. Do you want to borrow some aloe vera?" Amelia came up to Liv and scrutinised her sunburn. Liv nearly threw herself overboard in shock. She wasn't aware that Amelia even knew her name, let alone gave a damn whether she was pink or purple with blue dots. She'd assumed that Amelia only spoke to the beautiful people. "Have a cranberry juice at least; vitamin C's great for the skin." She handed Liv a tall glass of juice rattling with ice cubes and sat down next to her on one of the navy chenille deck chairs.

"Thanks." Liv turned into the class square who could only talk about algebra and who never made it to the netball team again. "It's a lovely boat."

"Well, you know, anytime you want to come and spend the afternoon on board you're welcome. Just give me a tinkle and I'll get the harbourmaster to let you on."

"Well, that's amazing, and thanks. Again," Liv moved her deck chair slightly away from Amelia's and hoped she was downwind. If Amelia got a whiff of her best cream, which had been lavishly plastered onto Liv's body by her boyfriend in her bedroom, Liv thought their new and beautiful friendship might come to an abrupt halt.

"So Alex tells me you run Greta's Grundies on Paddo Market. I've got a few pieces from them. And Ben's bought me some gorgeous stuff there. And he loves this pair with ties at the side . . . so he can just—whoosh—undo them." She laughed dirtily. Liv gulped as Amelia reclined and pulled her sun hat over her face. Talk about hiding your light under a bushel. Still, there were the legs and the gently concave stomach and the prettily manicured toes to show off when the face took a break.

"We're thinking of expanding. I'd like to get a catalogue

thing and a Web site going, but it might take a bit of time. We'll see. It's a small business and there's loads of really fierce competition," Liv said to get away from whooshing knickers.

"Well, you know I'll be happy to help publicise in any way I can. I have a few contacts on the fashion scene," Amelia said breezily, and then nodded off to sleep. Amazed, Liv's mind drifted off to little bylines in Australian *Vogue* next to a Greta swimsuit. Or Madonna wearing one of the old-fashioned bathing suits on holiday at Whale Beach. And all because Amelia had chosen to put the word about. Somewhere in her business brain Liv was grateful she'd just done the decent thing with Ben (well, after a brief flirtation with indecency that hardly counted except that she'd treasure it forever, amen, et cetera), because it was looking as though being on the same side with Amelia was going to be very important indeed if Liv and Alex were going to make a success of Greta's Grundies.

Chapter Thirteen

Love and Romance 1¾ Miles

I don't want to talk about it!" Liv nearly yelled down the phone at Dave. "If I didn't put him off before, I have done now, and if the truth be known, I don't regret it for a second. I'm dedicating the foreseeable future to my career."

"What do you mean, you put him off? Did you come on too strong and scare him away? Did you give up the goods, Liv?" Dave nearly cried at the other end. His protégée might have severely stuffed up her mission.

"No, I did not. I told him that I wasn't interested, and I'm not bluffing, Dave. I really am not interested. I can't afford to be. I know you're right and he'd drop me like a hot potato if I let him have his way, so I just threw in the towel." Liv sighed.

"Oh, my angel, you are a genius. Okay, I'm coming round and we're going to plot the next dot on the map."

"No, Dave, you don't understand. I really don't want anything more to do with Ben Parker," Liv protested, but it was too late—Dave was pulling on his cycle helmet and hopping on his mountain bike by the time she put the phone down in despair.

* * *

Liv was busying herself with tea bags and milk in the kitchen as Dave made himself comfortable on the sofa. In his cycling shorts, T-shirt, and stubble he looked about as far away from Dorothy, Cher, and Greta as could be. And he looked very handsome.

"I'd rather talk business if you don't mind. Now I know James is happy with the proposal that Alex and I made for the takeover of Greta's Grundies, but are you prepared to sign the documents?" Liv asked as she studiously avoided his gaze and put two cups of tea down on the table.

"I might be. But you have to hear me out first."

"What I'd really like to do is to expand the swimwear line and get some sort of Web site going. I think that could work, don't you?"

"Why are you backing off, Liv? The truth." Dave picked up his tea and watched Liv as she sat down opposite him.

"Because I believe you should quit when you're ahead. By some weird fluke I played all the games you told me even though I didn't mean to, and so by default I made Ben Parker chase me for almost a whole week. I got him to call me and I got him to kiss me and, believe me, it was heaven." Liv paused at the memory. Dave could imagine.

"Which is all great."

"But you know that both Tim and Will took what they wanted from me and then kicked me to the kerb, as you so delicately put it, and I don't want that to happen again. And the thing is that I like Ben. Listen, I've spent the weekend literally bashing my head against walls and tables in abject misery at the thought of what I've given up, but I know it was the right decision. Ben Parker's never going to be in love with me and so what's the point? I'm not so cool that I can just make do with sex. I wish I were, but I want to be liked, too. Anyway, Ben might be perverse enough to want to snog me because he thought I wasn't interested, but really that's as far as it would ever go. I really think he's the sweetest, most handsome, brightest guy I've met in ages, but the second I let myself go I'll fall for him so hard that I might never be able to pick myself up again. I don't want to risk that, Davo."

"Sweetheart, that's giving something away because you're afraid to lose it."

"Damned right it is. I'm going to lose it anyway, so better do it with some dignity and pride left intact," Liv reasoned reasonably.

"If you want to make him fall in love with you, then you can," Dave assured her. "Got any biscuits, by the way?"

Liv wandered over to the kitchen and picked up the indispensable TimTams.

"Look, even if I'd wanted to take this any further, I gave him such a brush-off yesterday that there's no way he'll even think about calling again." Liv bit into a biscuit.

"Okay, how about we strike a deal? If he calls again, then I'm right. It means that dog handling works and you have to go with it and follow it through. Make him fall in love with you."

"It's just completely unlikely, Dave," Liv assured him.

"Then you won't mind shaking on it." He held out his hand and Liv looked at it hesitantly.

"Guess not." She shrugged, "Now will you please sign my contract for the takeover of Greta's Grundies and then when I'm still single at ninety I'll at least be able to afford to pay my gas bill." She held out her hand and shook his, and Dave signed the papers that confirmed that Liv Elliot and Alex Burton were now the rightful owners of Greta's Grundies, Inc. Something to celebrate at least, she thought miserably.

Laura sat in front of her shrink biting her nails and making them bleed.

"Perhaps we should address why you bit your nails in such a destructive fashion this week, Laura." Suzanne examined her own perfect cuticles and looked with disdain at Laura's. She did think that people would have fewer psychological problems if they just kept up with their basic grooming, but then that wouldn't be great for business, she supposed.

"It's self-loathing," Laura remarked. "I did a really awful thing this week."

"Would you like to share?" Suzanne made a note on her pad to book an eyebrow wax.

"It's my neighbour Liv. I've been sabotaging her social life." Laura looked up from under her paint-strewn fringe in embarrassment. Suzannah did a "share away" pout and waited.

"Well, the thing is that she's involved with someone who I know is trouble and I'm really trying to protect her."

"How do you know this person is trouble?" Suzanne asked.

"Because I was involved with this person myself."

"Is this The One?"

"The one I had all the trouble with? Who broke my heart? Yes." Laura's hands had begun to shake and her cuticles no longer had a hope in hell of surviving the latest onslaught.

"You know I don't approve of that term, Laura." Suzanne frowned disapprovingly.

"The person who caused me temporary emotional trauma, then. Well, I just happen to be able to hear their phone from my hut and just sort of overheard this message that this person had left and deleted it. I'd hate to see her hurt in the way I was. Was that right?"

"I suspect you know that it wasn't. That it was you being controlling and not respecting your neighbour's right to make her own decisions."

"Yeah, you're right. I'll tell her as soon as I get home, then. Sorry." Laura broke into a sweat and moved on to discuss how her father flushing her dead goldfish down the toilet when she was five had left her with unresolved feelings about her own mortality.

Liv hadn't been able to get a sensible word out of James or Dave all afternoon. It was four and the beach was still hot as the three of them topped up their vitamin D levels in preparation for the night of mayhem they were planning.

"You two are like a couple of kids gearing up to go to a birthday party. I've never seen adults so excited." Liv grinned as Dave covered his face with a towel so that he wouldn't catch any more sun and not be pale enough to be Greta Garbo tonight.

"Just you wait, young lady; this is the party of the year. You'll see," James berated her.

"Well, I'm not likely to know, am I, as you can't seem to get me a ticket. I thought you were supposed to be the Queen Bee, and you can't even get me in. I have no faith in all this Pink Power you claim to wield," Liv complained.

"Sorry, babe, queers only. Anyway, you should be grateful I got you into that roof garden party on the route. I'll wave to you from my float. You'll be sipping cocktails all night and dancing with boys dressed in angel costumes, and you're complaining?"

"Yeah, I guess. But I'm not going to know anyone there, so I may feel a bit . . . well, left out. Won't all be gay, will it?" Liv wondered aloud.

"Not even slightly, honey. But very exclusive, so stop whinging and count yourself lucky. Besides, I gave you a guest ticket, too—haven't you invited anyone?"

"I'm going to ask Alex. I'll make her put on her nipple tassels."

"Fab. Get her to swing them in my direction when we go past," said James.

★ ★ ★

Liv lay on the sand and made angels' wings with her arms. Little grains had lodged under her fingernails and her hair was gently baking. Life felt good. She wasn't sitting on a dark commuter train somewhere under Victoria Station and she'd begun to realise that life as a single girl was not too horrible at all. In fact, the future, now she'd managed to eliminate all the male distractions (Tim, she had heard, had been spotted in Sainsbury's with a new girlfriend, to whom he was *so* entitled, she told herself; I mean how much further from buying mushroom quiche and cold meats with a marketing executive could she be right now? Will had been consigned to the scrap heap of bad-mannered boys who didn't return phone calls after they'd slapped your bum during sex, and Ben Parker had a perfectly valid girlfriend and had duly shown that dog handling was clearly a load of rubbish, as he hadn't even begun to stalk her despite the fact that it was at least a week since she'd told him she didn't want anything to do with him—and there you had it, the male status quo, not exactly a cause for celebration, but with the sun shining and Mardi Gras hours away who gave a stuff, frankly?), was a promising landscape in which anything could happen. So Liv had just decided to trust in fate and get on with her fabulous career, enjoying her friends, experimenting, and experiencing life as she'd always wanted to do. Nobody to stop her from wearing too-short skirts, sleeping all day, eating pizza for breakfast, going out for morning coffee wearing her pyjamas and stilettos, no one to make her feel guilty for only reading the showbiz section of the newspaper; she could do whatever she wanted.

"Okay, I think it's time we made a move. Let the beautification begin," Dave said as he pulled on his shirt and covered up his gloriously smooth chest. His grooming habits put Liv to shame and he seemed to positively enjoy his regular back, sack, and crack waxing sessions, much to Liv's horror.

"Liv, we're off, but we'll wave to you from the float—we're sixth along, just after Dykes on Bikes, and I'll be at the helm of the ship, of course," James reminded her—he was The Little Mermaid and was going to be surrounded by hordes of seamen, or semen, whichever way you wanted to look at it, and they were all going to dance to the throb of "In the Navy." "And I'm going to leave you a bit of a treat to get your party started. Have fun, angel; we'll call you to check in tomorrow."

"Wish us luck!" Dave called back as they headed for their van.

"Break a leg, boys. You'll be gorgeous!" Liv yelled as Dave and James went off like love's only slightly raddled dream into the sunset.

Liv sat on the beach a bit longer, finished reading *Vanity Fair*, and decided that she, too, ought to head home and slap on a bit of war paint. She gathered up her stuff and shook the sand from her towel.

"Rob. I didn't expect *you* to be here," said Liv as she bounded into the kitchen at home. "Is Charlie here, too, then?" She poked her head around the corner and found Alex in her dressing gown on the sofa with her hair in a scruffy ponytail and her nails devoid of polish.

"Oh my god, you're practically naked!" Liv squealed, realising that Charlie absolutely couldn't be here if Alex was looking so dishabillé.

"Charlie's away playing polo." Rob came in behind Liv and handed her a large goldfish bowl–sized glass of wine.

"Yeah, so Rob's keeping me company. Isn't that sweet?" Alex tucked her feet under her and took the proffered glass of wine. "It's an amazing Sancerre—try it."

Liv sank back into one of the beanbags on the floor and

decided that despite appearances to the contrary and guilty-sounding protests, there was no way that Alex and Rob were having an affair, because Alex had made sod all effort to look attractive. Unless it was a Frumpy Housewife theme party. It wasn't that Liv was opposed to anyone being an un-made-up slouch, just that for Alex the groomed thing was an occupational hazard and she'd never been seen in public before without her Laura Mercier primer and foundation.

"Now do you guys want to come to Mardi Gras with me tonight? I've got the hottest tickets in town," said Liv.

"Actually, we've just got back from a bit of a day trip to the Hunter Valley, so we're a bit knackered. Sorry, Liv." Alex did actually look a bit whacked, but that could be the lack of primer.

"The Hunter Valley. Isn't that the wine region?"

"Yeah. We thought that another Saturday in Sydney was a bit pathetic. I was going to ask you, but Laura said you were at the beach with the boys," Alex assured Liv. "She said she'd been waiting to speak to you. Sounded a bit desperate, actually."

"Do you think I should go and see her now?" Liv wondered aloud.

"Oh, she went out about ten minutes ago. To some theatre thing. Anyway, she's always desperate. I wouldn't worry."

"Yeah. I'll catch her later. So how was the Hunter Valley?"

"So beautiful, Liv, you can't imagine. We had this amazing lunch in a vineyard and got a bit sozzled. We really shouldn't have driven back, but . . ." Alex and Rob looked at each other and smiled at the memory. "Rob's parents have a place there, don't they, Rob?" said Alex. "But he wouldn't take me. I told him not to worry; my parents lived in a really small house when they were alive. It's nothing to be embarrassed about. I just wanted to meet his mum and dad. They sound so nice."

"Yeah, well, another time, hey, doll," said Rob. "And, Liv, you'll come with us, right?"

"Sure. But right now I need a date for tonight, and as neither of you look fit for anything other than bed I should go and get ready. Guess I'll just have to go alone," said Liv.

"Alone? Are you sure? Liv, you hate going to places on your own." Alex was feeling a bit guilty. "I can always pull on some clothes and come with you if you like."

"Nah, it's fine. It's weird and I must be growing up or something, but I actually quite like it. Not knowing who's going to be there, who I'll meet, and there's the distraction of the parade anyway. I'll take some photos of the boys," Liv assured Alex. Actually, she was quite looking forward to an evening alone on the prowl: she could dance as badly as she wanted without anyone she knew being emotionally scarred by the experience. "Hey, I'd better get ready. You've got plenty of glitter I can borrow, haven't you?"

"Sure thing, babe—on my dressing table. Help yourself."

Thankfully as Liv raided Alex's wardrobe and lamented the loss of her waist since she'd arrived in Sydney she discovered a great Fat-Day sheath dress that performed all the necessary tricks demanded by a girl whose gym membership was less lapsed than never opened. In fact, so hypereffective were all Alex's wildly expensive lotions and expensive glittery bits in making Liv look like a girl, not a bushpig, that she was ready in twenty minutes. She decided that her dancing needed a bit of a helping hand, so as Rob and Alex roared with laughter over some inane dating show on television she put on a CD and practised a few moves—full dress rehearsal in high mules to Techno beat.

"I am happiness on toast. I am sex in a sheath dress. I am J-Lo in silver trainers." (The high mules had caused her to dance in a jerky parent-at-a-wedding fashion.) And after a few bounces around the room and mouthfuls of wine she started to feel distinctly nifty on her feet. Of course there was no mirror handy, but, well, the furniture was still standing and she hadn't any visible lacerations or bruises yet, which was novel. She let out a little squeal of delight and shimmied her hips to celebrate.

"You okay, Livvy?" Alex turned round from her place on the sofa and looked puzzled.

"Really well. Actually, I'm fantastic. Feeling wonderful."

"Good."

Alex and Rob looked at her with curiosity.

"Hmmm. So I'll be off then." She smiled like a very happy Osmond child and made her way to the front door. "Ciao."

Liv arrived at the party and as she climbed the stairs to the roof terrace was longing for the Mardi Gras parade to begin. All up and down Oxford Street people were lining the route, standing on milk crates, wearing fabulous costumes: men in glitter hot pants, stray Chers, lots of moustachioed hard men in leather chaps, but also lots of children and teenagers and accents and real policemen mingling cheerfully with those with the buttocks of their trousers cut out. The fun was infectious and everyone was waiting for eight o'clock and the start of the parade.

"Cocksucking Cowboy?" A voice next to Liv's ear asked as she leaned over the edge of the roof and watched the crowds and strobe lights sparkle below.

"Love one." She smiled at the Cruella De Vil waiter.

"Coming right up." Cruella winked and vanished.

"You don't call; you don't write; you don't phone. How am I supposed to know if you're dead or alive, eh?" another voice behind her said over her shoulder and kissed the back of her neck.

Liv swung round to be confronted by Ben Parker, for

heaven's sake. "You?" She scowled as though screwing up her face would make him vanish like a mirage.

"Me. This is the hottest ticket in town—did you think me and my prestigious girlfriend would go anywhere else?" He smiled sweetly. "There's a crowd of us over there. Come join us?"

"Where?" Liv stood on tiptoes in her silver trainers and didn't have to look for very long before she spied Amelia and her reams of beauteous friends shimmering in slinky fabrics and dazzling the waiters with their sparkly eyelashes.

"You know what, I'm fine just where I am, thanks," Liv told Ben. Despite the little kiss he'd just bestowed on her neck (which may have been a trick of her disco-dazzled brain), she felt comfortable with him for the first time since she'd arrived. Clearly they'd dispelled any misleading sexual tension by having a bit of a snog, she'd then set him straight about her intentions, and he hadn't called her. So no weirdness—just friends. "But it's sweet of you to offer. I'm so glad we can be friends, you know. I do think you're nice."

"Well, I'm glad. I think you're nice, too." He laughed and Cruella brought over Liv's drink. Just then the lights went down and the music began as the MC announced that the parade had just begun. "Well, I'd better be getting back over there or I'm likely to be missed. See ya later," Ben said, and patted Liv's arm in what could only be described as an avuncular way. Worst luck but definitely for the best, Liv thought as she craned her neck to see the Dykes on Bikes on the street below roaring into gear with their boobs wobbling proudly. And as the music struck up, as the lights flashed up from the street and from the ceiling above her, Liv began to experiment with her hips a bit. She jutted one in one direction. Then the other. She shifted her feet on the floor and shot a glance shyly around the room to see if anyone had noticed. If they had, then they seemed unfazed and not especially terrified. The police may have been alerted, but she didn't think so. So Liv got a bit more flash with her moves. She jiggled her arm like she was pulling a fruit machine and then caught sight of herself in a nearby window. She was dancing. Not reinventing the boogie or anything but definitely dancing. Which set her off all over again. I can dance! I can dance! she cheered in her head as years of miserable school discos and sitting out the Scottish dancing at weddings melted into happy oblivion.

As the parade continued, as float after float of overt sexiness was paraded before her, as she watched the guests on the dance floor behind her, the teenagers snogging in the street below, Liv began to feel a bit hot under the collar. She had exhausted her hips and was suddenly seeing the point of a dance partner. She shot a few glances over her shoulder and noticed Ben dancing—not wave-your-arms-in-the-air-and-let-rip stuff but just a bit of hip swaying, a foot here, a hand on someone's waist there. He was laughing and looked all ease. Alex was right: he was sexier than any man had a right to be. So sexy it was wrong. Especially tonight in his linen trousers and his trademark T-shirt and trainers. Amelia was really getting it together on the dance floor with her modelly mates, but he was unperturbed and seemed happy to just ease around the edges, one eye on the floats and music outside, one on the party. Liv was beginning to feel a bit left out, wishing it were last week again and she had Ben panting at her heels like a dog. I mean here she was totally ignoring him (apart from the sly staring) and she wasn't having a bit of luck. She looked forward to reminding Dave how wide of the mark he'd been on his dog-handling theories.

She took herself and her drink off to the loo so she could come back in five minutes and reinvent herself in another spot in the room—where nobody had seen her before and she would look like somebody who'd just stepped away from the fray to be alone for a second or two rather than a sad bint who'd been on her own all night. She was about to lock herself in a cubicle in the ladies' when she heard the door shut behind her.

"Why didn't you call me back?" She looked around and saw Ben standing there, his back against the door holding off the rest of the party. A tap dripped and Liv clutched her bag and took a hasty look around the loos to see if anyone else was there. They were alone.

"If you don't ring I can't call you back." Liv took a step or two back towards the cubicle. Subtly, but putting the distance between them nonetheless.

Ben was looking closely at her to discern whether she was telling the truth. "I called you on Sunday. I left a message on your machine."

"Oh. God, well, I'm sorry. I really had no idea."

"I can't stop thinking about you." He didn't move from behind the door, but she knew that he was about to get much closer than ever before. She could feel her resolve rinsing away, and though she tried to remember what her objections to kissing him were meant to be they, too, seemed to have evaporated. Ah yes. She knew.

"You have a girlfriend," she said. Almost firmly.

"You're very busy," he reminded her while looking at her lips.

"You're a player and only after one thing and when you've got it I won't see you for dust." She moved another pace away.

"You don't want a boyfriend right now." He moved a pace closer.

"My heart was broken and I don't want it to happen again."

"I want you, Liv."

"Of course you do, because you can't have me."

"Can't I?"

There was a tap on the door behind him and they both

froze for a second. Liv opened the door of the loo behind her and motioned for him to go inside quickly. They could swap places.

"What's going on in there? Open the door," a woman called out shrilly. Liv took over holding the door shut where he'd been standing. Before he moved into the cubicle he touched her cheek. Liv closed her eyes for a moment and then, after he was securely locked in the loo, she moved away from the door and let the woman outside in.

"What the bloody hell were you doing in here? I'm standing out there dying for a pee." A shimmery girl whom Liv recognised as one of Amelia's cosy posse burst through the door.

"Sorry. I was just hitching up my tights and didn't want anyone to come in." Liv grinned inanely.

"Yeah, well." The girl looked Liv up and down as though she were just a weirdo and then shut herself away in the next cubicle for a very long and loud pee like a horse. Liv tapped lightly on Ben's door and he opened it. She joined him and they smiled conspiratorially at each other and locked themselves in.

"Hey, you got any dunny roll in there?" The horse pee girl rapped on the door.

Liv leapt a foot in the air and Ben sent a roll sailing under the partition.

"Here you go." Liv giggled.

"Ta very much."

Liv and Ben were now only a foot apart with nowhere to step back to. Liv looked at her feet and then her handbag and Ben's feet and everywhere except his face. His trousers, she noticed, were made of a particularly lovely rough-hewn linen, probably Italian but then again, maybe Egyptian cotton. And beautifully hemmed.

Meanwhile there was a flush next door. A great deal of

primping sounds and teasing of hair into place in front of the mirror and then the banging of the door and silence.

"Thank god for that. I thought she'd never go." Liv laughed.

"So where were we?" He put his hands on her arms and she did feel stupidly small and pathetically lacking in willpower.

"It was never going to happen," she said quietly.

"Exactly." Ben nodded and then leaned down to kiss her, his hands tightening around her arms and his body moving next to hers. "Let's go outside." He had been kissing her hard and she, this time, had not been resisting.

"Outside?"

"In the street. It's buzzing out there. And it's pretty rank in here." He took her hand and kissed her one more time for the road. "Come on."

Liv was glad she hadn't revealed to him that having sex in a loo was actually one of the things on her list of Experiences I Must Have in Life. Along with dancing in public and Ben Parker. So she figured it didn't matter too much if she skipped just one of her things to tick off just for tonight. Didn't want him to think she enjoyed doing rank.

Ben laced his fingers through hers and led her out of the fire escape down some back stairs onto the street. They'd totally bypassed the party and Amelia and, thankfully, hadn't crashed into anyone on the way.

"Aren't you afraid we'll get caught?" Liv asked rather naively. The look he gave her told her that this might be precisely the thrill he was looking for. Instantly Liv knew that this was probably not the path marked "Love and Romance 1¾ miles." This was the hot, sticky, slippery slope to momentary thrills and feeling like shit tomorrow. But whereas unbaked Liv would have hesitated on the street corner, thought of Dave's wise words, and said thanks, but no thanks, the half-baked version of herself felt the balmy evening envelop her, took one look at Ben's face, thought screw tomorrow, and followed him through the crowds.

The parade was in full swing and with each float that passed another disco hit filled Liv's head. She was happy to be jostled by the crowd with their whistles and cans of beer and shrieks of excitement and she couldn't help but dance along as she and Ben stared upwards to see more camp than several hundred rows of tents grinding and pouting away. Every so often Ben would rest his hands on her waist as he stood behind her and she could feel his knee brushing the back of her legs. She was absolutely beginning to get the point of Cock-sucking Cowboys by now. They fuelled her on her journey. Even if she didn't know her destination, as she was so tipsy. But just as she was getting into Barry White rasping "Hang On in There, Baby," Ben put an arm around her waist and led her away from the throng and onto a quieter street.

"A bit of peace and quiet at last," he sighed as they strolled past the darkened, silent houses in Paddington, smelling the jasmine and enjoying the warmth of the night until the noise of the crowds drifted away.

"Absolutely," Liv said. Though suddenly she missed the buzz. It had matched her mood, the energy that was still bristling through her. She was still high from earlier, and part of her wanted to keep dancing and moving. Still, here was Ben. All to herself. Couldn't really complain.

"I don't know what it is about you, Liv, but since you arrived I haven't been able to stop thinking about you. I mean truly, I have never been this distracted by anyone. There's something different about you. . . ." He stopped and turned to her, pushing her hair gently back from her face. She was looking slightly blankly at him. "Oh, I know that sounds like a line, but it's not. . . . . It's like you're not even aware of how great you are and—"

"Ah, you see, I have a theory on this." Liv moved around

to the other side of the tree and began to pull the leaves off it. Then the odd twig. Breaking it up into pieces. "Ha, look, I'm pulling apart this poor tree. Anyway, the thing is . . ." And she was away. Straight off the starting block her mouth was running the 100-metre sprint in Lycra shorts and very serious trainers. Fuelled by the booze with fluorescent go-faster stripes. Liv talked. And how. "What you have to understand, Ben, is that I was with my old boyfriend for years. I mean ages and aeons and practically generations—almost since Victorian times—and so I'm not exactly what you'd call experienced with men and I know that I'm not supposed to admit this, especially to you, but I think that what you like about me is this quality that—"

"It's a kind of innocence," Ben said as he watched her carve her name on the tree with her fingernail.

"Totally innocent. I mean really, how many people have you slept with in your life, Ben?" she asked as he rested against the tree and began to stroke her shoulders. "Actually, don't answer that, I don't even want to know, but the point is that I've slept with . . . well, not many, and if I were to tell you how many then actually you might—"

"You're talking complete rubbish." He was holding her hands and standing a breath away from her.

"I know; I'm sorry. I think maybe I'm a little high. Shall I shut up?" she asked through a haze of cocktails and fresh air.

"Just give me a minute," said Ben as he moved in closer and began to kiss her bare, burned shoulder. "Or two." And he kissed her neck.

"Okay," she conceded, and closed her eyes just for a moment.

"Too much bloody Chardonnay, I reckon. I'll be fine. Just need a gulp of fresh air." Back on the roof terrace Amelia waved the horse-peeing friend away, and picked up her handbag before heading down into the street.

"Where do you reckon Ben's got to?" murmured one of the glossy posse when she was out of earshot.

"I saw that English girl in the dunny. You know, the one with the market stall." Horse pee raised her eyebrow and the glossy posse decided they wouldn't want to be the English girl with the market stall when Amelia got her hands on her.

"Oh, and this one, the one just below my shoulder blade. This one's from the time when I was seven and I fell off a dustbin." Liv and Ben had progressed to an intimate history of each other's scars.

"It's shaped like a boomerang." Ben smiled and ran his finger over the shiny white mark on Liv's back. "In fact, you are my boomerang. You've come back to me, haven't you?"

"Oh, that feels lovely." Liv shuddered. "Can you do that with your tongue?"

"I guess so," Ben said gamely, but he was beginning to worry that Liv looked a bit unstable on her feet. He'd seen her knocking back a few cocktails and they were pretty ferocious. And now she was being unusually flirty with him. He had wondered for a moment if perhaps she wasn't better off tucked up at home in bed. Then he looked at her warm, soft shoulders, the smooth skin on her arms, and the curve of her elbow, which he particularly loved. And he carried on kissing her. After all, he went out with Amelia; he was used to manic, insane women who talked complete nonsense and never shut up. So he began to press his lips against Liv's scar. To kiss her shoulders. To ease the straps of her dress down and move his knee between hers.

Amelia stepped out into the street and pulled a packet of cigarettes from her Marc Jacobs bag. As she lit one and took a deep drag a small group of worse-for-wear revellers nearly crashed into her. One of the young women half smiled at Amelia, not sure if she knew her from her feng shui evening class or if she'd seen her on the television but knowing that she knew her all the same. Amelia smiled back and stepped out onto Oxford Street with a tentative strappy sandalled foot. Last year a friend of hers had slipped on half a hamburger at Mardi Gras and broken her ankle. Then she'd put on loads of weight because, obviously, you can't exercise when your leg's in traction and you have to eat hundreds of poached eggs in hospital. Amelia was very cautious of foot.

"Wouldn't go down there, love. Never guess what we've just seen," one of the men laughed over his shoulder as Amelia made her way down a back street into Paddington.

Amelia took another lung-crushing drag on her cigarette and then tossed it to the ground and squeezed it underfoot. "I bet I would," she mumbled as they walked off. "I bet I bloody would." She forgot all about soggy hamburgers and marched, her bag clinging onto her shoulder for dear life, towards the scene of the crime.

Chapter Fourteen

Pets Win Prizes

Liv woke up and began to wallop herself around the face. She could feel a giant mosquito perched on her right cheekbone.

"Get off. Go away." She slapped away until it had to be dead, then lifted her hand from her cheek to witness the gore in a satisfied way. She looked at her hand. It wasn't a mozzie at all. It was a spiky, glittery false eyelash. Ugh. And she'd just completely given herself a headache by whacking her face like that. She leaned over to pull a pillow from the other side of the bed to hide from the glare of the Sydney weather. Instead her hand hit skin. Unmistakably skin. Human. She slowly turned her head, wondering if maybe she hadn't just got what she'd prayed for at her Tim altar all those months ago. To wake up and find that it had all been a dream, they were still engaged, and he was lying next to her in bed. But as she opened her eyes she realised that no, her prayers hadn't been answered. Well, not the Tim one, anyway. But maybe another one. Had she, she tried to recollect, ever prayed to see Ben Parker wearing reckless ruby lipstick with the sibling of her glittery eyelash stuck above his left eyebrow while lying buck naked in bed next to her? Not specifically, she thought. But maybe in one of her dirtier, more daring moments this scenario might have crossed her mind fleetingly. Anyway, the point was it had come true. Thank you, God, for answering my prayers.

She had had sex with Ben Parker. She had died and gone to heaven. She was now a whole woman. Complete, fulfilled, extended, delighted, and satisfied by the man of her dreams. The only hitch being she couldn't remember a moment of it. Not a kiss. Not a lick. Or a squeal or a groan. Nothing. Nada. Rien. Naff All. She had somehow managed to have sex with him and completely forget it. How could that be? Then she remembered the Cocksucking Cowboys. Of course. She could have cried—she had clearly been a miserable, philandering good-for-nothing male in a previous life to warrant this sort of bad luck right now.

Then just as she thought it couldn't get any worse she remembered dog handling. She'd slept with Ben Parker. She'd totally and utterly messed up her plans. How could one person be so breathtakingly stupid? There was now absolutely no way that she would ever get him in the sack again. He was as good as gone. In fact, if she closed her eyes and opened them again in six seconds he would probably take the opportunity to sneak out of her life and vanish. She had given away the goods. She was the cheap floozy. The scarlet other woman. She took a deep breath and wondered what the correct position to assume was when you were about to be kicked to the kerb. Maybe head between knees like aeroplane crash landings. Certainly she wanted to avoid eye contact when he did it. She decided to go and take a shower to give him a chance to leave without having to endure the whole embarrassing thing about letting her down gently. She peeled her sheets back as slowly and quietly as possible and made her way to the bathroom.

Once the shower was pelting hot against her skin and torrents of water were vanishing down the plughole along with leaves and twigs and soapsuds her mind began to clear just a little bit. Fragments came to her. Dave and James waving down from their float. Lots of men in thongs. Ben locking the door of the loo and kissing her. But that was it. There was a moment when she'd shed her clothes, that much she knew, and judging by the small forest blocking up her drain she'd had something to do with a tree. But the recollection of the untold bliss stubbornly refused to show its face. Maybe someone had seen her, she suddenly thought. Maybe she could place an ad in the newspaper and ask anyone who had to come forward and jog her memory with vivid descriptions. Or maybe they'd only had sex when they arrived back at her house. Perhaps Alex had seen or heard something. She'd ask her later. As she squeezed too much shower gel into her palms she offered up another prayer to God. Please, if I never ever imbibe vile alcohol again, will you let me remember The Bliss of last night? Just so I can rewind the memory and live it again in low, cat-feedingly lonely moments for the rest of my life.

As she was contemplating her future as a spinster with cats, not men, she heard some creaking and footsteps in the other room. He was getting up and grovelling about for his shoes, no doubt. Which he wouldn't put on until he was out the door in order not to be heard so he could make his getaway without being disturbed. She heard a low cough and a bit more creaking. In order to block out the scene she soaped her hair up into a foaming Mohican and began to whistle to herself. Soon he'd be gone and she could crawl around the cottage on her knees in misery, cursing her life and luck and parentage, which hadn't made her Amelia, and sobbing at the thought of what could have been. But right now she was focusing with all the intensity of a certified whacko on the tune to "Chitty Chitty Bang Bang."

"Liv, listen, I think I have to go, but I just wanted to say thanks so much. I had great fun and—"

"Arggghhh." Ben was standing in the doorway of the bathroom. Liv pulled the shower curtain round her. Futile, perhaps, after she'd bared her breasts to him last night, but she didn't really remember that and well . . . she was shy. "What do you want?"

"I'm sorry. Here, do you want this?" He passed her a towel, which she dived behind gratefully. "I just popped in to say thanks. I had fun and well—"

"Well, you're in love with your girlfriend. Of course you are. Why wouldn't you be? *I* practically fancy her and I'm totally off blondes at the moment." Ben looked at Liv as though she had shampoo for brains. "I'm off blondes because my ex was a blond. It's a reaction thing. Well, I'll be seeing you around then." Liv clambered from the shower still covered in soapsuds and a wilting Mohican.

"Bye then." Ben's shirt was still unbuttoned and he hadn't got around to putting on his socks yet. He had clearly not got his quick getaway down to a fine art.

"Yeah, bye," Liv said breezily.

But instead of turning on his heels and being grateful for being let off for his caddish laddish baddish behaviour, Ben was shifting his weight from foot to foot, smiling, and looking a bit awkwardly at Liv. "Bye," he said.

"See ya." Liv shrugged. Go on. Out, out, damned boy. And then he leaned in to kiss her. She shoved her cheeks at him in a dinner party greeting way. But he was going for her lips. Honestly, the things men feel compelled to do out of guilt, Liv thought. Then, when he put his hands around her waist and began to search out her tongue with his she thought that rather than guilt this was simply a case of blatant opportunism. Here she was looking for all her life like a packet of Just Add Water and Shag and he was a boy. What else had she thought might happen?

"God, you're even more lovely in the daylight." He moaned gently as he eased his shirt from his shoulders.

Beautiful in daylight was a barefaced lie. Well, at least she knew where she stood. Scarlet Other Woman that she was and since she'd missed out on last night's festivities and activities and she had already signed away her right to be treated well by having sex with him once, she might as well just tuck in now. He was never going to call again, so in for a penny, eh? "Hmmm, that's nice," she threw out as a sign of consent, and helped him with his belt buckle.

He dipped kisses over her neck and along her shoulder. This felt so good. She closed her eyes and felt his lips. She ran her hand down his back and traced lines on his smooth, firm buttocks. God, she felt as though she'd been Sleeping Beauty for the last five years and had just woken up to smell the coffee and taste the toast and honey, or something. This was what it was all about. This was the kind of lust that made grown women weep and men leave families and lives behind. Quite simply, it was the best.

"That was lovely, thanks," Liv said instead of letting him in on the secrets of her epiphany.

"Are you sure?" He brushed her hair back from his face and she could see tiny beads of sweat glistening on his top lip.

"Positive," she whispered as he carried on kissing her.

"Good." He began to push himself against her. All over again.

And an hour later, long after he was meant to have done the kerb kicking, Ben was sitting on the edge of her bed as he handed her a can of Tizer. She took a sip and, though she hated Tizer, it suddenly felt like the sexiest, most elixirish drink in the world.

"We could have lunch on Monday. Please. You can't turn me down again," Ben said.

"I'd love to. You have my number, right?" said Liv, abandoning all pretence of unavailability. Actually, she had a meeting with her suppliers in the garment district, but what the hell.

"Great," Ben said. "Now gorgeous as this is and much as I'd love to sit here all day and bask in the sun and have you by my side, I really have to go. But I'll call you. We'll go somewhere lovely. Maybe a picnic?"

"Sounds great. I know this place called Parsley Bay. We could swim and I'll make some Scotch eggs or something." She laughed.

"I'll bring jam tarts and squashed sandwiches and flat lemonade and we're away."

"I'll look forward to it," Liv said as she leaned over and kissed him good-bye one more time. "Oh, and I know this is not exactly a romantic thing to ask, but did we have safe sex last night? I mean I know you were careful just now, but we were pretty fucked up last night and I just wondered whether—"

"Last night?"

"Please say yes or I'll have to slap myself *so* hard on the wrists."

"We didn't have sex last night, Liv. Jeez, do you think I'd have taken advantage of you in that state? I mean I would have loved to, don't get me wrong, but call me old-fashioned—I just brought you home to bed."

"Oh," Liv said. "Okay, fine. Thanks. That was . . . sweet. See you tomorrow then."

Liv fell back to sleep again for another hour or so and woke up to Alex doing squat thrusts on her rug. She turned her head and groaned in pain. Clearly she'd still been pretty plastered when Ben was here. Now she was beginning to feel the ill effects of so much unprecedented immorality. "Well, now I know that It Girls are born and not made," Liv growled at Alex in her newfound sexy voice, which had just appeared from nowhere. Actually, her voice was the only good thing about her right now and she was tempted to leave messages on the machines of everybody she'd ever met just so they'd hear how gravelly and seductive she was. Because it wasn't going to last. The reason being that Liv wasn't going to last. Ugh, this was awful. She thought perhaps she had about six hours to live. Six hours' countdown before the knocking in her head exploded into an ugly mass of self-loathing. Lots of stuff would come out of her ears. Mostly brain but perhaps a few internal organs, too, as they did feel as though they were swimming part of a triathlon in her bloodstream.

"I've just had some homemade muesli and freshly squeezed orange juice. And the body-sculpt class is really making my arms firm. Squeeze," Alex taunted mercilessly as she sat on the end of Liv's bed and displayed a golden, toned arm. In just jeans and a T-shirt she'd come round to take Liv for lunch in Bondi.

"Too bloody perfect. Leave the room." Liv reached for a towel, which she wrapped around her face. "So you were out, right? You just got back?" Liv wondered if Alex had run into Ben, but no, she'd have said so. Liv saved it up to tell her later. Right now she didn't quite have the energy.

"You see, if you'd experimented with clubbing and dancing as a teenager like people are meant to, you wouldn't be in nearly so much pain. Your body's too old and broken down to deal with the onslaught," Alex said as she flipped through the Sunday newspapers.

"This is why people hate Cliff Richard. Being good is not attractive. Why don't you go and have lunch with another saint and leave me to explode in peace?" a muffled Liv said from beneath the towel.

"You're kidding. I've got a table booked at Ravesi's for twelve-thirty. Shrimp ravioli's just what the doctor ordered."

"Get out of my life. I just hope your day of decadence in

the Hunter Valley and subsequent evening in was worth me getting into this state. Because it is your fault. You should have been there to protect me," Liv whinged, fully expecting Alex to jump up and down on the bed and make her cry mercy, but she didn't. Liv lifted the towel to see if Alex was still there. She was, but she was looking very sheepish. If Liv had a brain she might have wondered why Alex was being so sympathetic instead of reminding Liv of the balance of pity that should be wasted on hungover Liv versus refugees in war-torn countries.

"Yeah, sorry, Livvy. Anyway, how about I run you a bath with some ginger and a pint of milk in it? It always works wonders with my hangovers. Also, you should stand on your head till it's done." And she vanished into the kitchen.

As Alex munched her way through the shrimp ravioli and ginger crème brûlée Liv realised that though it seemed to have been at least seven years since Alex had bounded into her room this morning she still hadn't managed to tell her that she'd had sex with Ben this morning. She thought maybe she'd wait until she'd had some coffee so that she could sustain a conversation that required more than three syllables. But Alex had clearly taken more vitamins than Liv that morning and was a little sharper.

"You are looking really well," Alex said as she scooped the froth off her cappuccino. "I mean apart from looking shit— well, you know what I mean—you're kind of shining in spite of yourself. Is there something I should know about?"

"Are you completely mad, Alex? The waiter keeps trying to clear me away with the dirty napkins. I look rubbish." Liv dribbled some more Tabasco into her drink and then choked to death loudly.

"No, you've got it together. Dishabillé. Natural, relaxed, beautiful. Sydney's agreeing with you. Or if Sydney isn't then something is," Alex said matter-of-factly.

"Have you got a guilty secret? Did you break my favourite bottle of perfume or something this morning and are working up to telling me?" Liv squinted.

"I was wondering the same about you," Alex said, peering at Liv over her spoon.

"I'm a grown-up now. I don't have guilty secrets," replied Liv, trying for the enigmatic response till she got her strength up.

"Last night?" grilled Alex.

"Last night was only a bit guilty and definitely not secret. I was just waiting for a caffeine hit before I told you." Liv wrote out a check for her three Bloody Marys and put it next to Alex's, or rather Charlie's, platinum Amex card.

"Tell me now." Alex grinned in anticipation.

"Okay." She took a deep breath. "I went to the party and Ben and Amelia were there and he followed me into the loo and—"

"Don't tell me you had sex in the loo. That's so rank." Alex screwed up her face.

"He took me outside. We hung around by this frangipani tree and I was too fucked up to know what I was doing, but anyway, when I was in the shower this morning he came in and I swear to god he is the best, most incredible lover in the whole world." Liv sank back into her chair and grinned goofily.

"Well, I'll take your word for that, but, Liv, that's so . . . that's fantastic. I told you, didn't I?" Alex said. "So what now?"

"Well, you know me—I need to be whacked over the head with a piece of wood before I really believe someone likes me—but I really think that this could be something. I mean at first I thought he was just making the most of having a naked girl in the bathroom before he'd had chance to get dressed properly, but well, I don't know. We had such a great time. You can't fake chemistry like that, can you?" Liv said with more emotion than was advisable given her current poor health. "We're having lunch tomorrow. I guess we'll talk about it all then." She sank back and smiled at the thought.

The future's so bright, I've got to wear shades, Liv decided with a smile as they emerged from the restaurant and out onto the Bondi beachfront.

"So now you have to tell me to get over it. He's a lying, cheating, scheming man just like all the others and I should steer well clear of him. And Dave's going to be furious with me because I gave away the goods. Especially as I thought I had but hadn't but then did anyway. But I think I was right to have some faith in him, don't you? I mean I've known him for years, really."

"Yeah, Liv, you're right to. There's something really romantic about you guys. Teenage sweethearts in a Provençal barn. I really think that this could work. I mean I've seen him with Amelia and I really don't think they're very well suited. She's so cool and he's so quiet and sweet."

"God, Al, is that you in there?" Liv tapped her friend playfully on the shoulder. "I thought you said he was a player and dangerous."

"I've watched him, and Rob really likes him, so I reckon he's probably all right."

"Can sunshine cause schizophrenia?"

"I've always been a romantic; it's just that I've never had much cause to believe before," Alex said, and smiled at the sky.

The girls walked along past the shopfronts and postcards and ordered large rock melon juices from a kiosk on the Parade. Alex thought for a moment before going on, "And I totally understand what you're saying. I know how sexy it feels—all that illicit stuff. The fantastic feeling of knowing that when you're in a crowded room nobody but you two know that you can still smell him on your skin and that you know what it feels like when you run your finger along his cheekbone and that later you'll be wound around one another in some dark room, any room you can find, to hell with whether it's a bathroom or a kitchen or a cloakroom." The girls had walked to the top of the cliffs, where they sat down on a bench and basked in the sun.

"Would you mind rewinding your conversation just a little bit there?" Liv turned abruptly to Alex.

"What do you mean?"

"The bit about crowded rooms and fingers on cheekbones and the smell on your skin and sneaking out to the kitchen. . . ." Liv paused and looked suspiciously at Alex. "Or how about we try the stables? And how about we make it the smell of saddle soap on his skin and hastily undoing the zip on his moleskins? Does he keep his riding boots on?" Liv's eyes were lit up now.

Blankness flashed across Alex's face for just one moment before she stood up and gathered her bag. "Better get back before we burn, hey?"

"How do you know what it feels like having an illicit affair, then?" Liv asked firmly.

"What do you mean? I imagine that's how you would feel . . . excited, charged, intoxicated. Isn't that right?" Alex said, not meeting Liv's eyes.

"Oh, come on, Alex, why don't you tell me what it's like?" Liv continued. "Because I have no idea if that's what you feel like when you sneak away to squeeze in a quickie with Rob." She waited for the denial.

"I think I'm having his baby," Alex said quietly, still not turning around.

Liv leapt up and promptly trod in some dog muck. "What?" she squealed, lifting her foot from the mush. "Whose baby?"

"Rob's." Alex turned around and instead of the pale face of a reluctantly pregnant woman who is haunted by visions of the workhouse and has fantasies about drinking too much gin and miscarrying, Alex wore a discreet smile. Her shoulders hunched slightly in a "I know; isn't it exciting?" kind of way that made Liv stare wide-eyed at her.

"How? What? I mean when?" Liv spluttered, wishing she'd had time to prepare questions earlier; it was the only way she'd be coherent.

"We've been having an affair since I arrived." She fiddled with the chain around her neck like a love-struck schoolgirl confiding details of her first fumble with the football captain in the year above.

"Why didn't you tell me?" asked Liv in horror.

"Because I wasn't sure. I mean I thought it was just a fling and I also know how bad you are at acting innocent because you feel guilty, and if Charlie had come round and you'd given the game away then neither you nor I would have had anywhere to live out here."

"You did it for me?"

"No, I'm sorry, sweetheart. I should have told you really, but . . . well, I'm telling you now."

"So how did it all happen?" Liv was too excited to know to care about Alex's secretive ways.

"I met him that first weekend. We were out at Charlie's place in the country at this barbecue and he opened his beer all over me. Completely ruined my pashmina." Alex was grinning from ear to ear now like a complete twit.

"You loved him for that?" Liv asked, thinking she'd have to make more of a point of borrowing Alex's pashminas if they were so dispensable.

"He took it to the kitchen sink and washed it for me. Said, 'Jeez, this must be worth a fortune, darlin',' and when I said it was he looked so concerned and dunked it in washing-up liquid and scrubbed away." Alex was raking her hand through her hair in the way Liv had only ever seen girls who were positively deranged with love do.

"Christ, didn't he ruin it?" Liv winced.

"Completely. But the point is that he didn't just say, 'Oh, I'll buy you another one when we get back to Sydney,' or, 'My cleaning lady will sort that out.' He cared about it, Livvy."

Liv kept her thoughts in and thought that maybe he'd rushed to the sink because he couldn't bloody well afford to buy her another one.

"I think there are quite a few men in the world who'd be interested in just how easy it is to make you fall in love with them. I mean if they knew they'd be queuing up." Liv smiled, still not taking in the pregnancy factor. She really did need secretarial minutes for this meeting.

"We want a boy. Don't you think it'll be gorgeous? Black hair and funny little black eyebrows and he'll definitely be tall but maybe not very academic, but we won't mind 'cause he'll be really good at sport. We'll teach him to ride on a teeny Shetland pony called Morty." She stopped for a minute and looked concerned. "But we don't mind if it's a girl of course. I mean we'll still be thrilled and everything and she'd be really cute and have roly-poly little baby legs. God, I can't wait," Alex said as the sun shone on her profile and picked out her pretty freckles.

"Does Rob know about this?" One horror was overtaking another in Liv's mind. It was a domino effect—what about Charlie? How did Alex know it was Rob's baby? Where were they going to live? What were they going to live on, because while it was all very nice dating men and getting Hermes leather goods in return, Alex wouldn't exactly be able to go back to work after the baby like mothers with office jobs or nice interior design careers could. What would she do? Ask for a Mothercare account card for her birthday or a year's supply of Pampers if she went with some banker for a week in Saint Bart's? Unless she knew some very kinky men who happened to have a thing for stretch marks and precarious pelvic flooring. But then what would Rob think?

"In fact, can we start again please? I got lost somewhere around the moment you fell in love with a penniless man who ruined your favourite item of clothing with fairy liquid."

When they finally arrived back at the cottage the crowds on the beach were packing up their ice boxes and rolling wet, sandy swimwear up in towels and heading home. On the kitchen table was a huge bunch of flowers, sunflowers, pink flowers, lilies, completely unarranged but big and so cheering.

"Charlie's going to be gutted, isn't he?" Liv said as she emptied the sand out of her shoes and onto the floor.

"I shouldn't think so. Half the time he can't remember my name!" Alex called back from the kitchen, where she was tracking down a packet of jammy dodgers.

"But he still sends you huge bunches of flowers." Liv leaned over and sniffed one of the lilies, managing to smear her nose with orange pollen, which would take a week to scrub off.

"What on earth are you talking about? Charlie wouldn't pick his nose for me . . . let alone flowers. Those are from Rob." Alex came back into the room proudly wielding the biscuits.

"Penniless Rob?" Liv wondered.

Alex shrugged. "It's love, I suppose."

Alex and Liv spent the rest of the evening watching bits of *Fawlty Towers* and dreaming up business schemes. Occasionally they'd have these nights, not quite of homesickness but more of homage to home. They'd put on Turnbull and Asser pyjamas (Alex's, not Liv's, as hers were wincyette and tended to melt and stick to her skin in the heat). Liv would wear a particularly floral shower cap from Portobello Market and they'd eat marmite sandwiches and watch English movies. Alex would read the *Spectator* and Liv would flick through the Style section of the *Sunday Times,* which was invariably two weeks old and cost seven dollars, but it was worth it just to be glad that they didn't have to buy floor-length coats in whatever colour the new black was and could strip off and run approximately six feet onto the nearest beach instead. *HomeSmug* was probably the word. Though it did give Liv pangs for the times she'd read Shelley Von Strunkel's horoscopes out loud to Tim at breakfast. But he'd always be just a bit too engrossed in the sports pages to care, so sometimes she'd read out Johnny Depp's horoscope instead and wonder what this week would have in store if she and Johnny were breakfasting together. It was usually the same: travel, love, adventure, for which Liv read Viper Room, Cannes, unresolved feelings for Kate Moss, et cetera. Life with Johnny was not simple.

"So Dave needs our cheques for the final instalment for Greta's Grundies by Thursday. He's decided that he's going to buy this record company or something and needs the cash!" Liv yelled as she went through into the kitchen.

"Okay, I'll talk to my accountant tomorrow," Alex said casually, "though I'm going to *have* to make this Greta's Grundies business work now. No crawling to Charlie or any man with my dry-cleaning bills in the future."

"Christ, you're really giving it up? Can't you just keep seeing Rob slyly?" Liv asked.

"Oh yeah, and whoops, Charlie, here's a baby I had earlier with your mate."

"Well, I don't know, but you have to get by." Liv was concerned. "What about Luke's university fees?"

"I've got enough in stocks to pay for him for the next couple of years; then he'll start work. So where's the point anymore?" Alex said as she wrote a list of people as long as her legs.

"What's all that for?" Liv asked as she made herself a glass of Ribena, another constant craving that could only be indulged on homage nights.

"Our launch," Alex said. "What's Laura's girlfriend called again?"

"Jo-Jo," replied Liv. "Did you say launch?"

"I thought at the end of the month. If we're going to be Judith Krantz heroines with shoulder pads and our own empire we have to live like that and have a launch. You know, flamingos in fountains of champagne, cakes cut in the shape of G-strings, beluga caviar eaten out of diamond-encrusted Jimmy Choo shoes. That kind of thing," Alex said as she handed the list over to Liv for approval.

"You're kidding?" said Liv.

"No. I think we should definitely change our names to flowers. Liv and Alex are so pedestrian. I think I should be Amaryllis and you should be Primrose. And it's good that you're brunette and I'm a blonde; otherwise one of us would have to dye her hair. Shame that you're not secretly royal, though; that would be good for business. Princess Primrose. No chance your mum had a quickie with Prince Charles in 1971? He wasn't bad-looking then," Alex spurted on as Liv lamented her mother's lack of sex with Prince Charles. Life as the love child of a royal must be great. Discreet holidays with Dad in heathery Balmoral and a storecard at Fortnum and Mason. Still the horses. She couldn't stand horses and their evil, knowing eyes. "Didn't you ever read *Princess Daisy* or *Scents* or any of those fabulous dynastic epics with strong yet frail, poor yet beautiful heroines?" she asked.

"Sure. But only the dirty bits," Liv admitted as she remembered sitting around behind the gym at school as the owner of the book read aloud and ten girls gasped at the notion of golden showers and the word *cock* in print. Perhaps that had been the start of all Liv's problems. Those women were forever having their g-spots teased or sex in Jacuzzis.

The only thing Liv had ever got in a Jacuzzi was a mouthful of water with a toenail in it.

"I thought we'd invite your old boss, Fay. And Luke really wants to come over; he's got this girlfriend in Adelaide," Alex said.

"Aren't you getting a bit carried away? I mean this is Greta's Grundies, not the launch of the new Elizabeth Taylor fragrance in Harrods."

"God, and what better press could there be? 'Former market stall owners Alex Burton and Liv Elliot took off their money belts and gave their voices a rest from caterwauling today at the international launch of their exclusive range of designer lingerie.' " Alex laughed, "Today Paddo Market, tomorrow Saks Fifth Avenue. Good, eh? And I've always fancied being a dot com millionaire, too." The fact that Alex had never once arrived at the market stall before lunchtime on a Saturday and would rather wear a noose around her neck than put on a money belt caused Liv to want to put up her hand and object.

"I'm an accountant, Alex. It doesn't work like that," Liv said as she scanned the list and noted with relief that her own parents hadn't been added yet. Her mother would die of pride and have to be resuscitated and Lenny would inform the assembled partygoers about the Marxian oligarchy that made all such ventures inherently flawed. Though of course he'd mean well.

"Rubbish. You've got to think big. Trust me. Now first of all we have to get the invitations done. I'll take care of that tomorrow. You just get the stock in order and make sure we have enough samples to send out to, let's think . . . about five hundred journalists and stylists and personalities. That should cover it."

"Samples of what?" Liv asked. She'd had her daydreams about Greta's Grundies being worn by movie stars, but she'd never really believed it. Which seemed, she realised, to be the story of her life. Oh well, if Alex could help her make one of her fantasies see the light of day then she'd be thrilled.

"I think a G-string each would be really nice. Just that sheer but not obscene fabric. Leopard print. Slutty but a little more Fifth Avenue than Frederick's of Hollywood." Alex drew a sketch of the G-string she had in mind.

"Fine," Liv said, biting back her financial reservations. "I'll do a costing and we'll find a way of buying the fabric."

"Good." Alex clapped her hands together and lay back on the sofa. "Now what are we going to wear?"

"Well, you'll probably have to make do with a tent," Liv said, and gave Alex a big hug. "So I think I'll wear your favourite little red Prada suit, if that's okay?"

Chapter Fifteen

The Nature of the Beast

As Liv lay in bed that night she tried to fathom out how she ever got to be so hopeless. That her best friend could be conducting an illicit affair under her nose with Rob of the Eyebrows and actually be heavy with child (well, not quite heavy—Liv hadn't even noticed an early-morning dash to the bathroom to throw up or a sudden interest in stories about curious places for your water to break yet) had left her speechless. As she looked through the window at the moon high above the city, the Southern Cross just discernible behind the drifting clouds, Liv had to fight with her new, liberated, experimental side not to wish she were lying here now with Ben. And maybe even a little Ben between them. How amazing to have such a dazzling man for a husband and father. Other women would fall in love with him, he'd flirt outrageously as he played doubles tennis with friends' wives, but he'd always be hers.

Then as the clouds blacked out the moon and darkness covered the sea, Liv remembered that this was Amelia's story. And yet didn't she feel sorry for Amelia, being humiliated while Ben flirted and slept his way into Liv's affections?

Didn't she remember what Alex had told her so often, what she had told so many of her friends over the years from the vantage point of Going Out with Mr. Perfect? That if you acquired a man via his being unfaithful to somebody else there were no guarantees? In fact, the only guarantee was that he'd be very capable of doing the same to you? In an ideal Spice World of tough talking and girl power Liv would just have the sex and shoot through. Still, Ben was different. There really was some connection there, Liv told herself. It was just in the eyes, the way they looked at each other.

"Oh, Liv, you're home. I've been waiting for you." Laura emerged from her studio with a remarkably realistic blood colour smeared across her face.

Liv was still stumbling around in her nightie and a bit taken aback. "Laura. Listen, I just want a quick pee and then I'll come and have a cup of tea with you," Liv croaked, and walked into the frame of the bathroom door. Ugh, the last thing she wanted right now was a philosophical chat about filling up your love tanks with vitamin S (for Self) and learning to accept miracles in your life. She'd had all the miracles she wanted on Saturday night and was very much looking forward to another this afternoon. Now, had she said she'd call Ben or was he going to call her? she wondered as she walked back out into the kitchen. All she wanted now was to know where their blissful lunch was going to be.

"So what did you get up to this weekend?" Laura twiddled her thumbs nervously at the breakfast table.

"Oh god, I had the most fantastic weekend. I think I'm totally in love."

"Wow. Erm, anyone I know?" Laura swiped another bloody streak across her temple.

"His name's Ben. The guy I was telling you about," Liv said. She knew that this was probably going to be a touchy subject, given the Amelia debacle that Laura had endured, but she had to broach it sometime. In fact, it could actually be good for her. Maybe it would give her closure or something Californian like that.

"Liv. There's something I have to tell you. You'll think it's awful that I've waited so long, but shit, I don't know how to say this." Laura took a chunk out of what was once her thumbnail but now looked like a prop in a horror movie.

"Oh, Laura, if it's about you and Amelia, then don't worry. I know. I don't know what she did to you, but I think you're probably well rid of her and Jo-Jo's gorgeous and I only wish you'd told me sooner, because the thing is . . . ," Liv puttered on until she looked up and saw Laura, who was now fiddling with a paintbrush that had been lying on the table, and her hand was trembling as though she's been on a pub crawl through every licensed establishment and a few illegal watering holes in the eastern suburbs last night.

"You can tell me all about it if you like," Liv ventured bravely. She feared it was going to be a long haul.

"It's Ben Parker, isn't it? The guy you're in love with?" Laura asked, her pretty eyes burning crossly from beneath the streaks of paint on her face. She rubbed her hand down her dungarees and took a deep breath. "Livvy, I'm sorry you had to find out like this, but we had an affair. Six months ago."

"You and Amelia, right?" Liv said, but she was no longer certain that Laura was talking about Amelia.

"The moment I met him I fell in love with him." Laura's voice was bitter yet calm. Liv imagined that she'd had this conversation in her head, doing role-play with her shrink, before the mirror, lying alone in bed, many, many times.

• "But you don't go out with men." Liv giggled nervously, trying pathetically to delay the moment of truth.

"Which is what made me so attractive. Ben clearly thinks that a lesbian is like a spare room—something you convert. He couldn't have me. So he went to town on me—phone calls where he'd just hang up, staring at me across bars, promises. And eventually I couldn't resist any longer. I really believed that he loved me. I was going out with this great girl called Estelle and eventually we broke up. . . ." Laura flashed a very fleeting look at Liv and it wasn't lost on her. She felt embarrassed that she'd ever said anything foolish about Ben being in love with her to Laura now. And even more insane for believing it. ". . . but the minute we got together, the moment we had sex, he didn't want to know me. He just pulled on his boxer shorts and fucked off." Laura was certainly firing on all cylinders, but she also looked damned cool. The trembling had subsided and she was pink with rage, with her red hair spilling out of her ponytail like lava from a volcano.

"I had no idea." Liv could no longer stomach a single mouthful of cereal. She felt sick to her stomach.

"I should have told you before. I've been trying to protect you by deleting his phone messages," Laura said.

"Okay. I think I need to go to my room and be by myself a bit. Thanks for telling me, Laura, I know it can't have been easy." And Liv stood up and went to her room, though her legs felt for all the world like they might just buckle at any second.

"Oh, and, Liv, don't say anything about this to Jo-Jo, will you? I think it might upset her a bit."

Liv couldn't imagine why this would upset Jo-Jo, but neither did she particularly care right now. She just needed to lie down.

After an hour of lying on her bed with every thought and feeling swirling in mind and still no phone call from Ben, Liv began to clean her room in a frenzy of activity—she couldn't take the cacophony of shock and confusion a moment longer.

"Displacement activities." Laura stood in the doorway and watched Liv as she tipped up three carrier bags of makeup and began to dust her lipsticks.

"Of course displacement activities."

"It may be different this time, Liv. He could have changed."

"Yeah, right. You've spent hundreds of dollars on therapy and you believe that's possible," Liv said sarcastically but not unkindly. After all, this wasn't Laura's fault and Liv was loathe to turn into the sort of woman who blamed the messenger and not the maggot who had perpetrated the crimes in the first place.

"Not really. But you're special. He really might be in love with you."

"Thanks for being sweet, Laura. I guess that's because women are from Venus, hey?" Liv said in a bid to appease her and make her leave.

"You're so right. Now, I know you've been damaged by this. You may not think so yet, but the thing is—" Laura had mysteriously edged her way into Liv's room and was now ensconced on the edge of the bed. In fact, she couldn't have been more ensconced if she'd brought her duvet, paintbrush, and a change of clothes with her.

Liv dredged episodes of *Frasier* for the right phrase; she played back *Oprah,* struggled for the psychobabble. "Actually, Laura, what I'd really like right now is some alone time." She was impressed with herself when it came out so well. So resounding. Such conviction. Psychobabble was great. It was like a microwavable meal. Just right with little thought or inspiration. Perhaps life would be easier if you saw the Shrink worldview. Men *would* be from Mars—you'd never trust them and be permanently suspicious. Women *would* be from Venus and be as deliciously ripe and tender as week-old peaches and be allowed to cry and rant. You could feel the fear and do it anyway and never ever, this was the best bit, have to have a single thought of your own. Anyway, it did the trick with Laura. She was gone in a heartbeat, leaving Liv with nothing more than an understanding pat on the shoulder.

Liv sank her head into the bed and contemplated tears. Laughter. Pillow rage. Still, it was only ten o'clock in the morning and maybe Laura was right. Maybe he did really like her and want more than sex and the conquest. Just because he hadn't called to confirm the details of lunch didn't mean that he was another sad example of a dog run amok.

"Dave, please, please, I'm sorry I poured scorn on your theories and I'm sorry I was the worst pupil never to graduate from dog-handling school, but I will try harder next time if you promise to meet me for a coffee in Sloane's. I'm a broken girl!" Liv wailed down Dave's phone. It was two-thirty and not lunchtime any longer and the phone had not rung.

"I have a job to do, honey. How bad is it?"

"I had sex with him and he hasn't called and oh, he has a history of this kind of thing. He did it to Laura."

"And why is this news to you, Liv?" Dave sounded almost bored. "It's the nature of the beast. But if you refuse to house-train him, then of course he's going to shit on your carpet. This was lesson one."

"Then I didn't revise hard enough for the exam. Can I do a re-sit?" Liv pleaded.

"Sloane's in half an hour. But this may well lose the company sixty-seven million dollars, you know that, don't you, you hopeless minx?"

"Sorry."

Sloane's cafe was heaving with teenagers who'd just spent the last dollars from their paper rounds and waitressing jobs. They were making their smoothies last as they pulled bottle after bottle of bath oil and nail polish and cucumber cleansing creams from brown paper bags, sniffing each one and passing it around. The waiter weaved in and out of tightly packed tables in his denim shorts and purple T-shirt and pointed Liv to the table where Dave was sitting sweating in his suit.

"Sorry sorry sorry." Liv sat down.

"My only consolation is that you look wretched," Dave informed her.

"You were great at Mardi Gras, by the way. I took about three rolls of film before . . ." Liv looked sheepish. "Actually, I think it's all your fault for letting me party alone. If you don't help me I'll just shop you to the police."

"Don't push your luck." Dave drained his smoothie and lit a cigarette. "So you fucked up big-time then?"

"Yes. But why do I want to say it was almost worth it?"

"I have a theory on that, too." Dave sat back and inhaled deeply. "Love causes the female body to produce the same hormones as childbirth, because though you were kicked to the kerb by Tim and then Will you seem to have forgotten how incredibly painful it all was. You've totally blocked out the agonising screams and the cries of, 'I'll never do this again; it wasn't worth it,' and instead, at the merest hint of an invitation to repeat the misery, you go all watery-eyed and say, 'Ooohhh, yes, please!' It's a huge design flaw that women have."

"I want to teach him a lesson," Liv said firmly.

"Because you still fancy him like mad and hope he'll love you?"

"Don't be ridiculous. I hate him and his kind."

"Then ignore him. Treat him with the contempt he deserves and never speak to him again," Dave suggested disingenuously.

"No, I mean of course I bloody well fancy him like mad, but I'm not a masochist. I think that he needs to be taught a lesson and the mean, bitter, resentful part of me that self-help books will never reach is just mad for revenge. And I need to know that I can have him before I dump him or my ego will resemble take-away food the morning after with a cigarette butt squashed on top. Is it too late?" Liv asked.

"I think we can salvage something from the wreckage. But you're going to have to be tough and stop being such a girl. Think Barbara Woodhouse, not Barbara Cartland. Okay?"

Chapter Sixteen

Barbara Woodhouse Lives On

W ill? Is that you?" Despite the fact that it was only six-thirty in the morning, Liv flashed her perfect newly minted smile and shook her pristine ponytail in an energetic manner.

"Liz?" Will the Weasel reared his sweaty head from beneath a punch bag and blinked at the vision of loveliness before him.

"I had no idea you were into boxing. Imagine." Liv watched him scramble to his feet for a few seconds and then spun on the heel of her new trainers (the sporty equivalent of Manolos in the way they flatter the feet and ankle, Alex had assured her) and made for the dumbells without so much as a backward glance.

"Got to catch them off guard," Dave had told her. "When they're peeing or bounding around in the park. Or sniffing another dog's bum. Then you show them the ball and walk away. It's the only way you're ever going to get that leash back around their neck." In light of which advice Liv and Alex had spent all week planning this predawn assault on

Will. Liv wished it weren't quite so early, because, well, if the truth be told, Will hadn't been much of an oil painting *after* his shower and morning ablutions, but his grey vest and his sausagey little legs exposed in shorts really created a very bad look. Liv couldn't believe she'd actually allowed him near her with a ten-foot pole. But there was the remarkable power of hormones for you yet again. When a girl needs to get laid a girl needs to get laid. And he was as diametrically opposed to Tim as day was to night. Which had helped at the time. Anyway, as Charlie was still Alex's boyfriend to all intents and purposes and he was also Will's boss at the news network, the girls had been able to wheedle enough information out of him to catch Will off guard at his gym at 6:00 A.M.

"Liz. God, how are you? It's been a while." Will arrived panting at Liv's side as she picked up the dumbells and swung them about in as Jane Fonda a way as possible.

"Yes, it has." She didn't smile, just watched her biceps intently in the mirror and shuddered at the thought of having to kiss Will again. Which wasn't even slightly part of the plan, but if she was going to have to have a date with him, as *was* the plan, then he might come over all presumptuous and lunge at her.

"You're looking great." He was just standing there with his tongue practically hanging out and his hair all plastered to his head after his fifty push-ups.

"You're a bit out of breath." Liv smiled patronisingly at him and then had to raise her fragrant, newly laundered, intensely feminine lilac towel to her face to hide her sniggers. This was so disgracefully easy that she wondered why she even had to bother to use Will for Ben Bait. Couldn't she just turn up on one of Ben's archaeological digs somewhere wearing a push-up bra and cycling shorts and skip this Will part of Dave's plan?

"Yeah, well, I, erm, actually, I was going to call you. Yeah, I mean I was going to ask Charlie for your number and then

I was going to call you because, well, you're looking really well and I wondered if perhaps . . ." Liv turned to him and raised an eyebrow that said go-ahead-you-worm-I-dare-you-after-all-these-weeks.

". . . we could have dinner."

"Like last time when you fucked me and then never called me?" Liv got down on all fours and did a few stretches that served no other purpose than to expose huge, gaping amounts of cleavage.

"Oh, Liz, I can explain. Actually, I'd just got back from Bosnia, as you know, and I think I was suffering a bit from post-traumatic stress disorder. You know it's really terrible." He did a hangdog big-eyed thing and Liv nearly vomited.

"Yeah, actually, I had it myself after I'd slept with you." She pretended it was a joke and smiled as she said it just so he didn't get too offended and bash her over the head with a boxing glove.

"Ha ha . . . that's, erm, really a great one. Not just a pretty face, eh, Liz? I love a woman with a sense of humour."

"You'd have to." Liv climbed to her feet and pulled herself up tall just so she was looking down on him by about an inch. "Oh, and by the way, Will, it's Liv."

When Liv arrived back from her surfing lesson she picked up the post from her box. Mostly junk asking her to eat more pizza at lower prices and a couple of bills for Laura. There was also a letter for Liv Elliot, Managing Director of Greta's Grundies. Liv sniggered and tossed the bunch of mail into her basket. Alex was getting too big for the boardroom again. Considering they didn't have one. Liv flicked on her answerphone. You never knew.

"You have zero messages."

Yes, of course you know. You always bloody well know. She made a contemptuous growling noise and went for her shower. At least her surfing had been good this morning. She was definitely improving. Certainly Justin seemed to think so. He'd led her out to the Bronte Express and let her surf in on her own. No matter that the waves were flatter than pancakes and that she spent more time under her surfboard than on top of it, she was getting better. And as she ran up the beach *Baywatch* style with her boogie board under her arm, her legs no longer wobbled in such an environmentally unfriendly way as they had a few weeks ago. Always a bonus.

Liv had her Just Right out on the deck. She also covered her shoulders and put on a sun hat so she didn't end up like Brigitte Bardot. Then she opened the letter from Alex. Except it wasn't from Alex; it was from Amelia. On perfect silver-embossed letterhead at the top of the hand-rolled rose petal–encrusted notepaper.

> *Dearest Liv,*
>   *I just wanted you to know that after chatting to Alex at some length about your business plans I'd be delighted to accept the role of the face and body of Greta's Grundies. I love your product and am very much looking forward to the launch. Can't wait.*
>
> > *With warmest wishes,*
> > *Amelia Fraser*

Liv read the note several times before she fully understood what it said. She also had to check it against some of Alex's writing to make sure it wasn't a hoax. No wonder she'd been so shifty at the weekend, Liv thought. Feeling guilty and running me baths and making me stand on my head and telling me I looked dishabillé. She'd invited Amelia into their business and not said a word to Liv.

"I don't want her onboard. The last thing in the world that I need right now is to spend my working day in the company of Perfect Amelia!" Liv yelled into Alex's mobile. "We don't need her."

"I have not invited Amelia Fraser to join our company, okay? Whatever she's said is her own idea. I promise, sweetheart. But having her as our spokesmodel isn't such a bad idea. Think about it. In fact, it could be the difference between a small-time company and an international player. Remember, Sophia Loren is her godmother."

Liv put the phone down and felt all meagre again. Why did she only have snotty nouveau riche godmothers who weren't icons of the twentieth century? Anyway, Alex was probably taking the whole thing too seriously. International player. The face of Greta's Grundies. Spokesmodel. For heaven's sake it wasn't as though it were the house of bloody Lancôme or Christian Dior, was it? But Alex was probably right. Amelia could secure them more column inches than Hugh Grant's blow job. If only it wasn't Amelia, Liv thought as she crossed off a few people from the party guest list. She didn't want her work and her revenge life to be all mixed up like this. Still there was the party. Liv consoled herself by drawing up a list that didn't include anyone who wore hipsters and was just beginning to draw up a for and against list for inviting her parents when the phone rang.

"Hello."

"Liv?" asked the voice. Not Ben, surely.

"Yes?" Liv sucked her pen hard and got a mouthful of Biro sludge.

"It's Tim."

"Tim who?" she asked absentmindedly, and then nearly swallowed the Biro whole.

"Erm, Tim Evans." Holy-stuff-and-ohmygod-and-how-hysterical-because-she-never-but-never-thought-that-the-day-would-come-when-she-not-only-wouldn't-fall-off-her-chair-if-Tim-called-but-not-to-even-recognise-his-voice-and-well-ohmygod.

"Tim. I'm sorry. Of course. Hi," Liv said without the use

of her tongue, which she was busy dabbing with a tissue to remove the Biro ink.

"So how are you?" Tim attempted valiantly even though it was clear that she was doing very nicely without him, thanks, despite her present navy-blue-ink plight.

"Yeah, fine, thanks."

It was weird hearing his voice after all this time. And it had been ages. No phone calls, no letters, no anything except the communiqué via Alex's old hairdresser about the girl he'd been spotted with in Sainsbury's. And he sounded odd. Slightly nasally and his voice in no way sounded sexy or heart-stopping or made her knickers melt. And he didn't sound anywhere near as drippingly wonderful as Ben did. If she was allowed to think that and still keep up her vendetta against Ben. "And are you well, too?"

"Yeah. I'm great. Thanks." Scintillating. Why ever hadn't they got married?

"So?"

"The thing is that, well, I've been wondering what to do with my airline tickets from the, erm . . . honeymoon for a while and I thought that I needed a break and the only place that's really sunny this time of year is Australia, so I'm coming out there for a couple of weeks and wondered if maybe we shouldn't get together. Have a beer or something. What do you think?"

"Sorry?" Liv had been cutting split ends off her hair with a potato peeler.

"We could catch up maybe. Now that we're on the other side, as it were. Now that we've moved on."

"Sure. Call me when you arrive. That'd be nice."

"Okay then, well, erm . . . see you in a couple of weeks then. Bye."

Did time really heal all wounds? Or had she just become a weird emotionless freak?

★ ★ ★

"I'm telling you I'm sure she'd didn't suspect that you had sex with Ben." Alex was actually on her hands and knees for a very different professional reason than the usual one. She was folding 500 G-strings and stuffing them into leopard-print envelopes that no fashion editor or department store buyer could fail to miss when they landed on her desk.

"But what if we're working together and somehow she finds out? I mean she must have noticed that both Ben and I were missing from the party at Mardi Gras. And why the sudden interest in my business if not to spy on me?"

"You're just being paranoid. Anyway, so what if she does know? It's over between you and Ben, isn't it?"

"Yeah, it's well and truly done. I just think that we should be prepared. I get the feeling I shouldn't mess with Amelia. Especially not as the future of our business and our ability to put our children through private schools depend solely on her support." Liv lifted her leg in the air and inspected her toenails.

"Well, I'm telling you she doesn't know or she'd have taken action. She's not a slouch. Which is how she's managed to score this *Vogue* photographer to do our catalogue next week. So just give up the ghost. Has Will the Weasel called yet?"

"Last night. He wanted to take me to dinner, but I told him he had to come to the pub tomorrow night instead. Are you quite sure all the guys will be there?"

"Positive. I asked Rob and he said there's some huge rugby game on."

"I hope Will doesn't manhandle me. He has cellulite on his elbows, you know." Liv closed her eyes in fear. But in the name of redressing the injustices done to women every-where, well, herself and Laura Train Wreck anyway, Liv knew that it was her duty to well and truly shaft Ben Parker. And if Will got squashed underfoot on the way then that was something he should have thought about earlier, too. Was there a Nobel Prize for Justice Meted Out? she wondered.

The photographer Amelia had persuaded to snap her for the Greta's Grundies catalogue generally liked to mutilate his models in the name of starting new trends—shave off their eyebrows, dye their hair red, and paint them green, the usual stuff—but naturally he loved Amelia just as she was.

"You're such a beautiful woman without makeup that you're practically a freak anyway," he told her. Or so she'd related casually to Alex and Liv in this morning's board meeting. *Bored meeting* more like, as all it seemed to consist of were how-much-my-hairdresser-loves-running-his-fingers-through-my-silky-tresses anecdotes and how many times she and Ben had had sex last night and how she was going to have to have the dining table French-polished again after a particularly ecstatic moment involving a jar of raspberry jam. Like I want to know, thanks. Liv tapped her pen loudly on the table and thought of England.

Not that either of the girls had much time to do any thinking at all recently. Whole days seemed to be eaten up with the organisation for the launch party and the need to get Greta's Grundies up and running in time. Not only was Liv constantly deluged with calls from fashion editors asking if they could bring a friend and had she any more samples she could send them, but Liv also had to organise the whole Amelia shoot. Which, unfortunately, meant she had to spend more time than was desirable (i.e., a minute) with Amelia. And the more time Liv spent with her the more appalling she became and Liv really did begin to feel a bit sorry for Ben, given that he had elected to spend the rest of his life with this monster.

"The photographer's coming round at seven tomorrow morning, so if you could come and just kind of make tea for the crew and sort out invoices and stuff that'd be really helpful," Amelia had said on Liv's answerphone. Liv had stomped her feet a bit, then stopped because Alex was starting to look a bit hassled and Liv didn't want to add to her burden and the whole "whoops, I'm having another man's baby" dilemma she was facing.

"What on earth am I going to say to Charlie?" asked Alex. It was the day of the shoot and she and Liv were standing behind the glare of tungsten lighting holding up reflective trampoline things to give Amelia even more luminosity and cheekbone than nature had blessed her with.

"You're sure that you're going to stay with Rob? I mean it's all going to work out?" Liv asked, not wanting Alex to end up homeless and Prada-less if Rob was just going to tell her to bugger off the minute it looked like it might be getting serious. And it was Liv's home at stake, too. Where on earth would they live if Charlie chucked Alex out on her ear?

"Rob and I are in this together. It's fantastic. And you know I can always move in with Rob and I know Charlie likes you and wouldn't mind letting you stay at the beach house. I mean he lets Laura stay. It's no skin off his nose." Alex tried to reassure Liv, "I mean it's not like I'm going to be able to hide it for much longer, is it?"

"True. Why not tell him tonight then?" Liv's arm was beginning to ache; she waved it around a bit to whip up her circulation.

"Oy, hold still. She'll end up with dark lines and a moustache!" the photographer yelled.

Liv was tempted to waft her arms around like Don Quixote but didn't like the look of the photographer's winkle pickers. Besides, she kept having to remind herself, this was not Amelia, Inc., that she was doing it for. It was Alex and Liv Get Rich. If the pictures were fantastic, then it was definitely better for business. If not for Liv's ego.

★   ★   ★

"Okay, now that the Polaroid's done. Take off your top, Milly, and we'll get Stella to dust a bit of blusher between your boobs. Gorgeous." Everyone on the set turned and admired Amelia's embonpoint chest. Liv put the kettle on.

"Now for the real thing." The photographer called everyone back to position and turned up the radio. So not only did Liv have nothing better to do than watch Amelia be desirable and desired, but she couldn't even bitch about it because the radio was so loud that Alex couldn't hear her.

"It's not much fun, you know, doing little comparisons in my head. Her tits. My tits. Her flat stomach. Mine. Not," Liv said later as she and Alex picked up all the empty canisters of film from the floor of Amelia's apartment. "Poor Ben, no wonder he never called me again, given what he was used to."

"Ssshhhh, she's here," Alex hissed, and plastered a grin to her face. "Hi, Millie."

"Don't I look fuckable in that one?" Amelia handed over a picture of herself to Liv. "Now, I wanted to talk to you about the party next week. Do you and Alex have a budget in mind for the dress you want me to wear? Only I've seen this Dolce dress . . . it'll be worth every penny." So bang went Liv's hopes of fiddling the books just enough to buy herself a dress from the market for the party, and bang went her hopes of outshining Amelia on the one night that really mattered to her. The night she intended to reduce Ben to rubble as the champagne flowed and the freshly picked magnolia blossoms scented the night air and the fairy lights sparkled from jacaranda trees.

"And, you know, I can show you how to stop your hair frizzing up like that. I know you're going to want to look your best for the party," Amelia gushed before opening a bottle of beer with her back teeth and offering Liv a swig.

* * *

When Amelia had been firmly deposited back in front of the camera the girls continued to get to grips with the nittier-grittier business of party planning.

"Now how many waitresses do you think we need to cover the party? Fifteen enough?" Alex asked.

The accountant in Liv's soul leapt up in horror. "Fifteen. Don't be ridiculous; that'd cost us half our yearly takings. You and I can take round a tray of canapés each. If Tim's coming, then he can make himself useful, and I'm sure a few of the fashion editors won't mind pouring out the odd glass of champagne for themselves. I can borrow the table Laura uses for wallpapering and set it up as a buffet," Liv improvised hastily, seeing no reason why they should bankrupt themselves before they'd sold their first bra.

"Style, Liv. Style. We can't be serving up Scotch eggs and jam tarts. It's not a picnic in Bournemouth; it's the launch of one of the world's most exclusive and desirable ranges of lingerie. That lot wouldn't pour their own champagne if you threatened to strip them of their Prada discount cards. And anyway, I'm not carrying bloody canapés and risking my unborn child's health. Do you think I'm some kind of barbarian?" Alex asked as she stole a drag of the photo assistant's cigarette and then spent five minutes patting her stomach guiltily.

"You're preggars, are you?" a voice squealed behind them. "Bloody oath! Well done, darling." Amelia leapt forward and hugged Alex in an unborn-baby-squashing way. "You've snagged one helluva bachelor there. Christ, you'll be the envy of Sydney. Of course we've all been in love with him since we were fifteen, but to father your child . . . good going, Alex," Amelia gushed forth with utter sincerity. Liv couldn't say that she'd noticed Charlie being the object of desire of every woman in the Southern Hemisphere before now, but maybe he looked gorgeous in the rugby scrum or when he was muddy from polo or something.

"Thanks, Amelia. Only you know I haven't told him yet. You know, waiting till the moment's right and all that. It's a bit delicate." Alex was obviously going to take the hush-hush approach to the whole thing and let them think that it was Charlie's baby. Just sit on the time bomb until it blows up under your bum.

"Of course I won't breathe a word. Trust me." Amelia put her finger to her lips and darted off to hear the photographer tell her one more time how photogenic she was.

"Well, I guess I'll just have to trust her, won't I?" Alex said philosophically. "Must say, though, I never realised Charlie was considered such a sexpot. I mean he's all right, but . . ."

"Would it have made any difference?" Liv asked, thinking maybe it wasn't too late for Alex to face practicalities and pass the baby off as Charlie's. So what if it wasn't tall and strapping and handsome and good with horses and women? He wasn't likely to notice until the child was in its twenties, by which time he'd probably have traded Alex in for a younger version or a new polo pony. "It's just that sometimes I wonder how you'll get by without any money or luxuries or even a decent education. Rob can't make any money doing what he does, and well, I know you and I have dreams of running a billion-dollar empire, but you can't rely on that to keep your baby in Weetabix and Pampers, can you?"

"We'll make it work somehow, Liv. Now we ought to crack on—we're supposed to be at the pub for your hot date with Fat Will in an hour." Alex and Liv ran out the door before they could be roped into agreeing to pay for any more massages or collecting any more dry cleaning for their new spokesmodel.

The girls wandered down Oxford Street to Fiveways to stretch their hunched shoulders and worked-to-the-bone limbs.

"I'm turning into a crone with all that bending and scraping to Amelia. Look, I've got a hunch, haven't I?" Alex said as they sauntered along William Street without so much as a peek in Colette Dinnigan.

"Did we just walk past Colette Dinnigan because you're pregnant and can't fit into her clothes anymore or because you can't afford them?" Liv asked Alex in wonder. They had never ever walked past Colette Dinnigan's shop before without entering the airy portals for just a few seconds to fantasise about scones with the vicar in a transparent navy blue polka-dot tea dress or a night of Elizabeth Taylor tantrums resplendent in a shimmering slip dress.

"Neither. I just want to see Rob and show him the photos of the ultrasound," Alex said as she also ignored the equally dream-inducing handbag shop on the corner.

"So when exactly do you think you'll tell Charlie?" Liv asked.

"Charlie's making his own getaway. I haven't had sex with him for a week and yesterday I found a pink Versace miniskirt in his apartment. He tried to tell me it was his sister's, but only weathergirls wear pink Versace miniskirts— and I think I know the one. Pretty redhead after the ABC regional news at six. I'll talk to him tomorrow," Alex promised as they rounded the corner and climbed the steps to the Royal. "We'll end it in a mutually amicable way."

The tables were steadily filling with the Friday night after-work crowd gearing up for a big one and men getting in the pints before the rugby game.

"Will must be quite keen if he's skipping the rugby to take you out." Alex grinned.

"I told you Dave knows what he's doing when it comes to the workings of men's minds." Liv waved over at Rob, who was sitting between horse pee girl and a girl called Kicca whom Liv recognised from the dinner after Mardi Gras.

"Hey there." Rob stood up and scooped Alex onto a bar stool and plonked a mineral water in her hands before she could say vodka lime and soda. He bought Liv a beer, which she gamely had a go at as they filled him in on the day's excitements and the current state of RSVPs for the party.

Liv looked around to see if Ben was feeding the cigarette machine in the corner or making his way back from the gents', but he didn't seem to be there. She kept her fingers crossed and tried to calculate how long it would take him to get from work at the museum to here. Any minute now, she hoped. Amelia had confirmed his appearance tonight by moaning about having to spend another bloody evening in the Royal while he watched the rugby. Good for some things then was our Millie.

Liv knocked back her beer and then ordered a Scotch. She needed a bit of fire in her belly if she was going to pull off this whole Barbara Woodhouse thing. In fact, even the idea of seeing Ben from afar and ignoring him was making her feel nervous and bringing out a rash on her neck. Of course she fancied him still and of course she'd do anything to have had him not behave like such a completely predictable dog, but he had and so here she was ready to administer the first whack to his head with a rolled-up newspaper.

"When he sees that the other dog's got his stick he'll go mad and start dribbling," Dave had assured her. So Liv simply took another sip of Scotch and waited for the two mutts to show so she could engineer a standoff.

And she didn't have long to wait before the first canine bounded in, hiding his mean, nasty fangs from view and instead looking for all the world like the most glossy, handsome, adorable creature she'd ever seen. In his moleskins and black T-shirt Ben looked around and caught sight of his crew in the corner and suddenly Liv found herself offering her kingdom for a comb.

"Hi, guys." He smiled and patted backs and shook hands and delivered the odd pair of kisses to Amelia's friends. But not to Liv and Alex, who were admittedly sitting at the next table, but still. Confirmation of the big postfuck freeze-out, Liv noted. The dog.

"So, Alex, I hear it's going to be quite the party of the year?" said Kicca, who had previously perceived Alex and Liv as two of the unhippest nobodies ever to grace the same coveted restaurant table as herself. "Well, I'm a huge fan of your designs. Can't wait. And is it true that the dress code's lingerie only?" she asked. As Alex filled a disappointed Kicca in on the fact that she'd have to wear a dress and not be able to show off her hard-earned six-pack Liv turned and watched Ben at the bar. He was getting in the drinks, laughing at something the barmaid was telling him. He didn't turn around for even a second to find Liv's gaze. Her heart sank slightly. And did he not even feel slightly guilty, she marvelled at his temerity and rudeness.

"I thought you'd at least be wearing a bikini, babe," Charlie said to Alex. "I've invited the rugby team to see it." Charlie laughed, and Rob, who was sitting quietly in the corner, didn't.

Alex was unfazed. "Oh, I don't think my figure's up to a bikini at the moment," she said innocently enough, but it was instantly clear that at least half the table already knew the gossip, because a few glasses of Chardonnay were raised to lips to hide sly grins and Rob looked proudly in Alex's direction. Though if Amelia had been responsible for playing bush telegraph in this instance then everyone was doubtless under the impression that Charlie was the eligible, irresistible father. Liv looked at him and hoped for the baby-to-be's sake that Alex hadn't got her dates muddled up.

Charlie was currently throwing peanuts into the air while watching a young soap star who'd walked into the bar. Well, he could thank his lucky soap stars that next week he'd be free to admire the soap star at closer quarters, though judging by the wink she flashed him and the way he spilled his nuts as she did, he was perhaps not such a distant admirer after all. In fact, minutes later, after the soap star had left the bar and could be seen moving up and down in front of some flowerpots outside the bar, Charlie got a call on his mobile. The soap star outside the window threw back her head and laughed just as Charlie mumbled, "Long time no see, eh?" wittily into his phone. Alex barely noticed, as she was still trying to persuade Kicca of the postmodern humour of the name Greta's Grundies and that Intimate Secrets wasn't the name that the fledgling business was crying out for.

"Liv, you are looking spectacular." Will put his pudgy little hands around Liv's waist and she nearly jumped two feet in the air.

"Will!" It came out high-pitched like a schoolgirl who'd had her pigtails pulled. "I booked us a table at Hugo's."

He gave her a peck on the cheek. "I just have to go say hi to Charlie and the boys for a second if that's okay, sweetheart. Now are you okay for a drink?"

"Fine, thanks," Liv muttered as she looked around to see if Ben had noticed that his stick had been pinched by another dog. Admittedly, one with the body of a pug and the face of a Rottweiler, but Dave maintained that it didn't matter that the interloper was never going to win best of breed. Dogs didn't notice stuff like pedigree. They only wanted their stick back.

"He's watching you," Alex leaned over and whispered in Liv's ear.

"Truly?"

"Staring. Oh no, he's looked away again. He caught me watching him."

"Can men really be so dumb, Alex? I don't want to believe it."

"Ssshhhh, talking of . . . here comes Will." Alex turned back to what passed for conversation with Kicca but was actually more of a living, breathing interactive flip through the pages of *Hello!* magazine.

"You looked incredible in your gym outfit the other day, Liv." Will sat next to her and began to fiddle disconcertingly with her knees. "Fantastic legs. I hadn't noticed them before," he remarked to no one in particular.

"I'm not a racehorse, Will. Or perhaps you'd like to check my teeth while you're at it." Liv had very little patience with Will and his knack of making her feel as though she had as much intellectual relevance as a lamb chop.

"Ohhh, you're feisty tonight. We like that." He chuckled and slapped her thigh. "Can't wait." Liv gulped down an ice cube from the bottom of her glass and told herself that this was all in a good cause. In many ways Ben had treated her like a lamb chop, too, and he deserved to know how it felt.

"I'll bet you can't, you fat fuck," Liv mumbled with the ice cube in her mouth.

Will wasn't sure whether he'd heard properly and looked puzzled for a second. "So is that body all pumped and toned and ready for me?" Liv spat out the ice cube and giggled coquettishly as she suddenly saw Ben looking her way. Unabashedly staring at her. Had she had her old romantic head, she might have mistaken it for a gaze. But no—it was simply the stare of a simpleminded mutt who is jealous because a body-of-a-pug-face-of-a-Rottweiler type is dribbling saliva all over a stick that he once chewed and spat out.

"We're off to supper then." Liv made a big deal of saying good-bye to everyone even though they'd never noticed she'd arrived in the first place.

"See ya, babe." Alex stood up and shoved Liv to one side a bit, hissing under her breath, "Please, whatever you do, don't sleep with him. We'd have to have you deloused and fumigated and maybe even put down. You'd catch some kind of doggy dysentery or something."

"Gross, don't even begin." Liv swiped a quick look at Will, who was staring at her deliberately-on-view-in-tight-trousers bottom in a way that suggested he wouldn't mind a good sniff. "I'm going to order shellfish and throw up in the loos after the starter. Piece of fish cake."

"Ben looks as though he's about to cry into his beer. I think we should write a book on dog handling. It works like a dream," Alex marvelled, and gave Liv a hug.

"Bye then," Liv threw behind her, glancing one last time over her shoulder and catching Ben's eye for the first time that night. God, he did look sad sitting there on his own. She almost felt bad. Almost.

"Liv, this is Ben. I'd really like to take you to lunch if that's okay. I think perhaps we should talk."

"I cannot believe it. Can you believe it, Alex? Can you believe that he's doing this?"

"You're not supposed to be outraged, Liv; you're supposed to be delighted that everything's going according to plan."

Alex and Liv were at Liv's the next afternoon indulging in a bit of MTV after their week of baby-sitting Amelia. Laura had gone up the coast with Jo-Jo, so they were taking advantage of the flat because Alex was feeling a bit of creeping guilt for staying at Charlie's mum's house given her present condition.

"But am I meant to call him or what?" Liv asked. "What's the dog-handling procedure on this one? I should call Dave." Liv picked up the phone. "Dave, can you talk?"

"I have two seconds to spare. So tell me, how was last night?"

"Perfect. Prawns. I munched them all down and listened to him droning on about the illegal trade in AK-47s for a few minutes, then ran off to the loo. I did method acting and was thinking about what it would be like to have him lying on top of me twisting my nipples again and I think I went a pretty convincing shade of green, because he took me home straightaway."

"And you didn't feel guilty?" Dave asked.

"I did a bit until he made me hang my head out of the window all the way along the Pacific Highway in case I puked inside his silver Jag."

"What a tosser. Okay, so now all we need to do is sit tight and wait for number-one dog to call."

"He just did. But I don't know what to do next. Do I call him?" Liv was beginning to feel a bit queasy about all this.

"No. More subtle. You haul your backside down to where he works. The museum, right?"

"Yup. Aboriginal artefacts until next week, when he has a dig in Bermagui. Amelia filled us in."

"Great. Well, off you toddle with a nice frock and no knickers—adds to the vibes—and just sort of bump into him. It doesn't matter if he believes it's a coincidence or not. But just be there and be aloof and then if he asks you out be a bit cool and then agree grudgingly. Like god, I have a million and one tastier fish to fry, but I guess it'd be rude not to. That kind of aura."

"What if he doesn't try too hard to persuade me?" Liv sounded worried.

"He's on the trail, Liv. You've got the ball again and you have to hold onto it this time. Comprendez?"

"Yeah, I think so. Okay, well, thanks, Davo. I'll check in later."

Liv wandered through the cool portals of the museum try-ing to look riveted. She stared closely at the delicate wood carvings covered with hundreds of colourful dots and then did a surreptitious head swivel every few minutes to see if she could see Ben anywhere. But for heaven's sake he was the archaeologist, wasn't he, not a beady-eyed security guard who sat out on view all day just waiting to be bumped into by some girl on a mission. She might as well go home now. The only people in evidence were a group of schoolchildren who were much more interested in one another's nits than the exhibit and some desiccated pensioners who had probably been around longer than the dots on the wood carvings. Liv had one last glance around her and then slung her bag over her shoulder to leave.

"Would you mind taking a photograph of us, dear?" one of the pruney pensioners asked.

"Not at all." Liv took the very swish and high-tech camera from the old man and stood back. "Smile, all of you," she said, and wished she'd put on some knickers. Imagine what they'd have thought if they knew, she thought in horror and deference to their pacemakers and frail hearts.

"Cheese." The prunes all put their arms around one another and smiled.

"Excuse me, the sign says that all flash photography's forbidden in here. Would you mind putting that away?"

Liv had already committed a crime by pressing the button. "Whoops, I'm really sorry. Have I done loads of damage?" She turned to the security guard to face the music only to find that they were playing her song. "Ben," she yelped, and nearly dropped the camera.

"Liv."

"God, I'm, erm, sorry."

A prune appeared beside her and tapped her on the shoulder. "Thank you so much, dear. Very kind of you." He retrieved his camera and scuttled off, not even attempting to stop her from being arrested.

"I was, er, just, well, I was having a wander round and—"

"I had no idea you were interested in stuff like this, Liv. I put this exhibit together, you know. Isn't it beautiful?"

"Oh, it's lovely," said Liv. Thankfully she'd had nothing else to do for the past hour other than swat up, so she could quite honestly say that. "The Eora—they were the indigenous people of Sydney, right?"

"Yeah. Would you like me to show you around? Give you some of the inside info, as it were?" he asked eagerly.

Liv knew that she was supposed to be here to smoosh him into an emotional pulp, but what was the harm in looking when he was clearly so excited about sharing this stuff with her? She could smoosh him later.

"So it could have been as long as a hundred thousand years ago that they landed here really. We have to say fifty thousand to be conservative, but when the first settlers came it was the ice age. Their whole culture was based around the sea—bit like Oz now really; pretty much everyone still lives on the coasts." Ben had his hand on the small of Liv's back as he guided her to the last display. "God, I'm sorry, are you bored?" He turned to look at her.

Liv shook her head. She'd hadn't been bored for a single second. "No, I feel privileged. I can't believe that you actually discovered some of these things. What an incredible job. Truly." Liv looked more carefully at one of the dotty plates and thought it the most beautiful thing she'd seen almost ever.

"Anyway, I suppose I should be getting off. It's lunch break and if I hang around here I'll get roped into translating for Japanese tourists or something," said Ben.

Liv suddenly remembered that she was here as a stalker and not a genuine art appreciator and felt fraudulent. Then she remembered that Ben had slipped his leash and she was meant to bring him to heel. He's a shit, she repeated in her head a few times, and drew herself up to full height. "I have to go, too. Thanks a lot, Ben."

"You could always come and have a sandwich with me. I mean maybe you've got heaps of other stuff to do, but—"

"Okay. I'm actually starving." Was that too eager? Liv wondered. No. Dave had told her that she had to get a date with Ben. And what was this if not success on a plate? Liv took a reality check and thought of her Sunday by the phone waiting for Ben to call her and clicked back into dog-handling mode. He'd done it once and you could bet your pants he'd do it again. Bad dog.

Okay, so it wasn't Doyles or Hugo's or some wonderful seafront watering hole where he would try to seduce her over Chardonnay and she'd resist and leave him panting. It was the museum canteen with plastic tables and wedges of carrot cake and bread baskets filled with bananas by the tills, but Liv figured it would do the trick just as well if all she had to do was lead him on and make him want her. They'd been chatting perfectly pleasantly about art and television and travelling and how they both wanted to drive across America someday, eat beignets in New Orleans at four in the morning, and nice stuff like that, and she was just psyching herself up to be mean to him when he threw her off balance.

"Actually, Liv, I don't know if you got my message this time, but I called you. I really wanted to talk to you about something." He put down his fork and looked thoughtful.

"Really?"

"Do you think we could go somewhere a bit more private and have a chat? There's a bunch of stuff I want to tell you." Ben looked very serious. God, he was good; she had to give him that. He really had that earnest baby-I'm-not-joking-I-really-feel-deeply-about-this thing down to a fine art. He was making her feel like she was the only girl in the world and that nobody else mattered. And he had the cheek to not seem too confident of her response, just reveal a ripple of doubt so she couldn't accuse him of being arrogant and cocky. Clearly he wanted another shag. But Liv wasn't quite prepared for this yet. Though she was pretty much easy access all areas without her knickers, she hadn't got round to discussing with Dave what happened after the date yet. She knew that she was supposed to tear Ben limb from limb emotionally and make him feel as used and cheap as he'd made her and Laura Train Wreck feel, but she hadn't a bloody clue how to do it.

"I've got to go." She suddenly looked at her watch.

"It won't take long," Ben said.

Oh, even better, Liv thought. He's not even pretending to be in the market for anything more than a very quick one. There's a sharing, caring kind of guy for you.

"In fact, I'm late for . . . something." She picked up her bag and her postcard of the Eora pottery and stood up. "Thanks so much for the sandwich. And the exhibition was lovely. I'll see you around." Liv walked away without so much as a backwards glance. Well, if she *had* cast a nonchalant, uncaring look over her shoulder she might have melted into a big knickerless puddle of longing, because he'd looked decidedly sexy with his cheese-and-ham baguette in front of him. But how convincing had he been? Wow. She was amazed at what a fantastic lying, deceitful bastard he was capable of being. Was there no depth to which he wouldn't stoop to make her want him just so he could pee up her leg all over again? Metaphorically, of course.

On the bus back to Bronte, Liv stopped herself from thinking what a nice bumping-into situation that had just been and focused instead on the idea that life never really turns out as you planned. A snack in the work canteen of the guy who'd fucked and chucked you and whom you were now responsible for reprimanding on behalf of women everywhere wasn't exactly what she'd had in mind all those months ago when she told Alex she dreamed of a knickerless lunch with a sexy man. But things had changed. Back then Liv had been a card-carrying romantic with a head full of pink slush. A stranger to thrilling and illicit things. Sadly, now she knew the truth. That thrilling and illicit was just like hopping aboard a handcart to hell, so the most that could be hoped for in a knickerless situation was that you didn't catch a draught or have a brain haemorrhage or anything that would mean going in an ambulance and being exposed as a cheap floozy. Grim but true. And how strong and controlled had she been by not sneaking off into a dark corner with him for a quickie? Very, she told herself. Ubergirl that she was turning out to be.

Chapter Seventeen

Best of Breed

Fantastic. You're going to be agent provocateur. You're going to be Mata Hari."

It was Saturday afternoon at the market and Liv was tidying up the lingerie on the front of the stall—now that she was the owner she didn't want a bra strap out of place. Alex was sewing silver Greta's Grundies labels inside the underwear. Dave had come by to throw his shareholding weight around.

"I thought I was supposed to be Barbara Woodhouse. Anyway, I'm not Mata Hari. Clearly. Because he hasn't called back yet. Did calling Mata Hari back score so low on men's lists of priorities? Somewhere beneath darn my football socks and get my ears syringed?" Liv asked. Could she have finally bored Ben to death by running out on him once too often? Drumroll—here she is, the Incredible Buggering Off Girl.

"I'm so glad you didn't just leap at the invitation and go home with him. So much better that you catch him off guard when he's all naked and vulnerable and then make him suffer."

"Dave, you're really sick, do you know that? What has poor Ben ever done to make you so cross?" Alex asked.

"Oh, you've just gone all fluffy bunny because you're preggars, haven't you? I haven't forgotten the days of hard-bitten cynicism when you'd have revelled in some wanker being taken down a peg or two."

"Dave just likes to imagine Ben naked, that's all." Liv laughed. "Anyway, I don't want to make him suffer so much as have my ego massaged by knowing that he wants me and that it's my call. So, Saint Alex, when are you going to do the dirty deed and dump Charlie?"

"Soon enough." Alex concentrated on her needle threading so she didn't have to talk about it.

"Do I detect denial?" Dave asked.

"He's having an affair with some soap star now. I'm just waiting for her to leave a long dark hair in his bed and then I can confront him."

"Sounds like an avoidance tactic to me. The baby's going to be seventeen before you know it." Dave picked up a G-string. "Can I have this? I'm Miss Pussy Whiplash tonight and need a bit of a charm to wow my boys with in the Albury."

"All yours. Is James coming to the party, by the way? I haven't heard a peep from him."

"Too right he's coming. He's been raiding my CD collection all week. You do still want him to DJ, don't you?" Dave pocketed the G-string.

"We'd love him to." Liv broke off to serve a customer. They only had to sell one more vest top and they would have broken even today. And it was only ten-thirty. Business was looking good.

"Okay, sweeties, I'd better get home before my *pain au chocolats* start to melt in the heat. Livvy, I'm on standby for you. Call me the minute anything happens. And, Alex . . . do the decent thing, honey, before it's too late."

★　★　★

No sooner had Dave left with his G-string than the only other person in the entire city who would look as good in it as he did strolled up to the stall.

"Ah, girls, just thought I'd put in a personal appearance."

"Amelia." Liv and Alex looked up at precisely the same moment.

"Oh, and Ben. Hi," Alex added because she knew Liv wouldn't.

"Hi," Ben said, and looked slightly cowed and shy.

"Actually, we were just shopping for a wedding present for a friend and started discussing marriage. Wondering what vows we'd take."

Liv could have sworn that there was something pointed about Amelia's delivery, but it was hard to tell with her superfashionable science-goggle sunglasses obscuring most of her face. "I told Ben I'd absolutely want him to obey. Wouldn't you say, girls?"

"Oh yeah, you should always go for the old-fashioned full complement of vows. And then some," Alex said. "Love, honour, cherish, obey, adore, worship, spot of reflexology."

"Oh, I get all those anyway," Amelia roared like a drain as though Ben weren't actually standing next to her. "So who needs marriage, eh? Wouldn't want some bloke ripping me off. I'd insist on a prenup for sure."

"Me either," Ben chimed in. "There's no way I'd let some scheming bitch get her hands on my collection of two-thousand-year-old Vietnamese shrunken heads." He raised a sardonic eyebrow and Liv couldn't help but laugh—poor guy, he didn't look like he was exactly enraptured by Amelia's company. More like a jaded, roughed-up man who was resigned to his horrible fate.

"Now can I have one of those bodices?" Amelia picked up a hot pink satin number and checked the label size. "Ben and I are having a lovely romantic dinner tonight, aren't we, sweetie?"

Was that another glare in my direction? Liv wondered.

"Well, we're going to Moncurs with six other people. But I guess that's pretty quiet and romantic for us, hey?" He smiled at Amelia and she ran her hands through his hair like an indulgent mother might do to her five-year-old.

"Have to be off. You guys can just whack this on my account or something, can't you? Ciao."

And with that Amelia was gone. Leaving Ben to pick up her corset, which Liv was wrapping up. He moved his face close to hers and whispered urgently, "Liv. Come away for the weekend with me. Please. Next Friday."

"What?" Liv looked around to make sure Amelia was out of earshot. She was—stroking the ostrich skirts in the next stall.

"Please. Say yes."

"No."

"You have to. We need to talk."

"Once bitten. Sorry."

"I'll call you."

"Ben, do you think this yellow would make me look like an Easter chick?" Amelia turned around and demanded to know.

"No, you'd look fabulous in it," Ben said quite truthfully, and strolled over to Amelia's side.

"What the hell was that about?" Alex asked excitedly. "God, those two couldn't be less suited if they tried."

"Was I imagining that or did Ben just ask me away for the weekend?"

"I know he's really a dirty, scheming, cheating rat, but he's pretty convincing. I mean if he hadn't already dumped you on your bum once and done the same to Laura Train Wreck I wouldn't believe he was a bad cad." Alex was still watching in disbelief as Amelia persuaded the Stall Slime to part with an ostrich skirt for nothing more than the glory of having Amelia Fraser wear it to Moncurs that evening.

"Yeah, well, I've seen both sides of his Jekyll–Hyde thing."

"So are you going to go?" Alex asked excitedly.

"I thought you didn't approve of me being mean to him."

"Well, you're not going to be too harsh, are you? I mean you're just going to let him know that what he did wasn't very nice and he should think twice before doing it again."

"Pretty much. I think it's more of an ego thing for me. If I can just get him to the point where I'm able to reject him—where I have the power—then I probably won't fancy him half so much anymore."

"Hang on a minute. You still fancy him?" Alex put down her needle.

"Well, I think maybe I do. I'm not going to do anything about it so it's completely irrelevant, but . . . well, he is pretty sexy, isn't he? And when there's no sex involved—like when we were at the museum and talking rather than fucking—well, he was as lovely as you can imagine. Why is it that the second sex is involved normally sane people go all weird on you?"

"Not all people, Liv. Remember that. If I can be a worm that turned then there's hope for everyone."

"I guess. I just have to find the only sane, well-adjusted, balanced, nondoglike man on the planet other than Rob then."

"I'll keep my eyes peeled. So in the meantime are you going to make do with a spot of nookie with Mr. Parker?"

"Well, a weekend away might be fun, mightn't it? Do you think I should pack my lucky silver knickers?" Liv laughed as she watched Ben trail Amelia with another three shopping bags out onto Oxford Street.

"I don't think you'll need them, judging by the look in his eye earlier."

★ ★ ★

As it was, Liv didn't actually pack her lucky silver knickers, because she was trying to give the impression that she travelled light. Ben had called her every day twice a day for the last week and finally, on Thursday, as planned carefully and for maximum effect, she capitulated and agreed to join him for a weekend in the Hunter Valley. But only if he could promise her that they would have separate rooms. She wasn't giving a thing away this time. He promised, and Liv packed. However, while Liv's luggage looked like she was an easy breezy travelling-light type, it was in reality a deceptively vast bag that could have comfortably housed a football team—while looking as though it contained only a toothbrush and a couple changes of underwear, in fact, it harboured fashion collections for every eventuality: wellies for flash floods, bikini for sunbathing but swimsuit in case of adventuresome water sport, pairs of shoes for day to evening and flopping around on beach, something to wear while breakfasting in bed that wasn't a prosaic T-shirt, but also a prosaic T-shirt to wear on way to the bathroom that looked very Calvin Klein casual-sexy and not too try-hard. In fact, she only stopped short of taking Alex's mink-lined Drizabone in case she was clubbed to death by any well-intentioned animal rights protesters who might be lurking in the shrubs outside the hotel. How would they know that the mink in question had belonged to Jane Russell and was bloodily slaughtered so long ago that it was no longer a cause for moral concern? And if she bothered to explain it to them would they see the glamorous side?

Thankfully Laura was still away on tour for a few days with *Hedda Gabler* when Ben came round to collect Liv. Though Liv *had* fortified herself and strengthened her dog-handling resolve by taking a long, hard look at Laura's bookshelves before he arrived. The poor girl, there must have been at least seventy self-help manuals stacked up, and those were the weighty shrinky ones and didn't even begin to include the ones about Fluffy Little Happy Thoughts to Ponder on the Loo. Yup, poor Laura had been turned into a human catastrophe because of this man. She'd provided half the psychotherapists in New South Wales with hubcaps for their Ferraris. She'd been utterly destroyed by Ben the Bastard. Liv could not let him off lightly.

"Do you want to come in a second?" Liv asked as she realised that Ben was actually quite nervous about being in the house. Obviously he was remembering his past misdemeanours, too, and wondering whether Laura was about to launch herself out of the cleaning cupboard wielding a machete.

"I've left the car running." He looked around hastily. "Best just get off, hey?"

"Okay." Liv grabbed her cardigan and let him carry her bag. She was tempted to yell out, "Bye, Laura!" just to freak him out a bit, but he was already halfway down the front path. Besides, she didn't want him to be so scared that he'd decide against taking her away after all and run back to the shelter of Amelia's clavicle. This was, after all, Liv's first dirty weekend away in about a hundred and fifty years and she'd even had her bikini wax renewed, so she was not about to bottle out lightly. Even though she'd decided that she mustn't have sex with him again, as that would cause a power shift, she still hadn't ruled out a little fooling around.

"So here we are," said Liv as she belted up in the passenger seat—ever on the nose with her observations.

"Thanks for agreeing to come, Liv. I know that you didn't want to really and you have every right not to want to so much as share the same planet as me right now, but I hope we can sort things out this weekend."

"So where's Amelia?" Liv asked disingenuosly. It also made

her feel stronger if she reminded him that he was being a fugitive boyfriend. Not bad that he should squirm a bit.

"She's gone to a spa for the weekend. That's one of the things I want to talk to you about—Amelia."

"Okay." Liv knew that it was just going to be an "I love Amelia and can never leave her, but in an ideal world I've decided that you are cheap and worthless enough to be the girl whom I shag when I feel like it and then ignore in the pub the next day. How about it, darlin'?" And if that was the romantic declaration she was meant to be waiting for then she could wait just a bit longer before she politely declined. "But why don't we talk about it over dinner tonight, perhaps?"

"Fine by me. Let's just enjoy the drive. God, it's good to have you sitting there, Liv. You'll never know." He smiled as he fiddled with the tape recorder and unearthed an old Cole Porter album.

" 'Something Stupid' . . . how perfect." Liv sighed meaningfully.

"Me. Totally stupid for letting you go all those years ago." He patted her knee and let his hand rest there, gently stroking her leg. Wow, that was almost sweet. She thought he'd be crass and treat her like a hooker and expect blow jobs en route, but this was almost romantic. They slipped along the Pacific Highway, the shimmering blue of the harbour on one side, the sunlight bouncing off the high-rises on the other.

"Couldn't really have worked out more perfectly, could it?" Liv smiled with her head resting back and her eyes closed. "I needed to get away for the weekend, preferably with a man, and there was one I road-tested earlier just hanging about waiting to be taken for another spin."

"Jesus, Livvy, I wish you'd give up on the heavy emotional stuff. I mean you're backing me into a corner with all this talk of commitment and marriage and kids." He laughed.

"Does it bother you that I clearly care so little for you?" Liv asked, quite getting into the swing of Mata Hari. Liv Hari. Perhaps she'd missed her calling as Alexis Carrington in *Dynasty*. Perhaps she could be the evil one in Alex's lingerie empire dynastic saga *Knicker Lace*—the one who yells, "Which one of you bastards deserves a good slapping?"

"I know you better than that, Liv. I know you're not so hard—that you do care."

God, step forward the arrogant prick on wheels with his sunglasses on and one elbow resting out of the window. You're the bastard that needs a good slapping. And he was so goddamn cool—the way he drove with one hand, the way he smiled easily. He was as calm as a swimming pool at dawn. And it was all alarmingly sexy. He took a bend, turned up the radio, and began to sing. Liv thought about two more hateful thoughts and then remembered how fantastic it had felt when he'd kissed her neck. So she joined Ben and Frank at the top of her voice, their tunelessness vanishing into the afternoon heat.

Four hours later, after Frank had been replaced by Anthony Newley, who had given way to Ella Fitzgerald, and they'd made a pit stop at McDonald's for a couple of extra-large ice-cream sundaes with hot fudge topping, they arrived in the Hunter Valley. They pulled up outside a small sandstone house and tumbled out, Liv dying for a pee and Ben unable to find the keys. He searched under flowerpots, in a small shed at the side, beneath a million bricks.

"I'll go and see if any windows are open." Liv ran off around the side of the house, hopping from side to side in a bid to appease her bladder. The cottage was surrounded by scrub and eucalyptus trees. It wasn't until she'd peeped in a few dark windows to little avail that she realised that they were on the top of a hill, and as she rounded the back of the house she looked down and saw sprawling acres of vineyards dotted with tiny dwellings and the occasional meandering red dust track crossing a property. A light aircraft spraying the vines hummed gently in the still afternoon. Liv closed her hands around her face as she put her head to the sun-warmed glass of some French windows; she could see the flagstone floors and a large dining table inside the shady house—but little else. And certainly no sign of keys among the ants at her feet. She turned the door handle in a futile move, and to her surprise it edged open.

"Ben, round here. I'll come up and open for you!" Liv yelled as she made her way into the cool darkness. The ride up had been easy and relaxed and she'd decided to put her meanness back for a few hours. Wait until he started his "come live with me and be my bit on the side" speech and then she'd give him what for.

She fumbled through the house until she found what she assumed was the front door and opened it. After a second of blinding sunlight she was confronted with not Ben and their luggage but the overpowering whiff of damp and a huge green swimming pool under the shade of a jungle of green plants and overgrown orange trees. In the water a few spiders lay inanimate on the surface, and what was probably a summer's worth of oranges had sunk to the bottom of the deep end. "Wow," Liv uttered as she made her way back into the hallway.

"Did you find a key?" Ben came towards her through the dark, his car keys jangling in his hand.

"Who does this place belong to?" Liv asked, diving into a downstairs loo and regaining her composure. When she emerged she realised that it was so dark because the windows were shuttered all through the house, so she moved through the rooms opening them. Each time, the light fell upon a room more surprising than the last, beautiful bedrooms that were more Louis XIV than Aussie farmer—huge satin quilts graced the carved French beds—and in the kitchen a rustic table was set with silver for two, including two swillingly huge silver goblets and a fruit bowl with an ancient array of mouldering quinces.

"Who does this place belong to?" Liv repeated, mesmerised by the overwhelming beauty of it all.

"It's a secret. But it's perfect because we can just walk down the hill to Robert's Restaurant and then scramble back up in no fit state later." Ben pointed out of the windows to a small cluster of buildings a couple of vineyards away.

"So it's Amelia's place then?" Liv assumed, getting the impression that Ben had stumbled drunk back up the hill on many an occasion and that the only family in Australia rich enough to be able to neglect such a stunning house and even leave the back door open all summer must be the Frasers.

"Actually, it's not. Belongs to a mate," Ben said vaguely as he scanned the wine rack and pulled out a bottle, dusted down the label, and smiled like the cat who ate the canary.

"Anyone I know?" Liv asked, sitting at the head of the table and gazing down over the valley.

"Can't say. I was only allowed to bring you here on condition that I didn't tell." Ben winked and took an opener to the bottle. "Needless to say, the guy owes me a favour."

"Who is it, Ben?" Liv stopped sniffing the gorgeously musky quinces and sat up.

"I'm never going to tell you, so stop asking." Ben sloshed the wine into first Liv's goblet, then his own. "To you and I renewing our acquaintance," Ben diverted the conversation, and Liv made a mental note to bring it up again later when he was better oiled.

"Perhaps." Liv took a sip and narrowed her eyes as she took in just how glorious he was. Well, in another life, perhaps.

*   *   *

Later, after they'd explored and dumped their luggage in their respective and very separate bedrooms, they decided to rinse away the dust and grime of the journey with a swim in the green pool.

"It looks like a biology experiment. Are you sure it's safe?" Liv asked as she dipped her toe in the water.

"Perfectly." Ben ran along the marble side of the pool and jumped high, his knees clutched to his chest, and landed with a fearsome thud at the other side of the pool.

"Is it cold?" she dithered, looking suspiciously at the insect corpses that drifted across the surface.

"Oh, just get in." Ben emerged from the deep end and scraped back his hair.

Liv pulled off her bathrobe and dived headlong into the unknown. "Gross." She came up for air and imagined herself with spiders' legs in her hair and dragonfly wings in her mouth.

"That's what I love about you, Liv Elliot. You're such a girl." Ben emerged from somewhere beneath her and secured her to the side of the pool with his arms. "Truly a different species."

Liv brushed her hair from her face and blinked at him. "Oh, it's that madonna-whore syndrome again—you boys love that—pure, virginal Amelia at home and then rough, loose Liv to play away with." Liv half smiled but wasn't joking.

"You've got this whole thing so wrong." Ben fixed his eyes on her. "When I'm with Amelia I can't think of anything except you. Sure she's beautiful, can be funny, always knows what to say—"

"If you've come here to tell me you're in love with your fabulous girlfriend don't bother. It's a given." Liv slipped under his arms and clambered onto the side of the pool, where she sat with her feet in the water and the sun magnified through the glass windows warming the tiny droplets of water on her back.

Ben eased himself onto the poolside and lay on the marble next to her. "She's also selfish and vain and wouldn't give a damn if I were to disappear tomorrow as long as she had someone to carry her shopping bags and be arm candy for the photographers. When I first met her I thought she was lively and fantastic. But I was caught up in the whole trip, Liv—her looks, charm—it can feel like the most interesting place in the world. But really when you scratch the surface it's unattractive and superficial. I'm not in love with her." Ben covered his face with his arm to block out the sun.

"The only thing worse than a cheat is a cheat who slags off his girlfriend to other women."

"I know. And if I were cheating on Amelia then I wouldn't be saying this."

"Oh, so doing some girl in her bathroom and then taking her away for a weekend is the dictionary definition of fidelity, is it?"

"I was going to leave Amelia anyway. But meeting up with you again just confirmed that."

Liv must have unconsciously rolled her eyes at this feckless male bullshit, because he sat up and caught her arm.

"I know it's none of my business, but I saw you leave the pub the other night with Will. Are you seeing him? Is that the problem?"

"Do you really think that's any of your business? And did it occur to you that even if I weren't seeing Will I wouldn't want someone who's already walked all over me?" Liv couldn't believe his audacity. She shook his arm loose.

"It's just that I don't know Will very well, but he does have a reputation for being a bit of a shit and no matter what happens between you and me I don't want to see you get hurt."

"You what?"

"Above all, I really care about you, Liv."

"Listen, Ben, we had sex," Liv helpfully pointed out just in case it had slipped his mind. "But you forfeited your right to even have me acknowledge your existence when you led me on by saying you wanted to take me to lunch and then never called. Until you saw me with Will. Now just because you're perverse enough to only be interested in what you suddenly can't have does not mean that I am at your beck and call any longer. So get over it. I'm not *such* a girl that I don't understand the meaning of casual sex. Can I just suggest that in the future you don't make promises to women that you can't keep?" Liv splurted.

"You can't even begin to know how far from the truth you are," Ben tried to interject.

"Oh, I think I'm depressingly close to the truth. Don't pretend that this isn't a pattern with you, Ben."

"What on earth are you talking about?"

"I'm talking about Laura, my neighbour, for starters. Even if, as you claim, you wanted me all along, isn't this a remarkably similar pattern to the one you established when you broke her heart less than six months ago?"

Ben looked shocked.

"Ha, got you with your hand in the cookie jar!" Liv wanted to yell triumphantly. Instead she pulled on a bathrobe, because she did feel slightly ridiculous trying to be intimidating while her boobs jiggled around. She lacked a certain gravity in more ways than one.

"So?"

He looked at her, sitting there with her hair dripping water down her alabaster shoulders, her wet eyelashes. "Have you spoken to Charlie about this?"

"Why Charlie?" Liv asked.

"I met Laura through Charlie. She was going out with this great girl and they seemed really happy. We all used to hang out a lot—Laura's a great cook and we had picnics and barbies the whole time. Anyway, I'm a guy and you know I'm not really into all that psychology stuff, but I think that what pretty much happened was that Laura became fixated on me.

Some sexuality blip. Not sure if she was gay or not. Called me a lot, kept turning up at the museum when I was working" (Liv couldn't imagine what kind of freak would do something like that!), "and then turned quite nasty on Amelia. It was rough. She split up with her girlfriend and Millie had to have a restraining order taken out on her."

"You're joking." Liv didn't know whether to believe him or not. I mean, Laura wasn't exactly a poster child for mental health, but she wasn't such a loop, surely? Wouldn't Charlie have told Liv and Alex? But then perhaps he was just being gracious and giving Laura a second chance by not telling Liv all about her. Still, maybe she would have turned dangerous.

"Was she violent or anything?" Liv asked tentatively.

"No, just a pain in the backside really. She made a few threats, but nothing too serious. More than anything, it was stressful and rough on Millie. But then she met this girl Jo-Jo who's a social worker and they really hit it off. She promised to get help and I thought things had got better. She hasn't called me for months."

"And she probably was better until I came along and started talking about you and getting phone calls."

"You talked about me?" Ben interrupted Liv, and brushed the water from her cheeks.

"Only libellous, malicious stuff. Nothing nice." She half smiled and then bit the inside of her mouth to bring herself back from la-la land. "Right. Well, just because we've dismissed the Laura situation as a misunderstanding I can't think of a single excuse for what you did to me."

"I was trying to protect you."

"What from? Being happy and having self-esteem?"

"From Amelia."

"God, I think you're the freak. Are you telling me that every woman you know has some subclinical behavioural disorder? What? Did Amelia have a fixation on me? Should

I take out a restraining order, too? Come on, Ben; you're really stretching it now."

"What did I do that was so bad?"

"Ben, you used me. I know it sounds crap and old-fashioned, but there's no getting around it. You behaved like a wanker. What has Amelia got to do with that?" Liv clung on the cliff face of logic with her fingernails even though she loved the way the sun was making her feel as it streamed through the sunroof. Even though she was being very distracted by the way Ben was stroking the back of his neck anxiously. "I'll do that," she wanted to offer. Shut up, Liv, she told herself.

"I can't tell you."

"Oh, you are so full of it."

"No, really. You just have to trust me on this one."

"Ha. I see. Trust you. No way."

"Okay, well, you asked."

"Shoot."

"She knows about us. Not about the boat, but she saw us at Mardi Gras. She followed us."

"Holy shit." Liv was no longer cool and sussed. She was flipping out.

"Shhh. It's fine; I've got it all under control."

"What? The fact that your girlfriend hates my guts and probably wants me dead?"

"I don't give a flying fuck about Amelia." He was no longer soft at all. In fact, he was angry. What was that primal turn-on thing about anger? It was sick, but somewhere very sexy. As long as Liv wasn't on the receiving end. "But I don't like being blackmailed."

"What do you mean, blackmailed?" Liv felt as though she were watching a particularly juicy episode of *Eastenders*. This was more drama than the omnibus edition.

"She said that if I saw you again she'd pull out of helping you and Alex with the business," Ben said gravely. "So I didn't call you again. You've no idea how hard it was, but I couldn't risk her finding out, Liv. She stuck to me like a limpet that entire weekend. God, I could have throttled her."

"And whenever we had a meeting she'd just talk about how many times you and she had done it last night. It was a bit gross." Liv thought back, not quite sure how this whole picture fitted together yet. So Ben wasn't in love with Amelia, but she was planning to ruin Liv's business if he ever saw her again. "But we're here. What if she finds out?" Liv shrieked.

"She's away at a spa like I said. There's no way she'll know about this. The guy whose house it is will keep it superquiet, I promise. Anyway, the thing is that I overheard Alex at the pub that night of the rugby talking about how well you guys were doing on the stall. She said that business was great and I realised that Amelia had probably overegged her own importance in your success. Ego gone mad. Also, I figured that just so long as she'd done the publicity photos and the party was all done with then you could do without her. I was going to end it with her after your launch."

"But—"

"It's over between us no matter whether you want to be with me or not, Liv. I know you're seeing Will and I don't want to pressure you and I know that business is important to you, but . . . I'm willing to wait."

"Will?" Liv could barely contain her disgust. She wanted to tell Ben all about dog handling. About how she'd thought that he wasn't interested and that's why she'd spent the last few weeks scheming to make him want her. But how on earth could she? For heaven's sake—oh, by the way, I was training you, bringing you to heel, making you sit up and beg. Holding onto your ball, as it were. She was mortified she'd ever been so dreadful. But then she remembered that she had been pretty fragile what with Tim and then Will and then Ben dumping on her from a great height, so let herself off just a bit.

"Ben, if I hadn't been so hard to get, if I'd been available to you from the very first night on the beach, would you have wanted me?" She held her breath and hoped that he'd say something that vindicated her like, "Never. You know us men: We never want to belong to any club that would have us as a member." Something along those lines.

"You have no idea how much. You were just like this amazing breath of fresh air with your naturalness and innocence and the fact that you had no idea how to work it. All the women I've met for years have been operators. They're like steel. They manipulate and control and it's all some huge game. It sounds pretty mad, but you had a purity about you, Liv."

"Ben, I think that . . ." Liv was about to try to make some sense of what she'd been doing these past few weeks. The manipulative, controlling, steely games she'd been playing. Oh, whoops.

"I'm sorry I put you through hell," he said, and kissed her.

Liv closed her eyes and lay back on the moss-coated tiles and decided that confessions could wait. This, on the other hand, couldn't.

And so events sort of took on a shape of their own. Liv quashed her dog-handling revelation as irrelevant now that the whole game was over, and they just sank into the spirit of their dirty weekend. They'd put any talk of the future to one side as it was so stressful. The Amelia hurdle to leap, the party to get through, Tim arriving in Sydney next week. All just too much. Instead they retreated into a world of wine and Cole Porter and doing silly dances in the garden in the moonlight and talking about the bullfights they wanted to hold hands through, the days they'd spend just chilling out and watching MTV on Ben's bed, the afternoons when they'd just lie on the beach back in Sydney getting burned, and the archaeological digs they'd go on with Liv warming baked beans up on a calor gas stove, killing the odd snake, and guarding the tent while Ben unearthed unimaginable treasure.

Their hands shook as they raised glass after glass of red and white and Chardonnay and a little drop of Penfold's Grange to their lips in yet another winery, under the eye of yet another vintner who watched the happy couple enviously and thought that maybe it was time to make a lover of the pretty Norwegian grape picker who was staying in the attic bedroom for the summer. His wife was too busy chatting up the estate manager to notice anyway. And as they took long walks in the late afternoon through the vineyards, they'd laugh and chase each other onto private land with the air of naughtiness usually only managed between George Peppard and Audrey Hepburn in Breakfast at Tiffany's when they emerged bright-eyed from their shoplifting spree.

In fact, by Sunday evening, as the sun dipped behind the horizon on yet another perfect, still evening and they toasted more bliss and sex with yet another bottle of Shiraz, Liv felt as though her life had been a seamless journey from the Provençal marketplace to Australia. She could barely remember a time in between. Somewhere she was terrified to be this happy—she tried to tell herself that anything she gained on this trip, be it a man or a business empire, was a bonus, but she mustn't treat this adventure as her everyday life. She mattered; finding out what she thought and felt and cared about and hated mattered. Wasn't she slightly missing the point if she didn't do what she wanted to do for once in her life rather than what was right or expected or made someone else happy? Yes, she should definitely go for it.

After the Shiraz, Liv kissed Ben on the forehead and went to get dressed for their Last Supper. Or what she privately hoped would be their first of a million suppers. She showered for an age and pulled on an emerald-green silk slip dress. Though it was a bit on the long side because it was Alex's, it still looked ethereal and lovely. And the wine had made her cheeks flush pink, giving her a Snow White look against her clean, shining black hair. She wondered if she felt beautiful enough to tell him about the silly, pointless, irrelevant little game she'd been playing. She'd tell him honestly that it was because she felt used and broken and fragile and she realised now how childish it had been, but she was sorry and hoped that he could understand. He'd made such a big deal about her honesty, her integrity, that she felt she had to live up to his expectations and come clean. Then they'd have a wonderful basis for a new relationship. Liv was beginning to feel ready to trust someone again. There was little for it now except to remember to put some perfume on and hope for the best.

As she walked out onto the balcony into the dusk Ben whistled slowly. "It just doesn't get any better," he said, and pulled her onto his lap.

"Wait and see," Liv teased as she allowed his hands to ease down the straps of her dress and he rubbed his cheek against her shoulder.

"You are so fantastic."

"You're all right, too."

"Liv, you have to say that we can give this a go. That as soon as I've told Amelia it's over then we can be together. You have to."

Ben was so close, she could feel his eyelashes grazing her cheek. She should tell him now. Just say it. He'd understand completely why she'd done what she'd done. Then she thought maybe better after a glass of wine or two. Oil the wheels first.

"The table's for seven-thirty. We'll discuss it later, okay?" Liv took his hands and pulled him reluctantly to his feet. They set off hand in hand down the valley, through the rows of vines, dusting their feet with red sand. Robert's Restaurant was just at the foot of their hill, and they entered through the rose-covered oak door just slightly breathless from the walk.

The restaurant was full of very quiet couples. They were all so sophisticated that Liv felt she'd come in her mother's nightie and high heels. Everyone was tête-à-tête, doubtless discussing the vintage of the merlot in hushed tones and agreeing that this year's grape may be pungent, but it lacked a certain je ne sais quoi.

"Doesn't it remind you of the school in *Little House on the Prairie?*" Ben whispered in Liv's ear as they were shown across the low-beamed dining room to their table. This of course was all the excuse they needed to break into ludicrous American accents and find themselves hysterically funny. They devoured their warm bread rolls and then asked for more as they suddenly realised that they hadn't eaten since breakfast. The waitress gave them a sympathetic look as though she were feeding the needy.

"Do you think we'll still behave like five-year-olds when we're seventy?" Liv asked, giving her first hint that she was prepared to talk about anything beyond tomorrow. Which, one glass of champagne down, was the first step to giving up her armoury of toughness and mantle of noncommitment.

"Seventy?" Ben asked, casting his imagination across the decades. "No, when we're seventy we'll be wandering around a farm in Devon scraping our gum boots on our grandchildren and kicking geese."

"Devon? God, I can't imagine a time without sunshine," said Liv. "Couldn't we stay here and have sandy children and mangoes for breakfast forever?"

"Sorry, you're barking up the wrong bloke. I've always wanted to live in England. Well, Russia, actually, but England's got all the miserable weather you can buy. I want a windswept, chilly old age with bleak skies and a library full of books. The sun's no good when you've got the body of a California prune and can't get your kit off without scaring off the local wildlife," Ben remarked as he offered her a bite of his asparagus.

"If you promise that I can have a blackberry bush and pond and you'll bring me duck eggs for breakfast you might have yourself a deal," Liv said as she imagined her grown-up self picking daffodils and packing the children off to school with perfect triangles of marmite sandwiches. But now obviously wasn't going to be the time to be grown-up because, as Liv tried to cut her way through her prosciutto to offer him a taste, her hand slipped and sent her wineglass tumbling, which set off a full-blown chain reaction incorporating the water jug and ending with the candelabra. In Ben's lap.

"That's not a good look." Liv tried not to laugh as the waitress wafted the smell of burning away with a large napkin and offered to douse Ben's trousers with a soda siphon.

"Thanks, I'll be fine." He was an adult for a second before the pair of them exploded into howls the second the waitress's back was turned.

"It all just happened in slow motion," Liv said by way of apology.

"Yeah, well, like I said, you set me on fire."

"I was wondering how long it'd take you before you came out with some atrocious line, Barry Manilow." Liv smiled as the waitress hastily took their credit cards before she got tangled up in a tidal wave or assassination plot or some other disaster that might befall the ill-fated Liv and Ben.

Despite narrowly averted injury, this had been the most fun evening Liv had had in a very, very long time. She wasn't really a druggy clubby girl. She wasn't an athletic, hearty, surfing type, either. She was much more mellowing-out-with-the-man-I-love. It suddenly occurred to her that it wasn't just a coincidence that she'd been in a relationship with Tim for five years. Being part of a couple suited her in the way getting pissed and staying up till five o'clock and crawling to brunch in combats with a hangover suited other girls. It would be unnatural to pretend otherwise. Liv decided that now was the moment to come clean. Then she'd be able to agree to what he wanted. What she wanted more than anything. They could at least give the relationship a try.

"Ben, I've been thinking. About us," Liv began.

"It's not so hard, Liv. You know all you have to do is say yes. I've never felt more serious about anything and—"

"It's not quite so simple."

"There's Will, I know, but maybe you can finish with him when I finish with Amelia—"

"I'm not seeing Will. That was just a rebound moment. There's nothing to finish, thankfully. No, this is a bit more tricky. . . ." Liv took a deep breath. "You see, I," but as she was about to launch into her dog-handling confession she was interrupted by the waitress, who braved life and limb and approached the jinxed table.

"Erm, do you have another credit card, Miss Elliot?" she asked quietly.

"What?" Liv looked up at the interloper.

"This one's been declined." She was a sweet waitress who looked embarrassed to have to ask. Liv the accountant had a bit of a problem.

"Oh no," she said, hunting through her purse for sufficient coinage.

"Here." Ben handed the waitress his card again. "Put the rest on here. See, that's God's way of saying if you'd let me pay in the first place . . ." He looked at Liv, who had just had a minor epiphany.

"That's God's way of saying I'm no longer an accountant and now I'm a fully fledged designer of small, tight swimsuits." Liv smiled proudly. She'd been longing for something like this to happen since she opened her junior savings account aged twelve.

"Congratulations." Ben leaned over and kissed her.

"It's actually a really big deal, because for the first time in my life I've been totally, utterly irresponsible and hopeless without having to try." She laughed out loud and the whispering couples thought it might be better for all concerned if the couple in the corner left. Which they did.

They clambered back up the scrub of the hillside with a bit of bruising and battering on the way. At the top they collapsed onto the back lawn and looked up at the stars.

"That was gorgeous," Liv said as Ben pulled a tin of tobacco from his pocket and began to roll a spliff. "And I've been thinking." He stopped for a second and looked up at her. "Me and you. I really would like to try . . ." Liv laughed nervously to fill the silence. Ben wrapped his tobacco back up and put it to one side.

"And I hope that when I tell you what I'm about to tell you—"

"Liv, that's so fantastic. You won't regret it. I promise." He gave the biggest rib-crunching hug and kissed her face over and over again.

Liv pulled back. "But I'm not so perfect as you imagine, Ben. I mean I'm really so far from perfect. I can behave badly and—"

"God don't I know it. You're remarkably filthy for such an angelic-looking girl. You know, the morning after Mardi Gras I was so beaten up and scratched and—"

"I am not filthy." Liv laughed as he kissed her neck and began to run his fingers up and down her spine. God, now was not the time to tell him, was it? She'd do it tomorrow. She promised.

"I've got you. I can't believe it—you're mine."

"Okay. But just a word of warning. If you play true to boy form and dump me brutally or break my heart I'll get my contacts in the gay Mafia to break your legs and boil your cat. All right?" Liv tried to look forbidding.

"So we're going out together?" He looked like his team had just won a test match.

"As of the moment you're no longer going out with Amelia," Liv added.

"Oh, she'll get over it." Ben laughed. "I'm sure she's already got her next target lined up anyway."

"My god, who?" Liv asked.

"Good with women and horses." Ben smiled, paying much more attention to stroking Liv's shoulder than the fact that his girlfriend was in love with someone else.

A lightbulb went on for Liv. "If you're talking about the person I think you're talking about, then Amelia would never survive. Not only is he about to father someone else's child, he's dirt-poor and he'd never be able to keep her in the manner to which she's accustomed." Liv was thinking of Rob and congratulating herself on having spotted Amelia's penchant for him the first time they ever met.

"Then you're thinking of the wrong bloke. This lucky bastard owns this place, for one thing. Along with seven stud farms in the Western Districts and a few department stores in the States."

"Then we needn't spare another thought for Amelia, had we? Who is this guy anyway? Guess he's out of the country on business a lot, hey?" Liv asked, looking out over the hilltop and down the valley. At least as it wasn't Rob, Amelia would be able to afford to have her highlights redone from time to time.

"Nah, he's a dyed-in-the-wool Aussie. Now what about us?" Ben pulled Liv towards him and gave her a slow, warm kiss.

★   ★   ★

"So, best that you don't come in, I think," Liv said as Ben pulled up outside the cottage early on Monday morning.

"No, I'll leave you to explain all this to Laura . . . unless you want me to come in and just sort of be there."

"She'll be fine. Leave it to me. And I guess this is it then. We don't get to speak till . . ."

"I think after the party's best, don't you?" Ben looked downcast. "To be on the safe side."

"Yeah, I guess. Well, until then . . ." She leaned in and kissed him one last time. "Thanks so much. I've had the most brilliant time, you know."

"I really, really do think you're incredible, Liv. I love the way you are."

"Bye." Liv picked up her bags and virtually sprang out of the car and up the path. Did life get much better?

Once inside, she collapsed onto the sofa with a goofy look on her face. Alex had left a note to say she was at the library and Liv wouldn't have to tell Laura until after the party at least. Until Amelia knew what was going on in her own private life then it was pretty unfair to tell anyone else anyway. Except for Alex of course. And James. Oh, and Dave. Oh god, she felt a lurch of shame when she thought of Dave. How could she ever have behaved so stupidly with all that dog-handling stuff? To use Ben like some experiment. To not return his calls. To be all the things he said he hated— manipulative, steely. Oh, hell. And she just hadn't been able to tell him this morning in the car on the way home. It was just so sunny and the music was just a bit too loud and they were having such a nice time it would have been criminal to ruin things. It all felt like she'd missed the moment. Still, what he didn't know was not ever going to hurt him, was it? And really, how bad had it been? It was just a stupid prank. Nobody got hurt. What was a little manipulation, a little massaging of the facts, between friends? Besides which, he was never going to find out—he thought butter wouldn't melt in her mouth and she was pure and innocent as driven snow. Try mucky slush, she thought, and put the whole matter out of her mind guiltily.

"Good weekend?" Laura walked into the room and smiled warmly.

"Yeah, really nice, thanks."

"Liv, I have a confession to make." Laura sat down and looked guilty. "I'm sorry, but I haven't been completely honest with you. . . ."

Liv didn't know whether to let Laura go on and tell her everything or just explain that she knew the whole story of Laura's Lunacy, but she didn't get a choice. Laura, unlike Liv, was in confessional mode and Liv could do nothing but sit back and hear her side of the story until she got pins and needles in her foot.

So Laura told Liv everything. Beginning with the fact that she'd been thrown back into old behaviour patterns when she talked to Ben on the phone. Like his voice had set off some reaction in her. She'd panicked when she heard him and lied to Liv about what happened because she couldn't face seeing him again—couldn't face the possibility that he might be calling by, staying over the night, bumping into her in the bathroom in the mornings. Liv explained that she was perhaps taking the scenario a little too far as he was still going out with Amelia, but Laura explained that there was little that was rational about her problem. Though she'd talked to her shrink about it and they were working through it. Above all, she was very, very sorry and understood if Liv wanted to throw her out. Of course Liv wanted no such thing and the girls ended up making up.

"Now there's not a single skeleton left in any closet, right?" Liv asked hopefully.

"Absolutely not. I know you think all this therapy is a bit

extreme, but it's really helped me," Laura confided. "Three months ago I wouldn't have been able to cope with this. I'd have been a complete emotional train wreck."

"Always look on the bright side of life then, eh?" Liv attempted. It was Monty Python, but it sounded sensible enough.

"Yeah. Life's a piece of shit when you look at it." Laura laughed.

And they began to whistle and sing the song until they were rolling off the sofa laughing in a completely bonded and totally insane way.

"Oh, Liv, by the way." Laura stopped for a second. "There was one more thing. . . ."

"Oh hell, what?" Liv asked as she caught her breath.

"A guy called Tim called. He said he's staying at the Ritz-Carlton and give him a ring 'cause he's dying to see you."

Chapter Eighteen

The Past Is a Foreign Country— They Do Things Differently There

Liv could very happily not have seen Tim. She had successfully pushed him to the back of some dingy cupboard in her mind along with the time her knicker elastic had given way during the egg and spoon race. He wasn't somewhere she wanted to go. Though she supposed that if she ever had to, then now would be as good a time as any. She was happy and glowing from her weekend away with Ben, and if she looked back to her "I Will Survive" days of misery and damp tissues and imagining her best-case scenario for bumping into Tim again, then this was it. She'd moved on completely and would no more want him back than put her own eye out with a knitting needle.

It was just that opening the cupboard would mean that she'd have to confront a few things—like the fact that she was still angry about the icy-blooded way he'd done it, still bitter about being replaced so quickly by the Sainsbury's woman when he'd claimed only to want space and freedom. And she still thought he was mean and pathetic and small. But maybe she should pity him because he did have the odd sprouting hair on his back (unlike Ben) and played golf (unlike war correspondent Will, who dodged land mines for exercise) and had spent his last few months in the frozen goods section, whereas she'd had forays into club culture, had drag queens lap-dance for her, enjoyed (?) a one-night stand and sex al fresco—something Tim had always refused to do on no grounds other than he couldn't see the point. Which made her a pretty remarkable and accomplished young woman in her eyes. And Tim was still just Tim.

All of which did not mean that she didn't want to look as amazing as she could and play her look-what-you're-missing card. So when she turned up at the Doyles' fish-and-chip cafe with a sundress she'd made herself last week but had decided was a bit too Hands at Home for her weekend with Ben, she expected to attract a bit of attention. The dress was a bit short. And low. And other attention-grabbing things. But instead Tim seemed to be the main attraction in the place.

Not that the place was big and gaping and full to the rafters; it was an outdoor cafe and fish-and-chip shop on the waterfront. Leaning across his table, her skirt riding higher even than Liv's sundress and her blond ponytail falling into his can of Coke, was the waitress. Sixteen if she was a day but nonetheless flirting outrageously. Liv just gleaned the tail end.

."Oh, I live down at Bondi; you have *got* to come and see my view. There's a party tomorrow—" Liv was about to clear her throat to announce her arrival and, she hoped, cause the Elle Macpherson in waiting to flee when she saw the two women at the next table were also peering at Tim over the tops of their menus. Unlike the waitress, these two were only sixteen in their dreams, but presumably intended to use their throaty cigarettey voices and clanking gold charm bracelets and ladies-who-lunch-but-never-cook nails to lure Tim back to their convertible BMWs. Liv was quite amused. Tim must have got himself some new aftershave.

She smiled to herself as she pulled a chair up at his table and leaned over to kiss him.

"Tim," Liv said, then stopped dead in her tracks. This was not the Tim she had known and loved and been engaged to. This was the new, improved formula. Until this minute she'd been so busy sniggering at the hordes of admiring women she had only really recognised Tim by his shoes and watch poking out from behind the waitress. The shoes and watch were, in fact, the only things of Liv's Tim that remained. Or so it seemed.

"Liv. Hi, darling." He leaned over and kissed her chastely (the indignity of it) on the cheeks. "You look gorgeous. Very sporty." Tim smiled as he sank back into his chair. "Just fish and chips; thought we'd walk along the beach and eat them," he said with quiet assurance.

Liv nodded weakly. Sporty? She didn't want to look sporty; she wanted to look heartbreakingly sexy. Beddable. Weddable. Once upon a time she had been. She wouldn't have minded getting the impression that he was just a tiny bit still in love with her. Not so he couldn't sleep and eat and stuff, but just a little "I'll always be a bit in love with Liv Elliot" type effect.

"So how have you been?" He spoke because Liv wasn't going to. She couldn't. It was actually just a physical shock to see him again. The cupboard door flew open and she nearly threw a vinegar bottle at his head for the pain he'd caused her. Instead she smiled.

"Fine. You look tanned already. Been to the Electric Beach sun-bed parlour on Fulham Road?" she asked as she wished she'd left her Hands at Home dress at home and worn one of Alex's ball gowns.

"We stopped over in Hong Kong for a week before we came," Tim said. "You should go. You'd love it. The food's amazing. And the markets. Right up your street." Hong Kong. Hence the tan.

"We?" she asked, preparing herself for the body blow of full disclosure.

"A friend from Freuds," he said mysteriously. Liv racked through all the girls he'd worked with at Freuds and saw only the Glamazons, not the mousy ones. Who was it? Who was he seeing, the elusive bastard? The waitress brought her legs over to the table to distract Tim and placed two bags of sharp vinegar-scented fish and chips in front of them. Well, she sort of threw them at Liv's foot because she wasn't looking at Liv; she was scribbling her phone number on the bill.

"Here. There's a trance party tomorrow night in Avalon. I'm Martha, by the way." She flicked her long blond pony-tail in Liv's face and made her sneeze seven times. She was clearly a witch.

As they walked along the beach Liv was grateful for the huge amount of chips she had to carry (Martha the Witch Wait-ress had given Liv a double helping of lard to improve her own chances in the Race against Tim) because it meant that her puzzled hands were occupied and didn't keep wandering out of habit to his back trouser pocket or tucking themselves through his elbow. Postengagement etiquette was a bit of a problem if you'd never actually made it as far as the altar.

"So I sprained my ankle in Vail; it's still a bit dodgy. Do you think I walk like an old man?" Tim limped ahead of Liv on the beach and made her watch him. She looked at his legs and realised with a huge sense of relief that though he may have set the waitress alight with his very Merchant-Ivory brand of good looks, his legs just weren't her type anymore. Whereas once they'd seemed impossibly elegant, now they only looked spindly. Now she preferred a more . . . Aus-tralian . . . leg. She marvelled at how clever the subconscious is to completely protect you from yourself. If she'd still found Tim attractive, the fact that he was here with the Freuds Glamazon whom he'd clearly fancied all the time he'd been going out with Liv would have been fatal. As it was, it was just irritating and made her curious. So Vail? Excusez-moi? Since when did Tim go to glammy American ski resorts with hot tubs and ankle-spraining activities? How dare he have had a soul-searching journey of his own?

"Looks fine to me," Liv said, "but then maybe your left one's a bit wonky. Is that the one you sprained?" Liv averted her gaze to the harbour. "Sydney's pretty amazing, isn't it?" she said as she sat down on the damp sand and watched the waves lap a few feet away.

"I knew you loved it here. I could tell," Tim said, crashing to the ground next to her and taking off his shoes.

"How?"

"The silence had something to do with it. I figured either you really loved it here or you really hated me." He laughed.

"Actually, it was both. I did hate you."

"You did?"

"Oh course I did, you fucker; you broke my heart and ripped my world apart. I mean I'm fine now and would . . ." She was about to say "no more want you back than put a knitting needle," et cetera, but thought it a bit harsh. "Well, I think we did the right thing by having space and experiencing life and learning about ourselves. It was right for me anyway." She looked at him and recognised the person she'd once known as he turned the sand over with his shoes like a schoolboy. Suddenly she wanted to tell him all the funny things that had happened. She wanted to ask him if he had gone through a phase where he was only attracted to women who were her complete antithesis—like Will had been Tim's antithesis with his sausage legs and black hair. She wanted to tell him how great it was to own her own business and not be an accountant anymore. She wanted to show him Sydney and her amazing new life.

"You hated me?" He looked shocked. "Liv, I thought we

were in agreement. I thought that what we did was right for both of us."

"Yeah, it was, but you were still an unfeeling arsehole. So out of the blue and then just never calling me. We were engaged, for Christ's sake."

"I just thought that I should give you space."

"And you did. Listen, Tim, I thought this might be weird, but actually it's not. Looking at you now, I know that I don't fancy you anymore. And if I'm truthful, I hadn't been in love with you for a while. So really it was for the best. I'm glad I've seen you because now I know it's really over."

"Oh."

"Yeah. We've both moved on. Life's good and I think we can be friends. I'm glad you came."

"You think we should just be friends?"

"Yeah. Now why don't we have dinner one night, you, me, and your"—Liv balked at saying "new girlfriend"; she wasn't *that* sorted—"person that you're here with."

"Okay. That sounds great. I just want to have a chance to see you properly and stuff."

"Sure." Liv smiled at him and felt remarkably grown-up and free. And she'd never noticed before how little she liked the way he sniffed all the time. Had he done that for five whole years and she'd never noticed or was it a new sniff?

"So have you met anyone?" he asked quietly.

"Not really." Liv shrugged. To tell or not to tell about Ben? she wondered. "But I do have a business empire. Well, more of an empire-ette. In fact, you're just the person I need to talk to," Liv said matter-of-factly. So she picked his brain about marketing initiatives. They talked business; their hands were waving around, drawing graphs in the sand, emphasising how important it was to have the right advertising budget. And as they walked along the small beach at Watson's Bay, up the hill towards South Head, Liv gleaned so much invaluable advice from Tim on the marketing strategy for the first six months of Greta's Grundies that she was beginning to remember that she'd liked him for his mind. He was sharp and she was certain he'd already increased her first year's turnover by a zillion percent. Which was a good enough reason for her to have an ex-fiancé.

Well, that and the fact that as they looked out over the Heads, onto the sea, he put his hands on her shoulders and gave her ego the friendliest stroke she could ever have imagined. He tried to kiss her.

"Tim, what are you doing?" She took a step back and looked at him in bewilderment.

"I still love you, Liv," he said.

"No." She couldn't believe it. Had the world gone mad? "Have you gone mad?" she asked.

"I'm sorry. I really am. I just . . . I just don't know if splitting up was the right thing to do. I still think about you all the time, you know."

"Bloody hell." Liv walked away from Tim for a moment's breather. "Just give me a minute, will you, Tim?"

She sat on the grass as he pretended to look around the old lighthouse keeper's cottage. What about the Glamazon? Could Tim really be serious? She also thought extra hard for a second because until that moment she and Tim had been getting on so well. It had been easy, fun, nice, and light, and she knew that even if they were to walk along the beach until they were fifty years old they'd still have something to say to each other, still laugh together. It wouldn't be all fluttery and Ben Parker wonderful, but it would be nice. Was she being mad, being in love with Ben? He still had to chuck Amelia; imagine if he couldn't bring himself to at the last minute. Then she looked back and watched Tim loping around the cottage, caught his profile, the way he smiled at her. And she didn't feel anything. She really wasn't in love with him anymore. No matter how flattering all this was, it was only that. Inconveniently, she was in love with Ben.

"Listen, Tim, I think we should be getting back." She stood up and walked towards him.

"But, Liv, that's why I'm here. I came to get you back."

"You know that's not what I meant. I have a meeting at four o'clock. Anyway, like I said, I don't know that I can ever forgive you for what you did."

"But, Liv . . ."

She remembered the shrine she'd built to him on her dressing table in London and how she'd meditated on his passport photo for a whole week in a bid to conjure him up by witchcraft. And he hadn't so much as called her to make sure she hadn't hurled herself under a bus.

"Besides, getting back with an ex is such a cliché. It's like fancying Brad Pitt or being turned on by a man driving a Ferrari. Sure, it happens, but not to people with any taste."

Chapter Nineteen

It's My Party and I'll Ruin It
if I Want To

Liv knew that her alarm clock was droning away for a reason, but through the fog of sleep she couldn't remember quite why. Not market stall. Even through the fog, she worked out that it wasn't Saturday. It was . . . ? What day was it? What had she done last night? Ah yes. Last night she'd had supper with Alex. Pizza. Beer. Not much out of the ordinary. So today was Thursday. No market stall. Ben? No, she hadn't shaved her legs so she knew for a fact that she wasn't planning to see Ben again until the party. On Thursday. Today. Tonight!

Liv caused trauma to every single one of her vertebrae as she leapt out of bed seconds later. It was more a cat on a towering inferno type leap than a cat on a hot tin roof jive. She was up and at 'em. Today was indeed the day when everything receded into the background apart from canapés, cocktails, RSVPs, having her hair professionally "done" for the first time in her life, and still making it to the venue on time. It was a displacement wedding. She was about to marry her career. It was make or break for Greta's Grundies. If only three fashion assistants arrived on their way to a book launch and the waitresses had to take home the canapés wrapped in bacofoil at the end of the evening, then Liv didn't have a job, a future, or an income. If, however, the supermodel snogged the politician in front of the Greta's Grundies' large pink cardboard logo and seven hundred people lined the street outside in a bid to squeeze through the doors of the over-crowded party, then Liv and Alex had a hit on their hands. The latter, of course, was absolutely the dream-come-true-but-first-you-have-to-sell-your-soul-to-Beelzebub so was a bit unlikely. Somewhere in between would be gratefully appreciated.

"Alex." Liv banged on Alex's bedroom door. "Getting up?"

"I don't feel well!" Alex called out.

"Morning sickness? Then have a glass of water. It's mind over matter," Liv chided as she took a dry handful of Just Right and threw it at her mouth, though most of it escaped to the kitchen floor.

"Laura. You will be finished painting the giant G-string, won't you?" Liv panicked as Laura walked into the dining room rubbing her eyes and still wearing her nightie.

"Sure." Laura sat down on the sofa and reached for the television remote control, flicking on MTV. How could she choose this moment to get over herself and become a normal human being again? How dare she stop obsessing about her work and running round like the cat fresh from the aforementioned towering inferno and instead be as cool as a cold thing?

"Is something wrong, Laura?" Liv asked as she took to her guest list with a pen and began counting ticks next to names.

"I'm fine. In fact, I really am fine. You know, this whole thing between you and Ben has given me closure. I'm really, really well."

"You mean you're better? No more shrink?" Liv asked, astounded yet horrified. Did this mean that Laura would no longer use work as a tool to manage her emotions and so Liv wouldn't be getting her giant painted G-string for tonight's party anytime this side of Christmas?

"I feel fine. In fact, I'm not even going to take a single beta-blocker before tonight's party. Isn't that great? I realise that Ben's just completely ordinary, farts sometimes, gets the odd spot, and has smelly feet bloke. I really like women much better."

"Actually, Laura, that's the man I love you're talking about," said Liv. "But if you go and paint my G-string now I won't hold it against you!" she yelled as she headed for the bathroom before new, chilled Laura had a chance to become a reclining redhead among the bubbles and commandeer the loofah for the day. Right now she looked so relaxed she might just slide off the sofa and evaporate into a puddle on the floor.

Thankfully Alex emerged from the bathroom before Liv could administer any more bossy kicks to Laura's behind.

"Ah, my partner. Thank god we're in this together," Liv proclaimed as she dragged Alex bodily into the bedroom to help her decide which dress she was going to wear tonight. "Then we have to go to the flower market, then the hall, and make sure everything's in place." They had decided to hire out an abandoned church in Woollahra on the simple grounds that they could afford nothing else. Thankfully all the pews had been stolen so they'd just have to decorate the place with twinkling fairy lights, sweep the floors, and fill it with flowers to achieve their desired champagne-fountains-and-marble-staircases effect. Well, almost. They were also borrowing a few of Laura's old sets of Venice and Umbrian hillsides and Paris by moonlight and other schmaltzy things that looked better than mouldy old church walls. That was if Laura ever surfaced again now she'd locked herself in the bathroom. Only violet wafts were coming out from beneath the door.

"Actually, we're not quite in this together because I'm not quite together." Alex sat on the edge of the bed on the exact dress Liv had just planned to wear and burst into tears. "I dumped Rob!" Alex wailed.

"You did what?" Liv didn't really have the time for a crisis, but this was pretty earth-shattering and potentially party-ruining.

"Late last night. I told him I couldn't marry him because I have to stay with Charlie."

"Why?" Liv sat on the bed beside Alex and put her arm around her shaking body.

"It's Luke—he's won this amazing scholarship to a sports academy in the States. His future's guaranteed. How selfish of me would it be to say he couldn't go just because I love Rob? In time maybe we can be friends. But I've got to do it. For Luke. I'm so proud of him. Just it's a fortune, twenty-five thousand dollars a year for three years. I mean our business is okay, but it's not going to make up twenty-five thousand dollars in the next few weeks, is it? I can't afford to leave Charlie. It's as simple as that." Alex sobbed.

"And you told Rob that?" Liv asked, stroking wet strands of hair back from Alex's face.

"Yeah. And he just left. You know what he's like, Livvy: he's uncomplicated. It had never really occurred to him that I was only with Charlie for the money. I mean Charlie knows that and to him it's not such a big deal, but Rob took it badly. I tried calling him all night, but he wasn't at his flat." Alex burst into fresh tears and clung onto Liv.

The minute Alex was tucked up exhausted and asleep in her bed with her pashmina over her and a glass of water and box of tissues beside her in case she woke up, Liv scribbled her a little note telling her to rest and sit in the sun for the day and that they'd work it out later. Then she stole Alex's mobile from her handbag and headed off to the flower market, calling her troops on the way.

"Dave, you've heard of Black Monday?" she said.

"I'm a stockbroker, I live in terror," he replied while also selling grain, just in case Liv had insider information she was about to impart.

"Well, today's Pitch-Black Thursday. Please help."

She also called James and said the same thing, only he said he'd never heard of Black Monday, but he had a fuck of a hangover so would gladly come and hang out in a silent, darkened church hall for the day. If she provided him with a can of Diet Coke and an Egg McMuffin he'd be there in fifteen. Result. Liv also called Tim, but he wasn't in his room. She imagined him in his green silk jacket on a Captain Cook Cruise on the harbour with his Glamazon, who didn't know that he also liked shorter, darker, less attractive girls. She left a message telling him where the church was and asking him to pull on some old jeans and come along. Cheeky maybe, but if ever there was an hour of need it was now.

So by the time Liv got back from the flower market with a fieldful of antique roses in the back of Laura's car there was a lineup of unwilling men sitting on the wall of the church, smoking and basking in the sunshine. Well, lineup of three, Dave, James, and Tim, and they seemed to be getting on well, with James using Tim's green jacket as a parasol and Dave and Tim locked in conversation.

Liv screeched the car to a halt and fell out before either could impart incriminating stories about her to the other. "Boys, oh, thank you so much." She ran around the back of the car and opened the boot to unload her roses. "I've got the key. James, will you open up?" Liv handed over the key and James creaked to his feet.

"Where's my Macca, Livvy? You promised."

"I'll zip down to Bondi Junction and get you one in a second. And, Tim? James? Big Macs all round?"

They nodded as they removed the boxes from the boot and carried them along the cracked concrete path to the church. As Liv lurched up behind them under the weight of boxes of fairy lights she wondered if she and Alex had done the right thing in hiring this place. It had only cost fifty dollars and she hadn't seen the inside yet. They should probably have taken Amelia up on her offer of her apartment, but given the circumstances Amelia might well find out the Terrible Truth and leave them high and dry.

Though it was looking terrifyingly as if they were high and dry now.

"Are you sure this is the right place for your rocking, glitzy party?" Tim asked as he looked suspiciously at the six-foot spider's web obscuring the rotting church doors.

"I think so." Liv was glad she'd given James the key and was about to offer him an extra cheeseburger if he opened the door for them. But thankfully his glasses were so dark that he couldn't see anything as minor as the bird-sized spider that was waiting menacingly for lunch in the corner of its web. Instead he lumbered straight into the doorway, bouncing back slightly as the web resisted him, but putting it down to bad coordination due to his hangover.

"Ooohh, bit unsteady there," he groaned as he broke through the web and tried to fit the key into the door.

As it creaked open on its hinges and a smell like an old tomb engulfed them, Liv decided this was karma for her affair with somebody else's boyfriend. Lust had brought her here, to this dark, festering hole, instead of to the camellia-scented Designer's Guild waftiness of Amelia's immaculate apartment. Liv was the Damned, Amelia clearly Exalted. With wings.

"Okay, who's going in first?" James said as even his some-what diminished senses railed against the stench from the tomb. The tomb where they were going to host tonight's party for three hundred of Sydney's best-dressed and most celebrated Clean People. If it had been vampires or smeggy hippies with dogs on string, no problemo. But they were Fashionistas. These were Exalted Amelia's friends in Colette Dinnigan.

"I'm off to McDonald's. Won't be long." Liv backed away from the potential horrors within and sprinted to her car, leaving the boys to deal. Which was presumably what boys were for.

As Liv picked up her three brown bagfuls of burgerish things Alex's phone rang: "We need Vim." It was Tim. "And Domestos. And a kettle to boil water so buckets, too, and cloths. Oh, and, Livvy?"

"Yes?"

"Humane mousetraps. But big ones. For rats," he said gravely. Though he could have said it in a light and trifling way and it would still have had the same effect on Liv's arm hair.

"Okay," she whispered, and hung up. She wasn't in the mood to hear about the vampire bats clinging to the rafters. Or was that what the Vim was for maybe? She made her way to the hardware store across the road from McDonald's and increased their annual profits by a lot.

And of course Sydney, city of sparkle and weather and the like, chose that lunchtime to have one of its downpours. Not sprinkles of pretty April rain like England in spring. Not even the added interest of an electric thunderstorm. Quite simply, it pissed down torrents. Elizabeth Street was inches deep in slapping, lapping waves of water. The drains gurgled like the underworld was about to pop out for an Away-Day break. Liv couldn't park the car near the church because she couldn't see if there were yellow lines or not. And by the time she made it back inside, the hamburgers were soup and the brown paper had disintegrated in her hands.

"Sorry, boys." Liv ducked through the church door in trepidation.

"Don't panic, Livvy. I think it'll be okay!" Tim called out of the darkness, but it was too late. Liv had seen it and should have been struck blind or turned to stone, so unspeakable was the sight. A hole in the roof the size of . . . ohhh, a tennis court . . . an Olympic swimming pool . . . something like that. Big.

"Heellpppp!" It was a wail from a deep dark place. Liv dropped the burgers to the floor and they floated away on a slipstream that, had she brought her boogie board along, she could have surfed beautifully. "What are we going to dooo?" she cried.

"We've got a plan." Tim came and stood beside her, seemingly ignorant of the rat that had just run off with his lunch, and looked at the church hall as though it were a house in Hampstead that just needed a lick of paint to make the pages of *World of Interiors*. "See, what we thought was . . ." He waved his arm around the room and began to describe his vision.

And Tim was right. All it needed was several hours of scrubbing and slopping out water and for the rain to stop and more Vim than you can shake a stick at and the dismissal of the rodent population to the garden of a nearby pub (yes, they had some bad karma coming their way for that one, but hopefully it wouldn't arrive till tomorrow) and a lot of sweeping and just a bit of weeping (James), and there they had it. A work of art. Well, maybe not. Maybe just a church with a few cracked stained-glass windows and no pews, but still . . . Dave rigged up some electricity (again courtesy of a cable to the local pub and not necessarily legal, but . . .) and Liv scattered her flowers liberally and then at three o'clock Laura arrived with Jo-Jo on the bus with the scenery. And at four-thirty Alex arrived with very puffy eyes and a bagload of scented candles. But she was there and everything was in place, and just as Liv was about to stand on a chair and thank her team from the bottom of her heart and stuff, she remembered. Hair. Five o'clock. Double Bay.

"Bye, guys. Love you all. Couldn't do without you." And she vanished into the humid afternoon leaving her troops without a leader, but all secretly relieved because they'd been wondering all day how they could broach the subject of her hair. Which was, to say the least, not the best.

The evening sun left only a glow on the golden sandstone walls of the church, and after the taxi driver stopped to let Liv and Alex out he wolf-whistled them and they turned and curtseyed to him.

"Good on ya, girls!" he called out as he drove away.

A man walking his dog on the other side of the street got himself into a bit of a huff because while he didn't mind the gays moving into his street if they were professionals and worked in advertising and the like, he did object if they came lowering the tone with their frocks and women's clothing and such. But thankfully Liv and Alex only looked like transvestites from a distance to shortsighted old men. Up close they were divine. Made in Barbara Taylor-Bradford Land Lingerie Queens of all the knickers they created. They walked arm in arm along the candle-lined path towards the church with their hair high and expectations soaring.

"Do you think there are many people there yet?" Liv

asked nervously as a taxi pulled up to the curb and two black-twined women with Dior bags stepped out.

"They might just be going to a dinner party down the road," Alex muttered as they kept walking bravely towards the door of the church.

"No, they're coming here. Help." Liv's kitten heels clicked *FEAR* in Morse code on the path. "Are you okay now?" Liv asked Alex as the Dior bags shuffled cautiously behind them. Well, they'd heard of some outré venues, but this one? This one took the low-fat biscuit and no mistake.

"I'll survive. Then tomorrow I'll have a nervous breakdown. But Laura was sweet and said some really useful things this afternoon," Alex said, and Liv wished she'd persuaded Laura to have a pyre for her self-help manuals this morning so that they wouldn't be handed down to her best friend. Who would swiftly become her ex–best friend if she so much as mumbled the word *closure* in her sleep. "I forgot to ask you what you thought of Tim and," Alex began, but the Diors had crept up on them and the door of the party loomed large.

"This isn't some sort of Rocky Gothic Horror party, is it?" the first Dior, who happened to be the chief buyer for an American department store, asked.

"God, I hope not. McQueen had one last week in London. Never want to see another black olive as long as I live."

The second Dior replied, "By the way, this is the Victoria Loftes show, isn't it?"

As Liv pushed open the heavy door she detected not a whiff of mildew. Merely an overwhelming draft of Annick Goutal scent gracing the assembled fashion tribe and the low throb of James's dance music.

"Weellllll," said the first Dior ambiguously as Liv and Alex stepped among the fray. The room was now a mission statement for Greta's Grundies: the walls were dreamily awash with views from the Bridge of Sighs, the chestnut trees along the banks of the Seine, and on the back wall above the altar a vision of hell, all red and raw and in flames, and the bar was cleverly disguised as a G-string, which you actually had to lean across if you wanted to be served any number of champagne cocktails. The little bit of leftover accountant in Liv shuddered as she noticed the beautifully clad young women knocking back the booze as though they'd mistakenly read that you should drink at least two litres of champagne a day, rather than the customary mineral water, for clear skin and thin legs. But they did at least seem to be having an amazing time. Charlie had pulled out the stops and brought along every single member of his polo team and a handful of young squillionaires, so the boy–girl dynamic was working out very well. Especially given the high quotient of boys who like girls with thin legs and girls who liked boys to buy them things. The presence of the G-string and alluring red of hell no doubt fuelling the erotic ambience and improving everyone's chances of pulling. So far Liv hadn't seen a single person she recognised, but she took that as a good sign.

"Drinks methinks," Alex said as she led Liv towards the bar.

"For sure. It's going well, isn't it?"

"It's what the Americans call a fanny bumper," Alex said. "Why don't you go and circulate and I'll bring your drink over."

"Okay," Liv said reluctantly. Circulate? She didn't know anyone and these people probably had no desire to have her crash their conversations about what happened last night at the International or who was dressing Nicole Kidman for the Oscars.

"Liv, this is awesome." It was Amelia, looking stunning. Looking so good that Liv would contemplate taking her home tonight, not to mention what every man in the room wanted to do with her. Her skin shimmered in that damp modelly way that Liv remembered was always described as dewy. Her hair had sheen; she reflected light and beauty like a human sequin.

"You look great," Liv said simply.

"Thanks." Amelia inhaled the compliment. "So what's all this about Rob and Alex splitting up?" Amelia asked without bothering to lower her voice even though Charlie's soap star was standing inches away from them, chatting into her mobile as usual.

"Who told you about Rob and Alex?" Liv asked, thinking erroneously that she was the only person in the world to share in the secret, not just of their breakup but of their affair.

"Oh, you know I knew. I told Alex that he was the best bloody catch in Sydney. She's a fool if she gives him up," Amelia said as she scanned the room for the photographer.

"You meant Charlie was the best catch in Sydney, didn't you?" Liv whispered.

"Did I buggery. Jesus, he's got ears like the World Cup. No, Rob's the man; he'll make a great father, too."

"Yeah, but he's not exactly, well, rolling in it, is he?" Liv tried to be tactful, but she thought that Amelia was bright enough to realise why Rob wasn't going to be the husband and father that Alex needed. "And the thing is that Alex has these family reasons for needing to be—"

"You're kidding, aren't you? Robbie not rich enough. Where did you get that from?" Amelia had to hold onto her glass for support as she shook with laughter.

"Well, he can't make much money as a stable hand, can he?" Liv said, lowering her voice even further as she saw Alex approaching with the drinks.

"Stable hand." Amelia clearly thought this the best joke since Bill Clinton and nearly fell off her heels.

"What's so funny?" Alex approached, a smile stretched

across her face, but there were visible signs of sadness; she looked tired and older than usual.

But before Liv could divulge all, Amelia was snapped up by the photographers who wanted to take her picture next to the G-string, so she never got to share her mirth with Alex.

"Have you spoken to Ben yet?" Alex asked as she and Liv clinked glasses on their venture and the minor triumph that was not having to host the party in a room full of rats and bats . . . though given the assembled photographers and fashion hags . . .

"I'll go and say hello when he's stopped talking to that girl over there," said Liv.

"I'd go over now if I were you, Livvy. That girl's Helena Christensen." Liv looked over and, indeed, resting her arm lightly on Ben's was another dewy temptress. Lord, the world was peppered with them.

"Well, I suppose I should just say a casual hello so people don't suspect." She looked over at him all crisp in his white shirt and the casual way he was chatting but not leering at Helena and her heart simply soared. She felt light and happy and awash with warmth. If not love. "I suppose if I completely ignore him that'll look even more suspicious," she said while praying for an instant five-inch height spurt. By the time she'd arrived at Ben's right elbow it still hadn't been granted, so she stood on tiptoes instead and smiled warmly at Helena.

"Hi, Liv. Great party," Ben said, and winked at her discreetly.

"Thanks. I'll see you around then." She was shaking and could think of nothing else to say. She swore he was laughing at her nervousness but felt she'd already overstepped the mark. But what the hell, she leaned over and patted his arm. "Good to see you," she added. She knew she'd be rendered asthmatic at her obviousness tomorrow, but right now she was, if not the Greta of Greta's Grundies, then at least the power behind the pants. And tonight she looked the part— she'd washed the sand out of her hair for once and was swathed in a long pale blue dress, her hair was pulled up into a froth of curls, and her lips were a very kissable ruby colour. Not bad for a lass from just outside Basingstoke, basically.

"You look beautiful," Ben whispered as Helena turned to grab a canapé.

"Thanks. So I'd better mingle, I suppose." She smiled.

"I'll see you later. I really can't wait," he added before she walked away with all the conviction of a yo-yo. Leaving a boyfriend-to-be alone with a supermodel was never going to be the highlight of any girl's evening.

So Liv had used up her can-only-be-seen-together-in-public-before-people-begin-to-talk allowance of forty-five seconds and would now have to spend the rest of the evening circumnavigating Ben as if he were a globe or the South Pole. Something to be avoided lest she crashed. But that didn't matter, as she needed to be networking or something very eighties like that. Wasn't everyone in the room supposed to be wondering who the business brain behind this starkly original lingerie line was?

"You are positively a wunderkind, darling. It's a genius idea," a gravelly fashion voice declared.

"You took the words out of my—" Liv turned and smiled a flashing smile of success at the voice.

"Thanks, but you know it's a piece of piss really. Just godda do a little drawing and run the thing up on the sewing machine. Nothing to it," Amelia was saying as she lapped up the praise graciously. Liv looked at her own pinpricked hands, a monument to struggle; each bikini she'd sewn with her bare hands was a triumph over unlikeliness. The accountant turned designer. Not an everyday tale of modern transformation.

"Well, I think it's fantastic. We'd love to put a photo of you at the loom or whatever on the cover of next month's issue, your hair kind of a bit skewiff from a night of toil but the glow of achievement in your cheeks. You know what I mean," said the voice.

"Yeah, right." Amelia grinned vacantly and Liv wept inwardly. Christ, she had the ego of a designer now, too.

To distract herself from the grisliness of Amelia and a roomful of untenably thin, gleaming girls, Liv headed over to the music corner where James and his decks were keeping everyone's hips swaying.

"Not a bad do, sweetheart." Tonight James was Shirley Bassey. His big wig and dazzling dress had already prompted one young designer to come and ask him if he'd be in his next show. James had said he'd think about it but was secretly planning his new life tripping in Cindy Crawford's footsteps: Concorde, hemorrhoid cream for the bags under his eyes, no food. Ever. Just cigarettes. "It's every suburban girl's fantasy," he informed Liv. "But do you think I'll need a body double for advertising work? Like Claudia?"

"They'd be insane if they insisted on one," Liv told him honestly.

"Listen, babe, Dave and I are just off to the dunny for a bit of a buzz. Will you look after this stuff for me?" James put a pair of headphones on Liv's ears and whistled Dave over from across the room.

"What do I do?" Liv yelled too loudly.

"Slip the Fat Boy Slim on next and look cool." And James and Dave vanished into the loos.

As she stood there looking like a mad hag with her headphones on, Liv tried to spot Ben. Just so she could gaze upon him. Watch him in action. Work up an appetite for the time when they'd be together. But he was nowhere to be seen. Still, at least Helena and Amelia were accounted for in the corner where they appeared to be gazing at their own reflections in each other's shiny cheeks.

"Here—you first," James said as he proffered his perfectly chopped lines on the back of the loo.

"Cheers. I'm proud of our girls out there. Doing pretty well, hey?"

"Yeah. So how was Liv's weekend away?"

"Dunno, I haven't spoken to her yet, but have you checked out the cheesecake ex-fiancé?" James took his turn. "She swears he doesn't so much as light her touchpaper anymore, though. Shame."

"Yeah, well, Amelia's bloke hasn't taken his eyes off her all night. How's that for dog handling? She played the game and reeled him in. And he fell for it, the stupid mutt. I wonder when she'll tell him he's been had," said Dave.

"Personally, I can't believe he was such a sucker to fall for it. I mean didn't he see that she was leading him on? I'd have seen it coming from a mile away—all that blowing hot and cold and not returning his phone calls. Do you reckon all straight blokes are so clueless?"

"Dunno. She did have the best tuition, though. I was pretty spot on with all my dog-handling advice—naughty, naughty, bad, bad dog." Dave laughed.

"I reckon she should lose him soon, though—it's pretty bad karma to keep him hanging on for too long when she knows she's just gonna kick him to the kerb. Still, it's been pretty entertaining."

"Are you gonna have that last line or me?" Dave muttered as he rolled his stash back up and put it in his pocket.

"All yours, mate."

Outside the toilet cubicle Ben stood stock-still and listened. Then he turned and walked back into the party. Looking for Liv.

In the corner of the room (well, now more the focal point

of the room as the voices and emotions scaled new heights)
stood Rob, in his usual muddy boots, denim shirt, and moleskins, waving a can of Foster's around in his hand to empha-
sise his point.

"Okay, I know that you were only trying to be honest
with me and I know that Charlie has so much more to offer
you than me, but I love [kind of came out as "lubb," but
everyone knew what he was getting at] you, Alex."

"What's going on, mate? You all right?" Charlie had approached Rob now and was trying to placate him. Liv
looked for Alex, but she was attempting to crawl behind a
Paris in the Springtime mural.

"Fucking oath I'm all right. Just that I love [again, "lubb"]
your woman here and she won't have me. She's having our
baby, you know?" Rob said as Alex disappeared completely
behind the Seine. Charlie nodded calmly, for which Liv
thought he deserved a few brownie points, or was he simply
about to erupt like a dormant World War I bomb discovered
in a garden in Streatham?

"Listen, mate, why don't we just go outside and talk this
through." Charlie put his arm out towards Rob, but he
shook it off.

"Come out here!" Rob yelled to Alex.

A foot appeared, then a chandelier-type earring emerged,
and then a shamed-looking Alex. "I'm sorry," she whispered.

"Oh, this is bloody ridiculous," Charlie said, and Alex slid
her glance down to the floor to avoid his eyes, "Do you love
Rob?" Alex looked petrified as he asked this. Liv gulped
down more air like a goldfish out of water and even the
dance music was having a bit of quiet time. Then Liv remembered. Hadn't Amelia said something about Rob not
being a stable hand at all? Liv cast her mind back to her rival's
earlier hilarity. Then she remembered. Rob was rich; he was
loaded.

In fact, it suddenly dawned on Liv that Rob was the catch

of the decade that everyone had been nattering on about for ages. Jesus, she really should tell Alex before she went any further and stuffed up her whole life monumentally by choosing Charlie because she thought *he* was the rich one who could help her support her brothers. Liv twitched her arm towards the back of the scenery, hoping to be able to take Alex to one side and explain so that she could be fully informed before she made this decision, which would affect the rest of her life. Alex barely noticed Liv. What else could Liv do to attract her attention? She pondered a rugby-scrum-type head-to-head but was too attached to her earrings to risk them. Instead Liv just opened and shut her mouth some more à la goldfish.

Alex looked soberly from one man to the other. She took in Rob, all strapping six-foot-two with mud on his boots and beer on his breath, and she took in Charlie, swish shirt, calm and in control and promising all she could want for the future of her child and family if he'd still have her after this embarrassing scene.

"Well, Alex, are you in love with him?" Charlie asked again, more gently this time.

"Yes," Alex said as she took in the oafishness of the father of her child.

Liv nearly leapt in the air and yelled, "Correct! That is the correct answer! Yippee! Score one, pink team." But only nearly.

"All right. And, Rob, you're in love with her, right, mate?" Charlie continued as Liv watched his steely eyes for the moment when he banged their heads together like a livid schoolteacher.

"Guess so," Rob said, breaking the mates' code of honour and risking eternal exile from the horsy set. But still Liv felt thrilled. Except for poor Charlie. His girlfriend was in love with someone else. And poor Rob, even though he was rich, he still thought Alex had preferred Charlie to him, and poor Alex, in fact, most poor Alex. Because Alex was now looking at Charlie with the fear of God etched across her face and her head filled with thoughts of her future in penury with penniless Rob.

"But what about you, Charlie? I'm so sorry," she said as she remained frozen to the spot. The dance music was now no longer as James was perched high on Dave's shoulders at the back of the crowd, his Shirley Bassey makeup petrified into a look of expectation along with the rest of the crowd.

"Me? Oh, sweetheart, I'm all right. I don't deserve someone as clever as you—you're wasted on me—and I'm certainly not ready for a kid yet. No, you and Robbie go off and make sure I'm godfather to the little bloke, won't you?" He went over and put a reassuring arm around Alex, who gave him a huge and grateful hug. "Anyway, I've been rooting this weathergirl for a while now, so don't worry too much about it." He laughed lecherously and all was returned to normal.

Well, not exactly normal. Alex and Rob hugged and snogged and patted the baby bump and the fashion crowd turned back to their complimentary bags of knickers and it occurred to Liv that maybe they should launch a perfume to go with the knickers. She was about to tap Alex on the shoulder to remind her to remind Liv tomorrow she should tell her about the great idea she'd had.

"Alex, just a quickie," she said but couldn't be heard. She tapped again.

"The thing is, I love you even though we're going to have to struggle through. I love you even though I'm going to have to sell my flat in London to pay for my brother's college fees. Because I do. I just bloody well love you, Rob, and I love our baby and I'm so glad it's not going to be spoiled rotten and given silver rattles from Tiffany for its christening and have a nanny and stuff because, well, I didn't and you didn't and look at us. We're great. We're dirt-poor and we're wonderful and we know the value of love." Alex was clearly on a roll and Liv thought it rude to interrupt her. Instead she scribbled the perfume idea on the back of her hand in lip liner and tiptoed away, thinking that very soon indeed Alex would be finding out the value of true love and it was around the billion-dollar mark.

"Liv, we need to talk." Ben tapped Liv on the shoulder and she whipped around.

"Ben, sweetheart . . . do you think we should be—?"

"Sweetheart?" Amelia screeched. "What the bloody hell is going on here? Since when has my boyfriend been your sweetheart?"

The music, now accustomed to such excitement, was trained to turn itself down automatically and the crowd resumed their places and faces of expectation as the promise of another scene beckoned. And they thought this was just some little launch party and that they'd all leave at seven-thirty and go to dinner. No way, this was better than *de la Guarda*. In fact, the editor of *Vogue* vowed that she'd sponsor Greta's Grundies' next party if it was going to be this entertaining. Liv looked at Amelia, who was looking at Ben, who was inspecting his shoes.

"Well?"

"Millie, I think we should go outside and discuss this one," Ben said as he shifted uncomfortably and shot Liv perhaps the filthiest look she'd ever received. What on earth was going on? Was he suddenly blaming her for all this? Oh hell, why had she let slip that "sweetheart"? How could she have been so slack?

"What, and disappoint our audience?" Amelia shimmered

again. But with rage this time. "We'd all really like to know what you and thingy have been getting up to. Wouldn't we?"

Liv took "thingy" to be her. Each audience member stared at the dandruff on the shoulders of the person in front of him or her—the well-bred equivalent of baying for blood. Liv wondered if she were about to be lynched.

She contemplated crawling under the legs of the crowd, between the sea of stilettos, the mass of Gina mules, beneath the Christa Davis skirts and bias-cut hemlines. But then she looked up and realised that she was being watched. Not by the masses who were much more curious to see the beautiful ones arguing than to gaze at the cause of the tiff, i.e., Liv in the borrowed dress and now-wilting hair. She was being watched by Tim. And she suddenly felt very embarrassed to be in this situation. Here she was, reduced to playing the Other Woman, in what amounted to a barroom brawl. So she looked away quickly and ducked down low, taking her first option and crawling under the legs towards the door.

As she stood up by the door and rubbed her aching knees she came face-to-face with—hell, how did he get here first—Tim.

"Ha," she said.

"Ha?" Tim asked.

"Ha. Interesting evening." Liv looked nervously over her shoulder in case the crowd were about to drag her bodily into the stocks.

"Interesting choice of boyfriend." Tim smiled enigmatically.

"You know I don't really have time for this right now, Tim. I may be about to die." Liv moved into an alcove in the church porch, out of harm's way.

"You didn't tell me you were seeing somebody." He looked offended.

"And neither did you." Liv wondered what Tim had done

with the Glamazon this evening. Was she all alone in her hotel room watching *Debbie Does Dallas* on cable?

"That's because I'm not."

"Oh, and who was the 'we' who were here?" Liv asked. "And who was the girl you were seen with in Sainsbury's by Alex's hairdresser?"

"I'm not seeing anyone. I may have had the odd miserable one-night stand here and there and may have popped to the supermarket with one of them to buy the Sunday papers and a carton of orange juice, but nothing more serious than that. I told you, Liv, I've missed you. There's nobody else."

"Oh, come on; you said you were here with someone from Freuds. Was it that Sophie Barker with the nutcracker thighs who wore stockings and suspenders even in winter? Had you swapped phone numbers with her in case you ever managed to lose me? You know: 'Sophie Barker, why don't you keep in touch with me in case one day I leave Liv behind on a bus or something?' Like an umbrella."

"I came over with George from Freuds. The guy with the pale eyelashes."

"George George?" Liv asked. Her hair now matched her spirits and was leaning, Marge Simpson–like, in Tim's direction.

"George George," Tim confirmed.

Liv winced. "I'm sorry. I just assumed."

"S'okay. So what happened with that guy? He was giving you some pretty dark looks. You in trouble?"

"With Ben?" Liv peered back to see how the drama was unfolding in the hall. "No. But I wasn't completely honest with you when we were out on the beach the other day. You see—"

"Being dishonest's a bit of a habit then, is it?" Ben had appeared from nowhere and was now standing in front of her. And if she wasn't mistaken he was shaking.

"Ben, what on earth's going on? Did I really land you in it? God, I'm so sorry to leave you in there, but I thought that it was probably for the best and—"

"So when were you going to break it to me, Liv?"

"What?" Liv looked at Ben, then at Tim. "Oh, you mean Tim. I should have introduced you. Tim's just my ex-fiancé. He's here on holiday. Ben, meet Tim." Liv smiled.

"Liv, cut the bullshit." Ben was deathly pale as he stood in the doorway. "I know what you were playing at. I know about your game."

"Ben, what on earth are you talking about?" Liv asked, but of course deep down she knew exactly what he was talking about. There was only one game. He had to mean the dog handling. She had no idea how he knew, but she suddenly felt sick to her stomach.

"Jesus, and I thought Amelia was immoral and shallow." He looked at her with undisguised contempt and walked down the path away from the party.

"Ben!" Liv called. "Wait a minute. I can explain. Please." Liv ran after him. "Please let me—oh shit—please just listen to me."

"Leave it," he snapped at her, and she stopped running.

"I listened to *you!*" she called out after him. "When I thought you'd been a shit and didn't understand the truth I heard you out. That's the least you owe me."

"I've had enough." He carried on walking.

"Tomorrow. I'll come and see you. Explain. You have to let me. Please, Ben."

He stopped, turned around, and looked at her with a cold-ness that made her feel so small and ashamed she could have cried.

"Four-thirty at mine. Then I'm going on a dig for six weeks. Thank god I won't so much as have to look at you again. And whatever you have to say better be an awesome reason or don't bother coming," he spat, and walked away.

Had Liv had a G-string handy at that moment she just might have hanged herself from the church doorway. The fashion editors and fractious couples would have had to bend under her dangling shoes and floppy body in order to leave the party. And let them look up her skirt if they wanted. She had nothing left to lose. Least of all dignity. No. There was no hiding place from the wretchedness that was her life.

"Been looking for you everywhere. You're a bit of a star, aren't you? Causing all that trouble. Wooh, baby. Go." It was James. He came equipped with a bottle of neatest, purest, most inviting whisky.

Liv looked at it and felt a longing in her heart. Here was a solution to her problems. "I can't tell you how much I need this right now." She yanked the bottle from James's grasp. "Ben knows everything, you know. How in hell's name did he find out is what I want to know? Do you think Amelia knew somehow and told him? I mean absolutely nobody knows apart from me and Alex and you and Dave . . ." Liv took a swig from the bottle. "What do you think? Where do you think he could have heard about it?" Liv looked at James with bewilderment and shock. Ben had just walked away and god knows whether he was ever going to forgive her. She should have told him about all this when she had the chance. At the house. Now she wondered if he'd ever believe her. "What am I going to do, James?" she pleaded. But James was gone. Scotch mist.

"Tim, I'm sorry. I should have told you about Ben the other day. I guess I just didn't quite find the moment. Story of my bloody life." Liv banged her head in frustration. How many people could she alienate in one day? She slid, followed by a concerned-looking Tim, out of the porch into the vestry. Well, what had been the vestry. It was now the resting place of a few down-and-outs, a lot of rats, and what looked suspiciously like a dead fashion editor but turned out on closer inspection to be a pile of clerical robes in lurid purple.

"Oh, it's fine. I forgive you. Now do you want to tell me all about it, my love?" asked Tim as he put his arm around her shoulder.

Chapter Twenty

It'll Take More Than a Triple Espresso from Starbucks . . .

The morning after. None of those eighties horror fables about nuclear war could possibly come close to the devastation that was Liv's life the next morning. It didn't take Einstein to work out that Liv was throwing up at eight o'clock because she'd been far too familiar with a bottle last night. God, what happened to high hopes and aspirations? Did they get flushed away down the loo with the rest of Liv's regrets and stomach contents? She had wanted so badly to be splendid last night. To be not merely a human sequin but a diamond among girls. And now her life was not a little train wreck but a seventeen-car pileup on the M25 complete with jackknifed trucks spilling kerosene.

"Bleugh . . . oh, help. Oh no." Liv puked again and sat back against the cool side of the bath. And as she remembered the look on Amelia's face she felt terrible. Truly horrible. Liv had been quite surprised, in fact, to find that Amelia didn't just laugh off the idea of Ben and Liv as a riotous joke in bad taste. Which was usually her favourite kind of joke. She actually looked shocked and hurt. Liv had somehow imagined that Amelia didn't really belong with Ben at all. She sort of thought it a case of first come, first served, and since she'd baggsied him at eighteen all latecomers could shove off. She'd overlooked the small matter of an engagement ring and a looming wedding. Dismissed them as inconsequential.

"Just because you're a shallow cow who doesn't recognise the value of commitment," Liv mumbled to herself. Then she remembered the episode on the porch. The bottle. Thank god Tim had been there to . . . "Oh god, and what about Tim?" Liv murmured as she flushed the chain.

"What about Tim?" Standing in the doorway of her bathroom wearing the boxer shorts she'd bought him three Christmasses ago was Tim. Smiling.

"Aghhhh." Liv knew it was a rude reaction but couldn't help herself. "What are you still doing here? Oh my god, we didn't . . ."

"Have sex? No, we didn't." Of course they didn't, she realised. I mean, look at the state I'm in. Liv ran her hands through her hair and contemplated another dash to the basin.

"This reminds me of the time you had bad cod in Brighton." He knelt down and looked at her closely. "Poor you." Obviously last night hadn't taken its toll quite so badly on Tim as it had on Liv. She couldn't imagine how she looked. He smelled like a shower gel commercial. Zing Man.

"Thanks, Tim."

"My pleasure." He smiled and handed her a wad of tissue.

"Oh sure, some philosopher must have said that the meaning of pleasure was your ex-girlfriend on a bathroom floor with whisky breath and a dry tongue and last night's earring all matted up in her hair. But it's only pleasurable because you're ecstatic to be rid of her and know that she's your ex."

"Oh, come on, Liv. You always get depressed when you've been drinking. How about you go back to bed for a few hours?"

"Okay," Liv conceded, and allowed herself to be picked up like a scrunched-up tissue and tucked back in bed to feel sorry for herself for a while.

An hour or so later Liv rolled over and the earring that had become a hairball skewered her neck. She yelled out in pain and flung the pillow out onto the balcony. Tim was sitting next to her reading the sports section but on call should she turn green or lose a limb to gout or something. And it was nice having him there. Not the sick to your stomach, can't touch food, grinning like a lunatic nice of having Ben around, but then her Ben situation wasn't so nice now that he thought she was the spawn of Satan.

Liv rolled over and looked up at Tim. "Do you think I've made a total mess of my life?" she asked dramatically.

"I think that's the bottle talking." Tim laughed and stroked her forehead.

"It's nice to have you around, you know. I'd forgotten how comforting it was."

"Ah, the old-shoe syndrome."

"Not old-shoe. It runs so deep with you and me, doesn't it? I mean we've shared a hell of a lot, Tim. I'd been pretending that that didn't count for anything and that I needed to do all this crazy stuff and that it was more important than quiet, easygoing love. But it's not. I miss it."

"I'm glad. I do, too. I still love you, Liv."

"Thanks." Liv held onto his hand and wished that you could choose who you loved rather than the big hairy perverted hand of fate pointing its finger in a different and stupid direction.

After Tim was sure that Liv was not about to swallow her tongue he had to go and rescue George of the fair eyelashes from the lobby of the Ritz-Carlton, where he was so bored he'd nearly had a perm in the hair salon. Liv squeezed Tim's hand one more time for luck and went back to sleep. She slept off the whisky and she slept off her sudden churning anxiety that maybe Ben was just another example of lust and it would all go horribly wrong a week after they'd started going out together. Maybe what she had with Tim was the real thing. Something to be relied upon. Maybe Ben was a complete red herring. The glamorous-looking dessert that would be no good for her in the long run. But then she thought of how she'd feel if she were never to see him again and not be able to work things out between them. No, she was completely in love with him. Potty about him. Which was insane and painful because she'd monumentally stuffed up and may never get him back. She just couldn't help it. She was mad about him.

When she woke up she still felt that hollow feeling. She saw last night's dress lying discarded on the floor and decided she was just suffering postparty blues. She tried to count her blessings—how could she not be thrilled with her lot? She was the majority shareholder in a business that, if Tim was telling the truth, was splattered across the social pages of every national, evening, and local paper today and that had even got a mention in Page Six (the breakup of Charlie Timpson's secret engagement to the blonde in the picture) and was on excellent terms with her ex-fiancé, who had, as Alex predicted, not been able to live without her. Oh, and she got to go round to Ben's flat this afternoon to discuss why exactly she'd been a bitch on toast and attempted to screw him over. And all that fun stuff.

The only way forwards was to get up and do something about herself, she decided as she headed for the bathroom. As she pulled on a bathrobe and walked across the living room she glanced at the clock. Five-thirty. Couldn't be. She wandered back into her bedroom and looked at her alarm clock. Five thirty-two. Ben was meant to be four-thirty.

"No!" she yelled, and picked up the phone and dragged it to the end of its cord as she cleaned her teeth over the bath. "Taxi. Thirty-four Sutton Street . . . as soon as possible? . . . Thanks." She spat out and rinsed her hair under the tap. Then rinsed herself under the tap. There wasn't time for much else. The taxi hooted in the street outside.

"Bugger. Bugger." Liv leapt into the nearest handy thing, which was her nightie, and tucked it into the only pair of jeans she had left that fit her. They happened to not do up, so she had to put on a jumper to cover the gaping buttons and the nightie, which smelled strangely of Tim and just a bit of sick.

"Coming!" Liv yelled as she slopped into some flip-flops and grabbed her bag.

"Ben, oh my god, I'm sorry." Liv ran down Ben's front path towards him.

He was standing at the front door with a bag in his hand. He looked at the demented sight before him with a frown. "So you were pretty concerned about this whole thing then, weren't you, Liv, to get here an hour and a half late? Maybe you were hoping I'd have gone, to spare you having to explain what the hell you thought you were doing." Ben closed the front door behind him and double-locked it. "I've got to go or I'll miss my plane."

"The whole dog-handling thing, Ben . . . I didn't mean it. I mean I don't know what you heard or where you heard it from, but I never stopped liking you. Never stopped wanting you. Just because I tried to manipulate events and—"

"Dog handling? So that wasn't just some label that James and Dave slapped on it. You really viewed what you were doing to me as training a dog." Ben looked at her with even more derision than he had last night. If that were possible. He pulled his car keys from his pocket and walked right past her towards the gate.

"It's stupid, but it wasn't serious. It was a game, sort of. . . . I mean it was a bit serious but only because I thought you deserved it and then—"

"What I'm really curious to know is how you could allow me to tell you how I felt and how much I cared about you and not say something about all this." He opened the car door and threw his bag inside. "Or perhaps that was part of the plan, too, was it?"

"Well, not exactly, but . . ."

"Thanks. That's all I needed to know." The car door slammed and Liv watched him speed off down the road.

Liv sat down on his front doorstep and rested her head on her knees. She didn't even have the energy to cry. And neither did she deserve the privilege of crying. She deserved every bit of Ben's contempt and she deserved to feel this hopeless, because she'd brought it all on herself. Why in hell's name had she done it? Had it been the power? Feeling desirable again? Why exactly had she not told him? Why had she believed that being deceitful was a means to any end other than misery? She pulled the Biro that was holding her matted locks in place out of her ponytail and grabbed a pizza menu from Ben's mailbox and began to scrawl a justification, of a kind, until she realised she couldn't justify her behaviour at all. She was a fucked-up, stupid twit and had got what was coming to her. Which she attempted to convey to Ben in a pleading note until she ran out of ink.

Chapter Twenty-one

You Always Get the Dog You Deserve

Liv sprinted out of the mouth of South Kensington Tube Station and along Pelham Street, pausing for breath by the phone box. As she rounded the corner onto Fulham Road she came to a halt beside the wedding dress shop. The door trilled open and Liv stepped onto the mat. The whole place made her think of the day she and Alex had seen the sexy Frenchman and his perfect girlfriend. She'd imagined that they had the most perfect love imaginable then. Now that she was a little more worldly and less rose-tinted she thought it more likely that the decree *nisi* would be about to go through soon and Roger would be free to marry the waitress he'd met in Corsica and his perfect girlfriend would be moving to Milan to pursue a modelling career. Still, that didn't necessarily make marriage a bad idea. And especially not in light of tomorrow's hastily planned celebration.

"Hi, I've come for the wedding dress." Liv gritted her teeth and smiled at Delilah, who had lost none of her sneering Frenchness. Heaven only knows what she thought of Liv now with her nose peeling with the last of her Australian tan and her surfer physique and a leftover fake tattoo from last weekend's trip to Byron Bay. Australia seemed a million miles away now as Liv pulled her old coat even tighter around her and reminded herself to buy some mittens.

"Ah, yes." Delilah pulled out a box and opened it for Liv to examine. Tulle and lace and tissue paper spilled out and all that could be seen of the dress was really the tiny embroidered rosebuds that decorated the neckline.

"That's the one," Liv said, and danced impatiently from foot to foot as the assistant packed the dress away and rang up a staggering amount on the till. Liv clutched the bag close to her and pelted onto the street to deal with the next task on her list.

Once outside the shop Liv pulled a mobile phone out of her handbag and tapped in a number.

"Hello. Is that Big Top Tent Hire? . . . Good. My name's Liv Elliot. . . . Yes, I know I never paid the amount in full, but I wonder if it's still possible to have the Bedouin one. With the midnight blue stripes? . . . Oh, only green left? Does it look like a tube of Aqua-fresh? . . . Are you sure? . . . Okay, I'll take it. . . . Yes, same date as before. This Saturday. One-thirty. . . . Thanks very much." And she thrust her phone back into her bag and crossed those two things off her list. Forget manicures and hairdos tomorrow morning. It was all Liv could do to make sure the guests had something to drink and a vicar to perform the ceremony. Now she knew why she'd been so daunted by all the preparation the first time around. It wasn't easy.

"Tim called." Alex yelled from the other room where she was lying on the bed with her feet up so that her swollen ankles didn't escape from beneath her trousers. "Said could you call him as soon as possible; he needs to firm up the plans for tomorrow morning."

Liv put the wedding dress down on a chair, unwrapped the layers, and wandered through into Alex's bedroom.

"Success?"

"Yep." Liv sat down on the bed and patted Alex's protruding little tummy. "How are you feeling? You'll be okay for tomorrow, won't you?" Liv asked nervously.

"Sure. Just a bit tired. Rob can carry me. If he ever comes back from the pub." Alex sighed. Pregnancy had made her just a bit tired and emotional and occasionally homicidal, but apart from that she was coping with her expanding waistline quite joyfully.

"So what shall we do for a hen night?" Liv looked around Alex's flat. Only the remnants of her past life remained. Now it was all boxes and suitcases and the stuff of transitory visitors like Walkmans and baseball caps and old pizza delivery leaflets. Everything else had been shipped out to Australia in preparation for the birth of the Little Bloke, as the bump was known, and Alex and Rob's new life in the country.

"There's Scrabble. Monopoly. *ER*. Pizzas and beer," Alex said.

"Yeah. Last of the party animals, eh?" Liv laughed. "Oh, and I got a message from Mum earlier. Said would it be okay if a couple of the guests crashed here tomorrow night, as our house is full. Mum's already got camp beds up in the garden shed."

"Not a problem at all. So let's start with Monopoly. Then if we feel like it we can head for Stringfellows, pick up a couple of underage lads, ply them with booze, and make them paint our toenails," Alex suggested.

"Our toenails?" asked Liv, wondering if this was a very sexy thing to do that she'd missed out on.

"But I don't think I can reach my toenails right now," Alex lied as she patted Bump.

"Oh, you're right—it's much harder to reach your toes

than to do thirty Salutes to the Sun every day and half an hour of shoulder stands, isn't it?" Liv nodded sarcastically. "In which case, let's skip underage lads. I'll paint your toenails, and you can hand-feed me pizza. Sound good?"

"Like a hen night made in heaven." Alex nodded.

The weather on Saturday morning couldn't have been better for a wedding. In the country Elizabeth woke up early, stepped in a half-eaten packet of biscuits, and went downstairs to defrost the chocolate cake that had been sitting in her freezer since last September.

"Finally found a use for it, Blair," she muttered to the cat as she removed the cake from the Tupperware container and placed it in the sun on the windowsill. "Thought I might have to give it to the old folks home at one point. Not sure they'd have wanted it, though. They're very strict about pensioners' diets these days. I imagine chocolate is a bit of a no-no. Though if I were old it'd be chocolate for breakfast, lunch, and supper."

Blair yelped for milk and Lenny put his head around the kitchen door. "Okay, well, we've got the tent in place. Looks a bit like a harem, but don't think she'll mind." Lenny had been up since five this morning clearing old climbing frames out of the way and salvaging tennis balls so the dance floor could be laid.

"I think that was probably the intention; then we can all be very louche and decadent. Must say I can't wait. You don't mind if I dance with a few of the young men, do you?" Elizabeth practised a few steps she'd learned in her ecstatic-dancing class. "You do think my blue silk dressing gown's okay, don't you? Only it's such short notice. I mean I'll wear a hat and it'll look like it's proper clothing, I hope?" Elizabeth asked somewhat spuriously.

Lenny always thought she looked a million dollars. "Last word in chic, my love." Only he pronounced it "chick."

He kissed the back of her head and made for the bathroom. Elizabeth smiled dreamily and looked out her kitchen window but could only make out the green stripes that were obscuring her view. Still it made a change from looking at last summer's barbecue, which was full of leaves and rain and a bit of vegeburger the cats had left in disgust.

"Mum, we're here." Liv came tumbling in the back door followed by Alex and an assortment of bags. They'd caught the early train from Waterloo because neither of them had been able to sleep a wink due variously to excitement, crazy pizza dreams, and kicking bumps.

"Ah, Liv, Tim's here already. He's just upstairs and should be—"

"About time, too. I thought you'd got cold feet." Tim put his head around the kitchen door and Liv looked at him and laughed.

"Oy, we're not supposed to see each other today. It's our wedding day—remember?"

"Oh yeah." Tim gave Alex and then Liv a peck on the cheek each. "Just as well we're not getting married then, isn't it, or it'd be a bad omen or something." Tim laughed as he helped himself to a handful of jammy dodgers and crammed two in at once.

"It really is sweet of you to come and help out, you know, Tim." Elizabeth patted him on the shoulder and handed him a mug of tea. "I do think it's a shame you're not going to be my son-in-law."

"Yeah, but this way Liv and I will always be friends. Instead of making some dumb mistake that we regret." Tim grinned. "Not that Alex and Rob are making a mistake—I can't believe how well you guys get on. All Rob talked about on his stag night was you. He wanted us to break into Hyde

Park Barracks to nick a couple of horses and ride to South Ken and serenade you on horseback."

"Are you sure he's still in one piece?" Alex asked nervously.

"Tucked up in my spare room like a baby when I left this morning."

"Thanks, Tim. Thanks, both of you, in fact. Isn't it just a bit weird having Rob and me borrow your wedding day like this? I mean it must seem odd . . . Liv wearing her wedding dress to be the bridesmaid, having the flowers that you chose together?" Alex looked at Liv and Tim as they went halves on the last garibaldi in the tin.

"Not even slightly," they both chimed up at the same moment.

"See, opposites attract. Tim and I are too much like brother and sister, aren't we?" Liv turned to Tim.

"Sadly, angel, I think you're right." Since he'd arrived back from Australia six weeks ago Tim had thought a lot about Liv and really did believe that they could be happy together, and they might have been. Except that the next week he ran into, of all people, Sophie Barker, whom he'd worked with at Freuds. And if Liv hadn't pointed out that Sophie had fabulous thighs like nutcrackers and wore stockings even in winter he might not have asked her out for a drink. But he was glad he had now, because on top of her Glamazonness she was also very sweet and surprisingly clever and had a golf handicap of eleven. Which Liv, in spite of all her wonderful qualities, was never likely to have. And besides, it was always much more fun being a guest at a wedding than having your own, or so he'd been told.

"Now, Alex, do you know if it's a boy or a girl yet?" asked Elizabeth.

Elizabeth and Alex chipped back and forth with baby banter.

"Oh, I remember how it was with Liv. Nine pounds, seven ounces. Bigger than our turkey that year."

"Oh god, Mum. It's probably a good job that I'm not getting married or any potential husband would have run for the hills with you reminding him of my heiferish beginnings."

"Now tell me, love, are you going back to Sydney after the wedding?" Elizabeth asked. She had no clue what Liv's plans were as they'd only spoken briefly on the phone a few days ago when Liv had called to ask if the offer of the garden and sausage rolls for the wedding still stood. Apart from that Elizabeth was clueless. Still, that wasn't an unusual state of affairs. She'd only learned about Liv's success with Greta's Grundies (dreadful name, she thought, reminded her of gym knickers) via a piece in *Woman's Own* about what the stars wore under their frocks. It had been a proud moment and the cutting had been on the fridge door. Though it didn't seem to be there anymore.

"I'll go back in a few weeks, yes. But I've got to go to New York next week to have a meeting with the woman from Barneys." Liv and Alex looked at each other and burst into shrieks of excitement. They still hadn't come to terms with the unprecedented success of GG. Thanks to the huge amount of publicity the party had attracted and then even more column inches when Amelia very loudly resigned her post as spokesmodel, things had been going really well. It had definitely set tongues wagging. And you know how these things are in fashion. One minute a cronky sewing machine in a bed-sit, the next Giorgio is asking you for a weekend in his palazzo. Not that this had happened yet exactly and Liv *was* paying her own airfare to New York and planning to stalk the buyer at Barneys and strew her path with bras rather than actually having an official appointment, but still . . . things were looking good.

"But as Charlie's said I can have the beach cottage for as long as I like, I think it would be silly not to go back. And

Sydney's so great. It's too beautiful to leave just yet." Liv finished her tea and thought of the colour of the sea and the sky and lunch on the seafront in Bondi and surfing in the early morning when the air was still sharp and damp and the balmy evenings and cicadas and jasmine trees. Much as she loved London, she wasn't ready to come back just yet.

"What about this gorgeous young man I heard about a while ago?" Elizabeth asked.

"I don't really want to talk about it actually, Mum." That was the other reason Liv couldn't bear to leave Sydney just yet. Even though Ben had shown less than no interest in seeing her since the night of the party, she held out hope that one day his feelings towards her might mellow just a bit so they could at least be friends. And just being in the same city as him made her inexplicably happier, even though she knew that she'd completely ruined any chance she ever had with him.

"Why not? Did you have a tiff?" Elizabeth was so uncomplicated. She would never begin to understand why Liv had even begun to bother with all that dog-handling game playing. As if life weren't complicated enough, she'd shrug, and shake her head at the whole thing. Pity she hadn't been around to advise Liv two months ago.

"Not exactly. Let's just say that he learned his lesson. He's much too clever to have anything to do with some immature, scheming idiot like me," Liv said, and it broke her heart to remember what had happened that night. "Still, who knows? Maybe one day I'll meet some guy that I love as much as Ben. Did I tell you, Mum, about it being Ben Parker who I met that year in Aix on holiday?"

"You're kidding! The boy in the cottage down the road with the dreamy green eyes? Oh my goodness, that's the most romantic thing I've ever heard. And you're not speaking? Oh, darling, I'm sorry. There's no hope at all?"

"He even refused to come to the wedding. Well, not exactly—he told Rob that he was away on some dig, but I imagine that it's because he doesn't want to set eyes on me. And I don't really blame him." Liv couldn't bear to think about Ben right now. It was so painful that it sucked the air from her lungs. That she'd lost him. That Dave had even seen him in a restaurant last week and tried to smooth things over and he'd simply said he had no idea how anybody could do anything so malicious and he really was sure that he didn't want to see her again. No, there was no hope at all. "Better go and get dressed then, hadn't we?" Liv looked over at Alex, who was totally wiped out. "Come on; I'll give you a hand."

The church was littered with camellias and ivy. From the back, as Liv looked down the aisle, at the guests spilling out of the pews, it was her vision realised. Feathers rose spectacularly from hats and there was a low hum of anticipation. Liv's stomach lurched for a moment as though she were the bride herself.

"Okay, sugar, let's get to it." They were already half an hour late, as they'd got stuck in traffic on the A3. Lenny had been driving and he wasn't known for his lawbreaking abilities, unfortunately. Still, they were here now.

"Now or never," Alex whispered, and held out her arm for Liv to slip her arm through, and they took their first step as the organ struck up.

Liv could see the cherry blossom bouquet in Alex's hand trembling as they tiptoed down the aisle. This really is the real deal, Liv thought to herself, with just a flicker of envy as she and Alex took their final steps. They smiled conspiratorially at Luke and James, who were the groomsmen, all scrubbed in their morning suits, and a radiant Rob. And standing beside him, unless Liv was hallucinating, was Ben.

"That's Ben. Alex, what's he doing here?" Liv gulped as the wedding march came to an end and the vicar cleared his throat in anticipation of the proceedings.

"I have no idea. I know Rob got drunk the other night and left some slurring message that he better get over here or he'd never buy him a beer again, but I can't imagine that would have made him come all this way," Alex whispered over her shoulder, and the vicar gave them a disapproving look.

"Dearly beloved . . . ," he began, and Liv stole another glance over at Ben. Who was looking at her. God, he had probably been granted the power of the evil eye and wanted to melt her in some reenactment of *The Omen*. She looked at her feet and tried to concentrate on her best friend's wedding. She had better avoid him at the reception, too. Of all the days she didn't want to get told off and called a malicious cow, today was definitely one of them. He looked so achingly beautiful in his grey morning suit with a scattering of freckles across his brown nose, his hair short and ruffled. In fact, he'd never looked more irresistible. And never been more inaccessible. Oh, why did he have to come, Liv wondered, and make me remember just how much I regret what I did? Ah, perhaps *that* was why he'd come. To make her suffer even more. Just as she was about to moan to herself that there was no God, she looked up and saw the crucifix and thought better of it. Nah, can't afford to fall out with him, too, she decided.

"If any of you know of any lawful impediment . . . ," the vicar continued, and after the tense moment when psychopathic exes are invited to leap out of the pews brandishing deranged reasons had passed uneventfully, the congregation drifted back into their various reveries, be that wondering if they'd turned the heating off at home or gazing mistily at the beautiful couple who had to cross land and seas and social divides to meet. On Rob's side you could smell the money mingling with the incense, and on Alex's side were many friends, some literary lions, and her tall, handsome brothers, who were a credit to her despite, the more senior members of the congregation thought, the rather uncomfortable-looking ring through James's left eyebrow. Because most of Rob's family had flown in from Australia they were determined to make the most of it and were already wondering when the fella in the dress would give it a rest and let them go and do what they did best: have a knees up.

It didn't take long. The bride and groom, having been in a bit of a hurry to marry because Alex couldn't face having to wear a flowing gown to conceal her tummy when a slinky one would do perfectly well, didn't have the time to write their own vows. This pleased the vicar. In his experience such vows were usually embarrassingly earnest attempts at second-rate poetry.

Alex and Rob could have got married in Australia, but Alex, having agreed to spend at least a few years of married life there to begin with, had decided that she wanted to be married in England and while she was reasonably svelte. So had it not been for the fact that Liv had fled England a few months ago and forgotten to cancel almost everything from the dress to the morning suits to the napkins to the glorious Bedouin tent that everyone was now dancing the conga in, then they might have had a bit of a struggle arranging things.

The Carpenters tribute band, which Liv decided she would not be having to play at her own wedding, if ever she had one, played on. But the racket from the "Mr. Post-man"–droning woman in the wig was so bad that the neighbours' dogs were joining in and the cats were under the beds. Between the melon balls and chicken in white wine sauce Liv made her way across the garden into the house and escaped to the loo. All the time keeping a look-out for Ben, whom she had so far managed to avoid by diving behind guests with large hats whenever he so much as looked her way.

The loo door was locked, so she sat on the step outside and rubbed the red patches on her feet where her new shoes were rubbing like crazy. Five minutes later the door was still locked.

"Excuse me. Could you hurry up? I'm busting." Liv rapped on the door.

"Hold on a minute," a woman's voice came from inside.

Liv imagined it must be a bit of a twisted-knickers-and-tights issue or something and took off her shoes for a second.

"In fact, I'd be really grateful if you could give me a hand." The door swung open and there, lodged between the cistern and sink with a great big plaster cast on her leg, was Fay.

"Fay. Oh my god. Look at you." Liv leapt up and ran to Fay's aid. She took hold of her crutches and looked down at a giant plaster cast and a toe ring on the bare foot. "I'm so glad you could come. Alex has heard all about you and was so grateful for you letting me go to Oz and keep her company that she had to invite you. But god, how did this happen?"

"Believe it or not, I was learning to ride bareback. In Hyde Park. Not Arizona, but still . . ." Fay used Liv as a lever to prise herself out from the loo and collapsed on the steps.

"It's great to see you, Fay. Only I hope you're not going to try to poach me back, 'cause I think I'm staying in Australia for a bit."

"Not a bit of it. I've got a much more efficient accountant who doesn't know how to use the Internet so she doesn't waste quite as much time as you did on Naked Brad." Fay laughed. "Anyway, Livvy, what about you? Did you find your jackeroo?"

"Not exactly. But I had my knickerless lunch and even

though I haven't been hip enough to do rehab I've re-nounced drugs and had a huge affair, but . . . well . . . it's all over now." Liv wondered whether she should fill Fay in.

"Ben?"

"How did you know?"

"Well, I tripped this very handsome boy up with one of my crutches as we were coming out of the church and he was looking for you." Fay nudged Liv and winked.

"Oh god, I wish it were like that, but miserably it's all gone more pear-shaped than me."

"Really? What happened?"

"Such a long story that I'm not even going to bore you with it. Actually, it's more of a Theban play than a story. Or maybe one of those medieval morality tales."

"Sounds nasty."

"No, really, it'll be fine." Liv put on a brave face in the presence of her glamorous wonderboss, who was perhaps the most inspiring person Liv had ever met. And that was just her hair. "And besides, I did what I went out there for. I got over my broken Tim heart. I lived life a bit rather than just imagining it and I'm not even nearly as old as the girls in *Sex and the City,* so I reckon I can afford a few more years of sin-gle and fabulous before I have to start worrying about set-tling down. And you know I still haven't had sex with a rock star. I reckon every girl has to do that before she meets the man of her dreams, right?" Liv looked pleadingly at Fay, who took her hand and smiled sympathetically.

"If I were being completely naff I'd tell you that for every door that closes a window opens or something." Fay laughed quietly. "But you know you'll be fine, don't you?"

"I know." Liv pulled a pen from her handbag. "Can I sign your cast? Right here, next to . . . Hey . . . when did you let Robbie Williams near your leg? Did you get his phone number?"

★ ★ ★

It was now one in the morning and Not-the-Carpenters had been replaced by a Boney M–playing DJ. The hardier guests were still giving it loads to "Rasputin" and Alex was sitting on Rob's knee and they were both having a very earnest conversation with the Little Bloke and patting the little bump.

"Liv, I've been looking for you."

Liv, who had flaked out on a chair having danced a polka with every male member of Rob's family and a couple of his young nieces, turned round to see Ben, whom she had forgotten to avoid in her whirling frenzy. "Ben, please don't let's have this conversation now. I'm exhausted. I know what I did was unforgivable, but do you think perhaps you could just not remind me of what a horrible bitch I am until tomorrow?"

"Three nights ago I was at home on my own, about to watch some documentary on the Discovery channel, and couldn't be bothered to cook." He pulled up a chair next to her and handed her a glass of champagne.

"What are you talking about?" Liv opened her heavy eyes and squinted at him suspiciously. "Have you been smoking crack?"

"Anyway, I thought maybe I'd get a Chinese. Then I thought nah . . . what I really want is an American hot."

"An American hot?"

"Pizza. From Arthur's. Spicy, pepperoni. Family-size and a Coke."

"Ben, I think maybe we should get Tim to take you back to your hotel room. Where are you staying?"

"So I knew that I had some flyers somewhere with Arthur's number on. I mean I can't believe that after all these years of vegging on the sofa I don't know it by heart, but then I guess when I was going out with Amelia we were more a sushi couple than your pizza types. What type are you by the way, Liv?"

"Four-eight-five three-o-three-nine." Liv had taken two

mouthfuls of champagne and was trying to ignore the fact that Ben was talking complete rubbish and simply be delighted that he was talking to her at all. It was clearly a drug-induced, temporary state of affairs, which was even more reason to take advantage of it. If he hadn't snapped out of it in five minutes she might even attempt to kiss him. Or put her hand on his thigh.

"What's that?" It was his turn to be puzzled.

"Four-eight-five three-o-three-nine. Arthur's phone number. I'm a pizza girl."

"I knew you were." He took hold of Liv's hand. "So I went out into the hall and rummaged through my drawer and found the flyer for Arthur's. And just as I was scanning the list, looking for my American hot, I noticed that somebody had scrawled all over it." Ben looked at her with such excitement you'd have thought he'd just worked out how to split the atom. Then he pulled a piece of scrunched-up paper out of his pocket and waved it in her face.

"My note?" Liv suddenly realised what he'd been going on about. "You found my note?"

"Only three days ago. I found your note. You see, until then I thought that you hadn't given a damn. You'd showed up late when I'd given you a chance to explain and then I never heard another thing from you. It was as if you just didn't care at all. As if all the dog-handling stuff had really been a game and once you'd got me, made me like you, you lost interest."

"Oh my god, you didn't really think that, did you?"

"What else was I supposed to think? Anyway, I didn't get your note until after I'd told Dave that I never wanted to see you again. After I'd told Rob that I wasn't coming to the wedding because I couldn't bear to be in the same room as you. And after I'd decided that I hated you."

"But—," Liv tried to interrupt, but Ben was kissing the piece of paper.

"And I know that I've been a stubborn bastard and that I

wouldn't listen to you and that whatever this dog-handling thing is, by the way, it is complete bollocks, because if you had ignored just one more of my phone calls I was going to give up on you completely."

"I'm so sorry, Ben," Liv said—but even though she *was* sincerely sorry and the whole thing had been a miserable disaster, a slow smile had begun to spread across her face. What he was saying was that he used to hate her but that now he'd read her note he'd forgiven her. This was possibly the best thing that had ever happened to her. How could she help but smile?

"No, *I'm* sorry. Really, Liv. Anyway, the thing is that what you did was pretty shitty."

"I know and believe me, I've regretted it every single minute since it happened. I'll probably regret it for the rest of my life."

"And because of that I've found someone else," Ben said gravely.

Liv's smile vanished. She nearly buckled as he said this. "So soon?"

"I knew that I had to do it. You see, I figured that if you were really into all this game playing, needed someone to manipulate, to jump to your commands—"

"Ben, I'm not like that; please don't think I am. I don't blame you for finding yourself another girlfriend, I know I've messed up, but—"

"Do you want to see a photo?" Ben put his hand in his jacket pocket and pulled out a photo.

"Actually, I don't think that I do. This is pretty tough on me because despite what you think, I really do love you. So no, I don't want to see a photo of some other girl you've met. Thanks all the same."

"You do?"

"Do what?"

"Love me?"

"Yeah. I do. Well, I did. And I always have. So I probably always will."

"Here, just have a quick look." Ben pressed the photograph in front of Liv.

She nodded miserably but couldn't make out the girl in the picture because her eyes were blurry with tears.

"What do you think?"

"Ben, please, could you just leave me alone now?" Liv disentangled her hand from his and was about to stand up.

"Isn't that the most beautiful shiny hair you've ever seen? And those legs . . ." Ben was gazing at the photo and laughing. Jesus, he really was a sicko.

"Bye, Ben." She stood up.

"And all ours."

"Ours?" Liv nearly fled. Near miss. What? He'd hired some girl for them to share? He was an ubersicko.

"He's called Felix. And I figured that while you had this thing about dogs, about training them, well, while Felix was living under the same roof as us then you wouldn't have to hound me so much." Ben laughed at his feeble joke.

Liv looked at him in disbelief. "What on earth are you talking about?"

"I bought us a dog, Liv. Look—he's kind of a mutt. I thought maybe they were a bit more intelligent. A bit easier to train, right?"

"A dog?"

"Called Felix. I hoped that even if you didn't want to move in with me when you got back to Sydney, then you could at least take him for walks on the weekends. Maybe you could even stay over sometimes. He'd probably like that. Or we could come and visit you if you like."

"Ben. You're insane." Liv pulled the picture out of his hand and found herself staring at the cutest, most hairballish puppy she'd ever seen.

"I mean I know it's a big commitment and stuff, but I

really am serious about you, Liv, and I figured that maybe we're ready to take this step and—"

"He's beautiful." Liv put her arms around Ben's neck and kissed him. She couldn't believe it. He'd bought her a dog. Them a dog. They were going to be a dog-owning bona fide couple with responsibilities and a life together, all three of them. "Thank you; thank you. Oh, Ben, you're so amazing. I mean this is wonderful and . . . what about Amelia?" She stopped for a brief reality check. Just in case something horrific were lurking round the next corner waiting to bite her on the bum.

"She's going out with a rock star." He grinned.

"Thank god. I mean good for her." Liv's smile got wider. "And you mean this? Felix is ours?"

"Yes. If you want him. If you want us." Ben had hold of her hand and was waiting for her answer.

"Of course I do." She kissed him and he was kissing her back. But then she stopped for a moment and looked closely and seriously at him.

"Ben?"

"Yes?"

"There's one condition."

"What's that?" He looked concerned for a moment.

"When I look back on all I've been through over the last few months, all the lumps and bumps and little hurdles and all the stuff that life throws at you, well, when I look back I think there's one lesson I've learned. One thing a girl must always put her foot down about."

"What's that?" Ben wondered if maybe this was Liv backing out.

She took a deep breath. "He can only stay if he promises that he will never ever take me to dinner and then not call me the next day. Is that understood? Because if he does that then I'm afraid he'll have to go."

"I'll tell him that." Ben laughed.

"You'd better." Liv smiled and raised her glass of champagne, "To dogs everywhere. May they get the owners they deserve."

"Oh, don't worry," Ben laughed. "They always do."

Read on for a sneak peek
of the latest novel
by Clare Naylor

The Goddess Rules

Available in hardcover from
Ballantine Books
Coming soon

CHAPTER ONE

In which Kate Disney receives two surprise visitors.

Kate Disney was having sex with her ex when the legendary Mirabelle Moncur first came into her life. Actually Mirabelle came into the wooden garden shed that Kate called home just as Jake The Ex's naked bottom appeared over the top of the sheets in anticipation of his last few, enthusiastic thrusts. This was the climax that Kate had been waiting for since she and Jake had broken up a month ago. Since that Sunday night she'd existed in a fathomless abyss of pain, memories of Jake, and tears. Until about an hour ago, that is, when Jake, in answer to her prayers and a good deal of amateur witchcraft, had shown up on her doorstep on his way home from a night out that had extended into the day.

"Hello angel, I've missed you." It was three in the afternoon and he smelled of whiskey and cigarette smoke, his shirt was half-unbuttoned and his jacket was torn.

"Jake." Kate had been cleaning her paintbrushes when she'd heard the tap on the shed door. She'd wiped her hands down her old T-shirt and unbolted it. Jake was the first and last person she expected to see standing there.

"It was my birthday yesterday," he told her and propped himself up in the doorframe. "And the only present I really wanted was you."

"Jake, you're drunk," Kate said. Though she knew he wasn't.

"You've got paint in your hair." He leaned forward to touch her fringe. Kate shrunk back but knew that she'd already lost the battle. She knew that she was going to let Jake in.

"You look terrible," she lied.

"Don't I even get a birthday kiss?"

"You're lucky I haven't punched you."

"I love you." Jake looked at Kate and she felt her will dissolve. Maybe he really meant it this time. Because even though she and Jake had been together on and off for almost three years, he had told her that he loved her only once before, the same night that he'd been signed to a small record label. And that night he really had been drunk.

"We're only going to talk," she said and stood back to let him through the door.

"I know." Jake pretended to believe her.

"I'll make some tea." Kate turned her back on him and with shaking hands filled the kettle in the large butler's sink in the corner. This wasn't how she'd imagined it would happen—Jake coming back to her. And she *had* imagined it—night and day, waking and sleeping. She'd hoped that it would be a bigger moment—that it would involve a declaration and a diamond rather than a cup of tea at the end of a long night out. But then after three years with Jake, Kate was accustomed to being underwhelmed. Thankfully the sex wasn't underwhelming. It was fabulous. It was even more fabulous right now because they hadn't so much as laid eyes on one another for a month. And as Jake kissed her neck and Kate trailed her fingers down his freckled, brown back, she forgot about the underwhelmingness, and about the note he'd written to her, telling her that it was over because he had nothing left to give; she'd even forgotten that it was Jake's fault that she was living in her boss's garden shed. Well not strictly his fault, but she and Jake had been saving for a place together and she'd agreed to give up her overpriced studio flat so that they could buy somewhere quicker and be together. But Kate forgot all these things and bit hard into Jake's shoulder and let bygones be bygones. Until Mirabelle Moncur walked in and ruined everything.

"Kate Disney?" she demanded, without so much as a knock on the door or a polite cough to announce herself first. Jake, who was lost somewhere in the vicinity of Kate's left breast at that moment, completely lost his stride and practically gave himself whiplash as he turned to see who was behind him. Kate gave a cry of pain as Jake crushed her right leg.

"Who the bloody hell are you?" Jake asked the intruder as he ungraciously wrestled the sheet from Kate's grasp to cover himself up. Kate suddenly remembered why he was her ex. Apart from the fact that he'd dumped her. He always put himself first. He was completely self-absorbed, not to mention, she noticed in the late afternoon sunlight streaming in through the shed window, a bit on the fat side.

"Oh, you don't need to cover up." At the foot of Kate's bed stood a strikingly attractive woman, possibly in her late fifties, with disheveled blonde hair, the sort of cheekbones that hold a beauty together no matter how far south her face gravitates, and deep green eyes, which at this moment in time were locked on Jake's crotch.

"You have absolutely *nothing* to hide." And with that she glanced the tip of her Gitanes cigarette with a lighter and raised an unimpressed eyebrow. Jake turned beet red and looked uncomfortable.

"Yes, who the bloody hell are you?" Kate demanded as she reached for an old nightdress that was lying on the floor to cover herself with and clambered from her bed.

"I'm Mirabelle Moncur," the woman said in a French accent as thick as nightclub smoke as she looked around the shed. "Do you actually live here?"

"I'm sorry, do I know you?" Kate demanded crossly. Knowing full well that she didn't. Though there was something familiar about Mirabelle Moncur.

"I want you to come and work for me," the woman said and watched unabashed while Jake stumbled into his boxer shorts, one leg at a time. Kate had never seen him so ruffled.

"Well you could have knocked first," he muttered under his breath.

"Look, I don't know who you are, or how you got in but this is actually a private residence and if you want me to work for you then you'll have to make an appointment and come back." Mirabelle sniffed the air in a way that told Kate that she didn't believe this to be a residence of any sort. Let alone a private one worth knocking at. She walked over to where a few of Kate's canvasses were stacked up against the wall and began glancing through them. "These are your paintings?"

"Yes, and as I've said you can make an appointment to come back later and see them. But right now, as you can probably see, I'm busy."

"They're a little old-fashioned but I suppose you'll do," the woman said. "I want you to paint Bébé for me. He's very beautiful so I suppose it'll be easy to do. Even for someone like you."

"Who the hell is Bébé?" Jake asked, not, Kate noticed, leaping to defend her work, which he'd never complained about when it was funding his cigarette habit, paying for recording studio time, and keeping him in whiskey and the cashmere socks he absolutely had to wear or his feet got too hot, for the past three years.

"Bébé is my pussy. He arrives tomorrow morning from Mozambique and you can begin work in the afternoon," Mirabelle Moncur filled in the gaps. Jake looked staggered.

"Right, well I'm sure that we can discuss my old-fashioned paintings later. And whether I'm prepared to paint your . . . pussy, but for now would you mind leaving me and my . . ." Kate always hesitated to call Jake her boyfriend, even before they'd split up, lest he get nervous and feel like she was trying to tie him down and put him under pressure. She turned to look at the man who was sitting on the corner of her bed, waiting for her to deal with their intruder so that he could get on with the birthday treat. ". . . my friend alone?"

"I'll come back later, if you prefer," Mirabelle Moncur said as she dropped a glowing cigarette butt on top of a yellow canister of fertilizer with a skull and crossbones on the lid. "There's nothing worth hanging around here for." She looked at Jake with a sneer and walked out of the door, without closing it behind her, leaving Kate to pick up the burning Gitanes or risk being blown up.

"Who on earth was she?" Kate asked as she went to the window and watched the woman disappear down the garden path.

"Mirabelle Moncur. Rings a bell," Jake said. "Now sweetheart, cute as you look in that little nightie, I prefer you without it."

"You do?" Kate laughed girlishly and made her way back to Jake's side. He pulled the white cotton slip over her head and began to kiss her tummy.

"Mmmhhhmmm," he said. "I'd forgotten what a great body you have." Kate smiled inside and ran her hands through Jake's hair. She, in her turn, forgot how ungracious he'd been with the sheet when that weird woman had barged through the door. Amnesia was a requirement with Jake as a boyfriend. If you remembered all the bad stuff you'd have to wonder what had happened to your mind. Because you certainly weren't in possession of it. Kate chose to concentrate on her body instead, and how good it was feeling right now.

About the Author

Clare Naylor worked as an editorial assistant at a major publishing house. When her first novel, *Love: A User's Guide*, was bought for the movies, she left her job to write full-time. She is also the author of *Catching Alice* and *The Goddess Rules*. With Mimi Hare, she is the coauthor of *The Second Assistant*. She lives in England.